Song of the Stag

R.M. Brown

Ringwood Publishing
Glasgow

Copyright R.M. Brown © 2024
All rights reserved

The moral right of the author has been asserted

First published in Great Britain in 2024 by
Ringwood Publishing

0/1 314 Meadowside Quay Walk, Glasgow G11 6AY

www.ringwoodpublishing.com
mail@ringwoodpublishing.com

ISBN 978-1-917011-02-0

British Library Cataloguing-in-Publication Data
A catalogue record for this book is available from the British Library

Printed and bound in the UK
by Lonsdale Direct Solutions

Praise for *Song of the Stag*

"R.M. Brown's *Song of the Stag* is a stunning debut novel. With characters that grip you and a narrative that moves with nuance, pace and drama, this novel tackles complex issues with grace and creative flair. At once curious and commanding, *Song of the Stag* is a glorious Scottish read."

— Imogen Stirling, creator of *Love The Sinner*

"*Song of the Stag* is that mythical promise made real at last — a novel in equal parts pacy and exquisitely evocative. Beautifully written throughout, the book is gloriously Scottish; a feminist fantasy odyssey of which our nation can be proud. Readers will fall in love with Cait as her journey towards self-determination mirrors that of her nation."

— Kirsten MacQuarrie, Novelist

"Those readers currently frustrated by the block on Scottish self-determination will enjoy spotting political, cultural and linguistic parallels while fans of the fantasy genre will revel in the mythology and timelessness of *Song of the Stag*."

— Mary McCabe, author of *Two Closes and a Referendum*

"A brilliant, multi-layered debut about the importance of truths, myths, and folklore around Scotland's past, and their continuing relevance for its present and future.

Song of the Stag will delight a vast array of readers across different interests. Fantasy book lovers will revel in it as a uniquely Scottish take on *Game of Thrones*. However, the main mass of readers will realise there is much more to this deeply insightful book than its surface-level tales of action and intrigue. Its brilliant evocation of Scotland's vast imaginative history of myths, legends, folk tales, and fairy stories — drawn from the author's lifetime dedication to collecting, recording, and renewing Scotland's vast folklore traditions — will delight, intrigue, and entertain this book's readers of all persuasions and nations.

Valid as these two perspectives are, the essential core of this thought-provoking book is its political allegory of the past, present, and future struggle for Scottish Independence. It highlights one young woman's journey from complacent unionism into gradual awareness of a desire for her country's freedom alongside an equal need to assert her own social identity.

Ultimately, what this book does — and what its much-anticipated sequel is set to do, too — is pose the key question faced by independence fighters for the past 150 years, from Ghandi to Mandela and many more: if you believe your country should be independent, what are you prepared to do to achieve that? What are you prepared to sacrifice?"

— Sandy Jamieson, author of *A Subtle Sadness*

To everyone who wanted a civil dinner and ended up receiving an impassioned speech. Sorry.

Chapter 1

Separatists

Stories and songs claim that the sky in Storran is a blue unlike any other. They say that in the days before trains and maps, when travellers crossed the border from Afren into Storran, all they had to do was look up to know they were home. Three years ago, on Cait's nineteenth birthday, her parents gifted her a dress in the same pale blue as the sky, and it swished around her calves and the tops of her boots as she scaled rolling hills under a thunderous border azure. She had never seen a sky other than the one that hung over home, but its blue quickly became her favourite colour.

In the bumpy train carriage, Cait smoothed her skirt across her knees. It seemed the further north the train ploughed from the rural borders, the more the brilliant blue sky was choked by clouds of smoke. She tried to find reasons to be excited about moving to Storran's capital — new people, new stories, new history — but she jumped at the sound of the train's whistle as it stirred old fears of war-torn streets, and the faceless Fox of Thorterknock high up on a barricade, howling with laughter.

The outside world snapped its eyes closed as the blind rolled down the window and cast the compartment in yellow shade.

'It's too bright. You'll hurt your eyes.' Kenzie sat back down on the bench beside her. The cushion gave a little huff of dust under his weight.

Cait removed her hat and ran her fingers over the ribbon. If the city was much darker, perhaps her sensitive eyes would ache less. That was one positive, at least. She only hoped she wouldn't stand out too much. In Briddock, people were used to her cloud-like hair and pale complexion, so she had been spared the whispers and stares for many years.

Kenzie stretched his legs out and bowed his golden head over that morning's paper. It had been delivered by the paperboy in Briddock, hurled over Kenzie's fence at seven twenty-one before the paperboy moved onto the other side of the village. Cait's mother received her copy at seven twenty-nine. At half past eight, the butchers opened.

But today, at nine, instead of greeting her mother's first patient of the day, something out of the ordinary happened: Kenzie knocked on Cait's door, picked up her suitcase, and led her outside. She walked beneath the dock leaf that hung over the threshold for the last time, and side by side they walked down through the village and over Puddock Bridge. By ten past nine, they were out of Briddock, and by ten, they were on the train. For twenty-two years Cait had been able to read her life like a pulse, but now she didn't even know what time she would be stepping off the train and into the city.

Cait glanced over at Kenzie's newspaper, whose front page declared, "SEPARATIST SHAMBLES: THORTERKNOCK SEES THIRD ATTACK THIS WEEK" in furious black letters.

Storran is and always will be a province of Afren. She held her mother's earthy voice in her mind. *We're one of the Five Realms. No amount of troublemaking can change that.* The words were once comforting, but with each mile that stretched between her and home, Cait's mind only filled with gunpowder and terror and Separatists.

'Did they catch them?' she asked. She couldn't help it.

Kenzie slowly shook his head, his eyes still roving across the page. He had the profile of a conqueror, all sharp lines in his brow and jaw. 'Not yet.'

'Was *she* involved?'

Kenzie looked at her with amusement. 'Who, the Fox?' He chuckled. 'You can say her name.'

Cait said nothing. Chief among her concerns about moving to the city, above the crowds and the strangers, and the tangled sprawl of urban life, was the Fox of Thorterknock. A ruthless firebrand. A Separatist menace. The press told of her countless terrible stunts, but the Fox had never been caught. She always vanished as quickly as she had appeared.

'Three hundred officers in Hart Hall, and not one has managed to get near her,' Cait had heard Kenzie mutter countless times. 'I'll change that.'

As the train's rhythmic *clack-clack, clack-clack* filled the carriage, Cait tried to let Kenzie enjoy his peace. She lay her head against his shoulder. She tried to recount which Thorterknock folktales she knew of, but the mention of the Fox only made her spill the question she had been swallowing since leaving home.

'Are you sure it's safe?'

Kenzie flashed her a brief smile before returning his attention to the paper. 'Of course it is.'

She knew she shouldn't keep pressing the same point, not today, not on *his* day, but —

'The attackers ... will they have been captured by the time we get to the city?'

Kenzie chuckled fondly and folded up the newspaper. 'Listen,' he said, cupping Cait's face in his hand and fixing her with his steadying gaze. 'If they are not captured by the time we get to Thorterknock, I will put on my uniform and have them off the streets by teatime,' he said with his usual self-assured confidence.

Cait grinned. In her mind, the Fox bolted at the sight of Kenzie, so very small and insignificant in the face of his confidence. 'Promise?'

'I promise, little dove.' Kenzie pulled her towards him and planted a kiss on her head. Cait hadn't liked the nickname when it surfaced years ago, but as time marched on she felt it break in like a pair of new boots. Now, it served as a comforting reminder of the world left behind. Everything was changing, but Kenzie was still Kenzie. She was still his little dove.

'The Separatists will collapse within the year, anyway,' Kenzie said nonchalantly, shaking out the newspaper again.

Cait's head whipped around to look at him. 'What, really?' It was a bold claim to make. Thorterknock had been struggling with its Separatist problem for going on fifty years.

Kenzie nodded and looked down his nose as he hunted for his place. 'We're getting much better at predicting their movements. They don't have long left.' She caught the way he said 'we' as if he had been among the Watch's professional ranks for years instead of an isolated volunteer in the countryside.

Cait's heart lifted a little. 'So, when the Separatists collapse, you'll be discharged?'

'When the Separatists collapse, they'll need soldiers to ensure they *stay* gone. The Queen's Watch is a long way from being disbanded.'

'Oh.'

Kenzie must have caught the disappointment in her voice because his ardent expression softened. 'How many times do I need to tell you before you'll believe me? You'll love Thorterknock.'

'I know, I just …'

The paper flopped backwards as he gripped her knee. 'You know I need you with me.'

Cait put her hand over his. She hadn't meant to be selfish, and she felt the guilt of it blooming on her cheeks. He spent so much time being sure of himself that sometimes Cait forgot that underneath the chase for Separatists was a boy who just wanted his parents to be there when he got home. She had been foolish to think that he'd let any harm come to her after the Separatists took his parents from him. She squeezed his hand. 'I'm here,' she said with a smile. 'And I'll have my big strong Lealist to protect me if I get scared in the city.'

Kenzie stiffened. 'Don't use that word.' He glanced at the compartment door. 'Especially not in Thorterknock.'

His sudden seriousness made Cait pause. 'Mr Blaine says it all the time.'

'Blaine's an idiot,' Kenzie muttered, returning to the paper.

The man who owned the corner shop in Briddock had a sense of humour that liked to see how far it could go before running itself into trouble. He'd taken to calling Kenzie *Lealist,* the Separatist word for members of the Queen's Watch, in a bid to antagonise him, and it worked, because Kenzie had spent most of his early volunteer days trying to expose him.

With Kenzie's nose back in the newspaper, Cait released the blind on the window. The countryside had given way to a heavy curtain of houses and workshops and factories. Chimneys clawed for the sky, belching out plumes of dark smoke. The haze turned the sun into a sickly yellow circle, and Cait found that her eyes were able to take it all in without aching. As the train's formidable pace eased, Cait returned to hunting for reasons why coming to Thorterknock was a good thing, but when she caught sight of the station clock pointing to twelve thirty-two, all she could think was that it was lunchtime back at the surgery.

*

When she stepped off the train, the sounds of the station swelled into a single wave and crashed over the platform, forcing Cait to drop her suitcase and cover her ears.

'You left this on the train,' Kenzie said, placing her hat on her head. 'Honestly, what are you like?'

Wincing as a whistle pierced the air to her left, Cait looped her arm through his and allowed him to steer her through the fray.

'What do you think?' Kenzie asked. She could barely hear him.

'It's …' The station's elegant trimmings masked an industrial backdrop: a windowed ceiling held aloft by thick iron pillars and bright emerald buttresses. '… handsome.'

As they pushed through the turnstiles and made towards the exit, Cait studied the commuters individually in an attempt to dissect the throng and make some sense of it. From pinstriped suits and sweeping hooped skirts, to greasy overalls and holey leather, the station bulged with people from all walks of life. Cait's focus fell on a lanky girl walking in her direction. She moved against the crowd, her cap pulled low, casting shadows across warm beige skin. Cait watched her carefully, noting the way her eyes flicked from side to side beneath the dark, broom-like fringe that escaped her hat. She walked with long, hurried strides, thumbs hooked through her braces, and shoulders hunched nearly to her ears. Cait wondered if the girl felt as nervous among the crowd as she did. A shout pierced the air somewhere near the exit, and the girl threw a glance over her shoulder. A heartbeat later she was running. Cait felt the brush of her jacket as she careened by.

Her heart thumped. 'What —'

Five figures erupted from the crowd, whooping and hollering. Cait pressed herself against Kenzie as they barrelled past.

'For the Ootlawed Keeng!'

'Lealtie Ayebidin!'

The sound of Old Storrian singed the air. *Separatists.*

The stream of travellers ground to a halt as the group leapt over the ticket turnstiles and onto the platform.

'Kenzie …'

He wasn't listening. He grabbed her hand to pull her back towards the platform and hurl the two of them against the turnstile.

'Stay back,' he said, pushing her behind him. She gripped the back of his coat to stop her hands trembling. She shouldn't be here. She should be at home, prescribing Mrs Aitken a balm for her cracked skin.

The commuters seemed to be in two minds; some scattered, while some, like Kenzie, stopped and craned their necks. The group of Separatists descended on a waiting cargo train. Two of them clambered onto the roof, wild smiles plastered across their faces. The others hurled stones from the ground. Fists met the air. Cait winced as stone met glass with a terrible *crack.* The lanky girl paced up and down the platform and cried words of encouragement to her accomplices. They wore no uniform. They blended into the crowd so perfectly. Cait had looked right at the girl, and she hadn't known what she really was. She clutched Kenzie furiously. His body locked with anticipation, gaze anchored on the Separatists.

'Separatist scum!' A man spat from beside Cait. His saliva rained across her cheek.

A driver emerged from the train, hands raised. His mouth moved in the shapes of calm negotiation. A stone arced through the air. A sick crunch. The driver's head snapped backwards as he toppled to the ground. The onlookers hissed as one, and then their outrage poured across the platform.

'*Kenzie.*' Cait tugged at his arm. She wanted to go home. She wanted the next train away from here. 'I'm scared.'

Kenzie didn't hear her. His eyes hunted through the crowd. 'They'll be here,' he muttered.

'Take the train!' the girl with the braces cried, and her co-conspirators lurched into motion. They hauled open the doors of the train, exposing the crates of goods inside, and started to raid the contents. With every sack that hit the tracks, the Separatists' cries grew louder.

Lealtie Ayebidin!
For the ootlawed keeng!

'Look!' Kenzie cried. He thrust a finger towards the furthest platform. Cait couldn't see what he was pointing to.

The Separatists' shouts died in their throats. They froze where they stood. From seemingly nowhere, a group of soldiers swept onto the platform. Black, hoodless cloaks lined in ruddy Afren burgundy billowed at their backs, fastened at their necks with golden chains. Cait sucked in a breath when she saw the rifles in their hands. The Queen's Watch. It couldn't be anyone else. The Separatists scattered, but a second group of Watchmen materialised in their path, and before long, the assailants were handcuffed and marched away. Cait only felt able to breathe again when the gunshot she had been waiting for never came.

Normality resumed as quickly as it shattered, and the crowds moved on with their commutes. It was only Kenzie who lingered, gazing at the Watchmen at work with a boy-like glow across his features.

'Did you see that?' he breathed.

Cait watched the poor train driver, who was being attended to by two officers. Blood scored down his face. He would be paying for that injury for months to come. She thought about the girl with the braces. 'What will happen to them?'

It was only when the last officer vanished that Kenzie seemed to come back to himself and look at Cait. The way his blue eyes gleamed set her racing heart at ease. 'They'll get the firing squad,' he said simply.

Cait faltered. 'They'll die?'

'It's treason, Cait.' He offered her his arm and they moved off through the crowd. 'They'd burn the whole world down if it meant getting their way. It's for the best.'

Cait clutched her suitcase tight and tried not to look too closely at each plainly dressed commuter. In Briddock, the slightest disturbance was catastrophic and would be the talk of the village for weeks, but the station seemed to have forgotten anything had happened at all. The city moved. The Queen's Watch, with their heavy cloaks, were a protective veil, and Cait tried to focus on that rather than the train driver with the bleeding head.

As Kenzie led Cait out of the station and into the open air, he looked down at her with a grin. 'Welcome to Thorterknock, Cait. You'll be quite safe here.'

Chapter 2

Thorterknock

Cait began to forget about smashed windows and hijacked trains as she settled into the flow of Thorterknock's full and easy streets. Red banking offices fronted by pediments and pillars brushed shoulders with regimented sandstone apartments, and people flitted from offices to cafes to retailers and back again. They talked quick and loud. Everything was quick and loud here. There were more people on this one perfectly manicured street than had ever lived in Briddock, and Cait had the sense of being swept into a wild and beautiful current.

Kenzie was already striding ahead, map in one hand, suitcase in the other.

'This is the New Town,' he explained once Cait had scurried to his side. 'We're headed across the River Cath into the Old Town.' His eyes fell to her hands, which smarted from hauling her suitcase, but he hoisted it easily into the same hand as his.

'The Cath,' Cait echoed, eyeing the twisting river that split Kenzie's map in two. 'Like, from the ballad?'

Kenzie grinned at her. 'The very one.'

Her father, a retired professor of literature at the University of Thorterknock, was a storyteller at heart and *The Ballad of Anndras and Cathal* was his favourite. The river took its name from the fearsome outlaw Cathal, whose severed head rolled down from the hills and sprouted a crimson stream. Dr Hardie had always meant to bring his daughter to Thorterknock in his years working at the university, but something always seemed to get in the way. If it wasn't a busy week at the surgery, it was Kenzie's brief time off from the farm, and if it wasn't that, it was fears of Separatists and their destruction that kept her feet on borders soil.

'Da offered to take me to work with him next week,' Cait would tell Kenzie, and Kenzie would hiss through his teeth.

8

'You sure, little dove? A civilian was injured on the campus just a couple of days ago.'

'Separatists?' she'd ask.

'Who else?' he'd say.

Each time she found herself with a quiet week and an invitation from her father, she and Kenzie had the same conversation. Those conversations became a routine safety net when she had no other excuse. She had let Kenzie affirm her fears and had settled on catching up with her father's stories when he returned from work at the weekends. Her guiding rule was that if she didn't acknowledge the city, it couldn't hurt her or the people she loved. She wasn't quite sure what to do now that she was entrenched within it.

Cait paused outside a grand building with golden gates and ivy dripping down its caramel walls. People in trim suits and velvet gowns passed through its revolving glass doors, handing their luggage to waiting employees wearing emerald ties. 'What is this place?' Cait asked.

'The Seymour,' Kenzie said. 'It's the most upmarket hotel in Storran. All the Watch's visitors stay there.'

The crowd trickled away as Kenzie and Cait stepped into a peaceful square. A wide granite building with needle-like spires that rushed to the sky loomed over them, casting the square in cool shade. Cait eyed the two officers in trim blue uniforms standing to attention by the door.

'Are they in the Watch?' She whispered, turning to Kenzie.

Kenzie snorted a laugh. 'They wish. They're the City Guard.'

As they moved off, Cait spotted a statue at the centre of the square. Distance blurred the details, but she'd know that silhouette anywhere: a man with his arms raised high, and a gap between his hands where a crown should be.

'Kenzie, it's Anndras!' She bounced on the spot before hurrying to the foot of the statue.

The First and Last King of Storran was cast in bronze. His eyes lifted to the space between his raised hands. The Antlered Crown of King Anndras was an image banned by the Watch several years ago in a bid to crack down on Separatist symbolism — that, along with the iconography of Storran's Great Stag.

'You *can* still see it,' her father had once told her as they discussed the crown. 'It's held in the Treasury Museum in Eadwick.'

'In *Eadwick?*' Cait had gasped. 'That's so far away.'

'Far enough away that most people in Storran won't ever get to see it, you see. So, it's quite safe there. Can't cause any trouble.'

'Why is it so important?' Cait had asked and her father had sighed the heavy sigh that usually indicated a story was coming as he lifted her onto his knee.

'The story goes that the antlers on the crown were gifted to King Anndras by the Great Stag of Storran, a mighty and royal beast. They say that anyone who wears the crown is imbued with the strength and valour of that stag. Unless, you're not worthy ...'

'What happens if you're not worthy?' Cait had prompted.

The light from the fire glowed in her father's glasses. 'Then the crown will melt you until you're nothing but ash!' he had exclaimed, tickling her until she squealed.

'Really?' Cait had asked when she had calmed down. 'Is the crown really magic?'

'Well, it's just a story, pet. Most things to do with Anndras are.'

Anndras, the First and Last King of Storran, who defeated the armies of Afren and secured Storran's freedom, was a well-known folk hero, but his history and mythology shared a complicated marriage.

Cait looked past the statue at the building behind him. 'What's the building for?' she asked.

Kenzie didn't need to consult his map. 'Storran's Parliament.'

'*Oh,* really? I didn't know we had one. It's beautiful.'

'It's a waste of money. There's nothing that's done in there that can't be done in Afren.'

'Like what?'

'Local affairs, mostly. Besides ...' His brow furrowed as he traced a finger along his map. '... It only encourages the Separatists. They should just tear it down.'

'Do you think?'

As Kenzie moved off again, Cait stared at the Parliament's dark windows. She imagined footsteps ringing on empty passageways and debate chambers full of ghosts, and it seemed like such a waste, but perhaps Kenzie was right. The building was beautiful, but it was dead behind the eyes. They followed Anndras' gaze out of the square and walked until they reached a bridge marked 'Aist Bridge' that struck out across the River Cath. When Cait looked over the side, she found the waters weren't red like the legend suggested, but murky grey, and as spirited as the outlaw it took its name from.

The Old Town on the other side of the river was like a completely different world. Gone were neat pavements and pruned hedges, replaced with the rattle and chatter of a working city that burst through each crooked cobble and foggy window. The sky criss-crossed with banners of washing, and Cait eyed the tenements warily as they craned their long, brown necks over the street below. When she spotted a man leading a mule that hauled a cart stacked with neat bundles of newspapers, she thought of home. She knew of Thorterknock's booming print industry and wondered if *The Border Record* started its journey here.

'Look, there's Hart Hall,' Kenzie said, pointing down a street that opened out onto a view of a castle crouched on the top of a hill.

Cait gawked at it. '*That's* the barracks?' It looked like it came straight from a tale in one of her father's books.

'Impressive, isn't it?' Kenzie pulled his glazed eyes away from the view and back to his map. 'Your inn should be around here somewhere.'

The map of the Old Town was a mess of little boxes that looked like they had been tossed across the paper like dice. The Queen's Watch barracks took up at least four times the space that a regular building on the map did and it would be easy enough to find even without Kenzie's excited circle. Cait wished she could stay in the fairy-tale castle, but Hart Hall was a military barracks and no place for civilians, according to Kenzie.

'Here it is.' Kenzie's finger came plunging down on a little mark that was hardly distinguishable from the other skewed squares. 'The Crabbit Corbie. Two streets from here.' Cait grimaced. The name rang with images of sticky floors and sleazy drunks. She eyed the expanse of map between The Crabbit Corbie and Hart Hall. The village square that normally separated them was about to become much, much larger.

'Is there nowhere nearer to you?' she asked.

Kenzie squeezed her shoulder and gave her a small smile. 'I did try.'

'Thank you,' Cait said, smiling for his sake. She pushed her shoulders back and took his hand firmly. 'I'm sure it'll be lovely.'

'Of course it will be,' Kenzie said, his gaze lighting up their smog-shrouded surroundings. 'It's *ours*.' Her soul warmed as he placed a kiss on her head. He shone in this new life, and it felt good that she had given it to him. Bravery tightened in her chest. He wrapped his hand around hers, but as they moved off, Cait's eyes happened to meet those of a man who was huddled in a doorway. His clothes were dirty, his hat upside down on the ground with a spattering of copper Bodles in it.

'Efternuin,' the man said with a polite nod of the head. Cait immediately fumbled for her coin purse. Kenzie's hand pressed against her shoulder.

'Come on, little dove.' He pulled her away and muttered in her ear, 'He's having you on.'

Cait's fleeting courage dissipated. The city spoke a language that she had never heard before, and soon she'd be without her translator.

*

'This is cheery,' Cait said, looking up at the faded signage that depicted a grumpy caricature of a crow outside The Crabbit Corbie. The hyacinths and white carnations in the window box did their best to lift the spirits of an otherwise dingy wynd.

Kenzie frowned up at the crow, whose paintwork had been peeled away by time, lending it a sinister edge. 'Could do with a lick of paint.'

'Maybe they have a suggestion box?' Cait offered.

'Hope so,' Kenzie muttered.

They were interrupted by a voice down the street calling Kenzie's name. They turned, and Cait could just make out the shape of three cloaks swishing towards them. Kenzie's face broke into a grin. 'Innes!' he called as one of the figures became a boy who grinned back up at him from under a peaked cap. His Queen's Watch uniform hung awkwardly from his shoulders, the smart jacket waiting for the body beneath to fill out. His heavy cloak, navy and lined with deep maroon, drowned his small frame. Cait guessed he must have been at least a few years younger than her. Innes stopped to catch his breath and he and Kenzie exchanged a brisk handshake that didn't match the look of wonder in the boy's round eyes.

'You look smart,' Kenzie said.

Innes gave a playful flick of his cloak, and his russet features seemed to burn with pride. 'I *do,* don't I?'

'Haven't seen you since induction. First day?' Kenzie asked.

'Second. You?'

Kenzie put a hand on Cait's shoulder. 'Cait and I just got off the train not long ago.'

'Oh, *you're* Cait!' Innes turned his lopsided grin on her and removed his cap, revealing short black hair shaved to the skull. 'Kenzie told me you'd be coming. You're going to love the city.'

Innes' companions appeared at his side, and Cait noticed the cascade of gold chains that draped from the cloak fastening at their shoulders to the buttons of their navy jackets. Innes' uniform was bare in comparison, and she wondered what Watchmen had to do to earn themselves a chain.

'Well, I'm glad you're finally here,' Innes said to Kenzie. 'You'll flush that Fox right out.'

Kenzie gave a meek roll of his eyes. 'If you say so.'

One of Innes' companions scowled like she'd heard all this before, but she didn't know Kenzie like Cait did.

'You heading to Hart Hall?' Innes asked. 'You should join us.'

Kenzie glanced at the inn and then at Cait. 'I wouldn't want to disrupt your route,' he said slowly.

'We're behind schedule, Addison,' one of Innes' minders muttered. She seemed to lean back on her heels as though she'd disappear up the street at any moment.

'Could you see yourself in, Cait?' Innes asked.

Cait felt her mouth open and shut. The answer should come easy, but when she thought about the man she had almost given her money to, she froze.

'Cait?' Kenzie said, looking down at her. There was a softness in his eyes that pleaded with her, a gentle and expectant parting to his lips. He looked back at the waiting Watchmen. 'I shouldn't keep you —'

Cait reached deep within her and drew from the well of courage in her chest, forcing her lips into a grin. 'Of course,' she said before Kenzie could finish, and his face burst with delight.

'There's a rose garden in the New Town. Meet me there at six,' he said, planting a kiss on her head and flashing her that heart-throbbing grin.

'Nice to meet you, Cait,' Innes said with a salute.

Kenzie winked at her. 'Wish me luck.'

Before she knew it, the four of them had swept away, leaving Cait on the doorstep of The Crabbit Corbie, with only her suitcase and a thousand fears.

'Wish *me* luck,' she whispered, and pushed open the door.

*

'Let me gie ye a haun wi that.'

As Cait struggled through the door, a plump man with thinning hair hurried over to help her. The room was dim and cosy. A handful of people were scattered in mismatching furniture around a roaring fire and at tables covered with full glasses and plates of steaming food.

'Oft, that's a lot of gear for yin lass,' the man said when he dropped the case next to the bar. He took a moment to catch his breath, then moved to the other side of the counter. 'Whit can a dae ye for?'

'A room, please.' She remembered that Kenzie still had her board money and added quickly, 'I can't pay right now but my partner can come by later.'

The man raised his eyebrows at her suitcase and said, 'Are ye staying foriver, like?'

'I — I don't know.'

The man's eyes crinkled at the corners as he muttered, 'Nae bather,' and Cait realised too late he had been making a joke.

'My name's Bram, at yer every biddin, should ye need us that is. And whit's yer name?'

'Cait Hardie.'

He scrawled some illegible words into a ledger before shutting it with a *thunk* and selected a key from the rack behind him. It made a hollow scrape as he slid it across the counter. 'Room Fowerteen. Best view in the hoose, jist for you.'

'Thank you.'

'That's a Boarders accent a detect oan ye. Whit's a country lass like yoursel daein in Auld Thorter, then?'

'I'm travelling with my partner, Kenzie.' She cleared her throat, suddenly self-conscious of the way she spoke. Until now, she had never thought she had much of an accent. 'He's got work in the city.'

'Ah weel, nae doubt ye'll settle right in. Great place is Auld Thorter, great fowk.'

Cait almost asked him about the Separatists and how often they had trouble with them, but the door to the inn clattered open, and Cait turned to find a man approaching the bar. Bram looked anxious, yet expectant.

'Jist a moment, young Cait,' he said, his peaty voice dropping low.

'Bram,' the newcomer said with a stiff nod as he leaned his elbows on the bar.

'Whit ye playin at, Tod?' Bram hissed. 'It's middle o the efternuin. Ah've punters here an aw.'

Cait stilled at the rolling sound of the old Storrian tongue. She could generally understand, but her mind had to race to keep up.

'Anno, anno, but ah picked up the gear this moarnin.' The man glanced over his shoulder and caught Cait's eye, and they both tore their gaze away. 'Ah brung it earlier but yi weren'y in.'

'Yi did whit?' Bram exclaimed, clearly louder than he had intended. His voice dropped to a whisper. 'Are yi daft, lad? Wi aw the polis and sodgers gaun aboot aw ower the place?'

'Ah wis dead sleekit, like. They sawna.'

'Jings, Tod. Yi've got me up tae high doh.' Bram waved a hand. 'Haud awa and come back the morn.'

'Aye, fine. Cheery, then.'

Cait tried not to let her discomfort show as the man slunk out of the pub. Old Storrian was for the uneducated, so her mother had always told her. *You have to be wary of those folk, Cait. That's the tongue of criminals and beggars.* And Separatists. For a moment, Bram seemed to forget Cait was there at all until he clapped his hands together and snapped out of it. 'Now, then, let's get this case up the stair.'

*

The bed in Cait's room touched the walls at top and tail. A small table at the bedside was propped up under one leg by a book. Two translucent shreds of purple fabric flanked a grimy window, and the whole place smelled of must. The room had ample storage, with a wardrobe against one wall, and a large cupboard door set into the other. Bram beamed proudly at it all. As he dropped Cait's case, the floorboards gave an ungrateful squeak.

'Well, young Cait, I'll let ye get settled. You ken whaur tae find us.' He bobbed out of the room, tugging the door across the carpet behind him.

The bed wobbled uncertainly as Cait eased herself down. She eyed the cupboard door on the opposite wall and wondered if she should start putting away her things, but immediately decided against it. She would put her things away eventually, but not yet. She wasn't ready for any of this to feel real. Instead, she glanced out the window. The best view in The Crabbit Corbie wasn't much more than a few mossy rooftops, a broken gutter, and the narrow street outside.

What am I doing here?

No. She'd left her doubts buried in the border hills for Kenzie's sake.

Only a few months ago, the two of them had sat shivering on a wall in the village square as the sun slid down between the hills. The air had bitten sharp against her skin and she could tell it was feeding time at next door's farm on account of the cacophony of bleating. Cait had never felt more at peace. She had meant to tell Kenzie she belonged in Briddock, that she didn't want to go, but instead she had breathed in a lungful of countryside air and chose the words, 'I love this' and he had pulled her closer and said, 'Me, too.' He had looked into the distance as if his heart had already bound out of the village, and he had laced his fingers through hers as he said, 'Our life is so close to starting.'

But Cait thought their lives had already begun. The villagers had laid it all out for them like stepping stones in fragments of gossip: they'd marry in June, have one child, then another, and then Cait would take over the surgery. All they had to do was step from one to the other, and now a great train had ploughed its way through, scattering the stones and leaving Cait pathless.

'I've been thinking ...' she had finally plucked up the courage to say the words she had been rehearsing as she brushed her hair, and ate her breakfast, and washed the mortar and pestle. 'Maybe I should stay.' She had kept her gaze fixed on the gold-drenched fields, but she felt Kenzie's eyes turn on her.

'What?'

Cait had squeezed his hand. 'There's nothing for me in Thorterknock.'

'I'd be there.'

The hurt that had entered his eyes stayed with her still.

She had looked down the path, towards the surgery, towards her home. 'I don't know ...' It wasn't just leaving home. The city was dangerous. The Separatists had killed Kenzie's parents.

'We're family,' he had said. Then, as if he had sensed that she was thinking about his parents, he added, 'You know I can't do this without you.'

Suddenly, she had felt very selfish.

*

Aside from the hurt in Kenzie's eyes, Cait's enduring memory of that evening was the cold. It had seeped into everything across the village, wreaking havoc on water troughs, and pipes, and pathways. It was, in Mr Blaine's words, a belter of a winter. Kenzie had asked her to join him in Thorterknock with gold leaves underfoot, and Cait had stewed on the idea as the ground grew crisp and the days grew short. Why, then, had Innes known she was coming when the last time Kenzie had seen him was at his induction during a balmy summer? A belter of a summer, as Blaine would say.

Cait shook all of it from her mind and reminded herself why she was here in this volatile city with its lopsided buildings, and confusing tongues.

I can't do this without you.

Chapter 3

Not Very Streetwise

It was creeping into late afternoon by the time Cait found a doctor's surgery tucked away in a dark corner of the Old Town. The sight was a relief, because something about this area had her checking over her shoulder and jumping at shadows. Unlike the rest of the city, the area hung in an eerie silence, and Cait hurried towards the door. She only paused long enough to glance above the threshold in hopes of spotting a dock leaf, but the spot lay empty. The symbol of removing the sting from an ailment was clearly only a borders custom.

Cait opened the surgery door and chaos spilled out into the street. The sound of discontent smacked her across the face, and she only just managed to dart out of the way as a stormy-faced woman cradling a screaming baby blustered past and slammed the door behind her. Cait stared at the churning waiting room. Every seat was full, and people jostled each other in what pockets of space they could find. It was obvious a queue had begun near the reception desk, but at some point, it must have fallen away, because Cait found herself at the back of what could only be described as a mob.

'I'm sorry, sir, but we do require a deposit upfront.' She could only just hear the receptionist over the hum of voices.

'Ah get paid next week. Ah'll bring it, then,' a man's voice trilled in response.

The receptionist's tone was the slow and unflinching march of someone who had done all this many times before. 'Then please come back next week and you will be offered treatment.'

'It's an emergency!'

'You will have to find another doctor who can cater to your requirements.'

'Yi've killed is!' he spat at the receptionist, then barged towards the exit, pausing only briefly near Cait to double over and hack into his arm. She heard his angry cough echoing long after he had disappeared up the street. Cait watched as patients were turned away one by one, and once half an hour had passed, and countless bodies had come and gone, a doctor appeared behind the desk. He clapped his hands once. The waiting room plunged into silence.

'We're full up today. If you are not already waiting to see someone, please come back early tomorrow. Come on, then, let's get this queue cleared.'

The waiting room erupted, and the queue shuffled forward as people crowded the desk.

'We came yesterday and the day 'fore that!' The man in front of Cait cried. The woman at his side cradled her arm in a sling made from a scarf. 'My wife's airm's in twae. She needs seen!'

The doctor wasn't listening. He turned away and disappeared into the safety of his office.

Cait shifted her way past the crowd until her fingers touched the wooden reception desk. 'Excuse me.'

'Please come back tomorrow,' the receptionist said.

'What happened?'

The receptionist only blinked at her.

'Was there an accident?' *An attack?* 'Why are so many people sick?'

The receptionist opened her mouth, but before she could speak, a fist pounded on the counter beside Cait, making the two of them jump.

'You'll see tae my wife!'

'There's another surgery near Wast Bridge,' the receptionist said. Her voice was steady, but her teeth dug into her bottom lip. 'You might have some luck there.'

The man spat a word Cait had never heard before and whisked his wife to the door. Cait gripped the desk to stop herself from being lost to the crowd. 'I'm new to the city,' Cait said quickly. A child screamed at the other side of the room, and she lifted her voice. 'I'm looking for work, my mam's a doctor —'

'We don't have any vacancies,' the receptionist said without looking up from what she was writing. Her grip on the pen blanched her knuckles.

'You look like you need an extra set of hands.'

The receptionist shot her a frosty glare. 'You're blocking the waiting room.'

Cait looked around at the people waiting. Some of them looked unbearably sick. 'You don't even need to pay me.'

'Move on,' the receptionist said. Cait hesitated, and in that hesitation, a new patient swept in front of her and hounded the desk.

*

Outside, Cait pressed her back against the wall and closed her eyes. There were so many people, so many *sick* people. At home, her mother had never turned anyone away. She would see five or six people a day, leaving time for walk-ins. Things were conducted quietly and orderly, and then the patients would leave their money with her father and be on their way. When she finally opened her eyes, Cait caught sight of the woman with the injured arm and her husband walking away up the street. She knew broken bones better than anything. The least she could do was look at it, and maybe find out what was happening in that waiting room.

'Wait!' Cait called and the pair slowed. 'Let me look at your arm,' she panted when she reached them. 'My mam's a doctor.'

The man eyed her warily and opened his mouth as if he might protest, but his wife sighed. 'Oh, Ken, I'd let a monkey look at it if it would stop it hurting.'

Cait guided the woman to the side of the road and they both crouched on the ground.

'Do you mind if I take this off?' Cait asked, indicating the makeshift sling. The woman nodded hesitantly. Cait carefully untied the knot and slipped the fabric away. The woman gave a hiss of pain under the arm's weight. 'How did it happen?' Cait asked as she inspected the forearm. She couldn't see any disfigurement, which was a good sign. The white skin had thrown up fresh purple bruising that told her the injury was still only a few days old.

'Leaving work. *Oh,*' the woman winced as Cait's fingers pressed a spot near her wrist. 'Slipped on the steps.'

When she was satisfied with the look and feel of the rest of the arm, Cait said, 'I'm going to need you to move your wrist. Slowly now.' The woman gently rocked her hand back and forward. It moved, but her face pinched as she did so. Cait pressed some weight on the arm, which she managed to hesitantly resist. 'Do you know what happened?' Cait asked. 'Why is the waiting room so full?'

The woman's husband grunted. 'S'always like that.' He frowned at her. 'Where are you frae?'

'Countryside,' Cait said, brushing off the question. 'But — how does anyone get treated?'

The husband merely shrugged. 'Let us know when you find out.'

At last, Cait wrapped the arm back in the scarf and secured it in place. 'It's not broken, but it is sprained. You'll need to rest it for a couple of days, but it should be good as new soon enough. Keep it elevated as much as possible.'

'How soon?' the woman asked immediately.

Cait saw the urgency in her eyes. 'A couple of weeks to a month at most until it's fully healed. Just be careful with it in the meantime.'

'Can I work?' she pressed.

Cait watched her carefully. 'Give it a couple of days, at least.' Then she laughed. 'It's a good excuse to put your feet up.'

The woman didn't meet her mirth. Instead, she blew out a breath through her teeth and nodded to herself. 'Ahright.'

'Gail —' the man started.

'It's fine, Ken,' she said stiffly. 'We're fine.'

Once she'd reiterated her advice, Cait watched the pair go.

The waiting room was *always like that.* Every day. The city either didn't have enough doctors or far too many sick people, or perhaps a lethal dose of both. If that woman had truly broken her arm, if the bone had pierced her skin, she could have suffered an infection before the surgery even opened the following day. Cait wondered how much it would cost to have a sprain looked at back home. It was always her mother that dealt with the finances, and their patients always seemed to be able to pay if not immediately, at least eventually. Cait shuddered to think about the coughing man and the disease that could be crawling through his lungs. His words wheezed on the wind as she made her way to more savoury parts of the Old Town.

Yi've killed is.

*

Cait put as much space between herself and the surgery as she could, but she couldn't stop noticing the children who played in the street barefoot, or the people who sheltered in doorways and begged for change on street corners. Kenzie said they were crooks, so she kept her eyes fixed on her boots and walked faster until she reached a busy square with brightly coloured market stalls. She browsed the wares: earthy smelling soaps, glazed pottery, dainty silver trinkets, and soon found herself at the back of a crowd. There was a restless energy about the people gathered, and their attentions seemed to be captivated by something at the front that Cait couldn't see. She slid between the bodies until she was at the centre, and squinted until a newspaper stand came into view. A young boy stood on top of it, ignoring the flustered newspaper salesman hollering up at him.

'We were free once, what's haudin us back this time?' the boy cried out. His voice strained against the disapproving rumble of those gathered.

'Aye, seven hunner years ago!' a man from near the front of the crowd laughed.

The boy sputtered. 'Afren colonised us!'

The man guffawed. '*Colonised*? Do ye hear this yin?' A chortle rippled back through the crowd. 'It's thanks tae Afren we're no all living in mud huts!'

'That's lies! We — we've got everything we need ... we — we — we have peat!'

'Peat doesny last foriver,' the man said.

For a moment, Cait was transported straight back to her parent's kitchen table where she was watching her mother and Kenzie set the political affairs of the Five Realms to rights over a brew.

The Separatists like to pretend they're rational by making hollow arguments, she distinctly remembered Kenzie saying one afternoon. Her mother had nodded fervently and said, *that's exactly the problem. It's nothing but hot air, and fools will fall for it.*

I'm not a fool, Cait thought. She had to leave. How long before the boy's comrades made an appearance?

'This is an embarrassment,' a voice hissed to her left. Cait glanced sideways. A young woman bundled in a long, brown coat glared up at the speaker. With her collar turned up, hair tucked in, and hands thrust deep in her pockets, she looked completely swamped under the leather.

'It's just hot air, but fools will fall for it,' Cait said, parroting her mother. At least the regular folk of Briddock and Thorterknock seemed to have one thing in common: an intolerance to Separatists.

The girl gave a start as if she hadn't expected to be heard by anyone. She looked at Cait, then back at the boy, and murmured, 'Gaun find yourself a different fool to preach at, hen.'

'You agree with him?'

The girl pulled a face. 'Maybe not after hearing him speak.'

The boy said something that made half the crowd roar in unison. These people didn't care about nationhood or whose flag they lived under. They cared about how much tax they were paying, and if they could make ends meet. Cait thought of the woman off work with her sprained wrist, and the train driver from that morning. How would any of this help *them*?

'We don't need empty promises,' Cait said.

'Naw, we don't.' The girl flashed Cait a wry grin. 'More importantly, we need a better speaker.'

Without another word, she walked forward, disappearing into the crowd. A confused mumble lapped through the air when she appeared at the front moments later and hopped on top of the newspaper cart, alongside the boy. He glanced nervously at her as he tried to choke out another sentence. For a moment, he squared his shoulders, then teetered and resigned himself to the ground. The woman regarded the crowd. Her coat collar had flopped down, revealing a narrow face. Straight red hair spilled out over her shoulders. Her lips curved into a mocking, hungry grin, and she sized up the crowd with a righteous glare that Cait found herself unable to turn away from. Cait had no doubt about who she was even before the words rolled from mouth to mouth: *The Fox? That's her!*

'If the good man has something to say, perhaps he'd like to step up tae the box?' she said, maintaining burning eye contact with the main heckler. The Fox's voice was not what Cait expected. Words flicked, barb-like, from the tip of her tongue, but there was something quiet and melodic that softened its edges. It captivated Cait long enough for the crowd to press in and leave her trapped at the centre. 'Anyone else care tae speak?' The girl's eyes hunted through the crowd. Her gaze settled on Cait for a moment, and Cait held her breath until it moved on. 'I won't keep you long, I promise,' she said, but Cait wasn't prepared to trust the word of the Fox of Thorterknock. 'When I was wee there was nothing I loved mair than stories about heroes. You know the ones. Underestimatit hero stands up against oppression.' She paused. The silence was heavy. 'How many of those stories do you think ended with the heroes running back to those oppressors?'

The boy had thrown his voice into the crowd desperately, like a fisherman at sea, but this girl, the Fox, didn't need to do that. The crowd clung to her every word. Cait wondered if they did so out of fascination, or fear. She wasn't sure herself.

'Oppression's a big word,' the same man who had heckled the boy clucked.

The Fox's eyes sparked as she turned on him, and Cait tensed.

'Come up and tell us all about it, then, the invite's still open,' she said. The man didn't respond. 'There's a sorry lack of self-confidence in this nation. I won't bore you with a list of our accomplishments or inventions, like the steam engine or gas lighting. I won't bother laying out how our money is used to pay off Afren's debt, because I suppose you're not here to listen. You lot never are.' The Fox laughed. 'But tell me this, why does so much of our money get pumped into maintaining the Queen's Watch? Why are our esteemed overlords in Afren so set on keeping us locked away like a big, bloody, dairy cow if we're so destitute that we wouldn't stand a chance ourselves?' A cough came from the crowd. A nearby cart wheezed on its brakes. 'They need our resources! They're feart to watch us go because we'd leave them behind,' the Fox exclaimed. 'We've got wains going hungry. We've got elderly folks on the streets. We've got people dying off because they can't afford medicine, but that's all well and good because at least Eadwick gets a shiny new train.'

This is the Fox of Thorterknock, Cait had to remind herself. *You can't trust a thing she says.* And yet, Cait couldn't will her feet to move. The Fox's words slid beneath her skin and prodded at a dormant indignation she had never realised was there, but it tasted so familiar. It tasted like the day the valuable peatland outside Briddock had to be signed over to Afrenian officials. It tasted like Briddock's library closing, and her father's wages stagnating, the result of something Cait didn't understand but her mother called *austerity*. It tasted hot. It tasted bitter. She could get drunk on the Fox's outrage, if she let herself.

'Storran is full of potential, and it's only Afren telling us that it's not.' The Fox was silent for a moment, then her voice raised ever so slightly. 'And you glaikit arseholes are willing to stand there and lap that shite up 'cause they said so.'

The spell broke. Anger erupted across the crowd.

'We've got what it takes, and only a cowart would deny it.' The Fox seemed to hesitate, and her eyes slid over the crowd as if she were sizing them up. Cait's heart hammered against her ribs as she waited for the Fox to decide she couldn't get through on words alone and opt for firepower instead.

'Ach, you've no got a leg tae stand on!' the man at the front called.

'Nae claim, nae right, and nae plan.'

Then the red-haired girl gave a small grin. It was the grin of someone who had just pinched all the left socks from the washing line. She studied the crowd carefully, then at last she said, 'I'll let you in on a secret. Just between you and me.' Her voice dropped its volume as she crouched low on the newspaper stand. Her smile widened until her teeth were bared in maniacal glee. Cait's heart thrashed. It was time to go. She'd stayed too long. She turned to find a way through the crowd, but they'd pressed in so close.

'We've got the heir of Anndras Àrdan,' the Fox said.

Cait stopped. She gasped as the breath caught in her throat. She'd misheard that, surely. The square hung in stunned silence until someone cried, 'Anndras died heirless!'

Cait turned back to face the Fox, and her eyes gave a satisfied flash. 'Our heir wears the Àrdan ring! He is Anndras' *blood,* and once we crown him, Afren will have nae choice but to accept our sovereignty.' The crowd erupted into shouts again, louder and more ferocious than ever. Cait pressed her hands to her ears. 'By Afren's ain laws!' the Fox shouted over the crowd, 'They must recognise him!'

The Fox had lost control of the crowd, but she looked over it with satisfaction. As the hecklers raged around her, Cait stared at the Fox, and their eyes met. The Fox lifted an eyebrow and gave a subtle bow. *How's that for a speaker?* she seemed to say.

Cait forgot the city and Kenzie and the truth that Storran was one of five united realms. She forgot the train driver from that morning, and the woman with her sprained wrist, and she forgot every fear she had about the city. All the politics of the earth and her mother's kitchen table turned to ash under the startling light of King Anndras the First and Last. Somewhere, an antlered crown called for its secret prince. A quickening of her heart told her that something great was near, that the storybooks of her girlhood could be true.

But it all fell away at once. The crack of a gunshot pierced the air to the right, and the Fox froze, panic flashing across her face. The crowd started to scatter before Cait knew what was happening, and the Fox dropped from eye line. Cait saw their cloaks and chains before anything else. A group of Watchmen closed in around the crowd, guns in hand. Her legs froze and she watched as they tackled the most vocal heckler from the front of the crowd. He thrashed helplessly.

'I'm no Separatist!' he shouted, but two Watchmen crushed his face into the cobbles.

Cait found the good sense to run. She turned but caught sight of a familiar face only a few paces away. For some reason, her first thought was of how heart-wrenchingly handsome Kenzie looked in his uniform. His eyes fell on her, and his steely focus shifted to confusion, and then a dark rage. Before either of them could work out what to do, Cait ran for everything she was worth.

*

Kenzie was late. Cait perched on a fountain in the New Town's rose garden and a breeze sprayed cool mist across her skin. Again, and again, she counted the Bodles scattered across the fountain's tiled floor. They reminded her of the coins in the homeless man's hat that morning. She wondered where he would go when night came. She wondered where the Fox had slunk away to.

There she was again. It seemed the Fox had disappeared from her plinth and taken to hiding in Cait's mind. Cait groaned as she tossed a pebble into the water, and the sound of approaching voices broke the surface of her thoughts. When she turned, she found Kenzie and Innes walking towards her. Innes was laughing, and relief sputtered inside Cait. They seemed in good spirits.

'Evening, Cait,' Innes said when they drew closer.

Cait greeted him quietly. When Kenzie's eyes met hers, she laced her fingers together and offered him a twitch of smile. Slowly, he walked towards her, and wrapped an arm around her shoulders. Cait looked up quickly and he grinned at her. 'Hello, Cait.'

They started to walk, and despite the relief that washed over her, Cait's voice was small. 'How was your first day?'

'Excellent,' Kenzie said. 'They started me on patrol, like Innes.'

'And you got to see some real action.' Innes' voice dragged with longing. 'I've been down the New Town all day. Nothing ever happens there.' Cait knew from her first steps in Thorterknock that he was wrong.

'Beginners luck, perhaps,' Kenzie said.

Innes jabbed Cait gently with his elbow. 'Your Kenzie here helped scatter a rally on his first day.'

'A rally?' She didn't think it was a rally. It seemed more like a gathering of people on the street. Most, if not all of them, had been fervently against the Separatists.

'Aye,' Innes nodded eagerly. He was so excited Cait might have assumed he had been there rather than Kenzie. 'He got in a few arrests, even a Separatist.'

'The Fox?' The question spilled out of her before she could stop it.

'No, a young lad,' Kenzie said. The boy who had been on the stand must have been about ages with Innes.

'What will happen to him?' she asked.

'He'll get the firing squad, and that's one less troublemaker on the streets,' Innes said far too easily. A flock of pigeons burst into the sky. Cait jumped out of her skin. Innes chuckled.

'What about the people listening?' Cait asked.

Innes pushed his hands into his pockets. 'They'll be investigated —'

'Not enough,' Kenzie cut him off. 'Those so-called investigations always take too long. Separatist ideas are dangerous. Anyone caught listening should be locked up.' Cait shivered. Kenzie looked down at her and pulled her in tighter. 'Are you cold, little dove?' He unclipped his cloak, revealing the handsome double-breasted jacket beneath. Cait's tummy danced at the sight. Kenzie draped the cloak around her, and it dragged on the ground as she clutched it to her chest.

They walked in silence for a few moments, the rifle shot still rattling around Cait's bones, then Innes turned to Kenzie. 'Did you hear about the team they're sending into Afren?'

Kenzie grinned at him. 'I did, indeed.'

'Are you going for it?'

'That's a silly question, Innes. Of course, I am.'

Cait's interest piqued. 'What's this?'

Innes' face lit with excitement as he launched into an explanation. 'There's rumours the Separatists are planning something in Afren. Something *big*. They're sending a squad down to investigate, and word is, Brigadier Cameron wants to send some new recruits.'

Cait gaped up at Kenzie. 'In *Afren?* What part?'

'Eadwick, most likely,' Innes said. 'I don't think they'd strike anywhere but the capital of the Five Realms.' *Eadwick.* A glittering metropolis buried deep in the heart of Afren. The seat of government, and the home of Queen Ana. 'Some of the boys in Hart Hall are putting money on what they're planning. I put ten Siller on them blowing up Parliament.'

Kenzie laughed scornfully. 'If they had access to gunpowder, I'm sure we'd already know about it. My money's on something more low-key.'

'Do you think the Fox will be involved?' Innes mused.

Kenzie didn't miss a beat with his response. 'No. They'll need her to keep eyes up here. I imagine we'll see her becoming more active while things are happening down south.'

Innes peered round at Kenzie from under his cap. 'Then surely there's no better time to catch her?'

'She'll still be here when we get back.'

'How long would this be for?' Cait asked.

Innes shrugged. 'As long as it takes, I suppose.'

'But ...' *Why Afren? Why so far away? Why, when we only just got here?* She bit her tongue, remembering that she was here to support Kenzie.

*

When they reached the end of the gardens, Kenzie told Innes to go on ahead while he walked Cait back to the inn.

'See you later, Cait,' Innes said, as he took off at the pace of an excitable hunting dog.

Once she and Kenzie were alone, Cait found the courage to say, 'Are you really going to Afren?' Kenzie said nothing. Cait turned to find him looking at her with a blank expression on his face. 'Whatever you decide, I'll support you, I just —'

He raised his eyebrows, but his lips were taut. 'Separatists, Cait?'

Cait winced, suddenly feeling foolish for even hoping she had been forgiven. She took a steadying breath, but her eyes already stung. 'Kenzie, I promise, I didn't know —'

'And that's why you were right in the middle of them.'

Cait bit back her tears. 'They were just talking, nothing happened. It was ... interesting.'

Kenzie scoffed. 'Don't be stupid.'

She felt her voice rise. 'Honestly, trust me! I was going to leave, but they started talking about how people can't afford food or medicine or ... I saw the waiting rooms myself. Did you know how bad they are here?'

'Cait —'

'They said they found the heir of King Anndras —'

'*Cait.*'

'Anndras has an *heir* —'

'Look at me,' Kenzie said, crouching to her level and placing his hands on her shoulders. He held her gaze as he slowly, carefully, formed each word. 'They're *Separatists*. It's a *fairy story.*'

'But —'

'They get into your head,' Kenzie said softly, placing a finger to his temple. 'It's what they're best at.' He straightened. 'Honestly, Cait, *think*. Charisma is a weapon.'

Cait suddenly felt violated, as if the redhead had pried her mind open and tinkered with her thoughts. She'd rearranged what Cait knew as truth: Separatists could not be trusted. Separatists harmed the innocent. Separatists were a menace that needed to be stopped. She'd planted pretty stories in their place, and Cait had lapped them up. She was just another one of the fools her mother despised.

'I'm sorry,' she gasped, winded by the force of reality. What if she'd been caught? What about Kenzie's career? What if the Fox had decided to strike? 'I didn't mean … I'm sorry.'

'Oh, Cait,' Kenzie said, smiling. 'Sweet Cait.' He pulled her close, and Cait leaned against his chest. She could trust this chest; it was warm and sturdy. He eased her away from him and softly brushed away the white wisps of hair. 'You're such a trusting soul,' he said quietly. Then his affectionate gaze hardened. 'I need you to understand. These people, that girl, they're experts at what they do. Her especially. You can't let her get under your skin.'

'I won't,' Cait said, trying to sound more confident than she felt. Not again, not ever again. She'd make Kenzie proud of her. 'I promise.'

Kenzie watched her for a long moment then nodded. 'It's okay, little dove. No harm done. Just be careful. They prey on your sort the most.'

'What do you mean?'

Kenzie cocked his head and grinned. 'You think the best of people. That makes you easy to lead astray.'

Cait laughed, though she didn't know why. 'I suppose so.' How would she get by if he went to Afren? She missed Briddock. Things were simple there. There, things made sense.

'Let's get you home,' he said, and for a moment Cait allowed herself to hope, but her heart fell when they arrived at the inn, and it fell further when she realised this was now 'home'.

Kenzie let Cait enter first and Bram's face lit up the gloom within.

'Young Cait, how wis your evening?' Her expression must have caught the lamplight, because his smile faded. 'Everything okay, lass?'

When Kenzie stepped through the door behind her, the innkeeper shrunk several inches, and his face hardened, but Kenzie didn't seem to notice. 'Evening,' he said, his usual charming smile plastered across his face. He strode across to the bar and put a hand out for Bram. Slowly, mechanically, Bram took it and shook once. 'You'll be looking after my Cait for the next while.'

Bram nodded as he said, 'Aye, she told me you were in toon for work.'

'I certainly am, so I hope you're not harbouring any Separatists back there.' Kenzie leaned forward to look behind the bar before giving a hearty laugh.

Bram laughed, too. 'Jist dinna go in my cellar.'

Kenzie chuckled to himself, but Bram kept glancing at Cait. Maybe he could see it on her face: the speeches, the ideas she drank up so willingly, fairy stories of long-lost kings. *What a silly little country girl,* he was thinking.

'How much am I due you?' Kenzie asked Bram.

'Ah, yi'd normally be seiventy Siller for the week, but I'll do yi it for sixty.'

Kenzie thanked Bram and turned to Cait. 'Go and get some sleep, little dove. I'll see you tomorrow.'

Cait bowed her head and hurried up the stairs. She heard the clinking of coins, the scrape of a stool, the smacking of glass on wood, and then Kenzie's voice, tight with a grin, 'She's not very streetwise. I feel better knowing someone's looking out for her.'

Chapter 4

Eat Your Cereal

When she was sixteen, Cait picked up her mother's newspaper while eating her breakfast of warm milk and brose. The results of a recent election dominated the front pages, but she skimmed by them until a headline caught her eye:

'*The new Borders Council has stressed the important role public money plays in ongoing projects such as the west Eadwick railway line. They state that contributions towards innovation should be made across the Five Realms.*'

Her mother entered the room and boiled the kettle on the stove.

'Mam,' Cait said, laying the paper down. 'Have you read about the election results?'

'Not yet, but I hear Prosperity won down this way. Don't tell your father. He'll be beside himself.' Her mother's eyes narrowed as she regarded Cait, the kettle hanging from her hand. 'Not like you to be interested in the news.'

Cait shrugged. 'It says here they want to contribute to the Eadwick railway line with borders taxes.'

'Mmmhm, and what are you thinking about that?' She poured herself a mug and sat opposite Cait at the table.

Cait didn't know exactly, but the story left her with a sense of unease. She assumed she was missing a vital piece of knowledge about the situation and considered letting it go, but if her mother had taught her anything, it was that if you didn't investigate a symptom, you would never know its cause. She wove her way slowly around the words. 'Don't you think it's a bit ... unfair?'

Her mother considered for a moment, her mug poised against her lips. 'I don't think so,' she said at last. 'Do you?'

'I just don't understand why we should pay for it. It sounds like something Afren should pay for.'

Her mother shook her head and began leafing through the paper. 'We're all on the same team, Cait. There's no *us* and *them*.'

'It's just that no one in Storran will get to use it. It's so far away,' Cait said.

'Maybe not directly, but I'm sure it will benefit us in other ways.' Her mother's eyes scanned down the page as she spoke. Cait admired her nonchalant confidence discussing current affairs.

'How?'

'Mmm?' Her mother looked up at her. Her voice went high, and she shrugged. 'Well, growth, of course.'

Cait frowned down at her food. She wasn't sure what 'growth' meant exactly, but it seemed to be the answer to most political questions. 'I suppose.'

After a moment of silence, her mother peered at Cait over her glasses. 'People down our way aren't likely to travel much up north, but some of our money still goes to maintaining the lines between Thorterknock and Carse. Is it not much the same?'

Cait thought hard. 'I'm not sure.'

Her mother turned back to the paper. 'Think of it this way: Eadwick is in the south of the country, and we're in the north. We work together.'

'So, you'd say we're from Afren?' Cait said slowly.

'Goodness, Cait, no. We're from Storran.'

'But, then, why —'

'It's too early for politics, lass,' her mother said. 'Now, eat your cereal.'

*

We're all on the same team, Cait. There's no us *and* them. Her mother's words were stuck in Cait's mind as she slowly became one with the skeletal mattress in The Crabbit Corbie. *Just get on with your life and stop worrying about all this nonsense,* she told herself. It was her second day in Thorterknock, and she had spent the night fighting to gain control of her own mind. The Fox skulked around the periphery of her thoughts, and just when she had been able to think of something, *anything* else, she found herself wondering about the Separatist prince. Where were they keeping him? What was he like? What did this mean for the future of the Five Realms? Then, she would remind herself of Kenzie's warning, and the process would start all over again.

Cait was exhausted.

When a soft knock came at the door, she sat bolt upright. She scrambled to comb her hair and make herself look presentable for Kenzie, even though she was still in her nightdress in the height of the afternoon.

'Abody hame?' Bram's muffled voice came from outside the door. Cait sunk back under the threadbare blanket and didn't say anything. 'Just thought tae let ye know I've popped a pot o soup on. Plenty tae go roond.' Then she heard the faint clunk of footsteps going down the stairs. Cait rolled over and brought the blanket to her eyes. She couldn't stay here forever, but the Fox and her words and Cait's overwhelming temptation lay outside. When the smell of Bram's soup slid its way under the door, Cait's stomach moaned and she decided that whatever lay outside this room, it was worth the risk.

*

Cait found Bram sat behind the bar holding a steaming bowl of soup. The room was muffled by a warm lull, and conversations bubbled away quietly between the punters.

'Ah, Cait,' Bram said when he spotted her. She clambered on top of one of the bar stools as Bram scooped some of the thick broth into a bowl and pushed it towards her.

'I'll get Kenzie to pay when —' Cait started to say, but Bram cut her off.

'It's oan the hoose,' he said.

Cait wolfed spoonful after spoonful, ignoring the way the heat stung her mouth. The meat was rubbery and the water too salty, but Cait didn't mind, she was just grateful that Bram had thought to share with her.

He chuckled. 'Slow doon, lass. There's plenty tae go roond.' Then, with a thump of understanding, she remembered Kenzie's words from the night before and placed her spoon down. Maybe Bram just didn't think Cait would be able to feed herself in the city. Maybe Kenzie had put him up to this. 'Not tae your taste? Ah willna pretend I'm cook but —'

Cait shook her head quickly. 'No, no, it's grand.'

Bram leaned one elbow on the counter. 'Then whit's troubling yi?'

'It's silly.'

'Try me, I'm a silly man,' Bram said, spreading his hands.

She sighed. The words were heavy. 'Did my … did Kenzie put you up to this?'

Bram stilled, spoon hovering between the bowl and his mouth. His expression softened quickly as he placed it down with a gentle *clink*.

'Listen, you,' he said. 'Dinna pay any heed to what that laddie says. You're plenty capable.'

Cait almost laughed. 'He didn't tell you about yesterday, then?'

'Young Cait,' Bram said with a firm look that reminded Cait of her mother when she was making a point. 'I gaither you're wary o the city.'

Cait smiled despite herself. 'What made you think that?'

'I've nivver kent anyone tae stomach more than an oor alone in one of my rooms.' He laughed from the belly, and it swelled into the quietest corners of the bar. A couple of the punters glanced over their shoulders at him. 'You think I've no seen his sorts afore?' He nodded at the door as if Kenzie were still there. 'He's proud. Awbody who puts that uniform oan gets that way, thinks they're the brightest this toon's seen. And this toon's seen some bright fowk.'

Kenzie *was* proud, but he had good reason to be. 'His parents were killed in a Separatist attack. He doesn't want anyone else to go through that,' Cait said.

Bram's small mouth twitched into a smile. 'You've kenned him a lang time, then.'

Cait nodded. 'We grew up together.'

Leaning back on his stool, Bram lifted his bowl again. 'And, if you dinna mind an auld man's nose,' his eyebrows arched. 'Will yi marry?'

Cait's face burned. 'Just think of the do you could have on the salary of a Lealist. An officer's wedding, that would be,' Bram muttered through a mouthful of mutton.

Cait's mind was only partly there, the other half grappling with the future. It had always been assumed that she and Kenzie would marry, the only question on the village square was when. Now that they were in the city and Kenzie was off chasing Separatists, Cait wondered if *when* was rapidly becoming *if*. 'Everything's a bit confusing right now,' was all she said.

Bram sighed. 'Aye, it often is. Just enjoy your soup. And tell me, whit's been your favourite part of Auld Thorter so far?'

The New Town was a marvel. The Old Town bustled. There was much to like on either side of the Cath, but a bold face and red hair passed through her mind. She shook the thought away and spoke the first words that came to mind. 'The statue of Anndras in the New Town.'

'Ah, the one ootside the auld Parliament?' Bram said. He nodded thoughtfully. 'Anndras an Cathal. It's an auld favourite of mine. One of yours n aw?'

'Thanks to my da, it is.' She smiled to herself. 'He tells it at least once a week.' As Bram slurped at his soup, an idea crossed Cait's mind. 'Are there any ... museums, or archives in the city?'

Bram nodded feverishly. 'Plenty, aye. Whit are ye efter?'

'Anything about the history of Storran,' Cait said.

'The Museum of Storran. Juist a short walk from the station. Looking for anything specific, lik?'

'My da does a lot of research about Anndras and Cathal and it's been a few years since he was last in Thorterknock, so I thought maybe there might be something for him in the museum.' One particular artefact, actually.

A stramash three years in its length
A Keeng withoot a throne
A chairge enshrined within the law
Fur freedom jointly owned.

It was perhaps the part of *The Ballad of Anndras and Cathal* that she knew best. She could still hear the way her father's voice grew clearer, his words more pronounced, as he retold those lines by the fire. She could hear him muttering over, and over, and over, those lines that he was *certain* held something valuable in them.

'Do they have any treaties in the museum?' Cait asked Bram. 'Something that was signed by a lot of people, maybe.'

Bram shook his head. 'They've got plenty of auld paper in there. Dinna ask me though, it's no my scene.'

Her father wasn't even sure if it existed. Encased in those lines from the ballad, Dr Hardie theorised that Anndras, unsure of what the future held and perhaps predicting his fate, penned a treaty that handed over the sovereignty of Storran to its people. He thought that the charge was an order, and the fact it was enshrined within the laws of Storran must mean it was some kind of legally binding document. Where it was, he didn't know.

'I wish you'd stop looking for that document!' her mother would say with a shake of her head. 'It'll mean nothing but trouble if it does exist and you find it.'

He'd been searching for years, and he'd had no leads. When she was young, Cait had viewed her father's research as some grand conspiracy, but the older she got the more she started to believe it was nothing more than a misinterpretation of the poem on her father's part.

'Ye know, I nivver understood Cathal's death in that tale,' Bram mused. Cait laughed. 'I always thought the same thing.'

According to legend, the Queen of Afren, eager to end the feuding between Anndras' army and her own, sent for Anndras to meet her in the forest. Cathal received the message instead and went in Anndras' place to meet the Queen. There, he was pounced upon by her men and stabbed through the heart. Anndras received the outlaw's head in a box the next morning.

'Yi'd think a tactician like Cathal would see richt through that. Makes you wonder why.'

Cait had asked her father why he thought a clever man like Cathal would walk into a trap, but his only answer was that folklore was fluid, and maybe the story was mixed up before finally being written down in the version they knew today.

'Did yir faither ever tell yi the tale o how Cathal slipped and cracked his heed half open on rock while runnin from the Queen's sodjers?' Bram asked.

'What?' Cait snorted, almost choking on her soup. 'He didn't do that.'

'Well-known story in my bit, so it is!' Bram chuckled to himself. 'Onyway, if it's history yer looking for, Auld Thorter is steeped in the stuff.' At the thought of venturing outside, Cait's stomach gave an awkward flip. She stared at her soup, feeling Bram watching her from the other side of the bar. 'Don't let the boy get tae yi, lass,' he said softly.

'It's not just that.' Cait placed her spoon down again, her stomach leaden. She kept her eyes on the stained countertop as she spoke. 'I ran into some Separatists yesterday.' Her voice grew quiet with shame. 'I stood and listened to what they had to say.'

'And that troubles you,' Bram said.

'It does.' She didn't know much about Bram at all, but she knew that the longer she kept these thoughts to herself, the more invasive the Fox's whisperings grew. 'I can't stop thinking about them, the things they said. I told Kenzie it was fine but ... I think they're in my head.'

She expected him to push the plate of soup aside, to pin her with a firm look and tell her she had let the city get the better of her, but Bram just blew gently on his spoon and shrugged. 'It's plenty understandable tae be wirried. The Separatists say things, but the officers in the Queen's Watch say things, too.' He took another spoonful. 'Whas tae say who has it richt?'

Cait fought to keep her voice level. 'I don't want to become one of them.'

Bram flashed her a grin. 'Then you've solved your own problem, lass. Yer mind is your ane, no the Separatists', and certainly no the Watchmen's.'

His words reassured her, but they didn't take away the sting of shame. 'Kenzie still thinks I'm a fool.'

'Listen, if I were you I wouldnae listen tae a word that Kenzie says, but I'm no you and I gaither you care a fair deal about pleasing him, so go out and enjoy yourself and prove him wrang.' Bram got up and started to rinse his bowl under the tap before drying it and tossing the rag over his shoulder. 'Everyone finds their way eventually, lass, and everyone always makes their way back tae The Crabbit Corbie.' He glanced up at the punters and braced his hands on his hips. 'Whither they like it or no, mind you.'

*

There was a woman selling luxurious scarves on Barter Bridge — a wide sandstone arch lined on either side by stalls where people chattered and bought and sold. As Cait made her way across the bridge, she paused and admired the lush, woollen scarves. The woman, who had a pinched look about her, stood behind the stall.

'Can I interest you in a scarf, lass? Straight from the mills in Carse.'

Cait gently stroked the doughy wool. 'It's Birkenweave?' She asked.

'Aye, the genuine stuff.'

Exclusively handwoven in the northeast city of Carse on looms made of silver birch, Birkenweave products were one of the world's favourite Storrian exports, second only to whisky. Kenzie inherited one from his mother, but one day as they were out hiking, it was swept away by the wind. He was inconsolable for weeks afterwards, the last treasured piece of his mother, ripped from him. Cait had hunted the lands around Briddock high and low, but the scarf had been claimed by the elements. The price on the scarves before her, twenty-five Siller, was affordable as far as Birkenweave went, but Cait's purse was empty. She complimented the woman on her wares and set off to find a surgery that might hire her so she could afford the scarf for Kenzie.

*

In her search for a surgery, Cait found herself in a corner of the city off the main thoroughfare. She was before a building topped by the flag of the Five Realms: the Afrenian boar's head roaring on a golden sun, backed by a field of deep maroon. The building, whose brass signage read *City Chambers,* held a stout authority about it. She was just about to move on, when a flash of red at the skyline caught her eye. Though her sight was hazy, Cait immediately knew the flared shape of the brown coat and the red hair. The Fox of Thorterknock slunk along the rooftop of the City Chambers, one hand stretched out for balance, the other clenched around a piece of navy and gold fabric that pulled at her hand as it tried to escape into the wind. Cait held her breath. Other than two city guards muttering between themselves a short distance away, the street was empty and still. The Fox teetered dangerously on the edge of the building as she pulled at the rope and brought the Afrenian flag down towards her and unclipped it. The wind had tugged her red hair out of her collar, and it flapped around her shoulders in the breeze. She looked like a flag herself. For a moment, she considered the Afrenian flag in her hand, and then released her grip. It ripped free and stole away on the wind over Cait's head. Standing tall atop the building, with her chin angled upwards and back straightened, as though the wind couldn't touch her, the Fox looked like she belonged on a plinth. She watched the flag go, and as she made to turn back to the pole, her eyes fell on Cait.

Cait froze. The Fox appeared to do the same, eyes wide like she had been caught under the hunter's gun. Slowly, Cait glanced to her right to check if the guards had noticed anything. The Fox must have followed her gaze, because when Cait looked back a moment later, all she could see was the tail end of the brown coat disappearing behind the rooftops. Without thinking, Cait hurried after the Fox. Her eyes followed the skyline even as the light pierced them through the smog. Her boots clapped against the cobbles. She ran blind, taking corners at random as she hoped for a flash of red hair, or brown coat, or any sign at all. Then the world went dark. Cait yelped as course fabric pressed against her face and snatched away her breath. She stumbled to a halt, hands clawing at her face. They'd caught her. She'd put her nose too far in their business and now they were going to drag her off and make an example of her. This is what happened when you pursued the Fox of Thorterknock. Cait spluttered as her fingers found a grip on the fabric and she managed to pull it away from her face. She blinked, tensing for the backlash, but none came. She was completely alone on the street.

What were you thinking? She looked down at the fabric she pulled from her face, and found it was the navy flag the Fox had been trying to hoist onto the flagpole. She ran it through her fingers, admiring the way the light caught the gold embellishments: a great stag with a deep, regal stare, one leg elegantly lifted. A crown hovered between its magnificent antlers, and sprigs of gorse framed the scene. Stitched neatly across the top were the words *Lealtie Ayebidin,* Storran's ancient motto.

Loyalty Eternal. Once, those words would have been a battle cry, the flag whipping through the air behind Anndras as he charged into battle. Once, for a short while, this flag would have fluttered from the top of castles in a free Storran, until the country ripped itself apart trying to fill the power vacuum left behind by the heirless Anndras. When Afren stepped in, the stag and its crown became outlawed, replaced by the boar. Now, these ancient words were whispered in the shadows, as Queen's Watchmen, *Lealists,* hunted the streets.

Lealists. Only now did her mind seem to catch up with what Bram had said in the inn.

Just think o the do you could have on the salary of a Lealist.

Surely, she had imagined it …

'Cait?' A familiar voice cut through her thoughts, and she shoved the flag in her bag, spinning around just in time for Kenzie to reach her. His eyes narrowed. 'What are you up to?'

Cait shrugged. 'Getting lost.'

Kenzie smiled as he offered her an arm. 'A man of the Queen's Watch can't very well leave a lady lost now, can he?'

'How chivalrous of you,' Cait said, looping her arm through his. The Storrian flag made her satchel bulge against her hip.

They wandered through the Old Town, and Cait tried to pay attention while Kenzie recounted his adventures of the day, half-listening to his tales of raids and patrols. Her eyes lifted to the rooftops, and she wondered if the Fox had another flag up her sleeve. Perhaps Cait was only distracting Kenzie from capturing her.

'Are you listening?'

'What? Yes …' she dragged her eyes from the rooftops. *Enough.*

They walked a short distance until they reached the river and crossed arm in arm onto a picturesque bridge marked "Daibh's Airch". Cait wasn't sure how she would form the word *Daibh* out loud. She suspected it was a fragment of the beautiful and faded language her father called Leid. It was more ancient even than Old Storrian, and apparently sounded like waves breaking across shingles on Storran's northern coasts. As far as Cait's father was aware, no one had spoken the language in years. *Old things eventually die a death,* he had shrugged. *That's just the way it goes.* But the bridge, flanked by cast iron vines and bearing its ancient name, was too pretty for decay.

'This is lovely,' Cait said. As they neared the middle of the bridge, she noticed ribbons tied to the railings, fluttering in the breeze. She had the almighty desire to untie them all and watch them all take off, like a scarf on the mountain wind.

Or a flag.

'You seem distracted, little dove.'

His voice, though tender, made her jump, and she realised she had paused at the centre of the bridge.

'Just taking it all in,' she said breathlessly. She turned to Kenzie and admired the smart angles of his uniform. She had barely had a chance to appreciate how radiant and *happy* he looked amidst her shame yesterday. He seemed to stand up straighter now, and it reminded her of a night, many years ago, when he had escorted her to a dance in the village hall wearing his father's suit. Cait had struggled to contain her giggles. She thought he'd looked so silly standing at her front door as stiff as a soldier in a grown-up suit. They'd danced for hours, and when they grew too hot and tired, they'd retreated outside and sat among the rhododendron bushes.

'Do you really think I look stupid?' Kenzie had asked, self-consciously tugging at a slightly too-long sleeve.

'Of course not,' Cait had replied, feeling guilty for her earlier laughter.

'It's not too big?'

'No!'

'Shadielaunds, I look like my dad, don't I?'

'Kenzie,' Cait had said, grasping his lapel and pulling his face closer to hers. 'You look perfect.'

He had grinned at her, and she had dragged his lips towards hers.

Now, older and adorned in his uniform, he looked as though this is who he was always supposed to be. She ran her fingers down the fine woollen jacket, skimming over the golden hammer-emblazoned buttons at his chest. The third button down hung limp from a single weary thread. 'How has this happened?' she said, touching it gently. 'It's only your second day.'

Kenzie looked down and chuckled. 'Look at that.' He cast her a winsome grin. 'I'm clearly working too hard.'

They stood in easy silence for a while longer, and then Kenzie told her that he had to get back to work. As Cait watched him march off the bridge and into the Old Town, she wondered if he had any inkling of what the Fox had been up to. She turned and made her way into the New Town.

Chapter 5

Lealtie Ayebidin

An eclectic mix of people passed through the wynd outside The Crabbit Corbie. Children who laughed and chased each other, workers fresh from the mills, salespeople dragging their wares home from the market. Cait watched them come and go all afternoon, her eyes trained on the cobbled street below her window. If she didn't, she would glance at the flag laid out across her bed and it would wink at her. The flag had been in the Fox's hands, meaning it knew all the secrets of the Separatists. It knew where the Fox made her den and how she avoided capture. It had seen the faces of other Separatists Cait only knew as passersby: bakers, bankers, innkeepers …

Stop. Cait snatched the flag up and crumpled it between her fingers, squashing the stag and its enquiring gaze. She needed rid of it. It didn't matter where in the room she moved, it watched her. It could not stay here. It was banned, and clearly for good reason. When she got downstairs, Bram was nowhere to be seen. She found the bins down a dark alleyway around the back of the inn, and stuffed the flag deep among the rubbish. Her hand came away sticky, but it was a small price to pay to be rid of the stag's eyes. Leaning back against the wall, she closed her eyes and let out a long sigh. The flag was gone. If she saw the Fox again, she'd ignore her. Bit by bit, she'd unstitch the curiosity the Fox had put in her, and she could stop doubting innocent innkeepers for careless language. *Blaine said the word Lealist all the time,* she told herself. It meant nothing.

The sound of hurried footsteps scuffed across her thoughts, and Cait turned to see the shape of a man skidding to a halt a short way down the street. From her place in the shadows, Cait was concealed, and she watched as the man hauled a clinking bag into his arms and pounded on the external door to the inn's cellar with his foot. Shortly after, the cellar door creaked open, and Bram's round face appeared.

'Took yer time!' the newcomer wheezed. Cait recognised the voice of the man who had spoken with Bram in Old Storrian the previous day.

'Ye werena spotted?' said Bram.

'Naw. Close call roond the corner. Watchmen all o'er the bit the day.'

'Aye, weel keep yer heed doon and yer mooth shut, ane o them's a customer o mine. Git in here, ye.' Bram's homely chuckle warmed up the alleyway. The man struggled down into the cellar with his bag, and an empty bottle fell out and clanged against the cobbles. 'Ach, leave it,' Bram said, pulling the man inside as he reached to retrieve it. The wooden door creaked shut behind him. Cait dug her nails into her palms. *He runs a bar,* she told herself, *maybe he needs some spare bottles.* Even so, news items about bottles filled with alcohol and stuffed with burning cloth lingered at the back of her mind.

Just think o the do you could have on the salary of a Lealist.

At the front of the inn, she met Kenzie at the door. An array of excuses instantly arose in her mind to counter the guilty heat in her cheeks.

'Cait,' Kenzie said. He removed his hat. His hair was messy, and a sheen of sweat glinted across his forehead, but it gave him a handsome tousled look.

'Did you run here just to see me?' Cait asked.

Kenzie pushed the door open and stepped back to let her in. 'We had some last-minute trouble nearby.'

'What kind of trouble?'

'Fire in a shop window. The bastards took us by surprise.' Kenzie fell into a chair at one of the tables, and Cait sat opposite him, her back to the bar. She schooled her features into innocence, afraid her traitorous thoughts were legible in the look in her eyes or the spots on her cheek.

'Tell me about the trouble,' she pressed. The flag was buried under rubbish, so she could bury her thought crimes under this conversation. 'Was it the Fox?'

'Not this time,' he said, then rubbed his hands over his face. 'I'll kill whoever taught them how to make bottle bombs.'

'Bottle bombs?'

Bram must have emerged at the counter, because Kenzie raised a hand to beckon him over.

'Where did they go?' Cait pressed.

Kenzie shrugged. 'No idea. They're like rabbits. They must have allies, places they can hide.'

Bram appeared and braced his hands on the table. 'Food or drink for yoursels?' His cheeks squeezed into a smile; his weight shifted easily onto one hip. Cait remembered the way he closed off and tensed up when he first saw Kenzie.

Kenzie looked at Cait and raised his eyebrows. 'Have you eaten?'

Maybe Bram's hospitable nature was overcompensating for something. 'I'm not hungry,' she said.

'Ah dae apologise, Kenzie lad. Seems my famed broth has robbed your Cait o her appetite.'

Kenzie rubbed his hands together. 'I could do with that. Busy day and all.'

'Richt you are.'

Cait watched him go out of the corner of her eye and turned back to find Kenzie watching her. 'You seem tense, little dove.'

Cait shook her head. 'Just tired.'

He reached out across the table and scooped her hands into his. She clutched them tight, then Bram appeared again and placed a bowl in front of Kenzie, and he pulled away. For a few moments, Kenzie ate in silence, until, without looking up from his broth he said, 'My troop's lieutenant is passing my name along to the Brigadier.'

'Why?' Cait asked. 'Have you done something wrong?'

Kenzie chuckled and rolled his eyes. 'Of course not, Cait. The task force, remember? Innes was close but I reckon I've bumped him to the reserve list.'

Cait gaped at him. 'Wait, what? You're going to Afren?'

'I told you this afternoon.'

'Did you?' She tried to swallow her panic, but it was like a marble. Had he told her? She thought back to the bridge, but her thoughts had only been of the Fox. 'We just got here.'

'Cait.' Her name was a low warning on his lips.

'It's just … it's so sudden.'

'This is important to me. It's important for my career,' Kenzie said.

'I know, I just —'

'Are you going to make a fuss out of everything I try to do?'

For just a moment, his expression was blank, and then he smirked and raised an eyebrow. It didn't matter if they were in jest, his words left a sharp bruise on her heart. He was right. She'd dragged her heels at every turn. She'd trifled with Separatist games. Her eyes clouded over and her lip trembled dangerously.

'Oh, Cait, not the tears,' Kenzie sighed, and she felt his hand fold over hers.

She didn't know why she was crying. Why did she always have to get upset? She took a steadying breath and blinked through the tears as she said, 'I'll come with you, then.' She'd heard wonders about the white marble spires and pillars of Eadwick, the colourful masks, the music and fashion. It was far away, but if Kenzie was with her, it could be home for a short while.

Kenzie watched her. She didn't like the way his eyebrows knitted together. 'This is a military operation. It would be too dangerous …'

'So, what am I supposed to do?' The plea burst out of her. 'Why bring me all this way if you're just going to leave?'

Kenzie laced his fingers through hers and his eyes filled with warmth. 'You'll be just fine, little dove. I'll be back and decorated before you know it.' He retracted his hand, then after a pause, he laughed to himself. 'Just try not to become a Separatist until then.'

Cait tried to smile. She rubbed her fingers over the place where Kenzie's hand had been. Without him here, she wouldn't need to hide from the Separatists' speeches. She could seek them out and learn more. She could listen to what the Fox had to say, and make up her own mind like Bram had told her to. But who was Bram? He had treated her well so far, but what about when he realised she might be a threat to him? Bram dropped something heavy and the thump on the wooden floor made her wince. It took her back to the Fox's speech, when the rifle had cracked through the air. That was the price of meddling in the Fox's game.

Kenzie had said that charisma was a weapon, but Cait wasn't so sure. It was more like bait, and Cait felt herself biting more with each moment she spent in the city. The Fox of Thorterknock was in her head, and the only way to keep her at bay was if Kenzie was at Cait's side. *Prove him wrong,* Bram had said.

'Kenzie,' Cait said quietly. He continued to shovel soup into his mouth. Cait cast a look behind her, but Bram was busy whistling away to himself as he mopped up his spillage. 'Kenzie,' she said again, and this time he must have heard the edge to her voice, because he looked up.

'What is it, little dove?'

'You can't go to Afren.'

A little storm passed over Kenzie's expression, and he placed down his spoon. 'I thought we were past this.'

Cait twisted her hands together. 'I think ...' She fumbled with her words beneath Kenzie's stare. Bram's language. The strange man with the bottles. The ease with which he spoke about Separatists. His coarse language. Behind her, Bram whistled his recognisable ditty. Maybe she was wrong. Maybe she should just watch Bram until Kenzie returned from Afren.

'Cait?' Kenzie's hand cupped around hers again. His eyes were soft as he looked at her. *Lealtie Ayebidin.* Cait knew who she was loyal to.

'I think Bram is a Separatist,' she gasped quietly, spitting the words out, wincing at their cruel aftertaste.

Kenzie moved in slow motion. She watched his expression change from concern to wide-eyed disbelief, watched him glance at the bar and back to her. She waited for him to question her, to call her silly or paranoid, but then his expression dropped into a steely determination, and he said, 'Pack your things.'

She hadn't unpacked, so it took her no time at all to throw things into her bag. Kenzie shut the door behind them, and they spoke in hushed voices as she shoved her nightdress into the case and crammed it shut.

'He called you a Lealist,' Cait said, fingers fumbling with the lock. She hadn't felt afraid up until now, but seeing Kenzie's reaction made her blood run cold. 'And he was speaking in Old Storrian, and there was a man this afternoon who —'

Kenzie stopped her and held her face in his hands. 'Shh. Listen to me. You did the right thing.'

'What happens now?' Cait whispered.

'I'll twist some arms and get you into Hart Hall for the night.'

That wasn't what she meant. 'What about Bram?'

'He'll have to be investigated. I'll see to it myself.'

'Won't that take a long time?'

He placed a strong arm around her back. 'Yes.'

'What about ...' *your mission in Eadwick,* she almost asked, but shame strangled the words before they could tumble out. If he missed this opportunity, it was her fault. She'd done this deliberately.

'What is it?' he whispered.

Cait smiled weakly up at him. 'Nothing.'

She burrowed herself against his chest, wishing his cloak would close around her like a cocoon and block out the charmingly crooked Crabbit

Corbie.

*

The evening was dark, and a steady rain pooled in the gaps between the cobbles. Cait spent the journey to Hart Hall huddled under Kenzie's cloak. By the time they reached the gates, she was shivering. Kenzie exchanged some words with the Watchmen stationed there, and soon they were hurrying up the cobbled pathway into the heart of the castle. At last, Kenzie opened the door to an unused room within the barracks. The walls were a time-stained, whitewashed brick lined with rows of bunks. An empty fireplace slept at the end of the room.

Kenzie placed Cait's suitcase at the foot of one of the beds. 'This will do until we can find somewhere new for you.'

Cait lingered by the door and cast him a hesitant smile. 'Thank you.'

After a long moment, Kenzie walked towards her. 'What's wrong, little dove?' he said, taking her face in his hand and turning it to her. 'You're safe now.'

Not the tears again, Cait thought as her eyes prickled. 'What will happen to your mission?' A look passed through his eyes. Disappointment? 'I'm sorry, I shouldn't have said anything,' she said. 'It was selfish.'

'No,' he said firmly. 'You did the right thing. I'm proud of you.' The words made Cait glow, and suddenly none of it mattered — not the Separatists, not Bram or the lengthy, uncertain investigation she had consigned him to, not the Fox of Thorterknock, only those words from Kenzie's mouth. *I'm proud of you.* 'You are my priority, Cait.'

You are my priority. Kenzie led her to the bed and sat at her side. It was hard and cold, like the walls, but Cait reminded herself that Hart Hall was a fortress built to withstand military force. Separatists were nothing in its eyes. The Fox's whispers could never reach her here. Once she had changed into her nightdress and slipped under a blanket that was thinner than the one in The Crabbit Corbie, Kenzie made to leave.

'Stay with me,' Cait said.

Kenzie hesitated, but nodded once and silently undressed, laying his cloak over her. He crammed into the little bed and wrapped his arms around her.

'How do you sleep in this?' Cait asked, squirming to get comfortable.

'I don't.'

'You haven't slept?'

'Not a wink last night, but I'll get used to it,' Kenzie's voice came soft and low in her ear. His breath was warm. She closed her eyes.

'See you in the morning,' she muttered, already drifting off to sleep.

The rain thrashed against the window. Somewhere out there, the Fox was skulking, and Bram was hiding things in his cellar, but here, she was safe.

*

A familiar nightmare settled over Cait as she slept. It was a memory of playground bullies who cornered her and made fun of her for her hair and eyes, only in the dream, the sneering children looked like horned beasts with sharp fangs. Cait backed into the stone corner as they leered down at her and ran their claws through her locks. Their invasive questions were delivered through a sickly-sweet mist that painted them curious to everyone except Cait. Cait buried her head in her hands and begged for morning.

'Oi, get lost!' When she lifted her head, a golden-headed prince stood between her and the monsters. They balked at his light and shied back into the murk from where they had come. 'Are you okay?' Kenzie asked, stooping to help her up. Cait hadn't even noticed that she had crouched to the floor. She nodded, and he brushed her hair out of her face. She flinched. 'Don't listen to them,' he said. 'They're idiots.'

'They won't stop,' Cait said quietly.

Kenzie's look burned. 'If they bother you again, they'll have me to answer to.'

*

Cait blinked the light out of her eyes and rolled over in bed. She shivered, a pronounced chill creeping all over her skin. She reached out to pull herself towards Kenzie and warm up, but then she realised that the only reason she had been able to roll over in the tiny cot was because he was no longer at her side.

She passed most of the morning watching the smart shapes of Watchmen cloaks swishing back and forward in the courtyard below and tried to convince herself she had made the correct decision. The longer the day stretched on, the more Cait wondered if she had spoken too soon. Bram had been kind to her. Perhaps it was the Fox talking when she decided that she should apologise to Bram and warn him of the coming investigation, but she didn't care.

*

When she entered The Crabbit Corbie, she was surprised to find the floor quiet and dark, the regulars' seats suspiciously empty. She hovered at the bar for a moment, running her hands along the counter, peering behind to see if Bram was lurking in some back room. For a while, she eyed the unlabelled bottles of liquor on the shelves, expecting Bram to sense the need for custom and appear. When he didn't, she called his name, but her voice was met with silence. Through the quiet, she heard voices coming from somewhere below her feet. Cait slipped around the back of the bar where she found the trap door to the cellar wedged open. The voices were too muffled for her to pick out Bram's familiar accent, so, slowly, she eased the trap door open and crept down the staircase.

'Cannae believe we came all the way down here and it's just the man's shitty whisky,' one of the voices said.

'What do we do?' the second voice was taut with panic.

'Wasnae us, like. It was the new boy spewing out back. I say we bolt.'

Cait touched down gently in the cellar. Two Watchmen stood with their backs to her. There was a putrid smell that clung to the air. It was only when Cait noticed the line of copper casks, and pipes, and dozens of empty bottles scattered about, that the realisation of her mistake struck her. Back in Briddock, Ailean Clark's basement had looked much the same because she liked to distil her own whisky. Bram wasn't hiding Separatists. The bottles hadn't been for bombs.

The first of the two Watchmen banged a fist against one of the metal vats and it retorted with a sonorous clang. 'Was probably selling this crap behind his bar.'

Cait's eyes followed the line of tanks until her gaze fell to the floor between the two Watchmen. At their feet lay a lump covered by a sheet. The truth of what had happened distilled in her blood.

'The Brigadier's gonnae kill us,' one of the Watchmen said. 'You'd better have a bright idea, Bell.'

A door somewhere slammed shut, and Cait heard an all too familiar voice.

'We tell them he attacked us. I found this around the back. It's all we need.' Kenzie stepped down from the hatch that led to the street, the Storrian flag Cait had discarded lifted triumphantly in one hand. He beamed at it, then his eyes fell on Cait and his smile died. The air in the cellar turned to frost. Kenzie stared at her. Cait backed away towards the stairs. She needed out of that cellar with its heavy air and clicking pipes and the stench she hadn't placed at first but now made her insides churn. Kenzie shoved past his colleagues. His hand reached out towards her, but Cait turned and scampered up the stairs. She just reached the floor of the bar when he caught up with her and spun her around.

'You shouldn't be here,' Kenzie said. His voice was too soft for the scene in the cellar.

Her breathing came in ragged bursts. She fought to look away from him, she couldn't meet his eyes. This was a rotten mistake. Her hands searched for something to cling to, and she wrung the sleeves of Kenzie's jacket between her fingers. 'I was wrong,' she gasped, staring at the trap door. 'I was wrong. He was ... he was innocent ... What did ... Why did you —'

Kenzie spoke slowly, as though his words contained a complex code for Cait to crack. 'He was a Separatist, Cait. He attacked us.'

Cait shook her head. 'No, no.' Bram was an innocent man. A harmless jibe. The nerves of a petty criminal faced with a uniformed officer. A well-loved story. Some illegal alcohol. Now, a cold body. 'His investigation ...'

Kenzie shook his head, gripping her shoulders tighter. 'Cait, look at me.' But she couldn't pull her eyes away from the trap door. He stroked her cheek and tilted her face up until her eyes met his. 'This man was a proven Separatist,' he said slowly. 'When we came to arrest him, he attacked us.' Cait's gaze brushed the flag crammed into his pocket.

'You said he would be investigated.' Maybe the more she said it the more she would believe she hadn't put those words in his mouth.

'I said no such thing,' Kenzie said. He put a hand on her head and pulled her into his chest. 'You must have misunderstood.' Perhaps she had been so desperate for Kenzie to stay that she had made it up. 'You're safe now,' Kenzie said, pulling her towards him, but Cait watched the trapdoor, imagining the two Watchmen hoisting Bram's body into the street, and she realised she didn't feel safe. What could possibly come between a soldier and a fair trial? Cait realised that for Kenzie, it was the promise of his trip to Afren. He'd cut a corner to please his superiors and Cait had helped him do it. She had given him the evidence needed to incriminate Bram, even in death. Kenzie would keep her safe and get to go to Afren. He could have it both ways.

Cait's nerves frayed, but she forced herself to meet his eye. 'You can't tell them he was a Separatist.'

'Little dove, you're in shock. He was a dangerous criminal.'

'No. I was wrong.'

'You're upset.'

Even after what she had heard in the cellar, Cait wondered if Kenzie was right, and she was getting emotional over her own rampant delusions. Kenzie pulled her in tighter, and she cried into his chest. Her tears soaked into his smart uniform. 'He was just making drink.'

'Another one of his crimes.'

Cait shook her head. 'He didn't deserve to die.'

'I told you that's what happens to them.'

'You're lying to me.'

She felt Kenzie's body still beneath her grasp and he eased her face up to look at him. 'Cait,' he said her name softly, but it ripped through her, like a blunt knife through bread. 'I'm trying to look out for you.'

Something at the back of her mind said, *no, you've left me to wander the streets. You've threatened to leave me here alone,* but her fears overruled this voice. *Selfish,* she told herself. Hadn't he paid for her accommodation so she could be with him? Hadn't he spirited her away the moment she felt unsafe? Hadn't he forgiven her after she had blindly taken in the lies of Separatists?

'I know,' she said. She wept freely, forcing her palms into her eyes.

'Let's get you back to Hart Hall, you can calm down there.'

She saw it play in her mind. Safe in Hart Hall, with her uncomfortable bunk in a cold barracks, with a misty window into the outside world. Kenzie would report to his superior, and he'd tell him that his squad had an incident and there was a casualty, but the man was a Separatist, so it was justified. He'd toss the flag over as proof. *Found this on his person,* he'd say. And then the Brigadier would smack him on the back for a job well done and send him off to chase Separatists in Afren, and Cait would be left alone to drown in her guilt. But if Kenzie had no proof that Bram was a Separatist, he would just be a trigger-happy soldier who shot a minor criminal three days into his post.

'The flag wasn't Bram's,' Cait said.

'Then where did it come from?'

'I put it there.'

For just a moment, Kenzie looked bewildered, then the smile reformed on his lips and his eyes softened as he collected himself. He put an arm out for Cait. 'Let's get you back.'

Kenzie made to lead her to the door, but she pulled against him. 'Give me the flag. Promise me he won't be made a criminal.'

Kenzie gripped her wrist. 'Enough.'

'*Please.*'

'You're in shock. How would you even get a Separatist flag?'

'The Fox of Thorterknock,' Cait said, and Kenzie's eyes flashed at her name. 'It blew from her hand, and I found it, and I didn't want to be caught with it, so I threw it out.'

Kenzie looked at her, and for a moment she wondered if he would call her ludicrous, but he just stared blankly and said, 'We're leaving.'

Cait swiped for the flag, and it flurried from Kenzie's pocket. After just a flash of hesitation, Kenzie's face turned to thunder, and he stalked across the room towards her. Cait scattered backwards, banging painfully against the bar, and getting her legs tangled in the stools as they fell around her.

'They're in your head,' Kenzie said. He brandished a finger at her. 'What did I tell you?' His grip curled around the flag, dragging them both towards him, but Cait seized it with both hands, fingers smarting with the pain.

'I'm sorry,' Cait wept. 'I'm sorry.' She'd stop meddling with Separatists. She'd sit quietly while he worked just like he wanted, as long as Bram would remain innocent.

'Stop fighting me,' he spat.

Cait gave an ugly sob. 'Kenzie, please!' She hadn't meant to scream, but she did, and Kenzie stopped wrestling with her. His body quivered, and his breath trembled against her skin. Then he raised a hand.

An almighty crash shook the room. The glasses behind the bar trembled. The tables shuddered. Cait tumbled backwards as Kenzie lost his grip on the flag. She stuffed it behind her back. The front door flung open, and a Watchman entered.

'Kenzie, attack. Two streets away.'

'I'll catch up. I need to see that Cait is safe,' Kenzie said, his eyes never leaving her face.

The Watchman hesitated, lingering in the doorway for half a heartbeat before saying, 'It's the Fox.'

Kenzie's eyes widened slightly. Cait's heart hammered as she watched him. He sighed, and slowly, he smoothed his hair with his fingers. When he looked back at Cait his smile had returned.

'I'll see you at Hart Hall.'

And then he was gone. He strode towards the door which snapped shut behind him, leaving Cait alone in the dark.

Chapter 6

The Fox of Thorterknock

All Cait wanted was her parents. She wanted her father's advice packaged in stories about fairies and kelpies. She wanted her mother's surgical logic, sharp and precise. Eventually, though she had no idea how much time had passed, she picked herself up from among the scattered barstools, shoved the flag into her bag, and wiped the tears from her face. She couldn't bear to face Kenzie's disappointment back at Hart Hall. She couldn't bear to see his face knowing what had just unfolded. She needed out of this city.

The world outside dizzied her. Everything seemed to ring with vividness and rain pummelled the streets. The sudden brightness outside the darkened inn made her eyes balk. Her legs carried her instinctively towards the River Cath and the New Town. There, the Southgait out of the city waited, and beyond that, the road to home, but she had no money for a train, and would have to travel empty handed, because to return to Hart Hall for her things would mean facing Kenzie. When she spotted the familiar sway of Watchmen cloaks up ahead, she dodged into a narrow side street and flattened herself against the wall. She squeezed her eyes shut as their voices drifted by, laughing about what they would drink that night and whose little flat they would sneak off to. When they passed, she took a moment to steady her pounding heart. It wasn't as if they would know who she was, but the thought of running into Kenzie wasn't one she could stomach. She was about to slip back into the street when Cait realised the air behind her felt heavy. A presence tingled down her spine, and she stilled. Someone breathed down her neck. Slowly, Cait turned and found a young woman a full head taller than her pressed against the wall at her side, her eyes fixed on the alleyway's opening.

'They gone?' the woman whispered. Cait gave a dazed nod. 'Good.' She bobbed her head at Cait before stepping past her. 'Ta'ra.'

Cait had seen her before; round, golden face with small eyes and dark hair scooped up underneath a swamp green flat cap. Under her scuffed brown jacket, which was certainly a few sizes too big for her, she hooked her thumbs through a pair of braces. The last time Cait had seen her, she was being led from the train station platform by a Watchman.

'Wait.' She wasn't sure what made her say it. 'You're a Separatist.'

The woman paused and gave a nervous laugh. 'I don't know what you're talking about.'

'I need help.' Separatists made it their business to avoid the Queen's Watch, and right now, that was what Cait needed.

'Look, I'm sorry.' She turned to face Cait and pulled at the lining of her pockets. 'I've got nay money.'

'I'm just trying to get home. Do you know how to get to the Southgait?' Cait cursed the weakness in her voice. 'Preferably, avoiding Watchmen.'

'Southgait's down near the port.' The woman tilted her head. 'Where's home?'

'The borders.'

She raised an eyebrow and studied Cait's dress, which by now was soaked through. 'Oh, aye? Hope you've got travelling clothes in there,' she said, nodding to Cait's satchel. 'Maybe take a train. Odds of not freezing to death are quite high by rail, so I hear.'

Cait shook her head. 'No money.'

The woman folded her arms. 'S'pose you don't know you need to pay to get through them gates, then.'

Cait's hopes plunged. Hart Hall was rapidly becoming her only option. 'Shit.'

The woman gave a loud laugh that made Cait jump. 'Ah, come on now.' She glanced over her shoulder then back at Cait, and considered her. She seemed to grapple with something internally, then shook her head with an exasperated roll of the eyes. 'Sod it. I'm headed south for a job. Catching a train tonight. You can come with us as far as Holt, then you'll have to find your way from there.'

Holt was the station where Cait had boarded the train to Thorterknock with Kenzie. It was just over the border into Afren, and a half an hour walk from Briddock, but she knew the way from there just fine. 'That's perfect.'

The woman turned to step into the street, but whipped round to face Cait and jabbed a finger at her. 'Draw any attention and I'll chuck you in the Cath.' Cait nodded silently. After a moment, the woman grinned and stuck out a hand. 'Jamie.'

Cait took it tentatively. 'Cait.'

As they slunk through the streets, Cait struggled to keep up with Jamie's long strides. She had been struck by the woman's accent, which was staccatoed with the full vowels of someone who lived a few hours south of the Storran-Afren border. 'You're from Afren. Why ... How?'

'How's that a problem?' Jamie said, raising an eyebrow as they paused opposite each other at the mouth of a narrow wynd. 'Got something against Afrenians?'

'No! Of course not,' Cait said quickly. 'I just thought Afren hated Separatists, that's all.'

Jamie peered out and scanned the street. 'There's a lot of people in Afren, love.'

They moved off again, but the going wasn't smooth. Their progress was broken up by sudden sharp turns and detours through dark streets to avoid Watchmen. Jamie's strides were long and purposeful, and Cait had to scurry to keep up. Jamie moved like a sparrow hawk. Cait bombed along like a pigeon in her wake.

'Shake a leg, Cait,' Jamie threw over her shoulder after pausing to let Cait catch up. 'Not got all day.' Cait was about to hurry straight past Jamie into the main street ahead of them when her bag strap tightened over her chest and dragged her back. 'Whoah,' Jamie whispered just as two Watchmen marched by the wynd's opening. Once they passed, she released Cait and tipped her hat. 'On you go.'

Instead of turning and making their way up the main street, Jamie led them straight across the street into another twisting wynd that sloped upwards.

'There are so many narrow streets. Thorterknock's a bit like a labyrinth,' Cait mused aloud.

'Hmm,' Jamie said. 'Never thought about it that way. Labyrinths are made of dirt where I'm from.'

'Dirt?'

'Sometimes rocks. Not pretty rocks, like. Mossy rocks. Good, moist, mossy rocks, with worms under them.'

Jamie led her to the main street that led towards the Cath and Barter Bridge. The shadows grew long, and the streets were now almost empty. Just before the bridge came into view, Jamie halted at the corner of a building and Cait almost walked straight into her.

'Here's the deal,' Jamie said, talking softly, glancing out around the corner. 'You're about to meet my friends. Tavis is fine, he's Talasaire, couldn't do conflict if he tried.'

'Talasaire?' Cait gasped, perhaps too loudly judging by the look on Jamie's face. Cait wouldn't have expected one to be in the city. She thought they all lived in woodland Groves where they studied the art of story and talked with nature. Some people even said they could do magic, but she wasn't sure if that was a fairy story or not.

'Pay attention,' Jamie said firmly. 'Calan won't be chuffed that I brought you along but looks like Aggie's late, so he should be distracted enough not to get *too* riled up.'

Cait blinked through the list of names, and before she could come to terms with any of them, Jamie pulled her around the corner and strode towards two people lingering at the approach to the bridge. As they drew closer, Jamie waved and an older man with a pointed beard at the end of his chin waved back. His white hair was stark against the rosy pink of his cheeks. He leaned languidly against the wall, his hands busy whittling away a piece of wood with a small knife. At his side, a young man scowled through a pair of round glasses at a pocket watch. He was a picture of elegance, his locks twisted into long braids that touched the hem of his velvet green waistcoat, his skin the burnt umber of a fine leather tome.

'Alright, Jamie?' the older man asked as they approached. His words danced with the blackbird-like lilt of a Prilwyn accent.

'Ey up, Tavis,' Jamie said.

The young man with the glasses glanced up at them, then looked back at his watch before double-taking. 'Who's this?' he said, gaze flashing between Jamie and Cait. His facade was a finely polished bureau, but beneath that facade he seemed like a bottle of fizzy juice that had been shaken too much and was primed to erupt.

'This is Cait, she needs out of the city, she's got no money, and I told her we'd drop her in Holt, don't shoot me.' Jamie seemed to spit the words out before the young man, who Cait assumed was Calan, could interrupt. 'Where's Aggie?'

The boy snapped his pocket watch shut with a frustrated huff. 'Late.'

Jamie grasped her braces. 'There was gunpowder involved, so I hear.'

Calan gave a withering look and rubbed his temple. 'Where did she find ... never mind.' He turned his attention back to Cait. 'We'd love to help but I'm afraid this is a sensitive matter.'

Cait opened her mouth and closed it again. 'I ...' Her plea fell flat. She couldn't hold her own against Separatists. 'I won't be any trouble.'

'Get going,' Calan snarled through bared teeth.

Tavis tutted. 'Come now, lad.'

'Look, she was hiding from a group of Lealists when I ran into her,' Jamie said. 'Is the enemy of our enemy not our friend?'

She looked to Tavis for support, who nodded approvingly. 'She's right, you know.'

'Can't argue with Talasaire wisdom,' Jamie said.

Calan hesitated and a satisfying *thwunk* came from Tavis' direction as he shaved off a large chunk of wood. Calan sighed and tossed a braid over his shoulder. Before he could say anything, Tavis nodded at the road ahead. 'Ah, the lady of the hour approaches.'

'At last,' Calan grumbled.

Cait peered in the direction they were looking, and for a while, all she could make out was a brown blur. As it grew nearer, her vision rearranged the features into an upturned collar on a brown jacket, and red hair tucked inside.

'The Fox of Thorterknock,' Cait gasped, heat rushing into her face when Jamie glanced at her sideways, and she realised she'd said the words out loud.

'Don't call her that,' Calan said. 'She doesn't need any encouragement.'

'Sorry I'm late,' the Fox said when she reached them. 'I had ... business.' Her mouth curved up sheepishly.

'We heard,' Jamie said.

'I believe the whole city did.' Tavis laughed, hooking his knife and whittling stick onto his belt.

'What part of 'channel your energy into recruitment' did you not understand?' Calan said with a scowl, and the Fox shrugged.

As the group moved off, the Fox's eyes fell on Cait, whose heart faltered. Up close, she could almost feel the heat of the flames that flashed behind her eyes. The Fox considered her for a moment, then said, 'If I didn't know better, I'd think you were following me.'

Cait tried to think of something clever to say, but all she could focus on was that the fearsome Fox of Thorterknock was at least half a foot shorter than her.

Aggie moved on without another word, with Jamie close on her heels. 'So, this thing with the explosion. What's that all about? Is it true?'

Tavis shook his head, but a fond smile pinched the corners of his beard. As they moved off across Barter Bridge, Cait hesitated. She watched after the Fox, wary of getting too close, wary of even knowing her true name.

Tavis appeared to her left and smiled down at her. 'She's not all that bad,' he said with a wink.

On the walk to the station, Cait kept her mind centred on home. In less than a few hours, she would be walking back up the road to Briddock. She'd wake her parents up with a rap on the door and they would usher her in and sit her down at the table. Her father would stick a pot on the stove and brew her up something to warm her hands while her mother set about lighting the fire.

'What's wrong, pet? What happened?' her father would say, and Cait would tell them that the city wasn't everything that she thought it would be. In the meantime, she just had to keep her cards close to her chest. To these people, she was just a girl running scared from the Watchmen. She was not involved with one, and she certainly never had a man killed after handing him over to one. The thought of Bram made Cait feel hollow. Home could take away a lot of the things that had happened since arriving in Thorterknock, but it could never change what had happened in that inn.

Up ahead, the Fox of Thorterknock said something to Calan, which drew the first smile Cait had seen from him. The smile became a laugh, and the Fox gave him a playful nudge on the shoulder. *Aggie,* Calan had said her name was. Soon, Cait wouldn't need to worry about the Fox's identity. She was Thorterknock business, and Cait wasn't for Thorterknock much longer.

When they reached the train station, Cait was surprised to find it was almost completely deserted other than a few handfuls of people lingering at the platforms. The dying light filtering through the glass ceiling turned the few people into darkened shapes. The Separatists gathered around a metal bench and Calan pointed out a train waiting at platform seven, a sleeper service bound for Afren. Within the next twenty minutes, he would pick the lock on the luggage compartment, and each of them would have to slip on without attracting the attention of the pacing conductor. He charged Jamie with keeping an eye on Cait. Cait watched Calan's shape move down the platform and disappear out of sight, followed by Tavis slightly after, and then Aggie, who actually made a point of talking to the conductor on her way over. Jamie rolled her eyes.

Cait looked over at platform five. The place where the Separatists had commandeered the train lay peaceful and empty. She glanced at Jamie, whose fingers had absentmindedly wrapped themselves around a pendant at her neck. Out of all the Separatists on the platform that day, she had been the only one not to throw stones, or board the train. She had simply lingered on the platform and shouted encouragement.

'I thought Talasaire were supposed to be pacifists?' Cait asked.

'Huh?' Jamie frowned down at her.

Cait nodded at Jamie's pendant. 'You're like Tavis. He's wearing a pendant just like that one.'

Jamie avoided her eye as she unclenched her hand from the pendant and tucked it inside her shirt. Before it disappeared, Cait caught sight of the Talasaire emblem: three branches entwined at their bases and fanning to the sky.

'What's that life like?' Cait asked.

'It's nice,' Jamie said bluntly.

'Did you live in a Grove?'

'Yep.'

'Did you leave to join the Separatists?'

Jamie picked at her nails. 'Uh-huh.' She only sounded like she was half listening.

'Can you do magic?'

'So many questions from the new lass,' Jamie sighed, signalling the end of the conversation.

They fell into silence, and Cait glanced at the platform again. She remembered how swiftly the Watchmen had cracked down on the Separatists, and how safe she had felt knowing none of them could cause any more trouble.

'I've seen you before,' Cait said, breaking the silence. She *felt* Jamie roll her eyes. 'Over there.' She pointed at the platform. 'How did you escape the Watch?'

Jamie shrugged. 'More of us do than they like to let on.' Then she pointed to the clock on the wall. 'Ready?'

Cait wasn't sure if 'ready' was what she was, but she followed Jamie along the platform. Jamie kept her hands easily in the pockets of her too-big jacket, but Cait suddenly couldn't remember what she normally did with hers. As they moved, she glanced over her shoulder once, then twice. On the third, Jamie muttered, 'Stop that. Did you miss the part of the brief where — bugger. This way.' She pulled Cait behind a tiled pillar in the middle of the platform and held her back. Cait heard a whistling and a jangle of keys and when she glanced out, she caught sight of the conductor pacing back and forth on the platform behind them. If they made a move on the train now, he'd certainly see. They waited for what felt like an eternity, but when it didn't seem like he was going to move, Jamie cursed and approached him. Cait watched their conversation from concealment: Jamie lumbering up to him, pointing at the other side of the station; the conductor's slow understanding; his slow wander away from them. Jamie gave Cait a grin and thumbs up as she wandered back, but Cait's attention was drawn over her shoulder to the station's entrance. She couldn't make out their faces, but the shape of five heavy cloaks swept through the dusky entrance. She could hear their laughter, and Innes' struck out the loudest of them all.

'Let's go,' Jamie said, appearing at her side. To the right, brakes screeched. A whistle screamed. 'Train's leaving, Cait!' Jamie cried.

She could tell which of the figures was Innes now by his bouncing gait. He glanced in their direction. Cait couldn't will her legs to move, and Jamie didn't wait.

'Suit yourself.' Jamie took off towards the train and hopped into the compartment.

Cait watched as the train started to pull away from the platform. Even if she tried to be discreet, Innes would notice her hair from a mile off, and then what? There was only one place she could be going if she was spotted boarding a train, and Innes would undoubtedly tell Kenzie. She could see it now: Kenzie showing up in Briddock, and then it wouldn't only be *his* disappointment she'd have to bear. *Separatists, Cait?* her mother would sigh.

But the Fox's voice was in her mind.

We've got the heir of Anndras Àrdan.

Suddenly, she was pelting down the platform, the train gaining speed at her side.

Cait forced her legs faster and stretched her hand out for the rail, but with every step, she fell more behind. The door to the compartment slid open, and Aggie's face appeared. Cait reached out again. She stumbled, her legs flying from under her. She braced herself for the slam of the hard ground, when a hand grasped her arm, and she felt herself being hauled upwards. With Aggie's help, she pulled herself into the carriage and fell face-first onto the wooden floor. The wind rushed through her hair and then someone slammed the door shut, plunging the compartment into darkness. For a long moment, there was only silence and the sound of heavy breathing, then Tavis struck up a small lamp, and Cait looked up to find Calan glaring down at her.

'And just what do you call that?' he snapped.

'There were Watchmen,' Cait said.

Calan considered her. 'We'll be at Holt in little under two hours.' He settled down against a pile of travelling trunks. 'Don't be here when I wake up.'

Cait felt the gazes of the others drop off one by one until she was left staring at her hands. Had Innes spotted her? She hadn't looked back to check.

'Something to occupy you?' She turned to find Tavis holding out a knife and a crude piece of wood.

'No, thank you,' Cait said.

Tavis nodded and resumed whitling away at whatever he had been working on earlier. The flakes fell away in pleasing white curls, and only now did Cait see the shape he was carving. 'It's a spoon?'

'Better than that,' Tavis said, raising his thick white eyebrows. 'It's a *soup* spoon.'

Cait laughed, but it stung to think of Bram and the soup he kindly shared with her, and how he had paid for it.

'Do you carve a lot of cutlery?' Cait asked.

'Mostly spoons,' Tavis said. 'I'll occasionally do a full set as a gift, so I will, but mostly spoons. I find they have a most pleasing shape.'

'How many have you made?'

'Overall, about …' He paused, looking into the middle distance, and his eyebrows gave a little wiggle as he thought. 'About thirteen hundred.'

Cait's laugh escaped as a snort. 'Wow.'

They fell into silence and Cait listened to the chug of the train, counting each thud against the sleepers, each a step closer to home.

'Try to get some rest, pet,' Tavis said to her. 'You'll be with your kind soon enough.'

*

'It's almost your stop.' The Fox's voice, though hushed through the dark, made Cait jump. She hadn't noticed time passing, her thoughts too wrapped up in Bram and whether Kenzie would appear at her door, and if he did, how she would explain it to her parents.

'I thought everyone was asleep,' Cait said.

Aggie leaned against the compartment wall, her hands still buried in her pockets. 'I stopped trying an hour ago.' Cait opened her mouth to ask why, curious to know what kept the Fox of Thorterknock awake at night, but the Fox spoke before she could. 'Why are you running from the Lealists?'

'Why do you call them Lealists?'

The Fox quirked an eyebrow. 'They're loyal to Afren and not their own. It's irony. You avoided my question.'

Cait searched her mind for another way out, but there was none so she settled on, 'I made a mistake.'

The Fox grunted, and the carriage fell into silence again, only punctuated by Calan's quiet snoring. Cait couldn't pull her eyes from the Fox. The last time they had been so close, she hadn't known who she was, but now she was stark and vivid, even in the dark; a human who couldn't sleep, a girl with a name. Aggie.

'You're going to Afren, aren't you? It's about Anndras' heir.' She asked the question before she could think better of it.

Aggie looked up at her and frowned. 'How do you know about that?'

'I saw you speak in the city.'

Aggie looked taken aback. 'Right enough, you did.' She squirmed straighter. 'What did you think?'

'You ran loops around them.' Cait's smile fell when she realised the way she had said 'them', as though the crowd were other, as though she were one and the same as Aggie: a Separatist.

Aggie grinned to herself. 'I do remember that,' she said. 'Shadielaunds, Calan would kill me if he knew I mentioned the Anndras situation. Do me a favour and don't tell him.'

There was a restlessness about her, but not in the same way as Calan. She was like a candle on a long wick: small, but thrashing on her little pedestal, burning bright. The train slowed down beneath them, and Cait decided to press her further. 'Tell me about the heir.'

Aggie glanced at Calan who was slumbering with a frown across his face, his glasses tilted at a skewed angle. For a moment, her eyes lit up, but then she looked back at Cait and said, 'I can't. Not if we won't have tabs on you after tonight.' Her restlessness now was the same as it had been before she broke the news of Anndras' heir to the crowd.

'But you want to tell me, don't you?'

Aggie looked pained for a second, like she had uncovered some deliciously scandalous gossip that she was forbidden from spilling. Apparently, the temptation won over, and a bolt of excitement seemed to pass through her. 'The borders aren't a big place. If we're betrayed in Afren, I'll find you.' She sat forward, eyes flashing, mouth fighting a wide grin. Her words came in a brisk whisper. 'By the constitutional laws of Afren itself, the direct descendant of King Anndras has a right to Storran's throne. Any coronated heir to Anndras would inherit Storran's sovereignty.'

'So why go to Afren if you have him already?'

'There are a lot of people in Storran who wouldn't fall in behind a man they had never heard of before. Flesh is impermanent, but metal represents history and legacy. You've heard of the Antlered Crown?'

'Of course,' Cait said.

Aggie's grin broke free. 'We're going to break it out of its case. Its destiny was never being leered at by snotty-nosed tourists who don't understand what it represents. It's coming home. It's being returned to the rightful king.'

Cait tried to tell herself the chills down her neck were because of the draughty train, but she knew better. Aggie's excitement seemed to buzz in the air between them, and Cait felt it quickening in her chest. The things Aggie spoke of didn't belong to the mundane world. They belonged to a legend, a story that she would have read in her father's copy of *Songs of Storran*. 'You think it will work?'

She needed Aggie to say no, it was hopeless, this was a fool's mission. Instead, Aggie fixed Cait with a gaze so ardent it could cleave the land in two. 'With all my heart.'

And just like the day she saw her speak in the city, Cait believed her.

'With Anndras' crown, we'll win over the people, and with his blood, we'll win over the state.' The train slowed again, and Aggie looked at her pointedly. 'We're almost at Holt.'

Holt. Home. She couldn't let herself forget that it was the path laid by the Fox that had led Cait to betray Kenzie's trust in the first place.

'Why bother?' Cait asked.

Aggie's eyes narrowed slightly. 'If you need to ask, you're no paying attention.' When Cait said nothing, Aggie shuffled around to face Cait and jabbed a finger against the dusty floorboards. 'Picture this. We're married.'

'What?' Cait's voice squawked out through the carriage.

Aggie cringed and hushed her. 'Stay with me. We're married, and we both have jobs. We pay our money into the same account and I'm in charge of the finances.'

'Okay,' Cait said slowly.

'You earn 50 Siller a week. I earn 70. *But,*' she pointed to herself. '*I have a gambling habit.*'

'What has this got to do with —'

'Hear me out,' Aggie said. 'Each week, I go through the finances and divide up the money between us. Once I pay off some of my gambling debt, I get 50 Siller to spend. You get 30.'

'But I got paid 50,' Cait said, seeing where Aggie was going but playing along with her game regardless. 'Where's the rest, then?'

Aggie smacked her lips in pretend pity. 'Paying off my debt, silly. We're a partnership. But, each week you struggle to get by on that 30 Siller, and there's nothing you can do about it because I keep the purse strings tightly drawn.'

'I get it,' Cait said. 'You're Afren.'

Aggie gave a victorious nod and sat back against the wall. 'There you go.'

Cait supposed the reasoning was fair enough, and she couldn't think of a retort, not even when she tried to imagine what her mother would say. 'What if your plan with the crown doesn't work?' she asked, remembering Kenzie's assertion that the Separatists would fold within the year.

'It will.'

Kenzie had warned Cait that this sort of rhetoric was what Separatists were best at, *especially her.* For just a moment, Cait allowed herself to forget that *charisma is a weapon* and allowed herself to wonder *what if it does work?* What if the purse strings weren't drawn?

Cait pushed the words out before she could take them back. 'Take me with you.'

Aggie's eyebrows lifted in surprise. 'I don't think it's your scene.'

'I know medicine,' Cait pressed. 'If someone gets hurt, I can help.'

Aggie shook her head slowly. 'We all know a bit of first aid.'

The train slowed and they both watched the lights under the door ease to a halt. The train fell still.

'It's your stop,' Aggie said, her expression unreadable. Cait thought she had been prompting her to leave, but Aggie didn't so much as move to open the door, or usher her off into the night. Cait realised she was hoping. She was hoping that Aggie would tell her that she had to stay, that she knew too much, and it was safer to keep her under close tabs, but she remained silent. The Fox of Thorterknock only watched her.

She could put thoughts of home and Kenzie on hold, for now. Cait sat still as the train crawled away from the station, and the little strip of light began to thrum quickly under the door as Holt drifted quietly into the night.

The Fox of Thorterknock smirked as she pressed her head against the wall and closed her eyes. 'Welcome aboard.'

Chapter 7

Good Press

Calan's plan had been to sleep away the journey and wake when they arrived in Eadwick the next morning, but his grasp of time was completely thrown off when he opened his eyes to find Cait snoozing over a golf bag. He turned to Aggie and asked if they had passed through the borders yet, and her head lolled to face him from where it had been resting against the wall of the carriage. Her lips stretched with barely suppressed glee. Mischief winked in her eyes. 'We're almost at Eadwick.'

'The plan was to send her on her way at Holt,' Calan said firmly. He glared at her, but she didn't seem to notice at all.

'She had a change of heart.'

'She can't come with us.'

'She *wants* to come with us.'

Calan scooped up his braids and tied them in a tight knot behind his shoulders. 'There could be a very good reason she wants to come.'

'Please, Calan,' Aggie said, fluttering her eyelashes. It made Calan recoil. 'I'll take care of her all by myself, I'll walk her and feed her, and —'

'We're sending her straight back to Storran the moment we get off this train.'

She scowled at him. 'I seem to remember you telling me to channel my energy into recruitment.'

'Yes —'

'So, I recruited, didn't I?'

Calan pinched the bridge of his nose. He hadn't anticipated a headache this early in the day. 'That's not what I meant.'

'Look, she knows medicine. She could come in handy.'

'We all know a bit of first aid,' Calan said, shaking his head. He didn't need to look up at her to know she had a stupid, smug expression on her face.

'We both know that you're no good at it, and I didn't bother showing up to the lessons.'

Calan threw up his hands. 'Fine. She's your responsibility. And if she turns out to be a spy, I'm leaving you here.'

'In *Afren*?' Aggie said, her voice full of mock outrage. 'You wouldn't.'

Calan pursed his lips and shook his head as Aggie smiled sweetly and blew him a kiss. Keeping tabs on Aggie was almost a full-time job, and Calan's only regret was that it wasn't a paid one.

Though still early, Eadwick's train station was alive with activity. People with briefcases and suitcases wearing fine, tailored suits walked in straight, purposeful lines. Despite the sun only just rising through the sky, it cast a dry, stifling heat over the city, which was already thrumming with foot traffic. Calan told the group to meet near the museum's ticket booth at midday. That was peak time, when it would be easy to blend in among the tourists. As the group dispersed, Calan made to slink away to the offices of the *Peninsula* tabloid, but Aggie pinned him with a suspicious stare.

'Where you off to?'

Calan dodged the question as he had rehearsed. 'To see a man about a suit.'

Aggie's frown deepened and she lifted her chin. If she knew he was lying about the suit, she didn't let on, and Calan was relieved. If there was one thing Aggie loathed more than Afren's rule, it was journalists.

Eadwick didn't seem to have a single downtrodden quarter. It was all bright white marble and glittering canals, monuments around every corner, and a skyline flanked by spires. Everything seemed to be for show, from the offices belonging to local councillors, to the magnificent temples where people prayed for peaceful passage through the Shadielaunds, or *Shadowlands* as they said in Afren, when they died. The city lay in stark contrast to the humble hamlets his family had flitted between when they first arrived on Afren's shore, and certainly a far cry from Thorterknock, the first place he ever felt safe. Still, the gleaming metropolis seemed familiar, which Calan thought was odd since he had never stepped foot in Eadwick before. It hit him as he passed a gaggle of school children crowding around the window of a sweet shop: the grand-standing, free-wheeling nature of the city reminded him of what Iffega had been like before the war. He didn't have many memories of his homeland, and it sickened him that it had been reduced to merely an echo of Eadwick in his mind. One day, he'd see it for himself again. Until then, his priority was security for himself and his family. They would have a home in Storran. He'd have an oak-panelled office. Maybe even a swivel chair. He shook himself out of the dream. To be that person, Storran first had to be free, and before that could happen, they had to survive this mission — which was looking less and less likely judging by his steadily increasing blood pressure over the last few hours.

Lister Burke, the official-unofficial head of the Separatists had spent months scrutinising his work, until, by the fifth draft, he entrusted Calan with a team of his own choosing. It was his chance to show Lister what he was capable of. It was his chance to go down in Separatist history. All he had to do was swipe the Antlered Crown from under the noses of Afren's elite, and the rest would follow. Of course, his first choice for a teammate was Aggie. There was an unspoken fine print on their friendship that stated she had to be included in all his schemes. He wasn't sure she would ever forgive him if he left her behind. Besides, she was a good actress. Tavis knew Eadwick's history inside out, which would be important once they got into the museum. He didn't know Jamie very well, but he heard that she was wily. She kept a tally on her bedroom wall of the number of times she had slipped the Lealists.

Then there was Cait, whom Calan hadn't chosen. She was soft, with alabaster skin and hair, harmless at first glance, but she had been the first wildcard of the trip and Calan wished he hadn't left Aggie alone with her. He should have known she would waste no time in spinning her usual tales and making lofty promises until the wide-eyed girl had no choice except to come with them, but he hated to admit that Aggie was right. If the girl *did* have medical experience, she would be good to have around. She was a liability, but she was a useful liability. He would just have to be vigilant. Cait didn't have the face of a liar, but good liars seldom did.

When Calan reached the address that he had scrawled on the slip of paper in his pocket, he straightened his waistcoat and wiped his forehead. He had expected more of the infamous Heather Bruce's office, but what he was met with could easily be mistaken for a block of flats similar to the expensive ones he always eyed up in Thorterknock's New Town. By Eadwick's standards, it was a hole. Heather Bruce was a popular tabloid journalist, revelling in the gossip and outrage it brought with it. She enjoyed scandal, and he could think of no one better for his request.

The bell above the door tinkled as he entered, and the woman behind the desk snapped to attention and hastily shuffled the papers in front of her.

'I'm here to see Heather Bruce.' He buried his loose Storrian accent under a stiff Afrenian one.

The receptionist poised a pen on a blank piece of paper. 'Have you got an appointment, sir?'

Calan dipped his head. 'Yes.' For effect, he checked his watch. 'Though I fear I'm early.'

The receptionist frowned at a calendar on her desk and looked like she might query this, then seemed to decide it wasn't worth the effort. 'I'll fetch her,' she said, disappearing through a door next to the desk. Shortly after, the door opened again, and the receptionist hurried back behind the desk as if she were afraid to stand next to Heather for too long. Heather didn't cross the threshold but looked at Calan expectantly. Her blonde hair curled neatly under her chin, cheeks rouged, brows arced flawlessly, all in eerie perfection. He braced for her to scold the receptionist for wasting her time with an appointment that didn't exist, but Heather nodded Calan through the door and he followed her up a dark set of stairs that reminded him of the streets in Thorterknock.

'I don't have a nine o'clock appointment,' Heather said. Her voice was like a silk noose.

'No,' Calan said as they reached the top of the stairs and Heather showed him into a dark office. The sight was familiar: books stacked twelve high, papers scattered across the tabletops. His attic room in his family's most recent home, just outside Thorterknock, had looked much the same. Heather crossed the room to a window and opened the blinds. Startling sunlight poured into the room. She indicated a chair, which he lowered himself into, and she perched on the windowsill with a stunning view of Eadwick's skyline at her back. The building was west facing, and the eastern sun lit the buildings of Eadwick in deep red, so the spires looked like they'd been dipped in crimson ink. The city seemed to stretch on for eternity. The canals formed a complex weave as they twisted between the magnificent buildings. A monolith of a settlement. Calan wasn't sure how anyone could settle somewhere so hulking.

'It's nice,' Calan said, nodding at the view.

Heather sighed, looking out over the city. 'It's the only good thing about this ghastly building.' She flicked something off her fine tailored trousers.

'I assume you have your sights on bigger and better offices.'

'Who doesn't?' Heather turned back to him, blue eyes piercing. 'Why are you here?'

Calan took a steadying breath and pushed his glasses up his nose. 'I have a story for you.' Heather looked unamused and he quickly added, 'Well, not so much a story, but something of a project. I believe that there's something you can do for politics.'

She chuckled. 'Politics is such a petty sport.'

'Not necessarily —'

'You're boring me,' Heather snapped. Calan bit back his words. 'I've taken time out of my busy morning to hear you, and thus far it isn't proving to be worthwhile.'

'If you would just let me finish —'

'Give me something worth letting you finish.'

'The Five Realms isn't working,' Calan said. He saw Heather's eyes snap quickly to him and off again. Despite this fact, she kept her face angled towards the window. Calan started to count the reasons on his fingers. 'Our resources and money are siphoned off to Afren, we're dragged into costly wars we don't want to be a part of, we're forced to accept close-minded foreign policies, we *never* get who we vote for, even when Afren isn't gerrymandering.' Heather opened her mouth to cut him off, but Calan kept speaking. 'It's not worked for anyone other than Afren for a long time, and no one's had the courage to say it.'

Heather gave a frosty snicker as she said, 'And with good reason. Prilwyn's lifestyle binds its residents to neutrality, and anyone in Storran lives under the thumb of the Queen's Watch. The people of Kerneth and Tor have heard about what happens to Storrian Separatists. I can hardly blame them for keeping to themselves.' She paused, and when Calan didn't fill the silence, she said, 'Anything else? Or did you only come to state the obvious?'

Calan sighed and pinched the bridge of his nose. 'Okay,' he said, straightening. 'Okay.' He let his pretend accent fall away as he said, 'I have travelled from Storran. I'm from the Separatists.'

He had expected Heather to react, but she didn't flinch. Calan scrambled for his pitch. 'The only reason the Watch have such a hold over us is because we're in the minority right now, and the only reason we're in the minority is because our press is poor.'

'You want me to be your good press,' Heather said.

Calan faltered. 'Yes.'

Heather tilted her head as she looked at him. 'Why here? Why come all the way to Eadwick, when I'm sure there are journalists with Separatist leanings in Thorterknock. It's the printing capital of the world, is it not?'

'The printing houses in Storran are owned by people who don't ... tolerate us, as such. An industry plant of ours would never get close to writing the content we need to sway opinion. You have a bold style, the people trust you, and I can be almost certain you don't live in Afren's pocket.'

Heather laughed darkly. 'I work for the free press. We all live in Afren's pocket.'

Calan ploughed on. 'There's a feeling that us, Separatists, that is, are anti-Afrenian, so we'd start you down here and dismantle that notion.'

'You *are* anti-Afrenian.'

Calan sucked an impatient breath through his teeth. 'No, we're anti-Afrenian *rule*. We've got nothing against you, or anyone else, for that matter.'

Heather raised a sculpted eyebrow. 'So, you have a press? You can afford the ink?'

Calan wiped his clammy palms on his trousers. 'No, but we could build up to that. Your columns are widely read in Storran. Until the time comes when we have the facilities, you could continue to work from here, drip-feeding our message into your current work, and then —'

Heather folded her arms. 'My career would be in tatters.'

'In time, we could move you to Thorterknock.'

'Thorterknock would be no use to me if I were an outcast.'

'You wouldn't be, not if things went our way.'

'I don't care for Storran or its politics. This is not worth sticking my neck out for.'

He understood, perhaps too well, and it almost made him bow his head and leave her alone with her ambition. 'You take plenty of risks already,' Calan said instead. 'It's what you're known for.'

'Yes, with idle gossip. Which politician is sleeping with whose wife. Not treason, or sympathising with terrorists.'

Heather watched him flounder for a retort. 'We are not terrorists,' he said with more conviction than he believed. 'We are desperate.'

Heather studied him for a long moment. 'Plenty of people have died at the hands of Separatists.'

Calan felt the heat rising in his face. 'And plenty more have died from Afren's neglect.' Family cast to the streets. Friends lost journeying to a better life. Rich cultures rubbed too long against Afren's cold, white marble until all semblance of what had been was scraped clean. He'd done his homework. He'd followed the trail of abusive policy straight to the Council of Five, which Afren held dominion over. And Heather's use of the word *terrorist* scraped at an old wound that just wouldn't heal. The freedom fighters in Iffega had been labelled terrorists, which gave the government a free pass to kill. He was sick of this. 'I'm giving you the chance to be on the right side of history.'

Without another word, Heather stood, snapping the blinds over the window, and purging the light from the room. 'Get out of my office.'

'If you would just hear me out.'

'I've heard enough, and my answer is no.'

Calan knew when a battle was lost. He knew that if he left now, Heather would hold her tongue, but if he sat here and protested all morning, he would become her latest scoop. He stood and gave her a brisk nod. 'Think on it.'

Heather was already sitting at her desk by the time he turned the handle on the door. Behind him, he heard the crank of a typewriter being loaded with paper. He was almost out the door when Heather's voice made him pause with reckless hope. 'Leave this Separatist business behind,' was all she said. 'You'd fulfil your potential much faster.'

Chapter 8

Speak Properly

Unlike in Thorterknock, there was no smog in Eadwick, and the sky over Cait's head was a bright azure. The brightness of it dazzled her. She squinted furiously, regretting fleeing Storran without her hat. When her vision settled, she found the Separatists had dispersed, leaving her alone among the throng. The glimpses of the sky that she was able to snatch made her heart heavy. It was exactly the same shade of blue as the sky over Storran. It seemed the bold blue of Storran was a lie.

'Awright?'

Cait jumped at the voice and turned to find Aggie standing behind her, hands deep in her pockets.

'Fine,' Cait said. 'Just didn't know what I was expecting.'

Aggie stepped towards her. 'No, your eyes. You're squinting.'

Heat rushed into Cait's cheeks. She didn't want the questions. 'No, I'm not.' She lowered her hand, and quickly raised it to her eyes again as the light blasted in. Aggie raised an eyebrow and Cait sighed. 'It's called albinism. It makes my eyes sensitive.' It wasn't just her eyes. They had only been off the train ten minutes, and she could already feel her skin burning.

'Typical of Afren to be inhospitable. What would help? A parasol?'

Cait peered at Aggie, trying to discern her motive. 'I usually wear a hat.'

'Where is it now?'

'I left it at Har — home.'

Aggie seemed to miss Cait's blunder and looked about her. 'There'll be a hatter somewhere in this awful city.'

'I don't have any money,' Cait said.

Aggie's face broke into a roguish grin, and she tossed Cait a coin purse. 'Courtesy of Tavis. Lunch is on him, too.'

The scarred leather purse weighed gently in Cait's hand. 'Does Tavis know lunch is on him?'

Aggie shrugged innocently as she turned away.

*

Eadwick seemed to exude light. The canals glistened and every marble building glowed as though lit from within. On street level, shaded shopfronts sold colourful souvenir trinkets: twisting glassware, and clay jewellery, and novelty masks. A heavy purpose hung in the air, everything with its role in this place carved out in gold and marble. Cait could hardly believe how mellow Thorterknock seemed in comparison to the capital of the Five Realms. She kept her eyes trained on Aggie's coat as they walked. The Fox seemed to breeze through the crowd so easily, nimbly slipping between groups of tourists and workers, as though she could read them like music. She made no effort to bow her head or obscure her features, and Cait wondered how she wasn't well-recognised up and down the Five Realms by now.

'Have you ever been captured by the Queen's Watch?' Cait asked.

Aggie's fingers brushed a rack of pleated ribbons to her left. 'Nah.'

'But how?'

'When people think of the Fox of Thorterknock, she never looks like me. Myth makes for a good disguise.'

Cait supposed she had a point — Aggie's apparent normalcy was disarming. She was familiar with *Aggie the Fox*, who appeared as a flaming-eyed demon in her imagination, but *Aggie the girl* was so regular that Cait had mistaken her for just another resident of Thorterknock when they first met. *But she is still the Fox,* Cait thought to herself. Regardless of what skin Aggie had chosen to wear, the Fox was still inside her. She was still dangerous.

Aggie came to a stop beside a quaint little shopfront with pink bonnets in the window. 'Here we are.' She passed Cait Tavis' purse and gave a playful wink. 'Buy yourself something pretty.'

The hat shop smelled of sandalwood and rose. Mannequins lined the walls wearing hats in all kinds of styles, and the man behind the counter cast them a cheery grin as they entered. Cait stepped slow and light, but her footsteps still beat obnoxiously against the silence.

'These prices,' she hissed. The straw hat in front of her was 50 Siller. 50 *Silven*, she reminded herself, since they were now in Afren. The money between Storran and Afren looked different, sounded different, but was ultimately the same and carried the same worth. It always confused Cait.

Aggie shrugged. 'Welcome to Eadwick.' She replaced the bowler hat she had been eyeing up back on the mannequin at a jaunty angle. The shopkeeper's face soured.

Cait selected a sun hat that was on sale and lay it on the counter in front of the shopkeeper, who smiled modestly and said, 'A good choice, if I do say so.'

Cait handed the money over, and the shopkeeper's smile vanished when he looked into his hand. He slid the coins back across the counter. Cait blinked. 'Is that not enough?'

His expression hardened more at the sound of her voice. 'We don't take Storrian coin.'

Aggie huffed a laugh, and the maniacal glint in her eye told Cait she had been waiting for this to happen. Moreover, it was as though she had been planning it. 'And why not?'

The shopkeeper gave a single shake of his head. 'It's not done.'

'You cannae refuse us service,' Aggie said simply.

'This isn't Storran.'

'But it *is* the Five Realms, isn't it?'

The shopkeeper's jaw clenched as he repeated the words, 'This is not *Storran.*' The word slid from his mouth slick with oily contempt.

Aggie leaned on the counter and glanced at the door. She took her time to look around the shop, and then slowly looked back to the clerk. 'Your shop doesna exactly look like a hive of activity. Still want tae send us away for being frae up north?'

The shopkeeper closed his eyes and sighed. 'That's not what I said.'

'Then you'll take my friend's Siller, which was earned through fair work and can be exchanged fir goods and services anywhere in this happy wee family of nations.'

'We don't accept *Siller,*' he said the word through his teeth. 'I reserve the right to refuse service.'

Aggie rolled her eyes. 'Och, awa an bile yer heid.'

The shopkeeper's face scrunched, and he drew back ever so slightly. 'Speak properly.' His words were clipped. 'I can't accept your money. I won't accept your money. It's against the law.'

Aggie's eyes blazed. Cait took two steps back from the counter. She could see it now: the smashed shop window, the maimed clerk. This was a mistake. But Aggie kept her voice perfectly level, if menacingly lowered. 'Tak this up wi any judge you want.' She pushed the money across the counter with a force that sent a few coins rolling away onto the floor. Then she smiled and picked the hat off the counter. 'Keep the change.'

Before Cait knew what was happening, they were outside the shop, and Aggie placed the hat on Cait's head. 'Bampots,' she muttered, then looked at Cait and gave a satisfied nod, like she was pleased with a piece of handiwork she had just completed. 'Suits you.'

'It's not really illegal, is it?' Cait asked as they moved off, glancing over her shoulder for the shopkeeper.

Aggie gave a bark of laughter. 'Of course not. But anything from Storran is unwelcome down here, and they'll go out of their way to make that quite clear. They'd prefer we stayed in our muddy little pen up north.' She rubbed her hands together and said, 'What can I buy you next? Souvenir pearls?'

The look on the hatter's face when Cait had spoken stayed with her. *Speak properly.* She had never considered herself to have a very broad accent, but suddenly she felt other, like the way she rolled her r's or carried her vowels were somehow a mark that she didn't belong. The lash of the clerk's tongue as he spat out the word *Storran* reminded her of the crack of her teacher's ruler when she had described the drizzly weather out the window as "dreich." *Speak properly, Miss Hardie, or don't speak at all!*

Her own anger caught her by surprise, and when she glanced at Aggie, Kenzie's words came rushing back to her: *Charisma is a weapon.* If she wasn't careful, the Fox could turn her into a weapon, too.

*

As promised, lunch was on Tavis, and Cait and Aggie sat at the side of one of Eadwick's many canals, each tucking into a succulent pie. Cait dangled her legs over the edge, allowing her boot to skim the water as she watched silver fish swimming beneath her soles. Boats slid by, some packed with flowers and exotic fruit, and some carrying people in elaborate outfits who sipped sparkling drinks out of dainty glasses.

'What do you think?' Aggie said.

Cait shook herself from her thoughts. 'It's beautiful.'

Aggie chuckled. 'I've never heard someone describe a pie as beautiful, but I suppose you're right. That's one point — and one point *only* — to

Afren.'

Cait blushed. The *pie*. 'It's delicious.' It was more than that. The spices and juices burst across her mouth with every bite. 'But Afren is beautiful, too.'

'Eadwick is the posh part,' Aggie said. 'The rest is much the same as Storran.'

Cait realised that the Fox's voice was much softer than she had expected, even when she had been arguing with the shopkeeper. She also noticed how her accent slipped away around her companions, rising back hard and furious in front of strangers like she was trying to make some kind of point. It didn't roll off her tongue in the natural way Bram's words had. The Fox needed to work for it, throwing the odd piece of Old Storrian into her sentences where they wouldn't naturally fall for her. Cait glanced at Aggie out of the corner of her eye. There was something different about her here, with her legs dangling loose, unable to touch the water, pie juice on her chin. Being so far away from Storran seemed to have robbed the Fox of Thorterknock of all her intrigue, and now she was just a girl let loose in a city that was as many sizes too big for her as the coat on her shoulders.

'What happens next?' Cait asked. 'After you get the crown?'

Aggie flashed her a look and spoke through a mouthful of pie. '*We.*'

'Right.'

A distant, hungry look fell over Aggie. 'We'll take it to Gowdstane, and there we'll declare Aidan as rightful ruler of Storran.'

'*Gowdstane?*' Cait spluttered, almost choking on her pie.

'Big castle. Right by Clackhatton.'

'I know, but …' She had always wanted to see the ancient, gilded hall of King Anndras, but it was too far north to merit a visit. 'And Aidan? He's the heir?'

Aggie puffed her cheeks out. 'Calan'll twist ma heid if you end up being a spy.'

Cait laughed, but she was glad that Aggie had said too much. *King Aidan, the Second King of Storran*. It felt right, like she was reading his name in a well-respected history book that was yet to be written. Still, she struggled to imagine the villagers of Briddock celebrating a Separatist coronation. 'Will people really support him?'

Aggie's eyes flashed. 'Aye. If they're loyal to Storran, they will.'

'What about the ones who don't?'

'Traitors and cowards,' Aggie said on a shrug.

'You don't really think that, do you?'

'I do. They're betrayers of Storran. It would be wrong to say otherwise.'

'But the explosion yesterday ... isn't it just as bad?'

'If making Afren listen was as easy as writing them a love letter, do you not think we'd have done that already?' Aggie snapped, and for just a moment her demeanour changed, she closed off, her hackles raised. Cait suddenly didn't feel very hungry. Before she could say anything else, a passerby behind them tripped. Cait heard the scuffling of their feet on the stone, and a bag of shopping dropped to the ground, striking Cait's back.

'I'm so sorry!' the woman said, hurrying to retrieve the bag.

Cait reached for the bread that had fallen out practically in her lap. 'Don't worry about it,' she said, passing the bread to the woman.

On hearing Cait's voice, the woman recoiled. She snatched the loaf back so hard that a corner of it broke away in Cait's hand. 'Do we not give you enough charity without you stealing our bread, too?' she spat. Cait opened her mouth to retort, but the woman cut her off. 'Bugger off home and stop taking from us!' With that, she turned on her heel and marched off. Dumbstruck, Cait watched after her, then lowered herself back to the side of the pier beside Aggie, who continued to eat as if nothing had happened. Cait sat silently, staring at the pie in her hands.

Eventually, Aggie finished off the last of her pie and brushed the crumbs off her legs to the fish below. 'There was no explosion,' she said at last, picking up their conversation as if nothing had happened. 'But I did find some fireworks, and I did plant them in the house of a politician from the Prosperity Party.'

Cait's stomach whirled. 'Were they alright?'

'She wasn't even home. She would have had some ugly burns, but she'd live.'

Cait was terrified of fireworks even when they were in the sky, never mind in her home. She wasn't sure anyone representing anything should be maimed in that way, but she held her tongue and settled on saying, 'That's heinous.'

Aggie cackled. '*She's* heinous. Anyone who votes for their party is heinous. Did you know she supports sending Iffegan refugees home?'

'I didn't know that,' Cait said quietly. Her mother had always lauded The People's Prosperity Party's traditionalist stance and stringent economics. They ruled Afren, but never got far in Storran other than the odd stronghold. Briddock was quite in agreement over who to vote for. Her village had always seemed like a free-thinking, radical place in an otherwise careless world. The villagers were able to pass off blame about the state of affairs on other, less astute regions, and they lived in comfortable self-satisfaction. When Cait's turn to enter the shabby little village hall to cast her vote came, she chose Prosperity, because her life was just fine, and there was no need to heal a wound that didn't exist. Cait thought about the hat seller, and the woman from a few minutes ago, so repulsed by the sound of her voice, so quick to judge based on her being from a different part of the same peninsula. 'If we're such a drain on Afren, why don't they just let us go?'

Aggie threw her head back and laughed. Heads turned their way. "Cause they need us. They'd cut us loose if they really wanted to, but they can't. We have peat, for a start, heaps of it, and they sell it on our behalf.'

Cait was about to ask if this was just another Separatist line, when Aggie checked her watch and got to her feet. 'We'd better get a move on if we want to make it to the museum for noon.'

*

They met the others on a quiet street near the museum. Cait could make out the top of its tower peeking at them between the buildings.

'Look after this for me.' Jamie said, putting her hat in her pocket and passing her jacket to Cait. 'And don't go through the pockets,' she added quickly.

Cait pulled the jacket over her shoulders and watched as Jamie and Tavis slipped matching grey waistcoats on, the lining the same rich maroon as the Watchman cloaks.

Calan cast Jamie a level look. 'And the braces.'

'My trousers will fall down!'

He peered at her over his glasses. 'You are wearing a belt.'

Jamie grumbled as she removed her braces and Calan sized Cait up. 'Tuck your hair into your hat,' he said.

Cait absent mindedly reached for a strand of her hair. 'Why?'

'We need to blend in,' he said simply, tucking Jamie's braces into his bag. He passed Tavis and Jamie each a maroon flat cap which they slipped into their pockets. Cait wound her hair up and stuffed it under her hat. Her exposed neck prickled under the midday sun. Once the costume change was complete, they moved into line for the ticket booth. From there, Cait had a better view of the building. It was a lofty yellow tower at the centre of a wide canal. It gleamed against the sun like a gilded lighthouse, and boats ferried tourists back and forward in a constant stream.

'Why is it called the Treasury?' Cait asked no one in particular.

'It used to be where they kept the country's funds,' Calan said, though half of his attention was on Aggie who was busy returning Tavis' purse without him noticing. 'Now it holds other treasures. The World's Treasury, they call it.'

'Next joke,' Aggie snorted, and she opened her mouth as if to make another retort, but Calan silenced her with a glare.

They slipped through a metal gate onto the pier where a boat packed tight with visitors was waiting for them. They crushed on, and Cait's shoulders wedged between Jamie and a stranger to her left. She gripped the rail and watched the magnificent city stretch out behind them. The boat had no sails, and no black smoke churned up in its wake. It seemed to simply skip along the surface of the water of its own accord. When they reached the opposite shore, it was a pile-out. The crowd filtered along the pier and through a gatehouse guarded by soldiers in smart maroon uniforms. Their faces were covered by golden boar masks, with pointed little tusks, and huge dark eyes set with rubies. Where the eyeholes were for the soldiers beneath, Cait couldn't tell. It was hard to believe they belonged to the same army as Kenzie and Innes. A horrible, nauseous feeling swept through her at the thought of him. Whispers of long-lost princes were all well and good under the shadow of night, but now, beneath the glare of an unrelenting Afrenian sun, and so far away from home, Cait felt the first pangs of regret.

Her feelings must have shown on her face because Aggie leaned over and muttered, 'I know no one actually wants to be in Afren, but try to play the part of the enamoured tourist today.' They passed through a set of thick, black doors into a grand foyer, and Cait's gasp caught in her throat at the sight. The floor was checked with crimson and white marble, and the walls rushed up into a high ceiling bedecked with golden embellishments. At the other end of the room, a magnificent set of stairs swept up into the higher floors of the tower. They paused at the centre of the room beneath an enormous golden sundial inlaid with quartz and a ruby-encrusted crane. Hung on a wall inside, it was rendered useless, but Cait wondered what palace it had once sat in the grounds of.

'Afren has the loveliest taste,' Cait breathed, wishing that things like this could be found in Storran.

'It's not Afren's,' Calan said quickly. 'It's from Iffega.' He checked his watch and snapped it shut with a decisive *click*. 'We've got some time to kill.'

It was then Cait realised Tavis and Jamie were no longer with them. 'Where are the others?' She asked.

Her question went unnoticed as Aggie turned to Calan with a wide-eyed stare. 'We have time?'

Calan cast her a guilty smile, 'Just a little.'

*

They moved through countless halls of display cases as Aggie and Calan muttered excitedly to each other. There were artefacts from all over: mosaic pottery from Leja, ancient frescoes from Massila, skin bags and dice games, and complex alchemy sets from ancient civilisations Cait had never heard of before. As they walked, she kept her eyes on the cases, hoping to spot anything that could relate to the treaty her father longed to see.

'Why does anyone need to travel the world if they can just come here?' Cait muttered to Aggie. She had been to one museum, a little two-room affair in a village a few miles west of Briddock. It was dedicated to the history of the town and only stretched slightly further back than living memory.

'Most of it's looted. Look, you can practically see the scratch marks where they tore it from its owners' hands.' Aggie said, pressing a finger against the glass case of an old doctor's kit that Cait had paused to marvel at.

They climbed yet more stairs and filed into a long gallery where Cait found a beautiful painting of a masquerade in Eadwick. She was trying to pick out the landmarks she had seen that morning when she noticed Aggie looking at an unassuming painting nearby. There was a quiet focus about her, and Cait found herself drifting over.

The painting was no larger than the size of a small book. It depicted a familiar scene: a golden-haired Anndras standing on a decimated battlefield with the sun at his back. Just like the statue in front of Storran's Parliament, he lifted his arms high. Though tragedy had not yet struck and the arrow that would take his life had not yet been fired, there was a darkness all around Anndras' golden frame. Unlike any image of Anndras found in Storran, he held a pewter crown in his hands.

Cait gasped. 'The crown!' It had only just occurred to her that she'd never seen a depiction of the Antlered Crown, even though she had imagined what it looked like over and over.

'Must have slipped through the cracks,' Aggie said. 'I saw a replica of this painting once, on a school trip. It was much bigger than this. They just stuck an ugly mark over the crown, didn't even bother to blend the paint in. Calan was right, turns out. He said they would never do that to the real deal.'

Cait almost laughed. The Fox of Thorterknock went to school like any other person. 'You and Calan went to school together?' she asked.

Aggie smiled. 'Much to his bad luck, aye.' Cait struggled to imagine Aggie as a child at a desk, when the king in the painting before her was so reminiscent of the Fox on her newspaper cart podium. 'You want to know what my political awakening was?' Aggie asked, eyes still fixed on the painting. 'I was ten years old. We had to write letters to school children in Leja. They'd write back to us.' She paused, then looked at Cait. 'Ever tried to write *The Five United Realms of the Afrenian Peninsula* on a letter?'

'You could just write *The Five Realms*,' Cait said.

Aggie scoffed. 'That's what Calan said. But I'm no from five realms. I'm frae one realm, and that realm has so much wasted potential.'

Chapter 9

A Storyteller at Work

The simple, beige teapot in the case before them really was quite something to behold, but Jamie didn't seem to appreciate it as much as Tavis did. They had found a quiet corner to turn their waistcoats inside out, and place maroon caps on their heads so that they looked like one of the many tour guides moving about the museum, and now, Tavis was glad to have captured a moment to look at the displays before they got to work.

'You see, Jamie, it may not look like a work of art, but really the best teapots are designed with functionality in mind, not fashion.'

'But this yin looks like a duck,' Jamie said.

True, the teapot next to it did have a rather charming face and large orange feet, but it would never stand for practical use. 'The more fashionable a teapot is, the less tea-friendly.'

Jamie folded her arms. 'What do you have against the duck?'

Tavis could sense that Jamie didn't so much care for teapot practicality as she did for poking fun at him, but he wasn't one for letting poor craftsmanship slip by unchallenged. 'Well, the spout is all wrong, for starters,' he tutted. 'It should taper off, yet come to a decisive finish in order to prevent drippage. Why, the edge of the duck's beak is as wary as a new spring lamb.'

'My brew could drip as much as it wanted to if it was coming out of a teapot shaped like a duck,' Jamie retorted.

Tavis sighed. 'Such waste in the name of novelty.' He glanced across the room for the umpteenth time, and this time, he found Calan fixing him with a fierce stare as he, Aggie and Cait joined the queue that would lead them upstairs to the crown jewels. 'Right, Jamie. That'll be our cue,' he muttered, smiling at the pun.

There were two tour guides at the front of the line taking it in turns to escort groups of visitors up the set of spiral stairs. Carefully planned to control foot traffic and security around the crown jewels, the queue was a system. All Tavis and Jamie had to do was gain control of it. It was time to do what every storyteller did best: spin a perfectly believable lie.

When the next group had been led upstairs to the jewels, Aggie approached the remaining tour guide and her demeanour transformed into that of a confused tourist. 'Excuse me,' she said with a somewhat exaggerated Afrenian accent, 'I'm looking for a *very specific* Massilan mural and I wonder if you could point me in the right direction? You see, I'm writing a paper and —'

Beside Tavis, Jamie grunted. 'Someone needs to talk to her about that accent. It's offensive.'

'Quiet, now,' Tavis said.

Back at the front of the queue, the guide launched into a set of complex directions, which Aggie nodded her way mechanically through. 'You'll have to excuse me, I didn't follow any of that at all, the scatterbrain I am,' Aggie replied when the guide had finished. 'I'd appreciate it if you could lead me there?'

'I'm afraid I can't leave my post,' the guide said. 'There's sure to be another guide nearby that would be delighted to help you find what you're looking for.'

So, with a tip of his hat and a brisk tap on the guide's shoulder, Tavis, dressed as one of her colleagues, swept in. 'I couldn't help but overhear,' he said quietly to the guide while Aggie blinked on, doing an excellent job of seeming oblivious. 'But you see,' he indicated Jamie, who was doing a good job of much the same. 'I have a trainee with me today who hasn't worked the crown jewels exhibit before, and I'd like the opportunity to give her a bit of a show and tell.'

The guide frowned. 'Have we met?'

'Most likely not, lass, I don't usually work Wednesdays,' Tavis said.

Aggie made a show of checking her watch. 'I'm in a *bit* of a hurry.'

Tavis nodded eagerly at the conflicted-looking guide. 'Go on, we'll take it from here.' The girl's eyes flicked from the queue, to Tavis, and back again, before turning and leading Aggie out of the room. When her companion appeared at the bottom of the stairs with his own group of tourists, he frowned at Tavis and Jamie standing where his colleague had been. 'New start,' Tavis mouthed behind Jamie's back, and the boy nodded in understanding.

Tavis wasted no time garnering further suspicion. He clapped his hands loudly and projected his voice across the room. 'Right folks, we're about to go upstairs to see the crown jewels of Afren.' He paused, allowing a handful of tourists to respond with an excited coo, and he spotted Aggie slip back into the line. 'You'll have fifteen minutes with the jewels, and then we'll bring you out and let the next group in. Now, if everyone can please follow me.'

The spiral stairs were deceptively long. Glancing up at the intricate banisters that formed a curved spine right up the centre of the tower, any unprepared thief would be put off by the climb alone. Tavis was glad that the crowns were not stored at the top, and after just two turns on the spiral stairs, he led the group into a long hallway with an arched ceiling painted with gold stars. Each side was flanked by sculptures from Afren mythology which Tavis delighted in telling the stories of as they passed by. It didn't matter how many years had passed since he was a boy in his Grove, the stories of the Talasaire were as vibrant as ever: *The Serpent of Winborre, Lady Turner and the Ghoul of Drossop Downs.* He noticed as he passed the statues that there were figures from Prilwyn mythology among them. Their labels proudly declared Afren as their point of origin, rather than the green valleys of Prilwyn they had truly sprung from. Tavis cringed at the thought of ignorant tourists thinking that a story like *Brennan of the Shadowlands* belonged to anyone but the Talasaire.

At the end of the corridor, two boar-masked guards heaved open the doors and Tavis led his group into the dark chamber. Inside, dozens of plinths in glass cases formed militant ranks up and down the room. Lamps lit them from their best angles, giving each golden crown an ethereal glow. The tourists, who up until now had formed one excited gaggle, dispersed and fell into a reverent hush. To Afren, this room was not an exhibit, but a chapel. Each crown was unique, cast to represent the reign of its wearer. Tavis found Cait standing by a case that was elevated higher than the others. Inside was a bulky crown, made of angular slates of gold and embellished with the tiniest of rubies. While the other crowns seemed to make a statement with the size of their gems and intricate patterns, this one held its presence in its bulk alone.

'Ah, the crown of Queen Asha,' Tavis said, sliding into place beside Cait. 'It's quite something, isn't it? If ever I mastered the art of walking the Shadowlands I should think I'd like to meet her.'

'Are you a fan of her?' Cait asked.

It was Queen Asha who had finally put an end to the persecution of the Talasaire some five hundred years ago. Tavis found himself admiring her, but perhaps that was because, like Storran's Anndras, time had transmuted Asha from history into myth. 'It's a personal virtue of mine not to become a fan of statesmen.' He paused. 'That being said, hers is a wonderful story.'

'It is a good one,' Cait agreed. 'My favourite part is when the crystal palace grows a hundred feet.'

'Ah, it's different in the Talasaire version.'

Cait's eyes widened. 'Really? How so?'

Tavis would have loved nothing more than to continue discussing the mythology of Queen Asha, until he glanced across the room and saw Jamie struggling to fend off a group of enthusiastic tourists. He would have to get to know their mysterious newcomer another time. 'I'll perform it for you some day,' he said, winking at Cait.

Tavis spent the remainder of the time running through Afrenian history with the tourists, and when fifteen minutes were up, he called them to attention and led them towards the doors, which swung open as though they sensed his approach. As the crowd filed out, Tavis stopped at the door and spoke loudly to Jamie, as planned, 'I need a word with these two kind gentlemen here.' He gestured to the guards. 'Could you go downstairs and retrieve the next group?' Jamie nodded diligently and hurried to catch up with the tourists as Tavis turned to the guards. Out of the corner of his eye, he glimpsed Calan's face in the shadows of the chamber as the doors eased shut in front of him.

Tavis had come armed with a fanciful story about job cuts at the museum to turn the guard's attentions away from the coming and going of museum guests, because there was nothing that distracted a hard worker from doing his job more than the prospect of losing it. He dipped his head as he addressed the two guards. 'Afternoon, gentlemen …'

Chapter 10

The Antlered Crown

Even after the tourists left and the doors closed, Calan still felt like he was being watched. He had the uneasy feeling that the crowns of queens gone by had eyes and they would speak of the crime that they were about to witness. He felt in his pocket for the little key and flicked it into his hand with a *ting*. 'It's all up to old Howie now.'

Howie was the Treasury's head groundskeeper, a Talasaire that Tavis apparently knew from back in the day. Tavis had been visiting Eadwick a few months ago and just so happened to run into Howie, who he insisted should join him for a drink after work. As the ale flowed, Tavis took a keen interest in Howie's job, asking him everything from what his hours were, to how heavy his keychain was to carry around all day. Howie, several pints deep, allowed his old friend the honour of holding the ring of keys, and gladly answered Tavis' questions about which doors they opened. When a band struck up at the other side of the pub and stole Howie's attention, Tavis pressed one specific key into some soft wax. Calan only hoped it was the right one.

Calan, Cait, and Aggie hurried to the end of the room where the crown rested in its case. The dainty pewter circlet with its twisting antlers glowed spectral silver under the lamplight. Just like the other crowns in the room, Calan felt it watching him, only this one was in on the crime; it knew its destiny was more than this glass case.

'Is this it? The real thing?' Cait whispered, nose almost pressed against the glass.

'*They forged a crown in saicrecy, gray antlers for his bree,*' Aggie recited under her breath.

Cait gasped. '*But Anndras wouldna put it oan until his hame was free.* You know the ballad, too?' Calan glanced up to see her staring at Aggie with wide, misty eyes.

Aggie didn't answer. Instead, she continued in her hushed voice, 'They used to say the Queen of Afren stole the crown from Anndras' corpse, and the day it comes back to Storran he'll return for his revenge.' Her eyes were tethered to the crown, and her hands wrapped so tightly around the bar in front of the case that her knuckles were white.

'I've never heard that one before,' Cait murmured. 'Only that its wearer inherits the strength of the Great Stag.'

'Enough to wipe out armies,' Aggie said.

Calan bristled as he checked his watch. 'You can tell each other fairy stories later. You've got the decoy, Aggie?' Aggie removed the false crown from a pocket inside her coat. On close inspection, it would never hold up. While it was cast in pewter like its authentic cousin, its craftmanship left something to be desired. Its surface was uneven, and the antlers were far too small, but it didn't need to work forever, just long enough for them to get safely back to Thorterknock. 'I need someone to stand by the door and keep an ear out for Tavis,' Calan said. He directed the order at Aggie, but when it became clear she had no intention of lifting her gaze from the crown, he turned to Cait. 'Tavis is distracting the guards. When he sees Jamie bringing the next group of tourists upstairs, he will say Afren's motto. When you hear it, you tell us.'

Cait nodded quickly, her eyes glazed.

'Which is ... ' he prompted.

She hesitated. *'Afren ... Afren Prevails.'*

'Let's hope this time it doesn't.' Calan waved her off, and she hurried to the other end of the room. They had five minutes at least, seven at best, and too many minutes had already been wasted. With a slight tremble in his hands, Calan slipped the key into the display case's lock and turned it.

It stuck. He tried again, both hands, both directions, but the key wouldn't budge. He growled through clenched teeth. 'It's not opening.'

'Try again,' Aggie hissed, her attention still captivated by the crown.

Calan tried again, but his sweaty palms slipped off the metal. 'It's not the right key.'

'That's impossible. Howie —'

'Was drunk.' Calan wiped his sleeve along his forehead. *Think.*

'I'll break the case,' Aggie said.

'*No.* Just ...' He tapped an anxious hand against the glass. 'I might be able to pick it.' He swapped the key for the set of lock picks in his pocket, but he was no thief, and whether from inexperience or panic, the picks slipped from his fingers and clattered on the floor three times before he sat on his haunches and said, 'It's no good.'

'Let me try,' Aggie said, just as Cait cried out *Afren Prevails* from the other side of the room.

Calan straightened and righted his shirt cuffs. 'Let's hide.'

'We're waiting for the next group?' Aggie asked. Calan could feel her eyes trailing him as he hurried towards the door.

'No,' he said, 'we're getting out of here. We can come back once I've worked out the lock and —'

Aggie's voice iced over. 'You're not serious.'

'Aggie —'

'We don't have time to wait.'

'There's nothing we can do.'

'*Yes* there is.'

Calan turned to glare at her. 'Don't.'

'My priority is Storran.'

'And right now, mine is getting us out of here.'

'I can see them,' Cait said, face pressed to the slit in the door. 'They're getting closer.'

Calan looked at Aggie imploringly. *Please. Don't do this.*

He knew that look in her eye. It was the desperate and hungry look of the fifteen-year-old girl who had broken into his room and told him to forsake his studies and join an insurgent group in the city. But he had refused because he had things to prove and a future to make. He *still* had a future to make. The look didn't take over often, but it frightened him when it did. It reminded him of just how far she would go for Storran.

Aggie studied him from across the chamber for a moment, her fists clenched, feet pacing back towards the display case. She shook her head once, disappointment creasing across her brow. '*Lealtie Ayebidin*,' she spat.

As the doors edged open, Aggie lifted her elbow and threw her entire weight behind it. The glass cracked, sending a web of fractures across its surface. Calan threw himself behind the doors as Aggie crashed her shoulder against the glass, again, and again, until on the third attempt, the splintered pattern exploded, scattering silver rain across the room. As light from outside poured through the doors, Aggie raised the Antlered Crown for all to see.

Chapter 11

Your Move

Cait had done everything right. She was certain she had, so why was there now glass all over the floor and screams in the air? From her hiding place behind the door, she watched two guards rush into the room. Aggie charged forward and hurled the crown down the hallway. One of the guards turned and chased after it. There was a shot. Aggie rolled out of the way and a display case behind her exploded. The tourists screamed.

'Please, make your way calmly to the foyer,' Tavis' voice wove its way through the chaos, but the tourists' footsteps rang against the marble floors as they fled.

The remaining guard descended on Aggie. He charged, bayonet lowered. Seemingly from nowhere, Calan barrelled into him, and they both sprawled to the ground. A heartbeat later, Calan was on his feet. Red blood oozed through a tear in his sleeve. Aggie tossed him the guard's dropped rifle. There was a flash of hesitation, a moment where time seemed to be held in Calan's poised hand, then the bayonet came plunging down into the guard's thigh. The guard screamed, blood pumping from the wound instantly. Cait's instincts took over and she rushed forward to help the guard, but before she could reach him, Aggie steered her towards the door where they rejoined Jamie and Tavis.

'Calan MacKenzie,' Aggie said as the four of them pelted down the passageway. 'Didn't think you had it in ye.'

'It was just his leg,' Calan said shortly.

It *was* just his leg, but the first thing Cait's mother had taught her was the location of the arteries. They halted at the top of the stairs and were met with the sound of more guards clattering up towards them.

'Up,' Aggie said, already taking the steps two at a time.

They slammed into a locked door bearing a 'restricted' sign one floor up. Calan's lock picks were already in his hands, and mercifully, a moment later, the door sprung open. They piled inside only to find themselves at a dead end.

'Can you lead them away?' Calan whispered through the dark. Without a word, Jamie slipped out of the room and closed the door behind her.

They crouched in the shadows and waited. Cait tried not to think too far ahead. Kenzie and Innes' voices spun in her head, jovially discussing Separatists and firing squads. The footsteps below grew nearer, and Cait imagined the soldiers spinning up the spiral stairs towards them. Would they even grace them with a trial, or would they shoot on sight? Then the movement on the floors below seemed to grow more distant, and Cait kept her eyes screwed shut until the only thing she could hear was the ticking of a clock from somewhere in the dark. When the door to the office burst open, Cait almost choked on her own breath. Jamie appeared, wiping sweat from her forehead.

'They're away. For now,' she panted. 'You're welcome.'

Someone found the courage to light a lamp and Calan was the first on his feet. He turned to Aggie. 'Where is it?'

Aggie rose slowly, reached within her coat, and produced the crown. Even out of the flattering spotlight of its display case, it shone with self-assured radiance. It looked all the better for being free. Aggie grinned. 'They took the bait.'

Calan snatched it from her, as if it might melt if it stayed in her hands any longer. 'It won't be long until they realise it's not real.'

'Then let's get out of here,' Jamie said, checking over her shoulder as she bounced one leg impatiently against the ground.

'They've seen our faces,' Calan cast a pointed scowl at Aggie. 'We can't just walk out there like nothing's happened.'

As Calan muttered to himself and rubbed his temples, Cait looked down at the desk she had been hiding under. The surface was bare, other than a small book on a cushion with its yellow pages unfurled. Between bruises of smudged ink and jagged lettering that formed words she didn't understand, Cait recognised one name: *Anndras.*

The tingling sensation on the back of her neck told her Aggie was peering over her shoulder. 'What's this?' she asked.

Cait eyed the scribble at the top of the page that looked like it might be a date.

'Cait, pet! Read this, look what they found in an old wifie's house!' Her father had been practically bouncing off the walls the day he read the article. What was at first thought to be the diary of a recently departed widow turned out to have been written several hundred years earlier by a soldier in Anndras' army.

'Can you ask to read it, da?' Cait had asked, gripping her father's hands to stop them shaking.

Dr Hardie's eyes had twinkled. 'They're keeping it in Eadwick's Treasury. We'll go there one day, pet. Me and you.'

They'd never made it to Eadwick, but they'd talked at length about the diary and what might be in it. Now it was right here, laid on a plush pillow right before her very eyes.

'It's a diary,' Aggie said.

'It belonged to one of Anndras' men,' Cait said.

Aggie chewed her lip as she considered it, her brown eyes scanning back and forth. 'It's written in Leid.' She hovered a finger above the page. 'It says: *wi his left hand Anndras struck clean aff the heid of a wicked spy tae the queen. With his right, he held the fowks sovereignty.*'

Cait stared at Aggie. 'You can … read that?'

Aggie's eyes flicked up to her and back to the page. 'Aye.' She pointed to another passage. *"S e beinn de duine a bh'ann.* He was a mountain of a man. Strange. I always imagined Anndras was quite small. Lithe, you know?'

Cait just blinked, still processing the lilting language that had just left Aggie's lips. It sounded so rich and *alive*. 'Where did you … how?'

Aggie shrugged. 'I learned it. I heard it was dying, and I didn't want to stand by and let that happen.'

'Is it not a little …' Cait paused, trying to pick the right word. '… redundant? If no one else speaks it?'

Aggie glanced at her sideways, eyebrow raised. 'Leid wis here before anyone started bletherin in the Afren tongue. Same goes for Old Storrian n aw.'

Cait's cheeks heated as the sting of the belt ghosted her palms. 'Sorry.'

She read the words over and tried to make sense of them, but the idea of Anndras beheading someone sat about as right with her as Cathal wandering into an obvious trap. Perhaps answers lay elsewhere in the book. Cait reached out to turn the delicate, browning page, and Aggie sucked in a loud breath. When Cait glanced at her, she lowered her outstretched hands. 'You're meant to wear gloves.'

She dropped her hand and stared at the jagged handwriting.

'Someone must have been reading it very recently,' Aggie mused, nodding to the shelves around the room that were stacked neatly with boxes of artefacts of all sorts.

'Right.' Calan's voice snapped them back to attention. 'Jamie, switch your waistcoat round and put your coat back on. Same for you, Tavis.'

'Can I have my braces back?' Jamie said.

'We'll use the crowd for cover,' Calan said, ignoring her as Cait handed Jamie's coat back to her. 'What's it like down there?'

'Chaos. They're holding all the visitors in the central foyer.' Jamie stuck her hand out. 'Braces?'

Calan sighed and fished them out of his bag.

Cait glanced around the Separatists gathered in the little office. Now presenting more like civilians than tour guides, Tavis and Jamie at least looked somewhat different than they had before, but Calan was just the same, and the guards, or at least the one that was unmaimed, had caught a clear glimpse of Aggie. Cait wasn't sure how they planned to make it out of the museum, but she knew it wouldn't be easy. 'Give me the crown.'

A cackle burst from Calan's mouth. 'Not a chance.'

Cait removed her hat and allowed her hair to spill comfortably over her shoulders. 'People remember someone who looks like me. When they describe the criminals, they won't mention a girl with white hair because they didn't see her. I'm your best bet at getting that crown out of ... out of here ...' she faltered, acutely aware of Separatist eyes on her, Separatists who may very well assume she was making a stab at treachery.

Calan watched her for a long second, his expression inscrutable, then gave a single sharp nod. 'Aggie, wear her hat. Hide your hair. I'll need you to create a stir.'

Aggie gave a mock curtsey and the hat flopped as she bobbed her head. 'My pleasure.'

Calan's heavy gaze dragged over the rim of his glasses and settled on each of them in turn. 'Keep the guards off Cait. You see them so much as breathe in her direction, and I want you there.' Calan turned to Cait and glared at her, his words barbed. 'Get to the train station at all costs. Do not stop until you get there. Aggie?'

Aggie looked up from where she was admiring herself in a glass cabinet. 'Hmm?'

'Make sure she doesn't take off.'

He thrust the bag containing the crown in Cait's direction, and his grip snagged on it for a moment as it changed hands.

*

They hurried back down the way they came, and by the time they reached the museum foyer, it was packed with agitated tourists. The press of bodies stretched across the grand hall to the main door where those at the front were accosting the guards for answers. Calan nodded, and everyone other than Aggie melted into the crowd. Cait watched Aggie's stature fold in on itself until she seemed shaky and flustered. Cait wondered if she had ever looked that way for real.

'Oh, why won't they let us out already?' Aggie muttered to herself, positioned behind a woman who was already wringing her hands. 'Are they trying to have us all *killed*?'

The woman whipped round, face ashen. 'What's wrong? What do you mean?'

'I heard one of them guards, wasn't meant to, but they said the Fox of Thorterknock's here.' Aggie's eyes widened and her voice dropped to a whisper. 'They said she's got a bomb!'

'A bomb?' the woman trilled.

Chaos exploded around Aggie, and the wave of panic spread quickly to the front, where the guards struggled to keep the crowd in line. Aggie appeared at Cait's shoulder and whispered, 'Your move,' then vanished. Cait stepped forward into the crowd. With one hand firmly on the bag at her hip, the other buffered against the jostling bodies, she eased herself forward. Despite knowing Aggie's wildfire rumour was a lie, anxiety quivered through her limbs. She kept her eyes down, willing the guards to overlook her, and she was almost at the front when the crowd finally managed to burst its banks and pour outside into the courtyard. As Cait let herself be swept outside, the sudden glare of the Afrenian sun made her eyes balk and she trusted the crowd to lead her to the boats. When the wooden pier finally clunked beneath her boots, she glanced up to gather her bearings and stopped dead.

The crowd almost knocked her off her feet. Waiting by the boats that were being flooded with tourists were a group of Queen's Watchmen. Cait almost managed to look at the floor and pretend she was just another frantic tourist when she locked eyes with Innes.

'What are you doing?' Jamie hissed, materialising beside her as the crowd flowed around them. Cait tried to move, but she felt as though she were full of stone. Something tugged at the bag and Cait seized it to her body. She turned to find Jamie trying to prise it off her. From the group of Watchmen a voice cried, 'Them, over there!' The flow of tourists from inside the museum stemmed as the guards secured a handle on the crowd. The five Watchmen marched across the empty pier towards Cait and Jamie.

'Nice one,' Jamie muttered.

A group of museum guards emerged onto the pier. Calan and Tavis walked between them at gunpoint, arms raised. Behind them, Aggie was detained between two guards, her hair mussed and a snarl on her lips.

'You've caught yourselves a fox,' one of the Watchmen, a slender woman with silver hair and soft wrinkles, chuckled. One of the guards forced Aggie to her knees and she went down with a wooden *thunk*. When Cait looked back at Innes, he was staring at her, mouth hanging open wordlessly. 'Seize the lot of them,' the silver-haired woman growled.

Cait tried to back away, but she only bumped against one of the museum guards. It all unfolded in her mind: the Watchmen cuffing her, being led onto their little boat, being taken back to Hart Hall where she'd cry to Kenzie and beg his forgiveness. He'd be so disappointed in her. *'Oh, little dove. What have you done?'* Then she'd be lined up and shot with the rest of them.

Or would she? Kenzie wouldn't allow that to happen, not to his *little dove,* not if she had the crown to show for it …

'Innes!' she cried, before she had a chance to think. The Watchmen and Separatists alike paused and looked at each other, and then at Innes, and then at Cait.

'How do you know the girl?' The silver haired woman asked Innes. His mouth opened and closed as hesitation burbled in his throat. 'Quickly now, Innes,' the woman snipped.

'Friend of a friend.' He said the words like he wasn't sure of their truth.

Cait tightened her grip on the bag strap. Innes didn't move. She spoke quickly, trying to keep a step ahead of her panic. 'I was trying to get back to Briddock. They said they'd take me home.' Cait kept her eyes on him, determinedly avoiding Calan's glare. *I know who I'm loyal to.* 'I'll tell you everything,' Cait whispered.

'I'll secure her myself, boy,' the silver haired woman barked, marching towards Cait.

'Please!' Cait cried.

The woman's grip tightened around her shoulder when Innes threw up his hands. 'Captain Reid!' All eyes on the pier fell to Innes. 'I can vouch for her.'

'On your head, Addison,' Reid grunted, moving on to Aggie whose chin she cupped in her hand as she inspected her face.

Innes rushed the last few steps towards Cait. 'What happened? Kenzie is beside himself.' Cait shook her head absently, her mind blank. *I was duped,* she wanted to say, but she had chosen this. She was as responsible as the rest of them for the mess here today. It all started to catch up with her. Her knees went weak, and she steadied herself against Innes' shoulder. 'Whoah,' he said, and steered her towards a mooring bollard. As she sat down, Cait's hands started to tremble. 'You're shaking,' Innes said, taking her cold hands into his. They were soft and warm. 'Sit tight. It'll be over soon.'

She still had the crown in her bag, and it could stay there until she was back in Kenzie's arms. She glanced at the Separatists, at Aggie, defiant even in the face of the establishment that would see them dead. *We'll take it to Gowdstane,* Aggie had said of the crown. *There, we'll declare Aidan as rightful ruler of Storran.* Cait had imagined golden hair falling about the silver antlers after so many years behind glass. She had imagined Gowdstane's gilded walls, the castle alive and breathing once more. She had imagined answers to all of the things that had ever seemed ignored to her.

'Are you okay?' Innes' voice reached her from far away.

'Quiet!' Reid barked across the pier, and Cait glanced up to see Jamie and Tavis muttering to each other. Jamie shook her head at Tavis, who gave a solemn nod. He closed his eyes and spread his hands. His back straightened, his chin lifted, his lips parted.

Cait jumped, and so did Innes, as two new guards erupted onto the pier. 'The crown's a forgery!'

'Search them!' bellowed Reid.

Then Tavis started to sing. A low, singular *'ah'* that meandered around the same note until it melted into one a minor step higher, before cycling back again to the first. It reverberated across the pier, tugging on something ancient within Cait. It was the wind, and it was sea, and it was every folk tale she had ever heard by the fire. Reid's expression flashed with understanding. 'Silence him!' she ordered, already marching towards him.

The Watchmen made a move towards Tavis, but they hesitated as the moored boats started to bronco on the waves. The canal writhed. The air around them cooled.

'What's he doing?' Innes asked, rising to his feet.

Tavis continued to sing the same two notes, surrounded by soldiers, but as peaceful as an oak. With every note his voice grew louder, and the waves leapt with growing strength. 'He's Talasaire,' Cait breathed. So, the stories were true. They *were* magic.

Reid was almost on Tavis when the canal's level dipped and the water rushed up into a colossal wall behind him. It hung there, suspended between land and sky. The Watchmen ground to a halt. Two of the museum guards turned and fled back into the Treasury. Then, the wave folded in on itself, disappearing as quickly as it had formed, leaving them with uneasy stillness.

Jamie's scream smashed through the silence. 'Run!'

The pier burst beneath their feet. Water crashed up through the wood and dragged one of the guards down. Cait stumbled to her feet, and the wood groaned. Water pumped out across the pier, like the blood from the guard's thigh. The Separatists sprinted, water on their heels, towards the boats. A piece of pier beneath Cait's foot gave way, and she screamed and almost toppled into the water. Innes righted her.

'The boat!' Innes cried, and Cait followed him across the pier in the direction of the Watchmen's boat. A moment later, Aggie stepped in their path and shouldered Innes into the canal.

'Innes!' Cait screamed as she lost sight of him. A hand clamped around her wrist. She felt herself being dragged, the pier giving way to water, the rock of a boat beneath her feet, a mechanical growl as it shuddered to life. Cait gripped the back of the boat as it flew across waves that settled as quickly as they had raged. She searched for a glimpse of Innes, but the Treasury and its mangled pier were already a blur.

Chapter 12

Roots

A confused herd of sheep were their travelling companions on the train journey back to Thorterknock. The Separatists waited in brittle silence for the sound of Lealists ordering the train to be stopped, or for the door to be flung open to a forest of guns. But somehow, their waiting stretched out like a cat, the pistons picked up speed, and it was soon apparent they had made it clear of Eadwick. Jamie let her body sag against one of the sheep and buried her face in its wool.

Another bleated loud and low. Aggie burst out laughing. 'We did it,' she gasped, but she was the only one who seemed to be riding the wave of euphoria. The atmosphere in the rest of the carriage felt like heavy ash.

Jamie watched as Cait slowly held out the bag containing the crown to an utterly furious Calan. He studied Cait blankly for a moment then said, 'Is there anything we need to know?'

'No, I —'

'Are we going to find any surprises waiting for us in Thorterknock?'

'I didn't know they would be there,' Cait said. Her panic plunked the air.

'You could have fooled us,' Calan snapped.

Before this moment, Jamie would never have thought Calan was capable of tossing someone off a moving train, but now she wasn't so sure. When he turned to glare at Aggie and Jamie in turn, she decided that yes, in fact, he was *more* than capable.

'There's not a single thought between the two of you,' he said.

'Eh, wait a minute!' Jamie cried at the same moment Aggie also loudly protested. 'She asked for help, what was I supposed to do?' She waved an arm at Aggie. 'I wasn't the one who let her stay.'

'You shouldn't have offered in the first place,' said Calan.

Jamie spread her hands in frustration. 'You could have said no!'

'I tried,' he said through gritted teeth.

'This is on all of us, and you know it,' Jamie said.

'I'll get off at Holt!' Cait cried, and it snapped straight through their bickering. 'Just let me off at Holt and I'll go.'

Calan looked at Cait, but his words were aimed at Aggie. 'How much does she know?'

'Nothing,' Cait spluttered.

Calan held up a hand to stop her and turned to Aggie. 'How much does she know?'

Instead of lashing out, Aggie sunk into the collar of her coat. She looked the most sheepish out of all of them, which Jamie thought was impressive given the company. 'Enough,' she whispered, at last.

'We'll take her back to the Unnertoun,' Calan said, then shot Aggie and Jamie one last glare for good luck, before moving to the opposite end of the carriage. Jamie was certain he would have stormed out if he had the room, but he was forced to wade an awkward path through the sheep.

No one spoke for a long time. Aggie stared at the ceiling, Cait twisted a piece of her skirt around and around her finger. Jamie realised that there was something missing from the confrontation. She looked over at Tavis, who hadn't even tried to mediate. He just sat silently, gazing at nothing. She knew that something was wrong because her senses were tuned into every living thing around her, from Calan smouldering away in the corner, to Cait squirming with anxiety. But when she looked at Tavis, she felt like she was in a tiny boat on a glassy black sea. 'How does it feel?' She asked quietly, running her fingers through the wool of the nearest sheep.

She thought he wouldn't respond, but after a while he shifted where he sat. 'I won't lie to you lass, it's empty feeling.'

'Empty,' Jamie echoed, not knowing what else to say.

'When first we crossed the canal, I could hear the waves talking as clearly as you and I sat here now.' The feeling was familiar. Even now, speeding as fast as they were upon wood and iron, the wind called her name. 'On the way back, there was nothing. It's as though the world has gone silent.'

Talasaire's connection to the natural world had many names: the Cy, the Breath, the Song, life force, nature itself. But it was a delicate, fickle thing. Jamie closed her eyes and reached out to the wind whipping by outside, the trees that were there and then gone, the grass between the tracks. Her life would be so flat without its music.

'There was another feeling, so there was,' Tavis said. He sounded shaken, frightened even. 'There was a hunger. When I called the water to serve me, I've never felt more connected to the Cy. I felt like I was at the centre of all things.' He closed his eyes. 'I fear I will never be rid of the craving for another taste.'

'Did something happen to your magic?'

Jamie turned to find Cait peering at them. She had almost forgotten she was there at all, never mind that she might be listening. 'It's not magic,' Jamie said, rolling her eyes.

Tavis gave a weak chuckle. 'In some ways, Jamie, don't you think it is?'

Of course she did. Which was why she was so afraid for Tavis, and what it might mean for her if she ever made the same mistake.

'You sang, and the canal responded. It was like it was alive,' Cait said.

'Everything is alive, lass,' Tavis said. His voice was faint, like his breath had been snatched by the wind. 'People like Jamie and I just know how to speak the language.'

The first lesson a young Talasaire learned was how to tell a good story. The second, how to turn it into a song. *'Cycles, Jamie. Stories, Songs, and Seasons. They're all cycles. If you ever want the Cy to hear you, you'll learn the art of story first,'* Llyr, the old tutor from her Grove, had scolded her when she tried to make the fire leap the night of her first lesson. Talasaire training took a lifetime, and leaving her Grove after completing just one Cycle meant she would never be as sage as Tavis was, but she made a damn good bard.

Cait shuffled forward on her knees. 'What else can you make it do?'

'The Cy is not a tool,' Jamie said firmly, and then grimaced, realising she sounded exactly like Llyr. 'It's a partner. We're supposed to feel connected to the natural world by understanding it. We talk to it, it talks back. Our relationship to it is like a dialogue.'

Cait's head tilted to the side as she looked at Tavis. 'So, what happened on the pier? Was that not a dialogue?'

Tavis sighed. 'Not a dialogue, no. An order though? Yes, that's more like it. If we start acting like rulers and not ambassadors, the Cy has no reason to stay with us. It will retreat. Sometimes, forever.'

'Never, ever, use the Cy to your own ends.' That was the golden rule, and Jamie could remember countless lessons in the Grove, sprawled out in the clover, listening to elderly Talasaire preaching to them about what

would happen if they ever asked their tea to heat itself, or pleaded with the wind to dry their clothes faster.

'Use your abilities to protect the natural world and teach,' Llyr would say in his arthritic voice. It was a simple life, but it certainly wasn't dull. She would give anything to be sat around a fire hearing ancient folklore, or dancing at Midsummer while drinking someone's questionable home-brewed cider. How proud Llyr would be of her now, flouting all his teachings in the name of politics. *'Politics is the death of honesty'* was another of his favourite sayings. Thanks to some queen a few hundred years ago, Talasaire may no longer have been pyre-bound from the day they were born, but they certainly didn't do much with that privilege.

'Can it be healed?' Cait asked after a long silence.

'Sometimes you can regain its trust,' Tavis said, then added quickly, 'if not too far gone.'

'How do you know if it's too far gone?' Cait asked.

Jamie bristled and threw Cait a warning glare. She had too many questions. It was growing tiring. Tavis must have caught Jamie's look because he gave a weak chuckle. 'Now, Jamie, it's quite alright. We're teachers, are we not?' To Cait he said, 'We can tell, it's that simple really. Our connection feels like roots that keep us tethered to the ground. If you still feel tethered, there's hope.'

'How do *you* feel?' Cait asked.

Tavis smiled but didn't meet either of their gazes. 'Quite untethered.'

'It'll come back,' Jamie said. She'd decided it would, because she didn't like the alternative. 'You just need to focus on something else for now. The crown —'

'I rather think I'll lay low for a while,' Tavis said.

Jamie nodded. 'Aye. That makes sense, stay in the Unnertoun. Meditate.'

'I should go further afield, I reckon,' Tavis said slowly. 'Home to Prilwyn, perhaps.' His eyes went misty with nostalgia. 'If they'll have me.'

'You're leaving?' Jamie asked, aware that her voice quivered. 'For how long?'

'We shall see.' He gave her a smile which tugged gently at his beard.

She knew she couldn't ask him to linger if he felt there was a chance for his connection at home. Still, she'd miss him terribly. *All this for a stupid lump of pewter,* she thought. She almost didn't want to ask, not with Cait sitting there listening, but the question spilled out of her. 'Do you regret it?'

Tavis looked thoughtful for a moment, then Jaime caught it: a glance up towards Aggie. 'My duty is to Storran,' he said.

*

'It was brave of him to do what he did,' Cait whispered when it seemed everyone else had fought past their tempers and demons to get some rest.

Jamie scratched the head of the sheep she had made friends with, and it closed its heavy eyes. 'He might never return to his Grove after this.'

Cait frowned. 'Why? Wouldn't they look after him?'

Jamie sighed. 'We're not supposed to meddle with real-world things.' She nodded at Tavis, who was sleeping with a strained look on his face. 'This is exactly why.' It was brutal, but the punishment for losing that part of yourself had always been exile. That was how they stopped people taking advantage of their abilities. That was how they maintained their role as peacekeepers and makers.

There was a lapse of silence, but Jamie could feel Cait's next question quivering in the air between them even before she asked. 'Then why did you join the Separatists?'

Jamie stretched out her legs and pushed her face against the sheep's warm pelt. A really good story. That was the honest truth, but she couldn't very well sit here and tell Cait she became an outlaw for a legendary king and his secret heir. Instead, she said, 'Did you notice the boat to the Treasury had no sails? Or that there are no chimneys or smog in Eadwick?' Cait nodded. 'Most of Afren is powered by Talasaire. The government offer them a smidgen of money in exchange for their talents, but the money dries up in a matter of months. Most of the time, the Cy never returns to them, and they're left a shell of their former selves, and just as poor.'

Cait's mouth hung open. 'That's awful.'

Jamie shrugged. 'That's the Afrenian regime. Storran isn't the only place they exploit.'

'No wonder you don't like them,' Cait muttered.

'Understatement of the year.'

They laughed at the situation because it was all they could do. Jamie had to admit that Cait was growing on her. The questions were annoying, but there was no malice in them, only a craving for understanding. *I suppose we* are *teachers,* she thought begrudgingly. Tavis was always a better teacher than her. Cait's next query came right on cue. 'Don't your Groves provide for you?'

'Not every Talasaire wants to live in a Grove,' Jamie said. 'We have a harder time than most integrating, and that leads us straight into Afren's palm.' Jamie remembered a young Talasaire from her youth. She had forgotten his name a long time ago, but she remembered that he fell in love with a woman in the nearest town. He left the Grove to start a life with her among civilisation, but they must have fallen upon hard times because the next time she saw him, he was smaller, rugged. There was an emptiness that radiated from him where there should have been song. She shook her head and cast his dark eyes from her mind. 'Harnessing our abilities for industry is relatively clean. It stops the factories chucking smoke into the air, sure, and a healthy earth is pretty high up on the Talasaire agenda, as I'm sure you can imagine. But the fix for poisoning the earth shouldn't be found in stripping people of their soul.'

'And you think Storran being free will fix that?' Cait asked. Aggie might have taken that as an invitation to her soapbox, but Jamie understood. She was still asking herself the same question. There was no proof Storran would be better than Afren if allowed to manage its own affairs.

'I don't know,' she said, truthfully. 'But I do know I'm ashamed of how Afren acts. Dismantling their regime seems like a good first step. It only begins with Storran. It ends when the Queen of Afren is just the Queen of Afren and nothing else.'

'You want the Prilwyn free, too?'

Jamie closed her eyes, imagining the lush valleys of the Talasaire's home island, just off the east coast of the Afrenian peninsula. She'd never been there, but one day she hoped to go. 'I want all of them to be. Storran. Prilwyn. Kerneth. Tor. The Five Realms could exist alongside each other. They could work together.' She waved a hand, reciting another teaching from Llyr. 'Harmony, equality, respect. One cannot exist without the other.'

'I think that's beautiful,' Cait whispered. And then, 'I'm sorry about what they do to your people.'

Jamie buried her discomfort into the sheep's wool along with her hand and grunted with a shrug. She didn't want pity. She wanted change. She wanted Afren to pay for all the Talasaire whose lives they had ruined.

'I'm still trying to work out why I'm here,' Cait said quietly. 'I don't know. At first it was just the crown and the heir, but things are starting to make sense to me. They shouldn't, but they do. It's confusing. I don't know. I'm working it out.'

Jamie looked up at the pale girl with her legs pulled in tight to her chest. Tavis didn't sacrifice his connection for *don't know,* but perhaps recalling Llyr's lessons about harmony had had an effect on her, because she bit back the sharp remark that rose to her tongue. 'You'd better think fast,' was all she said.

Cait never replied. In the silence that followed, Jamie glanced at Tavis. If it hadn't been for him, they might be on a very different journey right now. And if she had been the only Talasaire on the pier? Jamie wasn't sure if she was selfless enough to dig up her roots for the sake of justice, or Storran, or even her friends.

Chapter 13

Unnertoun

Cait spent much of the journey back to Storran weighing up her chances of escape. She wondered how easily the iron bolt on the door could be undone, and how quickly she could disappear once she flung herself onto the platform. She told herself over and over that if the Separatists were asleep, she would take her chances, but the closer they got to Holt, the closer Calan seemed to watch her.

Calan ordered everyone to disembark at a station just south of Thorterknock. He said that the station in the capital would be too busy with Queen's Watch trying to intercept the crown, so they would walk the last few miles, split up, and enter the city covertly. She had hoped to travel with Jamie, but Calan summoned her with a glare and the two of them trudged in lumbering silence. Whoever's keeping the crown was now in, Cait had not been party to the exchange.

When they reached the outer suburbs of Thorterknock, their pace slowed, and Cait's nerves grew as rows of quaint houses popped up around them and streets fleshed out with citizens. Cait wondered what cunning trick Calan would pull to get past the heightened security at the city's Southgait, but he led her to a section of the city wall that was concealed by a cluster of gorse bushes, and as he beat aside the shrubbery, a rough hole revealed itself. Calan made Cait wriggle through first and her shoulders grazed the stone. In the moment she stood alone on the other side, she thought about taking her chances. She wasn't particularly fast, but with a good head start she could likely lose Calan to the city and make her way to Hart Hall and back to Kenzie. Her feet almost moved, but somewhere a whip cracked, and Cait suddenly, inexplicably, remembered Kenzie's raised palm.

'This way,' Calan said, on his feet again and leading her down a deserted backstreet.

Their movements through the New Town were stagnated by the increased presence of the Queen's Watch who seemed to walk slower and peer harder than they had before. The civilians seemed rattled, too, their quick voices frayed at the edges. The city was suspended in a restless haze and Cait felt like she was wading through it, leaving thick amber ripples in her wake.

'I'd fancy a look at the crown masel. I hope it stays in Storran for a bit when they find it,' one woman said as they passed.

'Bloody shame,' her companion clucked. 'Two folk died, you know? The Watch lost an officer, the museum security, too! I'm telling you, whoever's responsible needs strung up.'

Cait's heart twisted. Had Innes made it out of the water?

'Don't listen to them,' Calan muttered, but Cait felt like her guilt was stamped across her forehead.

She wasn't sure where Calan was leading her, but she followed him to a butcher shop just over Barter Bridge and into the Old Town.

'Calan,' the butcher said in a voice as flat as a board as they approached the counter. 'The usual?'

'Yes, fourteen pounds of the venison, if you will, Alec,' Calan said, checking over his shoulder as he leaned on the counter.

The butcher, a young man with a thick beard and curls of red hair on his head, chewed something with his back teeth and nodded at a door behind him. 'Aye, roond the back. I'll need a haund gettin it oot, like.'

They followed the butcher into a cool storage room, and Cait held her breath as they passed rows of livestock carcasses hanging from the ceiling. Their shanks brought to mind the blood spurting from the museum guard's thigh, so she anchored her gaze on the sleek ropes of hair shifting down Calan's back.

'Bin hearing all aboot this crown,' the butcher said. There was a hopeful twinkle in the look he tossed over his shoulder. 'Clatter aboot toun is we'll be free by the end o the year.' His rugged language made Cait shudder, then Aggie's sardonic frown filled her mind and she remembered the Eadwick hatter.

'We can hope. Though I'm sure whoever was responsible would enjoy a bit of discretion,' Calan said.

The butcher grunted as he shoved aside some boxes and heaved open a trap door concealed beneath. 'Not lang I howp! Long live the outlawed King.'

Calan glanced at Cait with a flash of exasperation before he nodded into the trapdoor. 'Follow me.'

Gazing into the dark and remembering what lay at the bottom of the last trap door she climbed down made Cait feel like she was swaying on a hook, but she followed Calan down the ladder. The door snapped shut above them before she had touched the floor, and her eyes only adjusted as far as the rungs passing through her hands. The air got colder, and she was beginning to think the ladder would never end, when her feet at last hit solid ground.

'Follow me,' Calan said somewhere beside her. His voice reverberated in the air around them.

As they walked, Cait's vision slowly adjusted enough to reveal a cobblestone passageway that sloped gently downwards. 'What is this?' she asked. A grim Separatist prison deep beneath the city? A crypt where they would lock her up and leave her for dead?

'We call it the Unnertoun,' Calan said. 'A hundred or so years ago they did some developments in the Old Town and a couple of streets were covered in the process. Lucky for us, our people found it first.'

Soon enough, a small amount of light from up ahead illuminated the passage, and the plain stone walls on either side of them became jaunty brown buildings, and the jaunty brown buildings gained little windows and doorways. Eyes appeared at the windows, and shadows shifted in the doors. Cait crept closer to Calan, but as the passageway levelled out, the shadows turned into people, and Cait found she was as good as walking through a street in the Old Town, only just below the surface.

'Do all the Separatists live here?' Cait asked. An old woman in a rocking chair smiled at Calan as they passed by, and Cait struggled to imagine her planting fireworks in someone's house.

They stopped walking halfway down the street and Calan ducked through a dark doorway into one of the buildings. 'Just the ones that need to.'

Cait almost banged her head as she took the stairs down into the building, and Calan lit an oil lamp which filled the room with a low, orange glow.

'Calan!' a high-pitched girl's voice cried. Cait jumped.

'Shadielaunds!' Calan shouted, clutching his chest. 'Elsie!'

The girl, who had been sat alone in the dark at a wooden table, stood up and rushed towards Calan. She had a pleasant, round face, and a wave of brown hair that curled at her shoulders. She grimaced. 'Sorry. The lamp ran out. I didn't refill it. Do you have it?' She glanced over Calan's shoulder at Cait. 'Hello.' Then her eyes were back on Calan. 'The crown, you got it?'

'That's not really your business, Elsie,' Calan said. Cait noticed him grip his bag tighter.

An impish and knowing glint entered the young woman's eye. 'Say no more, MacKenzie.'

When she lingered wordlessly, Calan raised his eyebrows and nodded towards Cait. 'Elsie. Can we have a moment?'

She muttered something affirmative and scurried out into the street. Cait already missed her, now forced to bear the brunt of Calan alone. She took stock of the room. It looked like the average kitchen, with its round table at the centre and rough counter space around the walls. There was a little window above the sink that at one time would have let in light, but now only looked out onto the darkness of the buried street. In the not-so-distant past, someone would have stood by that window preparing food, or washing plates. Now, it played host to whispers and schemes. It seemed remarkable that Thorterknock kept such a secret beneath its bustling pavements.

'Do you trust the butcher?' Cait asked. Surely a generous sum of money, or a misplaced word, and the Separatists would lose the one remarkable foothold they seemed to have.

'We just have to,' Calan said.

'And the Queen's Watch have no idea?'

'Not yet.' Calan cast her a warning glare, then gestured to a chair at the table and Cait eased herself into it.

Calan remained standing, his hands wrapped around the back of his own chair. His air seemed stiff and mechanical as he said, 'I hope you understand why we can't let you return to the city.'

Cait opened her mouth to protest. 'I —'

'You will not be a prisoner,' Calan said firmly. 'But I cannot overlook the fact that the Lealist on the pier knew you.'

Cait suddenly felt as though the walls of the quaint little house were closing in around her, entombing her beneath the city. She fought to regain control of her words, but they spooled out. 'I promise, just let me go home, I won't tell anyone, I'll never speak about any of this again, I promise, I —'

Calan looked at Cait over his glasses. 'Be honest with me. Were you sent by them?' Cait watched him for a moment, trying to think up any excuse that would separate her from his enemies, but there were none that fit. 'Who was the Lealist on the pier?' Calan pressed.

'He's a friend of a ...' She hesitated. 'Close friend.'

'This close friend, they're a Lealist?'

Cait nodded. 'I came to the city with him. We lived in the same village. We've been together for ... a long time.'

Cait's vision blurred. Thinking about Kenzie felt raw, like an untreated and festering wound. Kenzie had tried to protect her, he always had, and she repaid him by fraternising with his enemies.

'And why did you need to leave the city?'

Cait took a trembling breath. 'I was running.'

Calan watched her carefully, the same way Aggie had when she had asked Cait why she was with them in Eadwick. 'Why?'

'I don't know,' she said.

It took a while for Calan's stare to soften, but when it did, his shoulders sagged, and he sighed. 'Okay.' He looked down at his hands for a moment, then back at Cait. 'There is a place for you here. Whatever you're running from, you'll be safe from it.'

'Thank you,' Cait said. Then, in the silence that followed, like every silence since Eadwick, she thought about corpses with boar heads and drowning Watchmen. She had forgotten about the Separatists' reputation among their camaraderie. What was their promise of safety worth when the boy stood before her had recently taken a life? 'How many people have you killed?' Cait asked.

Calan looked startled. She watched him compose himself, rearranging his features into his usual even frown. 'None.'

Cait knew that wasn't true. 'The museum guard,' she said.

Calan gave a breathy laugh and shook his head, but his eyes refused to meet Cait's. 'I would think Afrenian medicine is capable of stitching a leg.' His fingers reached to something tied around his neck, and Cait realised it was a rusted iron key that fit neatly into his palm.

She chose her next words carefully. 'There's an artery up the inside of the thigh.'

Calan's eyes crushed close. 'Don't.' She watched Calan open his eyes, still avoiding her gaze. He arranged his hands in front of him on the table and looked down at them. Cait wasn't sure he'd ever see his own hands in the same way again.

'Can I treat your arm?' Cait asked. The blood on his clothes had dried, but she itched at the thought of leaving the wound beneath unclean and crusty.

Calan blinked through his apparent distraction. 'What?'

'The uh ... guard. He nicked your arm.'

Calan studied his own arm as if he had only just noticed he had been injured. 'That's not necessary.'

'Please, it's killing me.'

'First aid supplies in the top drawer,' Calan sighed, seemingly resigned.

Cait retrieved some spirits, dressing, and bandages, and pulled her chair alongside Calan's. He winced as she peeled away the sleeve and cleaned the wound, but she was relieved to see it didn't go deep. 'He only grazed —' she faltered, remembering that the 'he' who had inflicted the cut was no longer. 'It's just a graze.' She worked in silence to dress the cut, wiping away the dried blood and sweat, wrapping it in clean gauze, and securing the bandage with a sterile pin. For those short moments, she lost herself and felt her taut muscles release. It felt good to fix something.

'Was it worth it?' Cait asked as she finished. 'The crown?'

Calan sighed, rolled down his sleeve, and said quietly, 'It will be.' When he looked back up at her, his features had settled back into their usual stoniness. 'Regardless of where they stand, people respect the crown. Afren tried to erase its power by erasing its image, but by making it elusive, they've only added to its power. The people will understand its significance. And they'll want to see it for themselves. They'll want to hear us, if only to satisfy their own curiosity.'

He didn't suggest a revolution of fire and blood, he only spoke of being heard. Aggie had acted as though the crown were merely a symbol, but Cait could see now that it ran much deeper than that. Anndras' crown was an object of legend, and while the people of Briddock would never willingly seek out a Separatist king, she could imagine them flocking to earn a glimpse of the crown. An object of legend, both ancient and timeless, a gift from a god, and forged with terrible strength too, if legend was to be believed. She wished she could see it on a king's head, but not if the road ahead was anything like the road that had brought her here.

'I don't think I want to be a part of all this,' Cait whispered. The chill of the Unnertoun settled within her and she clasped her hands tightly.

Calan blinked slowly and gave her an almost-smile. 'You don't have to be.' He moved around the table and picked up the lamp. 'Follow me, I'll show you somewhere you can rest.'

You don't have to be. Cait held Calan's words in her mind as she followed him up a narrow set of stairs and into a dark room with a low ceiling. It was all the permission she needed to lie low for a while, and maybe then she could look to finding her way back home, whether that was Kenzie or Briddock, she wasn't sure. And yet, that night, she dreamt she was wearing the Antlered Crown, and no matter how she tried, she could not take it off.

Chapter 14

You Will be the Death of Me

When Calan returned to the kitchen, he sat at the table and carefully placed the satchel containing the crown on the table in front of him. He watched it for hours. His fingers touched the fastening, but he couldn't bring himself to open it. When he looked at the crown, all he saw was what they had done to get it. The black creases in the pewter told of churning canal water, and the antlers glinted like bayonets. His mind kept playing over the moment he knocked the guard over, how Aggie had tossed him the rifle, how his only thought before the bayonet fell was that if he aimed for the leg, it would somehow make him less guilty.

I don't think I want to be part of all this.

Most of the time, neither did he.

The door banged open and Calan jumped from his thoughts as Aggie appeared, a sack full of clothes in her hand. 'What's that for?' he asked, nodding to the bag.

Aggie ignored him and closed the door behind her. 'Where is it?'

Calan frowned. 'What are you talking about?'

She dropped the bag on the floor and braced her hands on the table opposite him. 'The crown. You still have it?'

'Yes,' he said slowly, fingers instinctively curling around the bag and pulling it towards him.

'Good. We need to leave.' She took a swipe at the bag and Calan lifted it out of her reach.

He laughed. 'You're not making any sense.'

She leaned closer, speaking in hushed, frantic whispers. 'I saw Lealists. They were sniffing around the entrance near Aist Bridge. I led them away, but it won't be long before they find us. We need to get the crown to Gowdstane before it's too late.'

Aggie's voice trembled with a panic that Calan had scarcely heard from her, and it unnerved him. He wasn't oblivious to the increased efficiency of the Lealists, who were always breathing down their necks. It was a threat they'd learned to live with. 'There have been plenty of close calls before,' he said it more for his own sake than hers.

'Not like this. They would have found us. And that's not all. Last week the Lealists paid Alec a visit.'

Calan frowned. 'He never said.' The butcher would normally be the first to mention anything untoward.

'That's what I thought,' Aggie said slowly. She held Calan's gaze with a look that was heavy with unspoken words. She had made up her mind about something, and she wanted Calan to reach the same conclusion himself.

'You don't think ...' he shook his head. No. Alec had been a stout ally as long as Calan could remember. He wouldn't talk.

'That's exactly what I think,' Aggie said in a low voice that sent a shiver through Calan. He knew exactly what Aggie was trying to do, still, he found himself running through the words he'd said to the butcher, if he'd left any hint as to where the crown was. He'd been careful to be discreet at every turn, but if Alec was in the pocket of the Lealists and they had intel on who had been at the Treasury that day ... He looked up to find Aggie gazing intently at him. She could see him thinking, he knew it. He brushed her stare from his skin. 'We've done our bit. All we can do now is let Lister know —'

Aggie groaned and threw her hands in the air. 'Fuck Lister!'

'And he'll collect the crown when he sees fit. Our job is to keep it safe until then.'

'Dae yi mind how long it took me to convince him tae make a move on the crown in the first place?' Aggie snapped. She must have been angry, because her words peppered with Old Storrian.

Lister Burke was a politician for the Enlighten Party, and he stood for Storran in the Council of Five. His involvement with the Separatists and the harbouring of the heir to Anndras Àrdan was, other than the Unnertoun, Storran's best-kept secret. Unfortunately, this time, Aggie was right. His support was firm, but his actions slow. Still, he was their leader, and he was a practiced politician. Calan had played his part. It was messy, but he had pulled it off, and now it was up to Lister. 'He knows what he's doing.'

'They're closing in on us, Calan!' Aggie growled. She started to pace.

Calan remembered the night she had snuck into his room, practically seething with these new, desperate ideas of joining the Separatists. She'd been young, only fifteen years old, but a decade later and she was still the same when she got her teeth into something. It had been the same then, the same when she convinced Lister to make a move on the crown, and it was the same now. 'Once the Lealists tear Thorterknock apart looking for that crown, they'll start moving north. Nowhere will be safe.'

Calan looked down at the satchel in his iron grip and muttered, 'I can't.'

'Shadielaunds, Calan, do you care about Storran or yerself?' When Calan said nothing, Aggie stilled. 'You are somehin else.' Of course she could see through him. She always had.

'I need Lister to trust me. He won't give me a place on his council at the end of it all if I go behind his back.'

'If the Lealists storm this place, there won't be a free Storran, never mind a *cooncil*. There won't be any opportunities left, and your family will just have one less son.'

Calan winced. This was history repeating itself: Aggie coming to his home, telling him they should join the Separatists together, and Calan sitting tight at his desk, pen clasped in his fist. *I need to finish my exams,* he'd said. When the University rejected him and no jobs came, he joined her, and devoted himself to becoming indispensable to the Separatists so that when Storran was free, he and his family could have a place in it.

'The sooner we crown Aidan, the sooner we can fight back,' Aggie said, then paused. 'The sooner you can get the recognition and power you deserve.' A wood-panelled office, an account for travel expenses. He didn't care what the job was — ambassador, negotiator. He'd write speeches for hollow politicians if he had to. He just needed to be more than he was. He reminded himself Aggie was no prophet, simply a girl who abandoned her family long ago, with no one but herself and Storran to worry about. Calan didn't have that luxury. They were waiting for him, *counting* on him to make something of himself. Aggie pulled up a chair and sat opposite him. 'Let me paint you a picture.'

Calan rolled his eyes to the ceiling. 'Aggie —'

Aggie spoke quietly. 'If we take this into our own hands, you will not only be the man who freed Anndras' crown from Afren, you'll be the man who brought it to its rightful owner.' She sat back and watched him. 'If Lister doesn't reward you for that, the rightful king certainly will.'

Calan stared at the table. This wasn't going to work on him.

When she gained no reaction, Aggie added slowly, 'If the Unnertoun is discovered, do you think Lister will hang around? It certainly won't be him that suffers. It'll be folk like me and you.' She tilted back on her chair. 'Besides, it'd be doing him a favour. We'd be saving him a trip.'

Perhaps Aggie was right. Lister Burke had very little to lose by waiting, but the same couldn't be said for the Separatists of the Unnertoun who had nowhere else to go. There were worse things he could do than steal a crown from Lister Burke. Most of them he'd already done. Calan let out a long exhale and peered up at Aggie. 'You will be the death of me, Agnes Allaway.' And he meant it.

Aggie's eyes flashed and she grinned. 'Say that name again and it'll be sooner than you think.' She stood, swinging the sack of clothes, whatever it was for, over her shoulder. 'See you in the morning?'

Calan nodded. 'Get some rest. We'll meet in Gelly.'

'I'll let the others know.'

Calan's head snapped up. 'No.'

'Why?'

'We need to keep this quiet.'

He expected her to argue, but she just shrugged and said, 'Understood.'

He drummed his fingers on the table. 'We can't take a train, the station will be swarming with Lealists ...'

Aggie grinned. 'I'll leave the details up to you. Where's Cait?'

Calan waved at the door that led upstairs, and when it had closed behind her, he rubbed his temples as his mind already started to spin through the next steps. Aggie was right, the Lealists wouldn't leave the city until they were certain they had exhausted their search. The Separatists' only hope of a head start would be to go by road. He'd need to secure a cart.

'Aggie,' Calan called. He heard her footsteps on the stairs still. 'Leave the city quietly.'

Chapter 15

Songs of Storran

The room Cait had been allocated was small and had no windows, not that they would do any good underground. It was lit by a weak oil lamp at her bedside, and next to it was a pile of books. When she finally gave up on her fitful sleep, she turned over and studied the titles. The well-loved selection of romance and history titles were piled upon a dusty looking book about political theory, and a green cloth-bound volume in the middle that she recognised. She eased it from the pile and read the gold lettering on the spine: *Songs of Storran.*

As she let her fingers dance across the pages, the sweet, woody aroma reminded Cait of home. She could see her father in his armchair by the fire, the very same edition of this book on his knee as he prepared to tell *The Selkie of Witteneuk* or *The Skeekit Mason,* or maybe even *The Ballad of Anndras and Cathal.* Cait knew she could recite the stories by heart if she tried, down to the accents and sound effects her father used. Each story was the same every time, yet they always surprised her. She let the book fall open in her lap and sighed with disbelief when it opened on *The Ballad of Anndras and Cathal.* The part of her that looked for signs and symptoms saw the wear on the pages, and the bend in the book's spine, and she could tell the owner loved this story particularly. She buried the small voice that told her it was fate. The words were in Old Storrian, but she knew the story well enough that it didn't cause an issue.

'There will be none of that language in this house!' her mother would chide as her father started to recite the ballad. Instead, he'd tell the story in his own words.

She skimmed the first stanzas which set the scene and introduced the main characters as boys of different worlds: Anndras, the son of the wealthy Laird Àrdan, and Cathal, a weaver's lad. As they grew, Anndras took over his father's estate, while Cathal travelled the land as a mercenary.

Appalled with how the southern nobility settled on northern land and stripped the local communities for their own gains, Cathal soon called together a band of supporters to drive the settlers home. Cait skipped to her favourite part: Anndras and Cathal's first meeting.

But Cathal knew he'd need some Lairds
Tae swear his solemn troth
Rich men the common fowk wad trust
Whas stock was of the north
Fine Anndras in the forest strolled

Ae crisp autumnal day
When spied the frichtsome Cathal there
Amang the birches gray

'Why comes the Bain o Kings tae me?
For though I am a Laird
My blood is o northern hills
For that, my heid be spare't'

'I want not for your heid today
You hae nae cause tae flee
Gie o'er your blade and o'er your gowd
For the north I want tae free

Call all your high and walthy friends
A mighty force they'll bring
Hoist yer banners for my cause
In turn we'll mak ye king'

Fair Anndras laughed and said to he,
'You'd mak me king o crime.
I'd rather that yi kilt me here
Than join ony cause o thine'

When winter swept in bleak as deith
Anndras, while in bed asleep
Awoke tae hear bold Cathal call
And through the windae creep

'I've come tae ask ye ance again'

The rebel he did say
But Anndras only shook his heid
And turn't Cathal away

'Come back and ask me ance again
When you have answers plain
Of how we should conduct oorsels
When we carve this laund in twain'

The Spring arrived with all its blyth
And Anndras hie tae ride
When Cathal rode astride wi him
'Sir, won't ye join oor side?'

'Will not our people starve tae death
If frae the south we split?
Ye cannae feed a hungry bairn
Wi just a proud spirit'

'You've made your point,' the rebel sighed
'I'll leave ye tae yer day
But you'd be wise tae be less feart
O what the cowarts say'

At last the year turned roon again
And Autumn flared up reid
The Queen sent oot a summons south
That Anndras gladly heed

The northern nobles bent the knee
And kissed the Hie Queen's feet
'I have a plan tae quell the north
And rebels tae defeat.

'For laund and riches in return
Just carry oot this deed
Purge all yer toons of their dissent
And mak those traitors bleed'

Guid Anndras he didna believe
In killing tae get rich

Or setting licht a hale village
Tae rid it o its witch

Four others left wi Anndras
Wha refused tae be sae bought
They departed under nichtfa
And Cathal's lair they sought

They found him high upon Oathlaw
And kneelt afore his baund
And Anndras tae the north he pledged
His sword, his life, his haund

A knock came at the door and Cait's heart sputtered to a halt as Aggie appeared. There was a sack in her hand and an inscrutable look across her face. Cait had no doubt the Fox of Thorterknock had come to punish her for what happened on the pier. Maybe the sack contained Separatist instruments of torture. She sat up straight, folding the corner of the page over. 'Aggie —'

Aggie glowered. 'Why'd you dae that?'

'I'm sorry,' Cait laid the book down. 'I swear, I didn't know they would be there —'

'Unfold that page, philistine,' Aggie said.

Cait looked down at the book, and then back at Aggie, who lifted an eyebrow in wordless command. Cait opened the book and smoothed out the corner of the page. 'I'll lose my place.'

'Mibbe it'll encourage you to get a bookmark,' Aggie said, and then tossed Cait the bag that she had been carrying. Cait caught it clumsily, and a holey jumper fell out across her lap. 'I thought you could use some clothes,' Aggie said. 'They came frae a washing line so you can be sure they're clean.'

Cait stared at her. 'Thank you.'

Aggie put her hands in her pockets and leaned against the door frame. 'Me and Calan are leaving for Gowdstane the morn.' There was a waiting silence, and when Cait didn't fill it, Aggie continued. 'I want you to come with us.'

Cait gawked at her. 'Go with you? To Gowdstane?' Her stomach gave an excited flip at the thought. 'Calan said I had to stay here.'

'And I've decided that's a rubbish idea.'

'Do I have a choice?'

Aggie nodded once. 'Of course. Either you can sit in this dour hole reading stories and ruining perfectly innocent books, or you can come to Gowdstane, and see where all those stories began.'

Cait shivered. To walk in the footsteps of Anndras and Cathal at Gowdstane, or to see the Crone of the Cruin with her own eyes ... It was something she had always dreamed of. But there was something on her mind. 'Why would you want me there after what happened on the pier?'

'Calan's not exactly well-versed on *The Ballad of Anndras and Cathal*. You're more fun to talk to,' Aggie said.

Cait blushed. 'But aren't you worried I'm going to betray you?'

Aggie tilted her head and studied Cait for a moment. 'Nah.' Cait only looked up at her, unsure whether that was supposed to be a compliment or not. 'Listen,' Aggie said. 'You can stay here, or you can come to Gowdstane, and there's always the third option where you escape the moment Calan and I have our backs turned and spill all our secrets to your Lealist friends.' She hesitated, then added quickly, 'You can understand why I'd want to keep an eye on ye.'

Cait looked down at the jumper in her lap and thought about all the times she and her father had conspired to visit Gowdstane, and all the times it had never happened. Still, was Gowdstane really worth entangling herself further with the Separatists?

'If you're coming, meet us in Gelly first thing tomorrow.' Aggie made to leave, then hesitated. 'And dinna tell Calan.'

Cait found her voice just before Aggie closed the door. 'What are you going to do if you win? How will things change?'

'Same way a wean learns to walk,' Aggie said simply. 'We'll stan on our ain two feet and work it out.' With that, she dipped out of the room and the door closed behind her.

We'll work it out. Cait had heard that phrase once before, when Kenzie first tried to convince her to move to Thorterknock. He'd listened to her fears and countered them all until he couldn't anymore, until *we'll work it out* was the only thing left to say. It hadn't reassured her. She knew now where *we'll work it out* led and she knew it was just another empty promise. Just like Cathal, Aggie had no real answers, and Cait decided she would take her chances the following afternoon when Aggie and Calan were gone and try again for home. She flicked through the pages of *Songs of Storran* to find her place again.

They sattled far up in the north
Beneath the Cronach crags
And called the leal tae come tae them
And raise the gowden stag

They built a ha upon the hill
And gied tae it a name
A fortress gilt just like the sun
Formidable Gowdstane

They forged a croon in saicrecy
Gray antlers for his bree
But Anndras wouldna put it oan
Until his hame was free

Fair Anndras led them toun by toun
Sly Cathal at his side
They sent the settlers hame again
And slowly turn't the tide

A stramash three years in its lenth
A keeng withoot a throne
A chairge enshrined within the law
Fur freedom jointly owned

The Queen, well keen to end the feud
For it was sair expense
Bid Anndras tae the forest come
Tae talk of recompense

But when the message came tae lie
At Gowdstane's tall bricht ha
Nane ither met the messenger
Than Cathal the outlaw

When Cathal heard the agent's words
He sensed a hunter's snare
He'd gang himself tae meet the Queen
So Anndras would be spare'd

The wood was still, the thicket calm

As Cathal he drew near
Then oot the dark wi a her men
The Queen at last appear't

As quickly as she ga'e the wird
Her soldiers swept aroon
Though Cathal felled some ten o them
The ithers beat him doon

Cathal watched frae whaur he knelt
The Queen unsheathe her knife
She held his cheek and pierced his hert
And took brave Cathal's life

Anndras found when he awoke
A gift tied with red threid
His grief pierced throu the quiet morn
For it was Cathal's heid

Doon it rolled through hieland hills
And sattled on a moor
And from his neck a bluidy spring
Became a crimson pool

So Anndras ca'd his men tae airms
And took up Cathal's sword
He picked a place upon the moor
And ca'd the Queen to war

By dawn the armies were laid oot
And waiting, stood at rest
The north assembled in the east
The southmen in the west

The northern men they tremmled
And some they turnt tae flee
For every man in Anndras' ranks
The Queen's army had three

'Don't turn yer backs my brithers'
Anndras proudly cried

'We'll serve them up a bluidy fecht
Then free men we will die!'

When the armies charged the field
Wi slauchter in their tracks
The sun rose bold and gowden
Upon the northmen's backs

The southern men were blindit
As dawn struck Gowdstane's face
They fell into the northmen's laps
And met their bluidy fate

When Anndras limped ower the moor
And watched the southmen flee
He liftit hie his pewter crown
And place't it oan his bree

The northmen sang and dance't wi glee
An raised up Storran's crest
Until an arrow brake the ranks
And pierced puir Anndras' chest

When Afren reclaimed Storran's launds
A hunner years had passed
And Storran murned her heirless king
Anndras, the First and Last

Cait stared at the page long after she finished reading the tale. A voice in the back of her mind whispered *come home*. She couldn't tell if it belonged to her mother, or father, or Kenzie, but it felt like a golden sunset on green hills.

Come home.

Or perhaps it was the voice of Anndras calling her to his golden fortress from deep within the verses of song.

Come home.

Maybe it was only Aggie picking the right words to recruit a new soldier.

She mulled over the final line of the ballad. If what Aggie said was true and Anndras really did have an heir, he would be part of Anndras himself. The Separatists' promised King was a living, breathing song. And Cait wanted to see that magnificent crown on his head. She wanted to see if he was worthy, or if it would melt his flesh like the legends said.

It occurred to Cait as she sorted through the clothes and packed a small bag that perhaps she had simply let Aggie's words get to her again, but she didn't mind, because she was going to see a king, and she was going to ask him how he would empty the waiting rooms and feed the hungry. She was going to ask if he would treat the Talasaire better than Afren did. She was going to ask him why it was that some languages were dirty, or why Storran was paying off Afren's debt, or why, indeed, her parents' taxes were funding the construction of a train so many miles from home. She was going to ask him if he was the solution.

When she thought she was packed, she hesitated, then shoved the *Songs of Storran* book in her bag, too. *I'll bring it back*, she thought. Maybe when she did, Anndras' legacy would live again. Her face broke into a guilty grin at the idea.

*

From the clothes that Aggie had given her, Cait chose a long lapis skirt held at the waist by a belt and a greyed white blouse with a gentle ruffle up the front. She shoved the threadbare jumper in her bag on top of medical supplies raided from the drawer in the kitchen.

The area around the Northgait was busy for such an early hour, with a steady stream of workers entering the city. They flashed permits at the City Guard as they passed, and a group of three Watchmen peered over them like buzzards. Cait had no money to pay the gate toll, but even if she did, there was every chance she would be recognised. Then, moving against the flow of bleary-eyed workers, Cait spotted her. She kept her head low, and her cap cast shadows over her features, but Cait could tell it was Jamie by her long strides and hunched shoulders. She stepped behind a cart as it stopped to pay the gate toll, crept between the wheels, and vanished. With a flick of the reins, the cart pulled out of the city, leaving not a trace of Jamie behind.

Cait knew she was no escape artist and whatever she tried was not likely to be so discreet. She took a deep breath and recalled Aggie's impersonation of a flustered tourist, then ran into the open. She pushed through the workers and stopped in front of one of the Guards who looked at her quizzically. 'I saw the Fox!' Cait gulped through a breathlessness that wasn't for show. 'She's here!' She paused, then added quickly, 'With a gun!'

'Where?' one of the Queen's Watch demanded.

She waved wildly behind her. 'Round that corner!'

The soldiers didn't need any further prompting, and they took off, their boots pounding the cobbles to a perfect beat. The two City Guards suddenly had a panic on their hands, and they fought to regain any semblance of order at the city gate as workers rushed in and fled the area. When the guards' backs turned, Cait saw her chance trotting briskly towards her. A carriage clattered past, and she lunged for the back. Cait gripped tight as it rolled out of the Northgait, leaving Thorterknock behind her.

*

The village of Gelly was four miles northwest of Thorterknock, and Cait clung to the back of the jostling carriage for three of them. By the time the road split and she hopped off, her hands were numb, and her legs tingled. Out in the countryside, the sun burned through the smog, and she kept the rim of her hat firmly lowered over her eyes.

'Oi, leal lass!' Half ready to run, Cait turned to find the voice belonged to Jamie, who jogged to catch up with her. 'Rumour this side of the wall is the Fox has gotten herself a gun.' Jamie raised her eyebrows at Cait. 'Know owt about that?'

Cait's face flushed. 'I'll be stealthier next time.'

'Aggie'll get a laugh, but Calan'll have it in for you, especially after your stunt in Eadwick. Speaking of ...' She stuffed a hand into her jacket and pulled out a piece of paper which she stuck in front of Cait's nose. 'What's all this about?' Cait's own likeness beamed back at her from the page, which trembled as she took it in her hands. The photograph had been taken a couple of years ago, when a photographer friend of her parents travelled in from Thorterknock to capture some family portraits. She recognised the one on the poster, with her blue dress, and wide grin as she perched on the garden wall. It was the one Kenzie kept in his pocket. 'You help pinch a royal artefact from right under Queen Ana's nose and you're just *missing*? You must be their favourite little spy,' Jamie said.

'I'm not a spy,' Cait said firmly.

'Well, the rest of us are wanted for the gallows, so you must have done summat they liked.'

Cait gazed at the beaming girl on the poster. She imagined Kenzie pulling up every cobble in Thorterknock looking for her, his *little dove*, the girl he loved, and the girl who was gone. The guilt chewed at her courage.

'I assume Calan hasn't seen it yet. I doubt he'd invite you along on this secret mission of his if he knew,' Jamie mused.

Cait thrust the poster back towards her and it crumpled slightly. 'I am *not* involved with them.'

Jamie grunted. 'We'll see.' Then she looked at Cait with an impish twinkle in her eye. 'Calan doesn't know you're coming, does he?'

Cait panicked. 'He does, I —'

Jamie crowed a laugh. 'I know you weren't invited because I wasn't either. But mark my words, if he thinks I'm gonna put in all the effort nicking that bloody crown and not get to see how it all plays out, he's got another thing coming.'

*

Gelly was opening its lazy eyes as they entered the village. The buildings were stout with lace curtains and colourful window boxes, and a lone man strolled by with his dog. The village was so quiet that the dog's padding steps filled up the street. It was such a far cry from Thorterknock's clatter, and Cait found herself missing unhurried village life. They found Calan and Aggie in the village square beside a piebald pony and cart. Aggie stood by the pony's head, quietly stroking its muzzle. Cait thought she looked almost peaceful.

As Jamie and Cait approached, Calan looked up and his face fell. 'No.' He strode towards them. 'No, no, no, no, no. You can't be here.' He flashed a glare between Jamie and Cait. '*Neither of you* can be here.'

'Haven't we done this before?' Jamie said with a roll of her eyes. She traipsed straight towards the cart, climbed into the front, and took the reins in her hands. 'It ends with you giving in, and your charming friend gets to bring along her mysterious companion. Aggie, wait 'til you hear about the riot Cait caused getting out of Thorterknock.'

Calan seemed to forget all about Jamie as he turned his scowl on Cait. 'What is she talking about?' He turned to Aggie. 'Was this your doing?'

Aggie shrugged and shook her head, then turned and smirked into the pony's muzzle.

'I brought first aid supplies,' Cait said.

Calan sputtered. 'So?'

'I won't get in the way, and if anyone gets hurt, I can help.'

'No one's going to get hurt.'

'What if your cut needs redressed?' Cait pressed.

'It won't.'

'*Shadielaunds*, Calan,' Aggie groaned. 'Do you want her to take an oath?'

'No, I want her, and *you*,' he levelled a glare at Jamie, 'back in Thorterknock, where I asked you to stay.'

'We have to leave now if we want a decent head start on the Lealists. Plus,' — Aggie cast a conspiratorial glance between Calan and Cait — 'she told me last night she was going to go running to her Lealist pals the moment your back was turned.'

'I didn't —'

Aggie shot her a warning glare. 'Your call.' She climbed up into the back of the cart. Cait stood here, hands clasped awkwardly in front of her, feeling very small under Calan's scrutinising eye, but eventually he sighed and nodded over his shoulder at the cart. 'Get in.'

As Cait approached, Aggie put her hand down and hoisted her up. She had expected the Fox of Thorterknock's skin to be like brimstone, but her hands were small and cool. As they trundled out of Gelly, Cait listened to the pony's hooves tromping on the stony road. Up front, Calan and Jamie bickered, but she couldn't make out what they were saying. Cait watched Aggie, who in turn watched the landscape. She had a strong profile, with a steep forehead and sharp nose. Her eyebrows always seemed to slant downwards. Beneath her still exterior, Cait could sense a churning restlessness.

'Calan told me about your Lealist lad,' Aggie said. Despite the blossomy softness of her voice, Cait jumped and realised she had been staring.

'I'm sorry,' Cait said. 'I — I promise you can trust me. I'm not —'

A soft laugh escaped Aggie's lips and she cast Cait a knowing glance. 'You're here now. You made your choice.' They fell into silence again, and Cait wished they were back at the canal-side, where talking to the Fox was as easy as eating an Eadwick pie. 'What's his name?' Aggie said at last.

Cait picked at a loose thread on her skirt. 'Kenzie.'

'Why are you running from him?'

'I — I don't know.'

'Is he looking for you?'

'I don't know.'

'Do you love him?'

'Yes.'

When silence fell between them again, Cait thought about Kenzie's parents. She found herself wondering how many had fallen to Aggie's small hands. 'This is the most north I've ever been,' Cait said quicky, desperate to stuff the silence with something other than her thoughts.

'The mair north you go the bleaker the weather gets. Don't be expecting any of the sunshine you almost-Afrenians enjoy at the border,' Aggie said. Cait had never felt like she was from Afren, and she suddenly felt a little ashamed to have been born so close to the border, though she wasn't sure why. Aggie's gaze remained fixed on the passing fields. The sun filtered through her hair and set it alight. *'On rolling hills the heather grows and my border lassie dwells,'* she muttered to herself.

'*The Border Lass*?' Cait said, grinning at the familiar lyrics.

Aggie started and looked at Cait with the same bewildered look on her face she had when Cait first spoke to her in Thorterknock. 'That's the only line I know,' she said quickly.

'It's practically drilled into us back home,' Cait said, remembering year on year standing before her classmates, reciting the famous borders ballad.

'Mmm,' Aggie mused. 'I never could get into borders minstrelsy. The Afrenian influences are *very* clear.'

There it was again, that stab of shame that Cait couldn't place. 'Cathal was from the borders,' she said, in an attempt to defend her rolling green hills.

Aggie laughed. 'If I had a Bodle for every place that claims either Anndras or Cathal, I could buy Storran's freedom.'

Cait reached out of the cart and let her fingers drift over the long grass at the side of the road. Her mind turned to Gowdstane, and the waiting king they pressed ever closer to. 'Have you ever met Aidan?' she asked.

'No, but I think about him a fair bit. What he's like, how he acts.'

'And what is he like?' Cait asked.

Aggie's gaze was fixed forward, to her King, and her freedom. 'Unwavering.'

A man like the one in the portrait of Anndras appeared in Cait's mind:

tall, with golden hair in a halo at his brow. He would be a serious man. No one would cross him, but everyone would respect him. In one hand he'd wield a blade of justice, and in the other a cup of grace. He wouldn't just speak for Storran — he'd speak for the people.

Chapter 16

Fox Hunting

'You guarantee it will load faster?' Kenzie asked, weighing the pistol in his right hand. The rain bounced off the cobbles and raced down his cloak.

The man in the doorway nodded profusely. 'Aye. It's best at short-range though, so dinna be trying to hit a target frae the far end of Barter Bridge.' He wheezed a laugh that tumbled into a cough.

Kenzie dropped two Sovereigns into the man's outstretched hand. It was a steeper price than the Siller he had anticipated parting with, but it would be worth it. 'Speak of this to no one.' The pistol wasn't military approved, but if he found the Fox, he wanted to make certain she could not slip away.

'Any sign of that crown?' the man asked.

Kenzie clipped the holster of the gun to the back of his belt and carefully covered it with his cloak. 'I'm working on it.'

Rain dripped off the peak of his hat as he walked back to Hart Hall. The city was dark and quiet, but he kept alert for anything that seemed out of place. He was quickly coming to know the pulse of the city well, almost as well as the Fox herself, he'd wager. When he reached the gates of Hart Hall, Innes was waiting for him, teeth chattering as he sheltered under the gatehouse.

'Where have you been?' he said. 'You're soaked.'

'Searching,' Kenzie muttered as they walked through the gate together.

Innes bobbed his head. 'Of course.'

Kenzie hated his pity. He had done his best to seem unruffled when the news from the Treasury reached Hart Hall. His fellow officers remarked in awe how well he handled the news that his lover was a Separatist, and Kenzie humbly waved off their condolences. The truth was, he seethed. Cait had made him look the fool, and it was all because the Fox had pounced on her dewy innocence. And at any rate, anger was a far more productive tool than the tender heartache that lay beneath.

'You should worry about yourself,' Kenzie said, nudging the conversation elsewhere.

Innes shrugged. 'I'm grand. Perfectly grand.'

He'd seemed strangely jovial since returning from Eadwick, but Kenzie wasn't so convinced. Innes had pulled a corpse from the canal. One of their comrades, Lieutenant Morag Smith, had fallen into the water and her cloak had snagged on the debris. She'd drowned before Innes reached her.

When they reached the door to the barracks, Innes paused. 'Brigadier Cameron sent for you.'

'He took his time about it.' He hadn't seen the Brigadier since he ordered the raid on the innkeeper and was scrapped from the Eadwick task force, though it wasn't for lack of trying.

As he turned to leave, Innes lay a hand on his arm. Kenzie flinched. 'If he gives you what you want, put my name down. I want to see her safe,' he said.

Kenzie managed a brisk nod, then turned on his heel and walked towards the Brigadier's quarters.

*

When he reached the door to the Brigadier's office, Kenzie removed his hat. He wiped down his hair and tried to ease as much water out of his cloak as possible. His fingers brushed the pistol, and he double-checked it was concealed. He suspected he was about to receive a rollicking on account of his persistent requests for an audience, and he didn't need a non-approved weapon muddying the water. The door creaked as he opened it, and the warmth from the office spilled into the dark passageway.

'Sir,' he said with a nod of his head.

The Brigadier stood with his back to Kenzie, staring up at the portrait of a military general in full regalia. The sound of ice clinking against a glass told Kenzie he was drinking. 'Bell,' he said, without looking at him. 'Come in.'

Kenzie stood before the Brigadier's desk with his hat tucked under his arm. There were two leather sofas in the centre of the room, and a roaring fire. He wondered what kind of people the Brigadier entertained in such a casual manner.

'When I took this post, we were slowly winning against the Separatists,' he said with his back still turned. 'I expected to put in a year, maybe two, and have the whole ugly affair dealt with.' He sighed and turned to face Kenzie with a bleary smile on his lips. 'It would seem the rats, or should I say Fox,' — he chuckled at his quip — 'have got the better of us.' Kenzie noticed the slight slur on his words and the faraway look in his eye. He wondered how many whiskies a man in his position had on a typical evening. The Brigadier moved slowly to his desk and eased himself into the chair. 'You've been ... incessant, Bell. Especially for a man on his final warning. We have an order to things here. Typically, a subordinate does not —'

'The Separatists have left Thorterknock,' Kenzie said.

The Brigadier stilled, glass halfway between the desk and his lips. He quickly reset his features into disapproval, but not before Kenzie caught the glimmer of interest. 'We are here to discuss your conduct.'

'There was a disturbance at the Northgait earlier today, an alert regarding the Fox of Thorterknock. She was never found.'

With a wave of his hand, the Brigadier slumped back in his chair. 'They're always disappearing. This is nothing new.'

'Normally that wouldn't be unusual,' Kenzie said. 'But I questioned the city guards on duty at the time.'

The Brigadier's eyebrows shot up, and he placed the glass down on the polished table with a gentle *thunk* that ate up the silence. 'Listen, Bell. I'm far too mellowed for shouting tonight, so I'll be straight with you. You've stepped out of line. Twice. That's twice too many as far as I'm concerned. Tell me why I shouldn't send you packing this evening.'

'They spotted a girl with white hair. She was with the Separatists in Eadwick.'

For a moment, the Brigadier looked like he would snap, but his eyes narrowed. He reported directly to Field Marshall Peck in Eadwick, and possibly Queen Ana, too. It was in his interests to stop the Separatists who had robbed the Treasury, and so far, he was failing. 'Go on.'

Kenzie unfolded the poster from his pocket at slid it across the desk to the Brigadier who frowned at it. 'Cait Hardie. She travelled to the city with me when I took up my post. My ... my betrothed.'

The Brigadier frowned up at him. 'What has this got to do with Separatists?'

'She's sheltered, easily led astray. I believe the group who took the crown are using her to transport it.'

'You believe this is the girl spotted at the city gates today?' He held the poster up to Kenzie, who maintained eye contact with the Brigadier. He had found the image increasingly difficult to look at since Cait's disappearance.

'I believe that she has been manipulated by the Separatists and they used her as a distraction,' Kenzie said.

The Brigadier let out a long sigh, swirled his drink, then leaned forward and interlocked his fingers. 'I'll trust you, Bell. You have good instincts. We'll send a squad north.'

Good. 'I'll prepare my things.'

Brigadier Cameron held up a hand and shot Kenzie a scathing glare. 'Steady.' The look ensnared Kenzie. He hated it. He knew it was meant to intimidate him. 'You forget why I asked you here.'

Kenzie bowed his head. 'The innkeeper. It was a mistake. I won't let it happen again.' His only mistake had been failing to cover himself, but this was what the Brigadier wanted to hear. The Brigadier only grunted.

'After my recent performance I certainly don't deserve to be involved, but you have to understand, sir. I only want to see Cait safe.'

The Brigadier was silent for a long moment. 'Bell, you have done nothing but push your charge since the moment you entered these ranks. I think you're sorely mistaken about the position you are in right now.'

He pushed his charge because no one else seemed to want to do the job properly, more interested in free meals and beds than actually stopping Separatists. He took a steadying breath. 'I have more information.' The Brigadier raised his eyebrows, and when he didn't say anything, Kenzie continued. 'A professor from my hometown has been doing some research into *The Ballad of Anndras and Cathal.*'

'This is the army lad. We don't do fantasy.'

'With all due respect,' Kenzie said firmly. He dropped his voice. 'This pertains to the Separatist heir.'

This caught the Brigadier's attention. Kenzie saw the spark in his eye. So, it was true. He had heard murmurs on the street, and when the crown was stolen it all but proved it. The Separatists had found themselves an heir to the throne of Storran. 'It's all nonsense,' the Brigadier said, draining his drink. 'The layman will be swept up by romance far more readily than fact, and the Separatists know this.' He stood up and paced around the side of the desk to Kenzie. The tang of whisky clung to his breath.

'But what kind of message would it send if we allowed the nationalists to crown their pretender?' He was inches from Kenzie, who could see every sweating pore, and the pupils that were wide with drink. 'What information do you have?' the Brigadier whispered.

'Dr Hardie has been studying an indication in the text that King Anndras had signed away the rights to Storran's autonomy to the people. If it exists, it will do us good to get our hands on it before the Separatists, or their heir. I already had Innes look into a document in Eadwick, a diary believed to have been written —'

'Oh, you did now?'

Kenzie lowered his head. 'Yes, sir.'

'Where would this investigation take you?' the Brigadier asked.

'Gowdstane, sir,' Kenzie said. 'Dr Hardie believes there may be answers there.'

'Gowdstane, hmm.' The Brigadier rolled the word around in his mouth. 'That's a name I haven't heard in a while. It's a ruin.'

'It was the seat of Anndras, and his tomb.'

The Brigadier studied him, and his pondering made his eyes dart from side to side. He was weighing up the stakes. He was weighing up whether Kenzie should be punished for his insubordination, or whether that made him just the man for this job. At last, he sighed. 'Go north, Bell. Take a squad. Do your research and find your girl.' He sat back down behind his desk with a heavy thud. 'But take the crown from them. No matter the cost,' he whispered, then added, loudly. 'Dismissed.'

Kenzie gave a short bow and made for the door, stopping just short. 'I believe the Fox to be with them.'

'Then happy hunting.'

Chapter 17

Long Live the Queen

Two days into their journey, they stopped at the town of Bonnetbrae for supplies. As the last town before they hit the thick of Storran's mountainous highlands, they'd need to stock up and load everything onto their pony, who Aggie had taken to calling Winnie, and ditch the cart. Calan had doled out tasks: Jamie was to find a buyer for the cart, while Calan went to find out the latest news from Thorterknock and buy a newspaper. Aggie was to gather some more provisions. Cait, meanwhile, had been given strict instructions to stand by the cart and not move. She hovered at Winnie's shoulder, and the pony stamped impatiently.

'Me, too,' Cait sighed, running her fingers through thick tresses of mane. Each time her fingers snagged on a tangle she gently teased it apart. Winnie was a stout creature. Her belly was as round as a drum, with four strong legs and a thick neck. Cait wondered where Calan had got her and what her life had been before. 'You have absolutely no idea what's going on, do you?' Cait muttered. 'You don't even know what a crown or a Separatist is. As long as there's a bucket of oats for you at the end of every day, you'll be happy.' She envied that fat little pony.

'She won't be happy when food coming from the Continent gets smacked with a horrendous customs charge and she can't get sugar cubes.' Aggie's voice made Cait jump, and she looked up to find her dragging a large sack beside her. She paused, fished into her pocket, and tossed Cait a white sugar cube. Winnie nickered excitedly and slobbered over Cait's hand as she fed her.

'Customs charge?' Cait asked.

'Afren's growing more and more closed off, less willing to work with other countries.' She rifled around in the back of the cart and her voice grew muffled as she leaned further in. 'It's only a matter of time before they burn every trade deal they've ever had.'

'That wouldn't happen,' Cait snorted. 'The Council of Five are too smart for that ... right?'

Aggie emerged from the back of the cart with a length of rope which she looped over her shoulder. She raised an eyebrow. 'Wanna bet?'

'No,' Cait muttered, shuffling where she stood. She watched as Aggie moved towards the sack.

'Mon, then,' she called over her shoulder.

Cait peered around the side of Winnie. 'Where?'

Aggie grinned, wide and rabid. 'To get your first proper taste of being a Separatist.' Cait gulped. Dread pooled in her gut. As if seeing her face pale, Aggie cast her a rue smile over her shoulder as she heaved the sack up. 'Don't worry, nae fireworks this time.'

'Calan told me to stay here,' Cait said.

'Calan needs to take the stick out his arse. Trust me, what I have in store will be much more fun.'

Despite her better judgement, Cait followed, keeping a tentative distance between herself and Aggie. She almost hoped Calan would catch sight of them as they slipped through Bonnetbrae and bring a stop to whatever Aggie had planned, but he didn't, and Aggie led her around the back of the town hall and through a creaking door. The back door led them to a kitchen with a set of wooden stairs that disappeared upwards.

Aggie heaved the sack onto her shoulder. 'Gie is a help up the stair.'

Cait's arms and legs trembled beneath the weight of the bag as they took the steps one at a time. While she pushed from the bottom, Aggie pulled the bag up from the front, grunting softly with every step. Through the course fabric, Cait could feel something dense and soft. Whatever it was, it smelled pungent. Her eyes watered as it took her back to Bram's cellar the day he had died.

The day he was killed, a voice said in her mind. She bit down on her lip and counted her steps. *Don't say anything. Don't even hint that the smell upsets you.* Telling Aggie what happened wouldn't earn her any trust, and they'd climbed enough steps by now that she didn't want to upset the Fox of Thorterknock. Still, she had to hold her breath, because each lungful of that awful smell trapped her deeper and deeper in that memory.

A door at the top of the stairs opened out onto the roof, and the breeze swept away the stench. She closed her eyes and took in deep gulps. Slowly, the inn faded from her mind. When it was gone, Cait wrapped her jumper around her and walked slowly towards Aggie. 'So ... that's in the sack?'

With one last grunt, Aggie heaved the sack up and spilled its contents onto the roof. Cait squealed and stepped backwards as a pig's head flopped to the ground, its grey tongue hanging uselessly from its mouth. 'Behold!' Aggie said, with a flourish of her hands. 'Her most royal highness ...' She fished inside her coat and removed what looked like a crude tiara fashioned from fencing wire. She crouched down and put the crown on the pig's head. 'The Queen of Afren.'

Cait kept one hand firmly over her mouth. 'What are you going to do with that?'

'Bonnetbrae's got an audience with her.' She said it as though the fact were plastered over the community noticeboard and Cait had simply failed to check. She beckoned Cait over and reached for the rope. Cait took her time approaching. She touched the pig with her boot.

'It's deed,' Aggie said. 'Butchered this morning.'

Cait eyed its severed neck. 'Clearly.'

Aggie explained how she wanted the knots tied, and they got to work in silence. Every so often, Cait's eyes snatched up towards Aggie to see her deep in focus, brow gently ruffled, mouth quirked slightly to the left. She wondered where these ideas of hers came from. She'd looked so serene in the cart. Had she been dreaming up how best to hang a severed pig head from a roof? Cait paused and held a knot in place as she glanced at the edge of the roof, too aware of how long she'd been away from the cart. She couldn't afford any more marks against her name.

'You're wondering how Calan's going to take this, aren't you?' Aggie said, without stopping.

Cait turned to her. 'How do you know?'

'I've been there often enough,' she said. 'Calan was something of a tyrant in his schoolboy days.'

Cait snorted.

'Aye, go on and laugh,' Aggie said. 'You think he's bad now, he used to drill me on numeracy like a bloody field marshall. Not that it did much good.'

'Sorry,' Cait said, but her snort had turned into a full-bellied laugh.

'You will be when he finds out about this.'

'Give him a break,' Cait said.

'Can't do that. Calan doesn't believe in breaks. He'd lose his mind wi boredom if I stopped keeping him on his toes, and then where would we be?'

Cait stopped to wipe her face and glanced up at Aggie. She seemed to beam with nostalgia. 'You must have more stories about him,' Cait said.

Aggie sighed. 'Wish I did. He was too well behaved. Got me out a few scrapes though, canny bastard.' She paused and looked out over the rooftops thoughtfully. 'I like to think he livened up after I left. Doubt it though.'

'When did you leave?' Cait asked.

'I joined the Separatists when I was fifteen.'

Cait lost her grip on the rope. 'Fifteen? You didn't finish school?'

Aggie shrugged. 'I was reading Dunning and Hewins by the time I was twelve. I could write. I could kind of count. What good was I doing studying for exams I didn't care about?'

'Dunning is an Afrenian writer,' Cait pointed out. Her father had a few of his essays back home.

'And he's very good. Credit where credit's due.'

'My da says he's a lot of overrated tripe.'

Aggie's eyebrows shot up. 'Your da's a bit of an academic, is he?'

'He was a literary professor at the University of Thorterknock, before he retired.'

'I would've liked to study literature,' Aggie mused. 'Maybe in another life your da would've been my lecturer.'

'Hope you like looking at sources about Anndras in *a lot* of minute detail, then,' Cait said.

'Oh?'

Cait suddenly became acutely aware of the pig's dead, blank eye watching her. She shouldn't talk about her father's research with someone like Aggie. The information could be a firecracker in Separatist hands, but there was a sweet satisfaction in Aggie being interested in what she had to say. 'He has this fascination — it's an obsession, really — with one line in *The Ballad of Anndras and Cathal*. He thinks it could point to some kind of, I don't know what he would call it, but like, a treaty, of sorts.'

Aggie watched her keenly. 'What kind of treaty?'

'He thinks the line that goes "*A charge en —*"'

'Chairge,' Aggie corrected.

Cait threw her a disdainful look. '"*A chairge enshrined within the law, fur freedom jointly owned.*" He thinks Anndras signed some kind of document that entrusted Storran's freedom into the hands of its people, so that they'd never need a king or queen.' She was still looking down at her hands, but she could feel Aggie's gaze burning into the top of her head. She shrugged and added quickly, 'He's never found any proof that it exists. It's just a theory.' Aggie went a long time without speaking, and when Cait looked up she found her hands had stilled and she was staring off into the distance, lips tracing silent words. 'What is it?' Cait prompted.

Without looking at her, Aggie muttered, '"*wis left haund Anndras strack clen aff the heid o a wickit spy tae the queen. Wis richt, he haudit the fowks sovereignty.*"'

Cait recognised the words from the diary in the Treasury. 'Well, see, that's what I think is more interesting. Why would Anndras be so quick to execute the spy? He's supposed to be merciful.'

Aggie cast her a look as though she had just scraped her up from the street. '*That's* whit you're most interested in?'

Cait leaned forward, then realised she'd placed her hand on the pig's cold flesh and immediately retracted it. '*And* why would Cathal just wander into the Queen's trap? He should've known better.'

Aggie's slight frown remained fixed in place. 'I always assumed it was his love for Anndras.'

This caught Cait off guard. 'You — What?'

Aggie's expression remained unchanged, her voice completely matter of fact. 'Cathal made the ultimate sacrifice for his King.'

Freedom for Storran and a thousand voices raised as one — how badly did Aggie want it? 'What did you sacrifice?' Cait asked.

Aggie picked up her knot-tying where she had left off and shrugged. 'A place at university. A few debating trophies.'

Cait thought about home and the promise of running her mother's surgery one day. These things might become barred to her if she continued meddling with Separatists, but there was something so thrilling about breaking the rules.

'What about you?'

When Cait came back to herself, she found Aggie watching her. 'What did I ...'

'Leave behind,' Aggie prompted.

A pit opened in Cait's stomach. She hadn't thought about it. On the journey to Eadwick, she had only wanted to glimpse the crown and go home again. Now, she supposed she was like Aggie: a runaway with a faded past. A sudden wave of grief swept over her. 'My mam's surgery.

She was training me to take it over.'

'Would you have gone to university?'

Cait thought about it. For a long time, her father had insisted she should, and she knew that if she wanted to do the work her mother did, she would need qualifications, but she had resisted, not wanting to leave Briddock and Kenzie behind. 'I think so,' she said. Then, with slightly more conviction, 'I would.'

'What stopped you?'

Cait bit her lip. The truth was silly when she was talking to the Fox of Thorterknock. 'I don't know, I just …'

Aggie looked up at her and raised her eyebrows. 'Boys?'

'Well, not just that. I was comfortable. I didn't want to leave the village.'

'What about when you came to Thorterknock wi, eh … what was his name? Menzies? What did he think of you taking over your mam's practice?'

Cait rolled her eyes. 'Kenzie.' She shrugged. 'He always said I could pay people to do that work for me. We always saw ourselves as business owners, and we'd hire staff to do the real medical work, that way I wouldn't need to spend time or money going to university. It's a solid plan.'

They'd laid in bed one lazy morning when Kenzie should have been at the farm and Cait should have been downstairs welcoming patients. They'd woken early but got lost in a conversation about the future delivered in conspiratorial whispers while gazing up at ceiling rafters. Cait remembered being relieved that Kenzie took such an interest in her family's business. She couldn't bear to give it up.

'It'll be hard,' Cait had fretted, 'I don't have mam's training.'

'We'll hire help,' Kenzie shrugged, unphased.

'Like, a secretary?'

'No, doctors, Cait. The more time we both have to dedicate to the business, the more successful it'll be in the long run. We might even have capacity to expand out of Briddock.'

Cait had gazed at him in utter admiration of his efficient mind. How lucky she was to know someone like him.

Back on the roof with the dead pig, Aggie said, 'Mmm.'

Truthfully, the thought of hiring other doctors had always made her a little sad. She enjoyed helping people and fixing things, and she admired her mother's skills. She had never picked at that thread of sadness before, afraid it would unravel the whole dreamy tapestry of their future together. She left it untouched once again and said, 'I suppose if I wasn't doing all the work, I'd have plenty time to look after the children.'

'Wains?' Aggie said. 'You thought about that?'

'Three. Kenzie would prefer one, but I'd like them to have siblings.'

Aggie watched her curiously. Cait couldn't work out what the expression on her face meant. 'What else do you have planned?'

'Well, we'd get married in May, and there's this little cottage on the farmland that's empty right now, but we'd buy that and live in it until we took over the surgery. It's not far from the school, so I could walk the children there on my way to the surgery in the morning, and Kenzie would keep working on the farm.'

'When he's not with the Lealists?'

Cait stumbled. 'That was before.'

They lapsed into a brief silence, then Aggie asked quietly, 'What else?'

'Why?'

'Curious.'

'Well ...' Cait thought through her back pocket of dreams. 'Once a week, we'd have tea at mam and da's. Da would sit around the fire with us, all cosy. He'd tell us stories, and the children would chip in with what *they* wanted to happen. The stories would be forever changed, we'd only tell those versions from then on.'

Aggie gave a fond laugh. After a short pause, she asked, 'Do you do a lot in the surgery already?'

Cait nodded eagerly. 'Oh, yeah, running the books and diaries and stuff. Mam started talking me through the business side of things, but a lot of it went over my head. Kenzie says not to worry about it, he'll handle the money.'

'Nice of him to offer,' Aggie said in a flat voice. Cait sensed she didn't truly mean it, but she couldn't understand why.

'Ready?' Aggie said with a grin as she tied her last knot.

Cait nodded, anticipation and adrenaline squeezing her cheeks into a smile. Together, they heaved the pig's head to the edge of the roof and secured the end of the ropes.

'Lang live the Queen, on the count of three,' Aggie said. 'One, two ...'

On three, they pushed the crowned pig head over the side of the building to the sounds of shrieks far below, and Cait cried out the words

so loud her throat ached.
> *Long live the Queen!*
> *Long live the Queen!*
> *Long live the Queen!*

Chapter 18

The Dorcha Pass

The Fisherman's Highway, affectionately nicknamed The Troot Route by locals, was one of two roads that led to Storran's highlands. Spacious and well-manicured, it rose slowly through a breathtaking vista of purple hills. The Dorcha Pass was far less welcoming. The path dipped into a steep valley and bucked up and down beneath a canopy of firs so thick it was difficult to distinguish between root and shadow.

Calan insisted it was still unsafe to take the train, and the Troot Route would be too busy, so the Dorcha Pass was their only hope of making it to Gowdstane. After parting with the cart and loading their bags onto Winnie's back, they set off on foot beneath the shadow of a hulking viaduct. Every so often a train rumbled by overhead and rained dust over them. As they trudged into the second hour of their journey, Calan scanned the newspaper he picked up in Bonnetbrae.

'We tried to set fire to the Treasury?' Jamie said, reading over Calan's shoulder. 'Blimey. That one passed me by.'

Aggie threw a look over her shoulder from her post at Winnie's reins. 'This is what we're up against. Afrenian lies.'

Calan's cheeks puffed out as he flicked through the rest of the paper. 'Afren are putting pressure on the Council of Five to tear up the Iffega Agreement.'

'What's the Iffega Agreement?' Cait asked. She racked her brain for a memory of her mother talking about it, but none came.

Calan quickly folded the paper up and slipped it into a bag on Winnnie's back. 'Something about refugees,' he muttered, before adding quickly, 'The Lealists left Thorterknock this morning. They'll be on our trail soon enough, especially after Aggie's scene in Bonnetbrae.'

Aggie scowled. 'It had to be said.'

Calan gave a defeated sigh. 'Said. Thrown. It always does, doesn't it?'

'I enjoyed it,' Jamie said. 'I liked it when you called 'em flag shaggers.'

Aggie smirked. 'That pissed them right off.'

But Aggie hadn't heard the same conversation Cait had. They had been hurrying back to the cart after their stunt with the pig head, when Aggie paused at a greengrocer's stall and became preoccupied with selecting only the best apples for Winnie. It was there that Cait had overheard a pair of townsfolk discussing the stolen crown one stall over.

'Makes you wonder, doesn't it?'

'Jist what are you wondering aboot? That's dangerous talk, you.'

'Well, the way I see it, it's one thing if they're just a group of troublemakers causing a racket, but a legitimate claim? Now, that could be something ...'

'Ah, king or not, we'd last a week.'

'Ah, you say that ...'

'I'll be calling the Watch on you if you're no careful.'

'Awright, awright. Tae wee, tae poor n aw that.'

'That's better.'

And that was when Aggie had swept in, drunk on the dregs of a conversation that otherwise carried a hesitant hope.

'Maybe they'll think twice from now on about spouting daft claims about Storran,' Aggie said, back in the Dorcha Pass.

'I'm not sure that's —' Cait said quietly, but her voice was drowned by the others.

'Next time keep your mouth shut,' said Calan.

'Or don't,' said Jamie.

'You can't stop me telling the truth,' said Aggie.

Cait wrung her hands as she lifted her voice. 'They were coming round, they just ... they just needed time.'

'Pish. They're aw the same.'

'Talk like that is *unheard* of down my way.'

Aggie scowled. 'Aye, borders folk. Yous are basically from Afren.'

'We're just as much Storrian as anyone else!' Cait snapped, and the spark of her anger caught her off guard. She blushed as the group fell silent and stared at her. Aggie opened her mouth to retort, and Cait braced herself for the wrath of the Fox, only for Aggie to grunt and turn away.

*

'Look! There she is. The Cruin,' Jamie said, piercing the frosty silence they trod through as she pointed up ahead. 'You can just see her head poking out.'

Cait peered through the trees, but the leaves were blurry, and the horizon was nothing more than a wash of greys and blues. It would be a while before she would be able to pick out the shape of Storran's highest peak. 'Her head?' she asked.

'Sure, d'you not know the tale?'

Of course she did, it was another of her father's favourites. 'The crone was once the wife of a sailor from Witteneuk,' Cait said. 'When her husband died at sea, she trekked into the mountains and climbed the Cruin, where she wails to this day.'

'My Grove telt it better,' Jamie said with a pointed toss of her head. 'When she got deep into the Cronachs, the crone gave up from exhaustion. The mountains felt sorry for her so made her one of their own. Every year the Cruin grows an inch with grief, and one day it'll reach the stars.'

'I suppose that's quite romantic,' Cait said. 'Horribly sad, but romantic.'

Calan smiled. Cait realised she hadn't seen him smile since setting off for Afren. 'Is it story time?'

For a moment, Jamie's eyes lit up, but she seemed to second-guess herself and folded her arms across her chest. 'Nah.'

'Oh, go on,' Cait pressed. 'I'd love to hear a Talasaire story.'

'It's not a party trick,' Jamie muttered to the ground. 'It's a spiritual art.'

Calan chuckled. 'It's a spiritual art until you've had a few too many down the pub and start rattling off rubbish.'

Jamie's eyes shot up. 'We met last week.'

'Your reputation precedes you.' He glanced from Jamie to Cait, and something about the mirthful look in his eye seemed to say forgiveness, or at the very least, toleration.

Cait looked up ahead and watched Aggie leading Winnie. The last thing Cait wanted to do was shatter the quiet fracture between them, but she was also yearning to patch it. Her clumsy feet had struck so many eggshells in her time that she had perfected the art of apology and the shame that came with it. When she approached, Aggie didn't react. After precisely twelve hoofbeats, Cait mustered up the courage to say, 'You're angry with me.'

'You —'

'I spoke out of turn, I —'

'What —'

'And I completely understand if you want to leave me behind, but —'

Aggie turned and fixed her with a searing glare. Her words were sharp. 'I'm angry at Afren. I'm angry at Lealists, and folk with no backbone.' After a moment when Cait felt sure she would burn to ash under Aggie's stare, her mouth turned upwards. 'You're flattering yourself assuming I've got any anger left over for you.'

Cait hunted for the riddle in her joke, or the threat concealed by her smile. 'No, I was out of line.' It was a test, to see just how sorry she was and make her admit her wrongs.

Aggie stared at her. 'You had something to say, and you said it.'

But Cait knew how poor her judgement could be. 'I didn't know what I was talking about. I was angry.'

'Anger always says it best.'

'I —' Cait floundered, unsure of what to say. No eggshells. No mess. She was left questioning why she had been so anxious to apologise. 'I don't like to talk about things I know nothing about.'

'And who says you know nothing about this?'

'I can respect when there are people who know more than me.'

'Like who?'

'You. Anyone.'

'You mean Kenzie,' Aggie said.

Cait threaded her fingers. 'And others.'

'But mostly Kenzie.'

She said it like there was something telling about it, as if the idea of Kenzie guiding her through this tricky world was inherently suspicious. Aggie didn't know Kenzie. She didn't know what they had. 'Ach, away and bile yer heed, Fox,' the lilt of Old Storrian fell awkwardly from Cait's lips.

'Excuse me?' Aggie snorted.

Cait cringed. 'That, I *will* apologise for.'

'I should bloody well hope so,' Aggie said with a laugh. Their eyes met, her smile faded, and she peered at Cait with a curious look on her face.

'What?' Cait self-consciously clutched the strap of her bag.

'Your eyes ... they look different.'

Cait's heart fell and she quickly turned her face to the ground and dug up her old explanations. 'I know. I was born with it, I —'

'No, I mean, they looked blue in Eadwick,' Aggie said. 'In the Unnertoun they were grey. They're pink now.'

'They've always been like that,' Cait said, using her hair and hat to shield her face. 'It just depends on the light.'

'They're bonnie,' Aggie said.

When Cait turned to look at her, Aggie's eyes were already on the path ahead. They trudged in silence for a short while, and Cait tried to think of anything other than those words. *They're bonnie.* She watched as Aggie gently guided Winnie through the Pass, giving her whispers of encouragement and gentle scratches when they traversed steep inclines or manoeuvred tricky corners. 'You're good with her,' Cait said at last.

Aggie smiled. 'I've always liked horses. Someday, I fancy having a wee paddock with a pony. Maybe I'll make off wi this one.'

The image would have had no place in Cait's mind a week ago, but now she couldn't think of anything more perfect than Aggie egging a lazy pony like Winnie through the hills. There was an unspoken softness about her, and Cait was starting to think the Fox of Thorterknock was a myth, after all. Winnie snorted, and the pair flinched as snot splattered everywhere. Aggie laughed as she wiped her cheek with her sleeve and kissed the horse's face. 'And the first thing I will teach you is some manners.' Cait was so focused on the cooing voice Aggie used to talk to the pony that she didn't notice the movement on the path ahead until Aggie tensed and muttered a low, 'Whooooah' to slow Winnie down.

Two figures approached. As they drew closer, Cait could make out a young woman and her companion who lay somewhere between boy and man. The boar and hammer of the Queen's Watch crest sat proudly on their chests, but their regular clothes told Cait they were only volunteers.

The woman didn't acknowledge them but addressed the boy. 'Search their bags.'

'Hang on a minute,' Jamie said.

'We're searching everyone who passes this way. You'll appreciate these are uncertain times, and we're just trying to protect the region.'

There had never been enough Separatist sympathy in Storran's rural areas to justify deploying real soldiers, so volunteers gathered intelligence in their local area to report back to the city headquarters. They wielded no true authority. Even so, that had never stopped Kenzie ruffling feathers and throwing his weight around in his volunteer days, so Cait held her tongue and prepared to comply.

'Did they not want you in the city, like?' Aggie snarled.

The woman's lip curled. 'Have I seen your face before?'

'I cannae think why you would hae.'

'Then you won't mind being searched.'

'And you winna mind if I —'

'*Aggie,*' Calan snapped. Out of the corner of her eye, Cait noticed him adjust his coat, so it concealed the bag that hadn't left his hip since Gelly. 'Let them do their job.'

The woman bore over them as the boy rifled through the bags on Winnie's back. She snorted again and he jumped.

'Good girl,' Aggie muttered.

'Where are you heading?' The woman asked no one in particular.

'Wittenneuk,' Aggie said without missing a beat.

The woman raised an eyebrow. 'Long way to go. Where have you come from?' and she turned her attention to Cait.

'Thorterknock,' Cait said quickly, then immediately regretted her choice as the woman's eyes narrowed.

'What's in Wittenneuk that you can't find in Thorterknock?'

'Fish,' Calan said.

'All clear.' The boy wandered back over to join his companion.

'What did you find?'

He shrugged. 'Supplies for the road. Some food.'

'Shocker,' Aggie murmured.

A look of panic, so brief that Cait wondered if anyone else noticed it, passed over the woman's face, then her eyes fell on the bag looped over Cait's shoulder. 'We're not done. Search their personal belongings.' With that, she left the boy to it and began poking around the bags on Winnie's back for herself.

'I'm sorry, can I?' The boy pointed to Cait's bag, and she passed it over him, watching the determined set of his brows as he peered through it. He must have been ages with Innes, too young to be playing soldier in the streets.

'You're a volunteer?' Cait asked quietly. The boy glanced up, nodded once, then looked back down at the bag. 'That's admirable,' she said. 'I know a Watchman in the city.'

His gaze snapped back to her, the bag forgotten about. 'You do? How did he get in?'

'He worked hard.'

The boy removed the jumper from Cait's bag and when he seemed unsure of where to place it, Cait held her hand out and took it from him. 'I hope I get a placement in the city soon,' he said, doing a poor job of hiding the grin on his face.

'I'm sure you will. You're protecting good people.'

He smiled bashfully. 'I believe you're good people. I'm sorry we disturbed your journey.'

Cait shrugged. 'You have a job to do.' As she said the words, the boy reached into her bag and pulled out a piece of cloth. Cait's first thought was that she didn't know what it was or how it had got there, until he let it unfurl in his hands, and the gold stitching caught the sun. The stag's eyes twinkled impishly. The boy scuttled backwards and dropped the bag and its contents. His hands flew into the air as if they had been burned by hot coals.

'Look what you've found,' the woman sneered, pacing over to them. In one hand, she held Calan's newspaper, and with other she lifted the flag to the light. Cait expected Calan to order them to run, or for the Fox of Thorterknock to lash out, or for Jamie to make the ground break beneath their feet and sweep the pair away, but no one moved. It didn't matter if they outnumbered the volunteers, if they didn't leave this place as innocent travellers, they'd leave a trail of rumour and blood behind.

'I can explain,' Cait blurted, and the girl cocked her head like an aggressive seagull.

'Make it good,' she said.

'I found it in Thorterknock, and I panicked, so I threw it away.'

'And yet it's still in your bag.'

'I'd put it in a bin behind the inn I was staying in, and the innkeeper got in trouble for it. I didn't want him to get in any more trouble, so I took it back.'

The woman let the flag drift to the ground and unfurled the newspaper. The image of Cait on the garden wall grinned blithely back at her. 'Is this you?' the woman asked. Cait shook her head wildly. The lie, or almost truth, not coming fast enough. 'There's a man hunting for you all over Thorterknock.'

'I don't know him,' Cait said quickly, but not so fast that the thought of allowing this woman to take her back to Kenzie didn't pass through her mind. How easy it would be for her eyes to fill with tears and for her to say she was far from home and so very scared.

The woman took a step towards Cait and spoke softly. 'Are you safe?'

She thought of Kenzie tirelessly searching for her, clasping her photo tight in the hand he had almost used to strike her. She didn't know what to say. She started, suddenly unsure where that thought had come from. The woman was surely asking if Cait was safe from the Separatists. Her hesitation lasted too long, because the girl removed a pair of cuffs from her pocket and tossed them to the boy. 'Start with the Fox.'

'*Bastards,*' Aggie snapped.

Cait wasn't sure what connection the girl had made to work out Aggie's identity, but Cait saw the hungry spark return to her eyes. Capturing the Fox of Thorterknock would earn her a place in the city, but in turning her attention to capturing Aggie, she had forgotten about the true prize. The crown was still safe in Calan's bag. As the boy clicked the cuffs over Aggie's wrists and locked her hands in front of her, Aggie slipped a pocket knife from her sleeve and into her hands. The woman marched over, seized hold of Aggie's wrist, and forced her to her knees. 'Try anything and I'll take you back as a pelt.' She snarled, tossed the knife to the boy, and looked down at Aggie. 'I thought you'd be taller.'

'You've got this all wrong,' Calan said.

The girl turned on Calan and her eyes fell to his side where his coat had slipped. 'Hand me your bag.' Calan only stared at her.

'You'll be rewarded for this, won't you?' Cait said. 'It doesn't matter if we're innocent. If you can pass off one ginger girl as the Fox of Thorterknock, you'll get your job.' Hadn't Kenzie tried to do exactly the same with Bram?

The woman ignored Cait. 'Hand. Me. Your. Bag.'

Aggie tried to scramble to her feet, but the boy grabbed her by the shoulders and fumbled with the knife.

'You're not allowed weapons!' Cait cried. 'If they know you broke the rules they won't have you in the city.' It was enough to make him hesitate, but not enough to deter him from holding the knife perilously close to Aggie's throat.

'We'll give you what you want!' Calan cried. 'Let her go.'

'Don't be daft,' Aggie hissed. Cait tried to wrap her mind around what Calan could be planning, but his expression only told of desperation.

'And what is it we want?' the woman asked slowly.

Calan's throat bobbed. He opened his mouth, then there was a cry as Aggie wrenched herself out of the boy's unpractised grip, swiping his legs from under him. The knife in his hand jolted upwards and nicked his shoulder, and he fell to the ground clutching the wound.

The woman's eyes widened. 'You've killed him.'

Aggie flexed her bound hands. 'It's just a scratch.' She bent to pick up the knife, but when she straightened, someone else stood in her place. She looked like the same girl who whispered to ponies, but in her gaze was ice, glacier thick. In those eyes, Cait saw every terrible deed she'd imagined the Fox of Thorterknock capable of. Maybe the Fox wasn't an urban legend after all, maybe she'd just been walking in Aggie's shadow. Aggie stepped forward. 'You Lealists are aw the same,' she rasped.

The woman took a couple of steps backwards. 'You're mad.'

Aggie walked slowly towards her. 'Afren promises you glory. Siller. Food. A place in this world. So, you chase those promises, because you don't want to end up trapped in the cycle, on the street, puir like so many ithers.'

'What are you talking about?'

'They tell you they're the fix. They're the saviour. We need them. You believe their lies and trample the very folk trying to dae the work underneath yer shiny boots.'

The woman's nostrils flared. Her fists clenched. Her voice wavered and picked up pitch with every word. 'I hope you get your freedom. I hope you ruin Storran so you can see how fucked up —'

A single movement: Aggie's eyebrow twitched. The woman backed off, slowly at first, then made to run, her face knotted with terror as she tried to flee from Aggie's vacant advance. Aggie was on her in an instant and the two grappled over the knife. Though Aggie's hands were bound, and the woman was much taller, the blade inched closer to her gut. Cait's mind moved quicker than it ever had before. *Not again.* She hurled herself forward. Her body collided with Aggie's and the impact of the ground knocked the air out of her lungs. Something stung in the palm of her hand. Cait looked up to see the woman hurrying away down the Pass without so much as looking over her shoulder. Beside her, Aggie lay on her side, dirt from the path flecked across her cheeks. Their shallow breathing marched in time, and Aggie stared at Cait. The Fox was gone, leaving Aggie's eyes warm and wide once more.

'You're bleeding,' she said.

Cait followed Aggie's wide stare to her hand where a shallow cut was blooming. It stung, but she wiped it on her skirt. The boy needed her help.

She left Aggie blinking after her. She reached the boy as Jamie helped him into a sitting position. He gripped his shoulder, breathing hard, but Cait was relieved to see his wound wasn't deep. She sent Jamie to fetch the medical supplies. When she returned, the boy whimpered as Cait poured spirits over the wound.

'You're going to be okay,' she said gently, though she knew she was lying to him. His shoulder would heal, but the look in Aggie's eye would live with him for a long time. Cait knew it would stay with her. 'You'll need to get this checked by a doctor as soon as you can.' She wrapped a bandage over his shoulder. 'Can you walk?' He nodded stiffly, and she helped him to his feet. 'Where is home?'

He hesitated, then said, 'The next village over.'

'Promise me that you will go straight home. This wound will need some proper attention.' The boy nodded, but Cait wasn't sure that he was listening. He stared up the path where his companion had disappeared. 'Are you both from the same village?' Cait asked. He nodded again. 'If I were you, I'd tell whoever you report to what happened here. Tell them she left you behind.'

She sent the boy on his way, and as quickly as they could, they set off again.

Chapter 19

A Familiar Story

Aggie slunk away the moment they set up camp for the night. The others huddled around a weak fire, sat in heavy silence. In the flames, Cait saw Aggie's zealous glare. She watched Jamie taking harsh swipes at a piece of wood with a knife and said, 'I thought Talasaire were nature lovers?'

'We are,' Jamie said, gritting her teeth and taking another pointed swipe.

Cait watched her chop away some more, until Jamie sighed and held the stick up in front of her. 'Tavis makes it look so easy,' she muttered. Where it looked like she had attempted to whittle down the thin neck of a spoon, she had shaved away too much and the whole thing looked poised to snap in two.

'Doesn't that … hurt it?' Cait asked.

The wood splintered as Jamie took another chunk out. 'Things are meant to change. Transformation and all that.'

The night was too still, and as Jamie returned to her whittling, Cait's thoughts scraped against her mind. Something had crept over Aggie, and it frightened her. She felt foolish and conned, like she'd fallen for some trick in believing the Fox's act. The fire popped, and it only reminded her of fireworks planted where they shouldn't be. She pulled *Songs of Storran* from her bag and walked into the night.

The highland hills were different. In the borders, they draped across the landscape and scooped walkers up into their green hands before lowering them gently down again. In the north, the hills seemed insurmountable. Scree scrambled down the sides, and dark heather huddled against the sharp inclines. The peaks, at least the ones she could see, were crowned by mist or snow. At home, the hills begged to be climbed, but here they dared you to do so. She climbed to the top of a low outcrop that overlooked a vast loch. Something in its surface pulled Cait, and she scampered down the hill to its shore where she sat cross-legged on the pebbles. She opened the book to *The Ballad of Anndras and Cathal*. Her eyes scanned the familiar verses and paused at the moment where Cathal walked into the Queen's trap. 'Why did you do it?' She muttered, as though Cathal could reach her through the verses. She had always believed in some noble intention, where Cathal sacrificed himself for a chance at peace, but now he twisted in the bonds of those well-known lyrics and transformed from a flawed patriot, into a menace. Perhaps he was only going to the thicket to have a stab at the Queen of Afren.

'I don't know what it's like in the borders, but stealing isnae looked kindly upon in Thorterknock,' a voice said behind her, and Cait jumped. She turned to find Aggie standing with her hands in her pockets. She nodded at the book in Cait's hand. 'It better no be all crumpled and clarty when I get it back.'

'I didn't realise …' Cait made to hand the book back to its owner.

Aggie shrugged. 'I know it by heart. Keep it.' She hovered there a moment, lingering on the threshold between unspoken words, then said, 'I'm sorry. I didn't mean to hurt you.'

'Thats okay.' Cait flexed her bandaged hand. It still stung, but it would heal soon enough and leave no scar behind. When Aggie turned to leave, Cait called after her, 'You did mean to hurt the girl though, didn't you?'

Aggie halted. A moment passed before she glanced over her shoulder and said, 'Aye. I think I did.' The moonlight made the worry-lines across her brow glow silver.

Cait turned back to the book and behind her, footsteps crunched slowly across the pebbles and came to a halt a few paces back. 'Do you know how the River Cath was formed?' Aggie asked.

'*From his neck a bluidy spring became a crimson pool,*' Cait recited without needing to read the words in front of her.

'Some say his head is still down there, singing songs of freedom to the fish.'

'Under …' Cait looked up at the dark waters of the loch. 'Under there? That's Loch Cath?'

She turned to find Aggie grinning at her. 'Follow it three days downhill, and you'll be back in Thorterknock.'

Cait pushed herself to her feet and moved to the edge of the water. She ran her fingers through it. It carried a slight red hue, and when she plunged her hand into the waterbed, she pulled out a fistful of red pebbles that bloomed against her skin. They reminded her of the blood on the volunteer boy's shoulder, and she let them plop back into the water. 'My da would love this,' she said. She didn't know why she was talking to Aggie. Or the Fox. She wasn't sure anymore.

Behind her, Aggie chuckled. 'Have I ever telt you that your life sounds like a biscuit tin?'

'What do you mean?'

'The quaint village. The rural surgery. Gathering around the fire with your twelve siblings to hear stories from papa. Did you ever sing songs around the piano?'

'I'm an only child.' Cait watched the surface of the water compose itself. 'Da always has a story. Even when he's not performing, it's always "Jim-down-the-pub-said" or "I-was-walking-home-from-a-client-and-you'll-never-guess-what-I-saw."' Shadielaunds, she missed him.

'Your da's the village gossip,' Aggie said.

Cait glanced back at her. 'Aren't all the best storytellers?' But the best storytellers were liars, too. Her father had told her the stories in that green book countless times since her birth, but he'd carefully avoided the less savoury parts. Cait hadn't known that Anndras was killed at the battle for Storran, or that Cathal had lost his head, until she was ten years old.

'Do your folks know where you are?' Aggie asked.

Cait shook her head. 'I never got a chance to write to them.'

'Do it when we get to Gowdstane, tell them you're safe,' Aggie said, then added quickly, 'Just dinnae put a return address.'

Cait laughed and almost forgot. Here was the girl who sat with her on the pier with pie juice on her chin, but she seemed different now. Cait sensed a conflict within Aggie, and she didn't want to be caught up in the crossfire. She had made up her mind. 'I'm leaving when we get to Gowdstane. I'm going home.'

Though she couldn't see her, Cait could feel Aggie's stare boring into the back of her head. 'Why?'

'I don't want any of this.'

'This is because of him. You're going back to that —'

Cait turned to face Aggie and looked at her straight for the first time since they left the Dorcha Pass. 'His parents were murdered by Separatists.' Aggie only stared. 'He was sixteen,' Cait said. She eased herself to the ground again and pulled her legs to her chest. The loch skimmed the toes of her boots, and the pebbles wet her skirt, but she was no longer at the loch side; she was far away, on the rolling hills with a golden-haired borders lad at her side. 'Our families were old friends, and my parents adored him. Everything was perfect. Then the attack happened.'

The memories didn't belong to her, but they were so vivid: Kenzie's parents stepping off the train, walking arm in arm to the square in Thorterknock's New Town. The fleeing crowds. The homemade explosive that shattered their bones and lives. 'We never found out why it happened,' she said. 'But it killed five.'

The other memories did belong to her. She watched as the news spread around the village, how it skirted Kenzie all morning, and how the villagers smiled to his face and shook their heads behind his back. *Poor boy.* Cait's parents sat him down in the late afternoon and broke the news with the same voices they used when they told a patient they wouldn't get well again. Cait stood behind the living room door and listened. He didn't cry. He didn't say a word. He simply put on his coat and walked out of the surgery. Cait had chased him all the way down the path and out onto the road, but he strode towards his parents' house, now *his* house, and closed the door. She didn't see him for weeks. That was until one morning when she opened her front door, and he was there on the other side.

'I'm going to fix things.' It was the first time she'd heard his voice since that horrible afternoon. 'I'm going to apply for the Watch. I won't stop until they recruit me.'

'Suddenly, it was all about Separatists, and justice, and making it into the Queen's Watch,' Cait told Aggie. She was glad Aggie was stood behind her so she couldn't see the tears that pooled hot in her eyes.

She remembered how his temper frayed each time he read news about Thorterknock, how he started to hate her going anywhere alone. Once, he failed to show at the surgery when he had agreed to help her father with a few things. When she asked him where he'd gone, he told her he'd had a lead on Mr Blaine.

'He's not a Separatist,' Cait had said.

'*Anyone* could be a Separatist,' he had replied.

'You said you'd be here, Kenzie. We needed you.'

'The community needed me. *Storran* needed me.'

'None of this will bring your parents back!' She lived to regret those words. They were spoken in heat, fanned by the frustration that she never saw him anymore, that hunting Separatists seemed to be the only thing he cared about.

'You have no idea what it's like,' he had said, hurt and disappointment scored into his face, and now into Cait's memory.

She vowed from that moment not to get in the way of his plans. She'd let him hunt. She'd let him apply to the Watch. She'd uproot her life and go with him to Thorterknock. He needed her. Sometimes, she felt sure he hated her. She could forgive him for that. She could forgive him for almost anything. She couldn't pretend to know how grief changed a person. 'I can't believe after what I've done, he's still trying to protect me,' she muttered to the loch.

The night received Cait's story in silence, until Aggie's footsteps crunched towards her, and she slowly sat down, leaving only a breath of air between their knees. 'That's a familiar story,' she said, staring out at the loch. 'I was fourteen when my brother was killed by the Lealists.' Cait almost argued that the Watchmen didn't kill people, until she remembered that wasn't true. Aggie tilted her head to the sky. 'My mam raised us single-handedly. She worked in the mills, and she started coming home wi this horrible cough. My brother got wind of a protest about the working conditions and mam telt him not to go, but he did anyway. I bunked off school to join him. He got there first. When I arrived, there were Lealists everywhere. There was blood on the ground. Lots of shouting. They wouldn't let me go to him.'

'You think they attacked the protest?' Cait asked.

'They were ordered to.'

'Why?'

'To silence them. To show what happens when you question authority.' Aggie looked down at her knees. 'That was the day I realised what the Lealists stood for. That was the day I realised what side of history I wanted to be on.' Cait wondered what Kenzie would do if he were ordered to attack an innocent protest. 'Mam died a few weeks later. I knew things had to change.'

Cait studied her, and the longer she looked at her, the harder it became to see the Fox of Thorterknock. Aggie was just a girl, grieving like Kenzie was. They were the children of something broken, and they hoped the blood shed by their enemy would numb their aching hearts. 'Is what happened in the Pass change?' Cait asked.

'Afren treats Storran the way that factory treated my mither. They give us scraps and tell us we'd be destitute without them, all the while poisoning us. Storran, Kerneth, Tor, Prilwyn: we're all just workers in

Afren's factory.' Aggie spoke quietly, then turned to face Cait, eyes bright. 'But what's an abusive foreman left with when all his workers leave?'

'All of this pain can't be worth it.'

Aggie's voice wavered as she spoke. 'Do you know what it's like to have to choose between food and fuel? Or to be forced to watch your mother work herself to death because if she doesn't, you won't eat?'

Cait remained silent, unable to find the words. There had never been a day she was hungry, never a day she was cold. She had never lost a loved one and had to live with the anger of knowing it could have been avoided. Her thoughts turned to the man with the hacking cough in Thorterknock. She wondered where he went to bed at night. She wondered if he was still alive.

'It just seems like everyone who supports the Five Realms is rooting for Storran's failure,' Aggie said. 'They want their own country to be poor, their own people to starve, their own children to get a bad education, just so they can turn around and say, "See? Told you so. We'd never make it on our own."' She closed her eyes. 'I'm tired. Hope is *hard,* but it's better than acceptance. For that Lealist girl to wish her own homeland suffering to justify her beliefs ... I snapped.'

'And do you regret it?'

'That's the thing,' Aggie said, and then, with great effort, 'I don't know.'

Cait didn't know what to say to that.

After a moment of silence, Aggie continued, 'My reputation is my strongest weapon. I let that fade, and I have nothing. I'm just a rebel with barely any education, and even less money. The movement needs the Fox. *I* need the Fox.' Cait watched her carefully. Her words alone had changed Cait's mind about so many things. Those words stuck with her still, dredging up doubts she never knew she had. Words that made her think. Words that made her uncomfortable. It was a discomfort she relished. It was power. 'You're cold,' Aggie said, and it was then Cait realised she was shivering. Aggie slipped her coat off and held it out to her.

'It's okay,' Cait said. The cool night was starting to gnaw at her bones, and she'd welcome an extra layer, but she was hesitant to wear the skin of the Fox.

Aggie raised her eyebrows. 'I can hear your teeth chattering.'

Reluctantly, Cait took the coat and draped it over her shoulders, burying herself into the residual heat. The leather smelled of old cigar smoke. 'Where did you get this?' she asked, wrinkling her nose as she pushed it into the collar.

'A casino, I think. I've had it years, and it still smells the same as it did back then. Trust me, I've tried to get it out.' She regarded Cait, and then, just as she had in Eadwick with Cait's new hat, tilted her head, and said, 'Suits you.' Cait buried herself inside the collar and fixed her eyes on her shoes. 'And one more thing,' Aggie said. 'Why did you apologise for calling me out earlier?'

'I told you, I spoke out of turn.'

'No,' Aggie said, and she looked at Cait with such intensity that it made Cait retreat more into that cigar-lined coat. 'The truth.'

'I don't know,' Cait said. 'Just a feeling.' Guilt. Shame. Not unfamiliar feelings to anyone. How else did you know you'd done wrong?

'Why does someone as smart as you feel the need to apologise for a perfectly valid point?'

Cait stilled. 'Smart?'

'Of course,' Aggie said. 'You know that, though.'

'I ...' but Cait didn't have the words. She didn't know. She'd never felt intelligent in her life, and it was only now that she was realising it.

Aggie cast her a pointed look. 'There's more to life than him. There's more to you.'

Cait wrung her hands and pretended she didn't know what Aggie was talking about. They sat in silence for a long time and watched the surface of the loch shift, moved perhaps by the songs of Cathal deep beneath its surface. Maybe Cathal *was* a menace, but he was loyal to his people and his King. He was a symbol of hope. 'And I think you're more than the Fox of Thorterknock,' Cait said at last.

Aggie cast her a sideways look and frowned. 'What makes you say that?'

'I ...' Cait leaned back on her hands and her fingers touched something metallic among the pebbles. She picked it up, and when she lifted it to her face, she found a little gold button with a string of navy thread still clinging to it. Its face was emblazoned with a golden hammer and boar, and Cait knew she had touched this button before, on a day not so long ago, stood on a bridge tied with coloured ribbon. Cait's hands trembled as she held the button out to Aggie. 'Kenzie was here.'

Chapter 20

A Small Price to Pay

Kenzie needed no evidence to kill Bram. This was the only thought in Cait's mind as she tore across the moorland after Aggie. If he could order the execution of an innocent man on suspicion alone, what would he do when he found the real Separatists with the crown in their possession?

Calan and Jamie stared at them as they delivered the news through ragged breaths, and before long they were urging a disgruntled and sleepy Winnie to walk as fast as her little legs could carry her. They travelled in silence until the night shook, and Calan peered through the dark behind them and said, 'They're coming.'

'Shadowlands, they're on horses,' Jamie hissed.

Cait wasn't sure what terrified her more: that the Queen's Watch soldiers were hurtling towards them, or that Calan, usually the first with a plan to hand, had his hands on his head and panic in his eyes.

'Go,' Aggie said, and Cait looked down to find her shoving a bag into her arms. 'Get this to Gowdstane.'

The bag containing the crown suddenly seemed to weigh too much. 'Aggie — ' Before she could protest, Aggie seized Cait by the shoulders and marched her to the hedgerow. For a small girl, her grip was strong, and Cait knew she would have no say in the matter. 'Don't hurt him,' Cait pleaded, but Aggie didn't reply, and Cait squealed as she shoved her into the bushes. The gorse grazed her skin, and branches cracked beneath her. She lay on her front as yellow petals settled over her, and she clasped the bag tight to her chest. Through its skin, one of the crown's prongs jabbed into her throat. Hoofbeats rattled the ground. Her view was obstructed by the delicate spines of gorse, but she could see the shapes of horses sweeping in a circle around the Separatists. The night masked the faces of their riders, but their voices rang out like church bells.

'It's them,' Kenzie said. His voice jolted through Cait, sending her heart into a frenzy. 'Restrain them.'

A cascade of rifles fell on the group. Cait braced for Aggie to slip another knife from her sleeve, or to swipe Kenzie's rifle from him, but three sets of hesitant hands lifted into the air, and she watched as the Separatists were marched away.

When she could no longer hear the horse's hooves or the soldiers' voices, Cait allowed herself to panic. The road north was clear. She could run as far as her lungs would allow her to, but what about when the Watchmen searched the Separatists and found no crown? Cait knew two things: that Kenzie would execute the Separatists when they stopped being useful, and that perhaps the only thing he might desire more than the crown was her. She could face him now, or she could face him later when her friends joined Bram in the gloomy cellar deep within her chest.

The ground was soft which made it easy to track where the group had gone, and Cait followed the hoofprints to a lonely bothy. She found the horses tied in a line around the back. The Watch horses stood with stiff necks and muscles rippling beneath sleek coats, and among them, sandwiched in with her head held stubbornly high, was Winnie. Cait approached carefully and cupped the pony's muzzle in her hand. 'I don't want to do this,' she whispered. Winnie snorted and gave Cait a firm nudge. She laughed, and it gave her a flicker of courage. She slipped out of Aggie's coat and lay it over Winnie's back, unwilling to meet Kenzie wearing it.

The windows of the bothy were fogged, and all Cait could see were the shadows of bodies moving against the weak glow within. The building was left unlocked for weary travellers, but it reminded her of old school lessons.

Sheep were more profitable, so the locals were forced to leave.

She remembered learning about the Afrenian landowners who evicted their Storrian tenants, and how she hadn't batted an eyelid at the time.

She pushed the door open and found herself in a room that was far too small for all the people gathered inside. The Separatists were pressed against the back wall, pinned in place by the barrels of five rifles. Cait followed the unpractised slant of one of the rifles into Innes' hands, and relief warmed her. The boy Aggie had injured in the Dorcha Pass stood beside an unlit hearth. Cait was pleased to see his dressing had been changed, but his eyes were haunted. He glared at the Separatists, and Cait, with accusatory anger. He looked like Kenzie after his parents' deaths.

Cait's heart stumbled as her gaze locked with Kenzie's. His hair was tossed from the ride, the lamplight gleaming against his skin. The sight of him caused her chest to clench. She waited foolishly for his mouth to fall into his usual charming grin, but he only stared at her with wide, desperate eyes. A feeling she had almost forgotten flushed through her veins, leaving her with the almighty desire to do what he wanted her to do, to make him smile. Behind him, a slight man with round spectacles not unlike Calan's peered at her from between the soldiers. Cait's breath caught in her throat. Surely, she was imaging him. 'Da?'

Kenzie stepped aside and her father hurried forward. He bundled Cait into a tight embrace. His tweed jacket, which still smelled of their peat fire and the pastes they used to ease burns, scratched against her cheek. After a long time, in which Cait forgot the Separatists, and the Watchmen, and the bothy around her, Kenzie rubbed his hands together and crossed the room to the fireplace. 'Let's get some heat in here.'

Cait furiously rubbed the tears from her eyes as she pulled away from her father. 'What are you doing here?'

'I came as soon as we heard. Kenzie told us everything, pet.'

'Da, I'm so sorry.'

Her father squeezed her hands tight and fixed her with a steady gaze, though his eyes glistened. 'Now, listen here, pet. You did the right thing. You complied. You kept yourself safe.' Cait shook her head, but she couldn't find the words to tell him she wasn't coerced here against her will. 'Let's get you home. All they want is the crown, and you're free to go. We can forget all about it.'

Home. Cait imagined herself going through the motions: agreeing to her father's plea, handing over the crown, and boarding the next train to Holt. They would sit in a real compartment, on a cushioned bench, rather than in a luggage car or surrounded by sheep. She'd tell him her stories before she drifted to sleep, and they would arrive home by sunrise as the paper boy was beginning his rounds. Her father helped her ease the bag from over her head, and they held it between them. 'That's it, pet. Well done.' When he saw Cait's hands shake, he released the bag and pulled her into another hug. 'I'm here. Don't be scared.'

The Separatists thought that their King would bring an end to suffering, but who was to say he wouldn't just bring more with him? She could hand over this crown, she could spill their every secret, and it would be finished. There would be no more orphans born from this twisted conflict.

'Let's hand this over and put the whole affair to bed,' her father said, pulling back and smiling softly.

But despite the pain she had witnessed, she was the daughter of a professor. He had taught her to read between the lines, to question what words told her. She was the daughter of a doctor. Her mother had taught her to heal. Deep down, Cait knew scuppering the Separatists' plans would only be a bandage. It would only serve to cover the ugly wound beneath as everyone carried on as normal and city waiting rooms swelled. She'd been ignorant to suffering once, but she couldn't look away now. She couldn't follow her father back to Briddock to live on the lid of a biscuit tin when she knew that things weren't right. Her father had once told her, 'We're very fortunate to have everything we need.' Cait remembered thinking it was odd that having everything you needed should come down to a stroke of luck.

The Separatists were offering something different, and Cait wanted to try. Cait stepped backwards. Her fingers locked around the bag. 'I can't.' Her admission of guilt released itself as a sob.

'You don't need to pretend anymore, pet,' Dr Hardie said, but Kenzie stepped forward and moved him aside. Cait stilled. Kenzie appeared as he had in every dream she'd had since they parted. His sky-blue eyes gleamed with love; his mouth turned down with worry. When he placed his hands on her shoulders his grip was tight and reassuring.

'Come on now, your father's right,' he said softly. 'You've done nothing wrong.'

'Leave her alone,' Aggie growled from the other side of the room. Cait didn't see what happened, but there was a *thunk,* a gasp, and Aggie staggered to her knees.

Cait shifted closer to Kenzie. The balm of his embrace started to take hold. Despite every mistake she'd made, despite how much she had betrayed him, Kenzie was willing to make it all go away. She knew his movements better than her own. He was her truth. Her roots.

'Cait.' His voice bearing her name filled her with peace. It burned away every uncertainty the Fox had planted within her. It stripped her clean, to simplicity, to that future she dreamed of. But perhaps it was just that: a dream.

She wanted to say so many things, but all she managed was one word. 'Bram.'

Kenzie bowed his head. 'The innkeeper.' He cupped her cheek in his hand, and his eyes searched her face. His eyes. He had such beautiful eyes. Storran's blue had been a lie, but Kenzie had always been her truth. 'You mustn't feel guilty.'

His response surprised her. 'I shouldn't?'

'Of course not. You were only doing what you thought was right,' Kenzie said.

'But why did he have to … Why …' She couldn't get the words out.

'I'm sorry, Cait. I really am. I regret ever going to that inn. I regret —' his gaze hardened the smallest amount, and apologies rose in her throat. 'I regret ever frightening you. I only wanted to protect you. It's torn me up. No, it's *fucking* destroyed me.'

Cait's tears slipped down her cheeks and Kenzie stroked them aside with his thumb. She buried her face into his hand. The things he'd done for her, the way she had repaid him. 'I just —' A sob broke free from her chest.

'Little dove,' he cooed. 'We love you, come home.'

Kenzie's actions always spoke louder than his words ever did, it was what she had come to know best about him. Cait felt his love when he protected her, and when he righted her unsteady course. She felt his love in the way he tolerated her stories and her questions. She hadn't realised how badly she longed to *hear* his love. Now that he had said it, she couldn't remember the last time she had heard it. Her heart broke, and she wept freely for everything she had done to antagonise him since coming to the city. 'I'm sorry.' He pulled her closer. A smothering peace cascaded over her. 'I'm so sorry.' She was getting his uniform covered in her tears. The fire in the hearth had worked up to a roar. Cait's face burned.

'Shh,' Kenzie said, stroking her hair. 'I'm sorry, too.'

But how could he forgive her when Cait had allowed the city and its strangers to warp her perception of the man who had been at her side all her life? The man who prioritised her safety the moment she voiced her fears?

The man who loved her.

She felt the bag being eased from her hands, and Cait glanced at the Separatists over Kenzie's shoulder. There *was* a sickness in this land, but the cure would never be found until the two groups found common ground. 'Wait,' Cait said. 'Promise me something.' Cait saw Aggie slowly shake her head, but she kept her eyes anchored in Kenzie's. She couldn't let the Fox of Thorterknock's thirst for chaos make her doubt any longer.

She had to throw her trust in Kenzie.

'Anything,' Kenzie said.

Cait took a trembling breath. 'Promise me you'll do whatever you can to get both sides talking. It can't go on like this.' She met Aggie's gaze. 'There has to be another way.'

Kenzie looked at Cait, and she prepared to apologise for having such a silly idea, but then he smiled. 'That's a wonderful sentiment.'

Cait clutched the bag to her chest, her pulse hammering through her hands. 'I don't want anyone else to get hurt.' Then she nodded at the Separatists and added quickly, 'Including them.'

'Of course.' He smiled. She glowed. 'You and your good heart.' He stroked her cheek again. 'I love you.' He paused, and his expression pained. 'I am really, so sorry. For everything.'

Cait grinned. She felt the ache of it in her cheeks. 'It's okay,' she whispered. 'We've both made mistakes.' At last, she passed the bag over to Kenzie. He slowly took it from her, patiently waiting for her hesitant grip to slacken. When he removed the crown from the bag and lifted it high, his blond hair caught the firelight, and Cait's breath stole away as she thought of the painting of Anndras. Her King of Storran, the only king she'd ever need.

'Spectacular,' her father whispered.

Kenzie slowly turned the crown in his hands. 'Isn't it remarkable how an old piece of pewter can cause so much upset?' he said under his breath. 'Can it really grant strength to its wearer?' For a moment, Cait thought he might put it on and claim its power for himself, but he lowered it slowly, and lifted his gaze to the Separatists. 'Now, which one of you is the so-called Calan MacKenzie?' Cait wasn't sure what Kenzie meant by 'so-called', but she watched as Calan stepped forward. 'Come here,' Kenzie said with a warm extension of his arm. 'Join me by the fire, please.' Slowly, Calan slipped between the wall of gunmen and walked towards Kenzie, his eyes scanning cautiously across the room. He didn't spare a glance at Cait. 'You've raised a few eyebrows at Hart Hall.' Kenzie said, raising the crown in his closed fist. 'To steal this artefact and get it so far north is no small feat.' He tapped his temple. 'You're sharp.'

Calan said nothing as he came to a halt before Kenzie.

'We could use that mind of yours,' Kenzie continued as he held out the crown to Calan, who looked at it for a moment, then slowly reached out and took it. Kenzie turned his back to Calan and jostled the coals in the hearth with a poker. The flames leapt with hungry fervour. 'Hart Hall *could* use you,' he repeated.

'I'm a Separatist,' Calan said simply.

Kenzie looked up and cast Calan a look that carried a meaning invisible to Cait. 'You'd have stability.'

Calan hovered there, the crown hanging between his hands. 'Even if you had any power at Hart Hall, why would you want me?'

Kenzie grinned and leaned against the fireplace. 'Because I know ambition when I see it. I'll pull what strings I can to get you a place at Hart Hall, your Separatist cronies will be spared the squad. There's really no better deal.'

Say yes, Cait pleaded with Calan in her mind. *He doesn't need to be so gracious, but he is. He's doing this for me.*

'What are your terms?' Calan asked flatly.

'No terms.'

'Seems unlikely.'

'Alright. Just one.' Kenzie waved a hand at the crown in Calan's hands. 'The Watch can give you the world. All you need to do is toss that crown, into this hearth.'

The entire room stilled. A breathy laugh escaped Calan lips. 'I'm not going to do that.'

'You will,' Kenzie said. 'I know you will.'

An uneasy feeling came over Cait, like when she stepped into the empty Crabbit Corbie. It didn't seem necessary to melt the ancient artefact now. 'It's okay, we don't need to do that —'

Kenzie cast her a firm but gentle look that told her to leave this to him.

Calan glanced at the crown and back at Kenzie. Cait couldn't see his eyes for the fire reflected in his glasses. 'What good will come from destroying it?'

'It's a small price for a life of peace,' Kenzie said. Calan just shook his head and held the crown back out to Kenzie, who sighed. Instead of taking the crown from Calan, he reached behind his cloak and his hand came away with a pistol, which he cocked with a horrible *clank* as he pointed it at Calan. 'You will melt this crown.'

'*Don't,*' Aggie said. She took a step forward, and the row of rifles around her twitched into motion.

'Kenzie?' Cait made to cross the room to Kenzie, but her father gently tugged her back.

'Leave it to the soldiers, pet,' he muttered.

'You should take her outside, Dr Hardie,' Kenzie said, still staring at Calan down the gun.

As her fathered tried to shepherd her into the corridor, Cait pushed against him. 'Don't do this,' she begged.

Kenzie's eyes snapped to Cait for a moment, and she saw a flash of the same anger he had on his face the last time she had seen him. 'Leave it, Cait,' he snapped. He took a step closer to Calan and straightened his aim. 'Do it, now.'

Across the room, Aggie took another step forward. 'Don't touch him!'

It was over before Cait realised what was happening. Kenzie turned the gun on Aggie. A loud bang pulsed through the room. There was a flash. A shock of smoke. Aggie staggered backwards with a yelp, her hand flying to her shoulder.

'You said you wouldn't hurt them! You promised!' Cait screamed. She tried to run to Aggie, but her father dragged her back towards the door.

Kenzie ignored her. 'What will it be, MacKenzie? Shall I put another hole in your fox?'

Calan's knuckles tightened around the crown. Kenzie squeezed the trigger. Then Calan lowered his head and stepped forward.

'Don't you dare!' Aggie screamed.

Calan's walk to the fireplace took an age. He clutched the top of the mantle, paused for a moment, then let the crown slip from his grip, and it was swallowed by the flames.

Moments later, a second shot rang out from Kenzie's gun, and this time, it hit Aggie straight in the gut.

Chapter 21

Duty

There was a foolish moment where Jamie trusted what the blond Lealist was saying about a peaceful negotiation, and then there was the first gunshot. The moment the flames wrapped their greedy hands around the crown, she knew there would be no negotiating with these people. There would be multiple executions today, and the crown was only the first. Jamie didn't spare a thought to the guns trained on them, or the sheer extent to which they were outnumbered, as she raised her shaking arms and swallowed a gulp of air. She exhaled on the note of the Cy and commanded the flames to part. All at once, it felt like every living thing rushed to her, and she spun at the centre. It felt as though strong roots spread from her feet and plunged through the earth, and they relayed so many whispers to her she almost bent like a willow in a storm.

Do not touch that crown, a voice from somewhere deep inside Jamie commanded. It was coming from her, but it was a part of her she had never met before. A part of her that whispered on dark nights about everything she could be, and one she'd never dare to call upon, until now.

Who are you? The flames spat in a thousand voices.

I am Talasaire. Now part!

With what reason? Who gives you the right?

I claim the right. I am commanding you to!

The flames watched her, then slowly uncurled their fingers from the crown, leaving it half-molten and perched on a bed of hot coals at the centre of the fire. A thousand voices filled her mind. They sang songs of lost secrets, told tales that only the oldest trees would know. They quenched a thirst within her, cool and deep. The invisible roots at her feet tethered her to everything that ever was, and ever would be. She was alone at the centre of all things. She was a god. She could use tree branches to strangle the Lealists if she wanted, summon the winds to tear the breath from their throats, call on the earth to swallow them up … hungry, her fingers twitched. The invisible roots at her feet tightened. They squeezed around her and surged down, and Jamie felt herself sinking into an empty chasm below, where there were no whispers of the Cy to be heard, only an endless silence. She grappled desperately for the Cy, but it retreated from her like a dog that had been whipped by its master.

The Cy is not a tool.

My duty is to Storran.

Tavis' drawn, white face filled her mind. Jamie couldn't live life as a shell.

She let go.

Her song choked in her throat, and she watched as the flames rushed in around the crown again. Before she had the chance to drop her hands, a second shot cracked the air. She flinched, and the flames still tethered to her leapt out across the room in a fierce, unrepenting breath.

Chapter 22

The First and Last

The air was abnormally cold for a May night, but he welcomed its sting. Once again, he had tossed and turned through dreams in which the silent King watched from afar. As he did most nights when Anndras disturbed his sleep, Aidan came to the ramparts on Gowdstane's southern walls, where all of Storran seemed to spill out below. In the stillness, the air sighed at his side, and he turned to find Anndras gazing out over the land that had once been his. The ghost didn't acknowledge him. He never did. A silent sentinel, everything from his broad hands to the crook of his nose, was poised and unflinching. There was a blade at his belt, but Aidan had never seen him touch it.

'I wis hoping tae find you,' Aidan said, unsure why he still hoped Anndras would respond. He braced his hands against the cool stone and studied the night for whatever Anndras was watching for. 'You're always here.'

The ghost of the King didn't do so much as blink when the night stirred below them. Aidan first heard the flitting hooves, and then spotted three figures hurrying alongside a piebald pony who had another figure strewn across its back. 'What d'you make of this?' Aidan muttered with a sideways glance at the King. For just shy of ten years, Gowdstane had lain forgotten while the struggle for Storran played out in the cities; it was a slumbering giant at the foot of the Cronachs, and no one cared for it. The group did not look threatening.

'Could it be ...' Aidan stilled. The crown wasn't supposed to arrive at Gowdstane for months yet. Without warning, Anndras pivoted seamlessly and marched slowly for the door back into the castle. 'Wait,' Aidan called. The King halted but did not turn. 'Is it time?'

For a moment, Aidan thought the King would turn and acknowledge him, but he started moving again, and Aidan could only follow. He had guests to greet, and his crown was finally home.

Chapter 23

The Haw Upon the Hill

Cait was certain they had brought a stranger to Gowdstane. Aggie was far too still. She lay on a low bed in the dark belly of the castle's infirmary, her brow was fevered, her skin a sickly grey. She had fought relentlessly to climb off Winnie's back until somewhere along the road, she slipped briefly into unconsciousness, and the castle's doctor gave her something to keep her that way. She looked peaceful. Cait hated it.

She could still hear the second shot ringing in her ears. It had been a constant drone since she had flown to Aggie's side and begged her father for help. She had rearranged her memories time and again so that it was the sudden blast of flame that parted them, and not her father's turned back. Together, Cait and Calan pulled Aggie from the burning bothy. She didn't have her mother's expertise, but she did everything she could. Aggie had struggled as spirits spilled across her bloody skin. Calan demanded she die quietly. Cait fought the blood loss from the wound in her gut. When she managed to stem it as much as possible, they bundled her on Winnie's back and walked as quickly as they could.

'Calan,' Aggie had said, clutching Calan's sleeve as she leaned down from Winnie's back. Her voice gritted past her teeth, and her face crossed with irritation, as though there was a word on the tip of her tongue she couldn't quite remember. 'You need to … you need … take the … take … crown to Aidan.'

'Rest,' Cait had said from behind Calan as she reached for Aggie's arm. Aggie looked at Cait as though she were a stranger. She shook her arm away, betrayal crossing her face. Then the pain claimed her. Her eyes fluttered shut, and she slumped forward in the saddle.

Half an hour from Gowdstane, they thought they'd lost her. Cait put her all into stopping the blood. Then they set off again. As they walked, Cait clutched Aggie's wrist and counted each pulse that staggered under her skin. She didn't let go until a severe man in a purple housecoat met them at the castle, and a young boy with black curls and too many questions buzzed around them. Cait snapped at him to move aside, then the doctor pulled Aggie away and slammed the infirmary door shut.

*

'Let oorselves in, did we?' A voice clanged against the cold walls and jolted Cait back to Aggie's bedside. The doctor, who would not be out of place in a forge, bustled down the steps, her arms pumping like a pair of angry pistons.

'How is she?' Cait asked, on her feet before the doctor had made it to the foot of the stairs.

'Ach, hale an fere,' the doctor grunted. She didn't pause to look at Cait as she moved to a cluttered counter and started grinding something in a mortar.

'Hale and, what?'

'Fere, lass. Perfectly healthy.'

'What's the truth?' Cait asked. She stared expectantly, until at last the doctor huffed a sigh and braced a hand on her hip. 'The bullet in her belly was in an oot. Easy mendit. Her shooder's a richt mess. Wound's fu o shrapnel and the bane's shattert. Not to mention the infection.' Cait's head dropped into her hands. The doctor's gaze hardened as she poured the freshly ground powder into a clear liquid and stirred it together. 'She'd have bin luckier if she'd bled oot.' Cait watched as the powder swirled and formed a bitty yellow solution. Her stomach turned. She'd fought so hard to claw Aggie back from the brink. Maybe she'd only prolonged her suffering in this bleak, lifeless state.

We're doing everything we can, her mother would have said. *It's a serious wound, but it's early days yet.*

She wasn't sure which verdict she preferred, but there was one thing she did know, and it was that if Aggie died, she died trying to defend the Antlered Crown, not lying sick on a bed.

The doctor clapped her hands together. 'Right-ho. I need to gie Mr Burke his draught. Dinna touch onyhing.' She was gone as quickly as she arrived, and Cait sat down at Aggie's side once more.

Her fingers felt empty without Aggie's wrist in her hand, and she worried that without her counting the weak pulse it would simply stop. She desperately needed something to distract her, because every time her mind strayed, a faceless king on a crumbling throne filled her thoughts. His eyes flared red when they fell on her. *You betrayed me.*

Cait pushed aside the panic that squeezed her chest and thumbed through the pages of *Songs of Storran,* which had lain unopened on her lap since she arrived at Aggie's side. She found the tale of *The Smithy and the Doo* and cleared her throat. 'You've probably heard this before,' she said quietly, unsure if Aggie could hear her and equally unsure if she wanted her to, 'but it was my favourite when I was little.'

The story was written in verse, peppered with Old Storrian, like *The Ballad of Anndras and Cathal,* but Cait used the lines as a prompt to tell the story as her father told it. In a voice no louder than a whisper, Cait began to read.

'There was once a handsome and skilled smith who worked for a Laird and was adored by all. His hair was golden, and his arms were strong, and his laugh could be heard ringing from peak to glen. Many of the local townsfolk tried to catch his affections, but he had only eyes for one lady: a soldier among his Laird's ranks. She was equal parts charismatic and beautiful, and when she rode a horse, she flew like a bird in flight. When the pair fell in love, the smithy lived dreading each day the Laird would send his love to battle. He scarcely breathed until she returned, and soon he learned to resent the work she cared so much for.

'One day, the soldier's troop were late in returning home. Rumour on the glen spoke of a terrible battle in the south, and that the field was stained with the blood of their own soldiers. The smith watched the valley for three days, until he finally caught sight of his lover returning to him. Not wanting her to leave his side again, he sought the help of the local henwife. When he explained his fears, she brewed him a special potion and said, "Mak yersel a sturdy cage and mix this amang her brose. By morn yer love will leave nae mare tae fight ony foreign foe."

'So, the smith set about making the finest cage ever seen. It was jewelled and golden, and the inside was lined with plush cushions. He worked through the night and finished just as his love was rising, and served to her the potion among her brose. She ate quickly, and soon fell weak with illness. The smith worried at her bedside all day and night, until the next morning he woke to find his love was missing. When he looked beneath her blankets, he found her strong arms had become grey wings, and her shining brown hair replaced by speckled feathers. Her pink lips were sharpened into a little beak, and her round eyes now small and beady and black. She squawked and thrashed as the smith lifted her and placed her in the golden cage, because he loved her so. She flapped, and flapped, and cried, until exhaustion took her, and she settled her head under her little wing. The smith spent his every day stroking her feathered breast.

'But each day the doo grew more listless. She slept most hours. She stopped eating. She even ceased cleaning her beautiful feathers. One day, the doo looked at the smith and blinked slowly. "Please, love. This room is hot from the furnace. Won't you open a window?" she cooed.

'So, because he loved her, the smithy opened a window.

"Love," the doo then said. "Let me out so I can perch on your shoulder and groom your sweet, yellow hair."

"That would be unwise," the smithy said. "There are cats and foxes that would have your blood." He would not put his love in danger, because he loved her so.

"Oh, let me out love, so I can kiss your cheek," cried the doo.

'The smith loved her dearly and had grown to miss her affection, and so gently he opened the cage and allowed her to hop onto his hand. No sooner —' The sound of the infirmary door creaking made Cait slam the book shut and bite down on her words.

'Don't stop on my account.' She heard Calan's voice before she saw him hovering at the top of the steps.

Cait's cheeks burned. 'It's a sad ending anyway.'

Calan slowly walked down the stairs and paused at the bottom. 'The doo flies away, never to be crammed into a tiny cage again,' he said.

'And then the smithy dies of hunger and heartbreak.'

'He should have thought about that before he spent all his money on building a cage,' Calan said. Cait looked down and worried the edge of a page before remembering that it was Aggie's book and she'd hate that. 'How is she?' Calan asked at last, though his eyes didn't leave the flagstones.

Cait glanced at Aggie's slate-grey face. Her mother was always careful to tell the truth with her patients, no matter how bad the news, but Cait found herself lying. 'The doctor says she'll get there.'

'Thank you for caring for her,' Calan said, eyes still trained on the floor. 'I wouldn't have expected you to do that.'

Because you're one of them, Cait finished his sentence in her head. Separatist or Watchman or innocent bystander, how could she have left

Aggie, bold and brazen Aggie, for dead? 'She's my patient,' Cait said simply.

She wanted so much to tell Calan she was sorry, but she was afraid of what he would say. Even now, she was still hunting for excuses for Kenzie, but she was coming up empty-handed. The truth raked at her heart. He had used her. He had used her, and she was worried that he was using her father, too. It was all too convenient; the diary left open on the desk at the Treasury, her father with Kenzie. She was almost certain that Kenzie was using her father's expertise to undermine the Separatists.

'Lister wants to see us. Aidan, too,' Calan said.

In Cait's mind, the King's red eyes flared. 'Oh.'

'I can't protect you from him,' Calan said. 'Even if I wanted to.'

Cait shook her head. 'I didn't mean to —'

'You *gave* them the crown.'

'I only wanted peace.'

'We might have had that,' Calan said quietly, though his words bit. When he looked at her over his glasses, Cait wondered if he had meant to glare, but he only looked shattered.

'I'm with you,' Cait said. Suddenly, she felt like the walls were listening and would carry her confession through the earth to Hart Hall. She didn't care. She remembered Aggie's raucous laugh in Eadwick. *They need us!* Cait hadn't believed it at the time, but now she was starting to see. Kenzie didn't need to melt the crown. He had them cornered. He could have marched them, and the intact crown, back to Thorterknock to the same result, but he'd been ordered to destroy it, because they couldn't risk the Separatists gaining a foothold. Afren's leaders abused Storran's people. They stole their money, stole their resources, stole their own, ancient words and national confidence. But that was because Afren needed Storran's people, too. They needed their peat, needed their access to full-bellied fishing waters. The melting of the crown revealed Afren's desperation to her. It was the same desperation that had driven the smithy to lock his love in a cage.

Calan watched her for a moment, then said, 'Lister's waiting in the library,' and turned to leave.

'Calan,' Cait called after him. He paused and glanced at her over his shoulder. 'I'm terrified.'

Calan only sighed. 'Me, too.'

*

Cait's visions of a sprawling, glimmering court had crumbled the moment she laid eyes on the decrepit castle that was Gowdstane. The passages that led to the library crawled with moss and mould and they toed a path around piles of rubble. The evening sun leaked in through holes in the ceiling, and Cait pulled her jumper tight around her as the highland wind whistled as they passed. The castle may have been a corpse, but it was bursting with life. Separatists of every age and accent gathered in the ancient halls, carried supplies down dark passageways, spoke in low and excited murmurs about the crown that had supposedly been returned overnight. Cait realised that while the Separatists of Storran's cities had been wreaking havoc across the lowlands, the Separatists of Gowdstane had been busy. They were building an army.

A man waited for them at the door to the castle's library, and Cait recognised him as the one who had been wearing the purple housecoat the previous night. His nightcap was gone, and his neatly cropped black curls were on show. Now that he stood before them in a fine suit and cravat in the plum velvet of the Enlighten Party, Cait recognised him as the politician Lister Burke. The only indication that he had noticed their approach was the deepening of his frown. Beside him stood Elsie, the girl from the Unnertoun.

'What is she doing here?' Calan muttered as she rushed towards them.

'You made it!' She gave Calan an unreciprocated jab in the ribs. 'Took yer time about it, didn't you? That you off to meet Aidan?'

Lister regarded her with mild distaste. 'Can we expect any other visitors from Thorterknock?' he asked.

'She's not with us,' Calan said.

Elsie fell into step with them and leaned towards Calan. 'I couldn't not see the crown.'

'He's waiting,' Lister said, then pushed the door to the library open. Elsie tried to follow them in, but Lister blocked her way.

The library was no grand affair. The bookshelves slanted and bowed, giving everything a crooked edge. A bone-deep chill ran through the room despite the stove that crackled away in the corner. Three people occupied armchairs at the centre of the room, and Cait scanned their faces, hunting for the regal glow of King Aidan. A woman with withered cheeks and silver hair sat next to a dark-haired lady with bright red lips, and a man with a horse-like face and red hair sat across from them. Cait almost didn't spot Jamie perched on the window ledge, her view blocked by a boy that stood by the window. As they entered, he spun to face them, and Cait recognised him as the boy who she snapped at the night before. He must have been around sixteen or seventeen, and his eyes were wide with worry.

'The Fox!' he blurted and took a hurried step towards them as they sat. 'Is she awright?'

Cait scanned the room, now certain that Aidan must be elsewhere, waiting to enter once everyone had arrived.

'She'll be receiving the best of care, I assure you,' Lister said.

'But —'

'Now *sit down*, Aidan.' Lister scolded the boy and Cait gave a start.

Cait watched the boy perch sheepishly on a footstool. His lips pouted as he pulled his legs in. She suddenly realised what she had been hoping to find at Gowdstane was the ghost of a king. She had hoped to find Anndras himself. King Aidan was no red-eyed warrior, or golden prince, but a sulking boy.

Chapter 24

The So-Called Calan MacKenzie

The so-called Calan MacKenzie hadn't felt this vulnerable in a very long time. *So-called.* The words the blond Lealist used to describe him writhed beneath his skin. It meant Kenzie had done his research, and it left Calan feeling exposed and skittish. It had been almost twenty years since he slept not knowing if he'd see the morning, through nights that rattled with gunfire. Since then, he had reinvented himself, but the phrase *so-called* took him straight back to the boy he had been. Kenzie would only need the right words and the wrong person to reduce his family's life to rubble all over again.

He looked around at the people gathered in Gowdstane's draughty little library. He recognised them, but he could not place why they would be here and how they could be associated with the Separatists and the boy king.

Margaret Gibb. Owns a munitions factory. Very wealthy.

Ranald Reilly. Lager merchant. Well-connected.

Fiona Brown. Owns a birkenweave mill in Carse. Very wealthy, very well-connected.

At the centre of it all, sat with a straight back in a stiff armchair was none other than Lister Burke. Calan was under no illusion as to who he had stolen the crown from, and he wished he had a wooden chair, rather than the soft couch that seemed to sink under his weight and cause him to fold in like a hermit crab. Everything in the world seemed to lean towards Lister, from the books on the shelves to the weak flames in the fire, and the assemblage of tradespeople watched him out of the corners of their eyes. Without saying a word, Lister slowly placed a newspaper on the table and opened it. The sound of the pages turning filled the room and sent a bitter shiver through Calan's teeth, as though it were peppering his bones with paper cuts. Lister took his time to scan down the page, lifting his eyebrows high.

'Well, then,' he said at last. 'Why is it when I opened this morning's paper expecting to complete the crossword, I found a story about a group of Separatists who melted a precious artefact recently stolen from the Treasury Museum in Eadwick?' Lister had a slow way of talking, meandering around each word, taking his time to form each breath. He spoke as though he had all the time in the world.

'That's not what — we didn't —' Calan croaked. It would seem the paper had beaten him to his spin.

'That isn't what *The Northern Herald* seems to believe,' Lister said.

Calan stuttered. He was off to an excellent start. 'You know as well as any how biased the papers can be.'

Lister levelled him a steely glare that made Calan want to drop through the floorboards. 'I'll give you two minutes to explain yourself, MacKenzie.'

'We were cornered. One of the Lealists melted the crown, they're obviously trying to cover for themselves.' The lie burned. He could still feel the singe of the fire on his fingers as the crown slipped from his grasp.

'Hmm.' Lister leaned back in his chair and fixed Calan with a dead look, then his eyes fell back to the page. 'This article tells me it was you who did it.'

Calan's skin turned clammy as Kenzie's words drifted through his mind again. *The so-called Calan MacKenzie.* What else did the article say about him? He imagined the journalist spinning a story about how once again the refugees from Iffega were unwelcome, destroying the heritage of the Five Realms. His crimes would be the crimes of every Iffegan. 'That's not true.'

Lister folded his hands and sucked on his teeth. 'So just how did it get into their hands?'

'It was my fault,' Cait blurted before Calan could pull on another untruth. Her small voice quivered, barely audible even in the silent room. 'I handed the crown to the Watchmen.'

Margaret Gibb frowned down a pair of half-moon specs. 'And who on earth is this, Lister?'

Lister's gaze ambled back across the room to Cait. 'I'd like that answer myself.'

'I was trying to negotiate.'

Lister glared at Cait, and Calan had to give her credit for weathering it, because it was enough to turn crops sour. 'Your name, girl.'

'My name is Cait.'

'And you're from the Unnertoun, Cait?'

'I'm from Briddock.'

Calan watched her carefully, unsure what Cait was planning to accomplish other than completely incriminate herself. 'I only wanted to help.'

'Well. Didn't you do a remarkable job?' Lister said simply. 'Mr MacKenzie, we had agreed that I would send for the crown once things died down in Thorterknock. What possessed you to take matters into your own hands?' And just like that, Cait was discarded and left at the wayside, Lister's fire blazing with its full ferocity on Calan once more.

Calan shifted on the sofa, though it seemed to only make him sink more. 'The situation in Thorterknock isn't good. The Lealists have been running rings around us for months. We were getting desperate. There was a reported near-discovery of the Aist Bridge entrance to the Unnertoun, so I —'

'Thought you would report it to me so I could deal with the problem in line with our wider strategy,' Lister said, casually scanning down the newspaper. His voice was too measured. Too steady.

Calan opened his mouth but shut it when he realised he didn't know what to say. Why had he taken the stupid gamble? Why go against his own instincts, this time of all times? He knew too well. Aggie. She'd painted him that pretty picture of an office panelled in glory and like a moth he'd swept towards it. But he had also noticed the way Lister always spoke of their next bold moves, and how those bold moves never seemed to manifest. They would be left waiting in the Unnertoun for their orders, suffocating slowly on the heat of their own zeal. Lister's strategy was all talk, much like his politics. He watched Lister lazily turn the pages in the newspaper. Calan spoke in a low voice, perhaps hoping Lister wouldn't hear. 'There had been too many close calls in the Unnertoun. It's thought that the butcher, Alec —'

'Who reported these suspicions?' Calan hesitated. 'Speak, boy.'

'Aggie,' he said quietly.

'Ah,' said Lister, with next to no emotion. 'Of course, this mess can be traced back to that nuisance.'

'She was shot twice trying to stop it,' Calan said curtly, unable to do anything for Aggie right now other than defend her. She'd do the same for him. The day they met, he had been standing by the entrance of the school kitchens eyeing up a bag of shiny, red apples on the counter. Aggie had been sitting at the other end of the dining room, watching him. He was no thief, but food was scarce at home that week, and his stomach ached. He stood there for an hour, but his hunger pangs weren't enough to carry his feet over the threshold and take one of the apples. So, he went to class. He was hunched over his paper when something slammed onto the desk in front of him, inches from his head. He looked up to find an apple on his desk, and Aggie standing above him. She earned herself the cane for that, but he'd never forget it.

'I would have preferred you brought me a crown rather than a dead fox,' Lister said.

He finally looked up, and Calan found himself wanting to be him. He wanted to strike the same fumbling fear into people that Lister put in him, to be so assured of his position and stability that he could afford to make enemies and stand his ground. But Calan didn't have that. He had to scrape for everything he had and place himself in the right pockets and bet on all the right horses, so he cast his eyes down to his tightly clasped hands. 'Yes, sir.'

Lister was quick to dismiss Aggie as a liability, and a liability she may be, but she would never sit back and let anyone tell her what to do. She reminded him every day why he was here and what he was doing. He wished she were here now. She would roll her eyes at Lister. She would wink at Calan like she had done from the opposing team's lectern at school debating contests. *You know what to do.*

Ever since the bullet left Kenzie's gun and they had hurried onward to Gowdstane, Calan had distracted himself from Aggie's weakening state with thoughts of *what next.* The crown was gone, and no amount of ridicule by Lister, or his strange collection of visitors, would change that. Lister claimed their momentum had never been stronger. Growing numbers of Queen's Watch officers on Thorterknock's streets told another story, but Calan had now seen the secret that Gowdstane was hiding: numbers. They wore no uniforms, and they looked untrained, but while the Separatists of the Unnertoun had been scrambling for even a crumb of credibility, Lister had been busy. And, judging by the people in this room, he had made some influential new friends. Cait had said that for anyone to take the Separatists seriously they would need to gain the public's respect. If what Lister said was true, and time was on their side after all, there was a different way. They wouldn't need the crown. They wouldn't even need the restless young boy before them who was masquerading as a king. He knew too well how quickly the battle for a throne could consume a nation. If they could avoid that, it would be preferred.

The room chattered quietly in urgent tones. Calan couldn't sift through the words, his mind too full of the thought that had been tugging at his gut all along. 'We don't need the crown,' he said, still looking at his hands.

One by one he felt their eyes fall on him. For a moment, there was silence, and then Margaret Gibb crowed a laugh.

'You ken fine well the power that crown held,' Ranald Reilly grumbled.

'Jist what do you plan on crowning him with, lad? A soup pot?' Fiona Brown chortled.

A chuckle rippled around the room, but Calan looked up at Lister, whose face was blank. 'We don't need a crown because we don't need a king,' Calan said to him.

Aidan piped up. 'But —'

'We need to change our tactics. We need the respect of the people, and right now, they're afraid of what our vision might mean for them.' Calan spoke fast, plugging the silence as quickly as he could.

All eyes slid towards Lister, who leaned forward. 'How do we gain the respect of the people when the state itself does not respect us?' He asked slowly. 'When the mere mention of separatism results in a death sentence?'

The debater in Calan was telling him to talk collectively, and maybe that's what Aggie would do if she were here. She would weave an inspiring tale full of metaphor and hyperbole, but Calan's instincts only said *spit it out*. 'Information. People want facts, *proof* their lives will be improved. They have everything to lose.' *Trust me,* he wanted to scream. *I know.*

'It's true,' Cait said. 'I'm from the borders. No one tolerates separatism there, but I *know* they might change their mind with the right message.'

'It doesn't matter how much we rebrand ourselves,' Gibb clucked. 'We could promise every person in the Five Realms a small estate in exchange for our freedom, and Afren still wouldna recognise it.'

Calan could feel the spark of debate carrying him now, he only wished he had the quick wit of Aggie when speaking. He could see the path of his argument ahead, but he stumbled and tripped on his words. 'Afren has power over the people because they're the status quo. *We* know that a free Storran will benefit us in a thousand ways, we just need to tell them. Once we convince the public, it'll become as normal as ... I don't know ... rain.' Calan paused, and when Lister didn't say anything, he kept talking, because he didn't know what else to do. 'We need the press. They won't take it from people like us.'

'People like *us*?' Lister said under the raising of eyebrows.

'Outlaws,' Calan said. A soldier wearing a boar mask with a bleeding leg flashed through his mind. 'Terrorists.' The word caused him physical pain to speak, but he knew it would garner a reaction. Lister merely grunted and lifted his chin, but his eyes said, *take it back.*

'I suppose there's sense in that,' Fiona Brown said. She wore a pink shawl of Birkenweave which she clasped at her heart with one delicate hand.

'That's not in your best interest,' Lister said, and Calan noted how his demeanour softened each time he addressed one of them. 'The press would never side with us. It would take years to get them on board, if ever.'

'I've already met with a journalist in Afren,' Calan said.

Lister glared at him. 'You'd do well to remember your place.'

Heat rushed to Calan's face. 'Yes, sir.'

'He might be right,' a new voice said. Calan looked up to find Aidan looking around the room. His shoulders were set like a warlord and his voice, deeper than expected, was measured and forceful, but the nervous tapping of his foot could be felt thumping through the floorboards. 'I dinna want to be a tyrant. I want people to come to me willingly.'

'That's quite enough, Aidan,' Lister snapped. Storran's promised King dipped his head and obeyed.

It didn't add up. If their movement had never been stronger, why was Lister so adverse to trying a new strategy? Calan thought back to the night Aggie had come barging into the Unnertoun with warnings of Lealists closing in. Had she seen through a weakness in Lister's armour without realising? It suddenly occurred to Calan that he was looking straight into a mirror: Lister was floundering. On one hand, he had a frustrated and increasingly desperate group of Separatists in Thorterknock, who demanded action, and on the other, he had this secret world of allies at Gowdstane who saw a measured man with a tactical plan. Prowling around it all, the Afrenian regime, who only grew stronger by the day. Regardless of what story Lister was spinning, the Lealists were closing in. In fact, the crown may not have made the slightest bit of difference in the end. But none of that angered Calan as much as the fact that Lister had allowed discontent to swell into violence on the streets of Thorterknock as a distraction for his political games in the north.

'I'll speak to the people,' Aidan was saying. 'Or send me to Afren. I'll meet with the Queen.'

'No,' Lister said simply.

'I've got tae try.'

Lister ignored him.

'I'll tell everyane the truth about what Afren did to the crown, and everyhing else they've done. They'll believe me, an they'll back my claim. Then we'll go to Thorterknock and do whit Calan suggests —'

'This is your last warning.'

'We've done *nothing* —'

'Be quiet.'

'Then what's even the point?' Aidan cried. 'What am I doing here?' He looked on the verge of tears. All pretence of authority the boy had held melted away.

Calan saw Reilly and Brown exchange a glance, and Gibb busied herself folding a handkerchief she had removed from her pocket. Lister's voice sliced clean through the air as he spoke quietly. 'You are not a strategist. You are not a politician. You are a figurehead. Your job is to be a figurehead. Now, sit down.' The last two words grated past his teeth. Aidan hovered in place for a moment, then his throat bobbed and he lowered himself into his chair.

Aggie's words came back to Calan then. *Do you care about Storran, or yourself?* This room contained wealthy merchants and a senior politician. They were people who had found a comfortable place in society and were using it to their ends. They had power, but they would never stick their necks out far enough to get the job done properly. Storran's independence was their side hobby, something they pursued because it might grant them more money or power down the line. Luckily, Calan had no such position to cling to. He touched the key at his neck that opened a door to a house that no longer existed. If the boy he was before had taught him anything, it was how to build from rubble.

'Announce that Enlighten support Storran's independence,' Calan said.

Lister's raptor stare landed on him. 'What?'

'You're the head of a well-respected party in Storran. That's how we get credibility.'

Lister watched him for a long time. Then he lifted his chin and spoke slowly to Calan. 'You should be careful, MacKenzie, or the wrong people might learn of your ... status.' A bubble of hot air rose in Calan's chest. Of course, Lister knew. He knew everything that entered his orbit. He might not know that Calan was smuggled into the Five Realms among sacks of coffee, but he did know that Calan was undocumented. As far as the Five Realms were concerned, Calan shouldn't exist. Lister stood up and tucked his chair in. 'One more wrong move, boy, and it'll be home time.' He swept across the room. 'Mark my words.'

Home. Not Thorterknock. Not Morburn, the town near Thorterknock where his family currently lived. *Home.* Calan felt sick. The room emptied, leaving Calan and Cait on the sofa. Calan felt like he was floating above his body, watching himself stare blankly at the space in front of him from above.

'I'm sorry,' Cait whispered at last.

'It's fine,' Calan said shortly. He was growing tired of her apologies.

'We can try something else, even if we're not at Gowdstane. We can ask —'

'Leave it, Cait,' he gritted out. He couldn't find the energy for anything else. There was no more room for mistakes.

'Maybe the crown survived,' a small voice said from the window, and Calan turned to see Jamie perched on the windowsill, her long legs pulled to her chest. He hadn't even realised she'd been in the room. She gazed blankly out the window. Despite the late evening sun casting a golden glow across her skin, she looked wan.

'It's made of pewter,' Calan said. 'If it didn't melt in the fireplace, it certainly would have melted in the house fire.'

'Is it not worth checking?' Jamie asked firmly. When she looked up, her eyes were glassy and grey. 'It can't be gone.' Calan wondered if she was talking about the crown at all, or something else.

'Have you felt anything yet?' Cait asked. 'The Cy?'

For a moment, Jamie looked like she wouldn't answer, then she pushed her head back against the stone wall and said, 'It's there, I can feel it, it's just out of reach.'

'Can you bring it back?'

Jamie shut her eyes. 'I have to.'

Calan got to his feet. He'd had enough of this draughty library with its shadows and angles and Lister's threats hanging from the walls. He made towards the door.

'Where are you going?' Cait asked.

'Back to the bothy,' he said, because either he was finding that crown, or he was running for his life all over again.

Chapter 25

Born of Ashes

Cait found Aggie's coat trampled in the dirt near the bothy. She shook out the hoofprints and brushed off as much of the mud as possible, then pulled it over her shoulders. While Calan surged ahead and disappeared into what was left of the house, Cait hung back with Jamie, allowing her to set a dreary pace.

'This is a mess,' Jamie muttered. She kicked a charred lump across the ground, and it bounced with a series of hollow *thuds*. Their boots crunched as they stepped onto the blackened grass surrounding the bothy. In the gloaming, the building looked like a grotesque creature prowling the outskirts of the charming countryside with its drystone walls and threading streams. There was no door for them to push open, and Jamie hesitated at the threshold. She stared at her feet and ash tumbled down her dark fringe into her eyelashes. 'I did this,' she said, blinking furiously.

'Listen,' Cait started.

'I thought …' Jamie gasped, 'I thought I could stop them, but …' her words trailed away and she waved listless arms at the shell of a building.

'I did, too,' Cait said quietly, then, 'The Cy. Can you feel it here?' She had hoped that being back in this place would give the Talasaire some connection to her faded power.

Jamie squeezed her eyes closed and shook her head. 'It's far off at Gowdstane, but I can feel it, like it's walking a few paces behind me. But here?' She shivered. 'It's like it's keeping its distance. And I'm *hungry* for it. I'm so hungry.'

'It'll come back,' Cait said. She knew how to dress a cut. She knew how to set a bone. She only wished she knew how to heal the loss that Jamie was feeling. 'We should find Calan.'

Jamie shoved her hands in her pockets. 'Go ahead. I'll meet you back at the castle.'

Cait hesitated and watched Jamie warily. She looked so listless. 'Are you sure?'

Jamie mustered a weak laugh that was trying its best to seem effortless. 'Take a look around. If there are any Lealists lurking about, they'll think twice before starting a scrap.'

Jamie's false pluckiness was little comfort, but Cait turned and walked into the bothy. The moment she had heard the voices from the cellar of The Crabbit Corbie she had known, gut-deep, what had happened. She had ignored it, unwilling to mar the perfect image of her golden boy. It had led her here, to this place of ash and choking shame. She found Calan rooting around in the rubble by what had once been the hearth. Cait hovered by the door, the place she'd embraced her father just hours earlier. Where was he now?

'Calan?' The only answer was his heavy breathing as he tore through the ash. '*Calan.*' He ignored her. 'Stop.' He sent up a spray of ash with a frustrated cry, and spluttered on the dust. Cait swept forwards and crouched in front of him, taking his trembling and dusty hands in hers.

'I should have burned it sooner,' he choked. His head was bowed, and his shoulders shook. For a moment, Cait wondered why he was laughing, until he looked up and she saw his cheeks glistening. 'I should've done it when he told me to. Maybe then he wouldn't have shot her.'

'That wouldn't have helped.'

'It's *my* fault she's hurt.'

'It's mine. If I hadn't been here … I'm sorry —'

'Stop apologising,' Calan snapped on a sniff. Behind the tremble of his grief, Cait sensed an insurmountable, icy stone wall. Even if she could comfort him, he would never let her in. 'That Lealist said you turned in an innkeeper for being a Separatist.' When he looked up, his red eyes glared over his glasses. 'All this time, you were just playing your cards right until you could lead him directly to us. Is that what you wanted?' he brandished a hand at the destroyed bothy. 'Is *this* what you wanted?'

'No.'

'What about this?' He threw a fist into the dust.

They both coughed on the ash that burst into the air, and when it had settled there was no point left in kidding herself. 'I suppose on some level, yes.'

Calan's head fell forward again. 'I'm a fool,' he whispered.

'No, you're not,' Cait said firmly. 'That's not the reason I came with you. I wanted to see the crown. That's all, I promise. But when Aggie told me the rest of your plans, maybe I also thought I could bring them back to Kenzie.' That moment on the pier, she had been so close to betraying them and handing the crown over. That couldn't have come from nowhere.

A flicker of a rueful smile appeared on Calan's lips and quickly disappeared. '*She's* a fool.'

Cait squeezed his hand. 'And you can tell her you were right when she gets better.'

'You were playing us.' Calan threw another fist into the ash and sent up another cloud. 'And I let you.'

'I wasn't playing you, Calan.' She hesitated. The truth unveiled itself slowly. 'I was playing myself.' She'd told herself her little adventure was for her, but deep down, had it just been for Kenzie? 'I'm not anymore.'

'What changed?'

'Honestly?' Cait said. 'A hatter in Afren turned away Aggie's money.' She laughed, despite it all.

And miraculously, Calan did, too. 'That'll do it.'

'And I saw that big, beautiful Iffegan sun dial in the the Treasury,' — like the doo in her gilded cage — 'and I realised that's all Storran is, just another shiny artefact. Things that I grew up thinking were normal stopped making sense, and I wanted to know why. I wanted to learn.'

'And what did you learn?' Calan's eyes looked heavy with an unspoken plea.

Cait thought on it for a moment. The answer was as thick and true as the ash that coated the ground, their hands, their hair. It had been for a long time now. Even in Briddock, surrounded by champions of the status quo. She'd asked so many questions about the way of things, and she hadn't been satisfied with a single answer until she met Aggie. She knew in her bones now that she was Cait: a doctor's daughter, a citizen of Storran, a Separatist.

'That I'm one of you,' she said quietly.

It didn't solve their problems, and it didn't make things right, and Calan's disappointment showed in his eyes, but it was true. She was a Separatist. And she wasn't ashamed. 'I still have a lot of questions,' she continued, 'and I don't know what I want Storran to look like on the other side, but what you believe, it's hope. It's the promise of something different.' It was the sign that there were people willing to fix things. 'But the fighting needs to stop. That's why I gave Kenzie the crown.'

She looked away. 'I really thought I could get through to him. He ... He promised ...' Her eyes stung, and she told herself it was just the ghost of smoke in the air. When she blinked, the blurriness in her vision spilled down her cheeks in hot streaks. *I really thought he would listen to me.*

Calan was silent for a long time, and when Cait finally looked up, she found he was staring at her. In his eyes, a dim glint of understanding. A single crack in the steep wall. 'I was born in Iffega,' he said. 'My family fled the rebellion and came to the Five Realms when I was young.'

'Shadielaunds,' Cait breathed. Iffega was almost legendary to her. It was the place that was always in the paper, always fighting, always the place people fled from. It had been, for as long as she could remember.

'Our first homes were all in Afren, and when we were no longer welcome there, we moved to Storran. My parents wanted me to fit in like I never had in Afren. They gave me a new name. We stopped speaking Iffegan. When that wasn't enough, I took elocution lessons. We stopped celebrating Iffegan festivals. We stopped wearing our Iffegan clothes. Every time someone made a comment, we changed. I could write the book on what it means to be an upstanding citizen of the Five Realms. By the time I started school, no one would have guessed I'd ever lived anywhere other than right here.' He fell silent, then took a shaky breath. 'What I'm trying to say is, the violence back home took everything from me.' When he looked up at her again, his eyes gleamed with fresh tears. 'It breaks my heart to think Storran could go the same way.' He cleared his throat and added, 'So trust me, I want the fighting to stop more than anyone.'

They sat in silence for a long time, Cait clutching his hands, wishing she could see the boy he had been before Afren sunk its teeth into him. 'We won't let that happen to Storran,' Cait whispered. 'I promise.' For Aggie's sake, for Kenzie's sake. For every other child who had lost something in the name of freedom, and for everyone who had to change the way they spoke to fit in.

'I don't think we'll have to worry about it for long,' Calan sighed. He straightened his back, rubbing his hands across his face, seemingly uncaring that it stained his skin grey as the soot stuck to his cheeks. 'The Queen's Watch will overrun the Unnertoun soon enough, then they'll move onto whatever Separatist bases exist in Carse and Witteneuk. They'll send their troops to every corner to make sure separatism is stamped out. They'll come to Gowdstane eventually. Lister knows it. We're out of time. Even if it survived, the crown wouldn't do us any good now.'

'So, what now?' Cait asked.

Calan bit his lip and shrugged. Calan MacKenzie *shrugged*. He looked down as his hands found their way into the ash again, smoothing it out into a flat plain. He brushed forward and back; once, twice, a third time, a gentle wave smoothing the destruction in its path. Then his hand stopped, quivering over the patch he had just levelled. Something pointed and silver peeked out at them. Barely breathing, they glanced at each other, and back at the little fin poking out of the ash. Calan began to dig, gently at first, until he was frantically pulling ash, and wood, and cinder from the ground, leaving a frail silver circlet perched in the cavity of the hearth.

Only a barely surviving knot of silver on the headpiece hinted that the distorted crown before them had ever belonged to Anndras. The pewter antlers had dripped downwards into petrified grey waterfalls, and the circlet's intricate patterns had melted into a single band of metal, but even distorted and misshapen, it was the Antlered Crown. It was their crown. Calan lifted it in his hands, and for the first time since she'd met him, Cait watched him beam like the Iffegan sun.

Chapter 26

Queen of the Heather

None of it was fair. He had done everything he was told. He kept himself hidden away, he let Lister take the reins, and make his secret deals, and carry out his secret plots. He hadn't even asked to know what they were. But what good had Lister's scheming come to? His crown was gone, and the Fox of Thorterknock was fighting for her life, and Aidan could do nothing but stew in his resentment. He should have been the one to retrieve his crown. He should have been the martyr. He rested his chin on his knees inside one of the vacant canon embrasures on the castle's battery and watched as night settled over the mountains.

'I don't want to talk,' he called when he heard soft footsteps approaching behind him.

'That's why I brought wine,' came a voice as cheery as bells. Aidan's heart lifted. *Bess.*

He turned to find her picking her way towards him across the embrasure, one hand grasping a folded blanket, and the other clutching a bottle of wine. Her tight, black curls swirled around her head in the breeze, and she let out a squeal as her balance wavered and she wobbled in place. Aidan reached up to steady her, and she lowered herself down next to him.

'You don't make it easy, do you?' she said, tossing the blanket over the two of them once they were huddled close. 'Here.' She thrust the bottle into Aidan's hands and rifled around a deep pouch at the front of her dress. The bottle was covered in a layer of dust and the label had words on it he didn't understand, so Aidan assumed it was fancy. Bess produced two wooden cups. 'If my father asks, I bought that in town.'

Aidan raised his eyebrows as she took the bottle and blood-red wine glugged into his cup. 'Lister's cellar?'

Bess' eyes flicked up to him with a guilty glint as she passed him his cup and started filling her own. Aidan laughed. Bess shared her father's amber eyes, his broad nose, his clipped Thorterknock accent, but her smile was all her own. Even under the cold spotlight of the moon, her face carried a warm glow, as if the sun spent its night nestled beneath her russet skin. Elizabeth Burke was radiant.

'The Crone's quiet tonight,' she said. He hadn't realised until she said it that the eeriness of the night was caused by the absence of wind tearing through the Cronachs. Bess rested her head on Aidan's shoulder. 'Where have you been all day?'

'Just, about,' he said. On the battlements. In the east wing. Anywhere that people weren't.

Bess huffed a laugh and turned to look at him. '"Just, about"? You've been avoiding everyone.'

'Clearly not well enough,' Aidan said.

Bess grinned and rolled her eyes. 'That's because I know where to find you.' He laughed. He could see her citrine gaze peering at him out of the corner of his eye, but he kept his eyes anchored on the Cruin and her gaggle of lesser mountains. 'You've been speaking to Anndras, haven't you?' Bess said at last, and Aidan cringed. Sometimes the way she could see through him made *him* feel like a ghost. He gave a bashful nod. 'Still won't answer you?' she said.

'No.'

'Bastard.'

'Bess!'

She shrugged on a swig of wine. Shadielaunds, he loved her.

Before he could stop himself, Aidan glanced over his shoulder, and Bess echoed with a frown. Anndras was not there. Aidan hadn't seen him since the meeting in the library, when Lister had snubbed him like an irritating child. 'What if he's just in my heid?' Aidan whispered.

'He guides you,' Bess said, watching the wine swirl around her cup. 'Does it matter what form he takes?'

'But if he's not real, it's jist me against Lister and —'

'Ah, that's why you're in such a mood.'

Aidan sighed and looked up at the clouds gliding faintly across the night sky. 'The crown's gone, and he's taken that as a sign to just do nothing.' He spread his hands. 'What am I meant to do wi that? How am I supposed to be a king if ...' He sighed. 'It should've been me.'

'What should've?'

He looked down at his hands, clasped between his knees. 'The Fox shouldn't have got hurt. It was *my* crown. I should've been there. If someone had to die —'

'Aidan, no.'

'It's true! How am I supposed to be king if I just let people die off for me?'

'Don't.'

'How am I supposed to get their respect?'

'Aidan!' Aidan turned to look at her and found her staring, no humour or warmth in her eyes. She glared at him. 'You can't get respect from anyone if you're dead.'

He stilled, immediately regretting the remorse that had entered her eyes. He took her hand. 'You're right. I just …' he sighed and looked out over the mountains. 'I just feel so useless.'

Bess watched him silently and took a long sip from her cup. Her lips came away red. He longed to kiss them clean. 'You have plenty time for all that kingly stuff.' Her hand squeezed his. 'Your time will come.'

He watched her carefully, eyes flitting to her wine-stained smile. 'I hope so,' he said. There were so many ways he wanted to change things, but he could do none of them until his home was free.

'Be patient,' she said. She turned towards him, and the blanket slipped off her shoulder. He reached out to readjust it. 'Trust my father.'

He smoothed the blanket across her shoulder and slowly let his hand slide down her arm, the crook of her elbow, her waist. She leaned into it. He closed his eyes. 'I don't know if I can.'

'You're … frustrated, but he knows what he's doing. He's done it all his life.'

Aidan's chest ached with a stifled, desperate scream he felt he had been gulping down for years. He longed to speak to Anndras. He needed to know that he wasn't just a convenient tool for Lister Burke to use, just because the Àrdan legacy happened to run through his veins. Aidan drained his cup. 'I just wish he would let me *do somehin*.' He reached for the middle finger of his right hand where he wore his mother's wedding band. Bearing the Antlered Crown of Anndras' house, the family heirloom was his only earthly tether to the King. It was the only remaining sign that he ever had a mother. 'It's in ma blood.'

'It is,' Bess said firmly, squeezing his hand tight. Her frown ploughed deep furrows into her forehead. She shared that with her father, too. 'But remember, he's a politician.'

'And what am I? A bairn?' he snapped before he could stop himself.

'Well —'

'You sound jist like him.' Aidan placed his cup down harder than he meant to, and it teetered over the edge of the embrasure, splashing dregs across the stone and falling into the gardens below. Bess' eyes followed it. She said nothing, and Aidan's chest filled with hot, sickly guilt.

When he'd first arrived at Gowdstane as a boy of barely nine, Aidan had hated it. The orphanage had been dire, but in the lumpy food, and itchy mattresses, and coarse camaraderie, he found home. Then a strange man armed with tales of long-lost kings and promises penned in the pages of fairy tales had appeared, and suddenly home was gone. Lister had sold Aidan a glorious con: that he'd have admiration and power, that he'd be a freedom-bringer, the architect of a better world so that no one else would meet his mother's fate. But Gowdstane was a shell, full of nothing but draughty passageways and holey ceilings, and only Lister's withering frown for company. So, Aidan had done what the heroes in storybooks do when they found themselves trapped: he'd run.

Aidan had just escaped the castle when he'd encountered a man. His clothes were strange, and a crown made of antlers rested on his brow. Aidan had noted the phantom ring on his finger that matched the very same one on his. Sometimes, when he was lonely, he'd speak to it as though it were his mother. It never had her blithe advice. Without so much as a glance in his direction, the man had marched past Aidan and made his way up the road to the castle. Aidan didn't know where he had been, but it seemed the King had come home, and Aidan supposed the home of anyone wearing his mother's ring could be his home, too. So, Aidan had done what the chosen ones in storybooks do when they are beckoned: he'd followed.

Five years later, Gowdstane breathed once again. Separatists had from all corners of Storran, and money had filtered in from somewhere that only Lister knew. On the first day of May that year, the Fest of Hawthorne, they had lit the fires in the Great Hall and danced, and Lister, more generous than Aidan had ever seen, opened his secret wine cellar. It was there that Aidan first saw her: a pretty girl with a bow in her hair the colour of Enlighten purple. No, it was *royal* purple. When she looked his way and laughed, Aidan finally felt at home again.

They spent each secret rendezvous dreaming about a world beyond these castle walls. Bess, not cooped up like Aidan, had brought him stories about his subjects from across Storran when she travelled with her father. She'd kept him informed of the world outside Gowdstane so he could be the king his people needed. She'd spoken with him about Anndras. She'd conspired with him when they grew bored. Bess had chosen Aidan. But Bess hadn't chosen Anndras and all he brought with him.

He was stirred from his thoughts by the warm brush of skin against his hand as Bess entwined her fingers around his. 'I've watched my father deal with dozens of statesmen,' she said quietly. 'Trust me, Storran could not be luckier to have you.'

He smiled at her, then quickly remembered the news that had reached them that day. 'It doesn't matter anymore. The crown's gone, and Lister seems to think that's the only way to get people to follow me.'

'We'll find another way,' Bess said. 'My father won't stop until Storran's free.'

Aidan looked up at the Cruin and sighed. 'That's been the case since I got here. What's that? Seven, eight years now?' he fell back on his back and pushed his hands through his hair. 'You should've heard what the Separatists frae Thorterknock were saying the-day. They said the Lealists are closing in, we're on borrowed time.' A horrible thought occurred to him. 'What happens if they come here?'

'We'll fight back.'

'I don't want that though.'

'Me neither.'

Aidan puffed out a long, low sigh, and after a moment of silence, Bess grabbed his arm and dragged him into a sitting position. 'Come on, you. Enough of that. Between you and my father, there's only so much politics I can take.'

Aidan raised his eyebrows at her. 'Then you're in for a world of pain when I *am* king.'

Bess sighed dramatically and looked out at the hills. 'Maybe I'll take my chances with the mountains, after all.'

'And leave behind dancing and socialising? You could never.'

Bess gave him a playful nudge, then returned to her cup. Aidan watched the way she sat with her shoulders back, lifting the cup delicately, even huddled up here with him. Her profile glowed against the moonlight, shining like a painting of a noblewoman. Bess shouldn't be here. Her father already disapproved of her joining him on his visits to Gowdstane, and he'd disapprove even more if he found out about her secret meetings with Aidan. She didn't belong to the rugged, cold world of Gowdstane and secret Separatists. She belonged in a glistening ballroom, dancing with a wealthy diplomat or politician who could give her the peaceful life she deserved. Every story he'd read about long-lost kings were filled with strife. He was certain his reign would never be easy or safe, and that he'd never have the peace to be a better man than the one who had taken his mother from him.

'What?' she asked on a nervous laugh, hiding her face behind her cup. Aidan settled on it then: Bess being at his side was like keeping a fine champagne in a dusty cellar.

'I canna promise you peace, Bess,' he said.

Bess' eyes, previously shining, grew serious. Her mouth turned down. 'That's a weird thing to say.'

He lifted his hand to show Bess the ring on his finger. 'I'm always gonnae be an outcast. Nothing will ever be easy.'

Bess' eyes trained on the ring, and slowly, she lifted her hand to his and wrapped his fingers in hers. 'I never liked this ring,' she whispered.

'I'm serious.'

'So am I. Dead serious. Wherever this road takes you, wherever Anndras leads you, I'll be there. Whether we're royalty or outlaws, it's you and me.'

'Your father —'

'My father doesn't know everything.'

'You said —'

She hushed him, fixing him in her golden gaze. 'You will be a great king, Aidan. You've got plenty to learn, and my father will help you with that, but listen,' — she lifted his hand bearing the ring and held it up to his eyes — 'you're more important than he could ever be. You were born to free Storran. You were born to be its King, antlered crown or not.'

'You know, you'd make an outstanding statesman,' Aidan said.

Bess gave an exasperated shake of her head. 'Shut up, I'm being serious. I'm choosing this life.'

'You don't know what you're agreeing to.'

'I do,' Bess said. 'And I'll prove it to you. Come with me.'

'Wait.' He reached a hand up to her warm cheek and pressed his forehead to hers. As her eyes closed, he ran his hand down her arm, over her hand, brushing his fingers over her warm skin. She sighed. He brushed his lips against her cheek, then swiped the cup from her hand and downed its contents in one go.

'Aidan!' Bess shrieked, snatching the cup back and peering into it. 'You've finished the lot!'

'Dropped mine,' Aidan said with a grin, and then with a huff of laughter, she pulled him to his feet.

*

Bess' laugh rang in the night as she pulled him across the moorland just north of Gowdstane, almost within touching distance of the Cronachs. If they just kept running, they could disappear and be swallowed by the mountains. If they kept running some more, maybe they'd reach Witteneuk. Maybe no ghosts of kings could reach them there. Bess led him just short of the mountains. 'Why are we here?' Aidan asked.

Bess stooped, and Aidan saw then the patch of rare white heather clustered at their feet. She picked two sprigs, then stood.

'A promise,' she said, passing him one sprig of heather. 'That when all of this is over, I'll still be here. That I'll be everything to you, a soldier, a …' her voice faltered, and she blushed. 'A queen.'

Aidan felt his mouth fall open. 'What are you getting at?'

'I love you, Aidan.' Her full, wine-stained lips were taut and serious. Aidan watched her, and he saw it all unfold before him. Bess in a radiant wedding dress, Bess at the altar, Bess the glowing and gracious Queen of Storran. Every hero in every story had a destiny, and a person who was their reason for fighting. To him, Bess was both. Bess reached out and curled Aidan's fingers around the heather. 'It's you and me, and Anndras is just going to have to get used to that,' Bess said.

Aidan's laugh escaped as sputtered relief. He realised he hadn't seen the ghostly King since the meeting in the library. Aidan felt untethered, light, free from his scrutinising stare. 'I want that,' he said. 'But it's too much to ask. It's —'

'You're not asking me,' Bess said. 'I'm asking *you*.'

To commit to a future with her, whatever it looked like. To have her at his side, no matter what became of his destiny. 'Bess,' he breathed, and he slipped the sprig of heather into his breast pocket. 'How are you so perfect?'

Bess rolled her eyes. 'Stop it.'

He stepped forward, scooped her hands in his. Her breath kissed his skin. Her hair tickled his face. He grinned. 'You just made history. This moment is going to be in *books*. The beginning of Storran's greatest dynasty.' Yes. He wanted this. He wanted her humour to soften the blows. He wanted her steadiness in treacherous waters.

'On second thought,' Bess said, casting her eyes to the sky. 'My father probably wouldn't allow —'

Aidan grinned and Bess squealed as he swept her into a low dip. 'I'm more important than he could ever be, am I not?'

Bess watched him. Her gaze meandered across his face. Her cheeks flushed with the cold. Then she tilted her head, rolled her eyes, and smiled. 'You're unbelievable.'

He pulled her to her feet again and they stumbled with the force. Suddenly, her hair was in his face and her arms around his shoulders. He spun her, allowing the wine to rush to his head and tilt the ground beneath his feet. 'Your crown will be *twice* as bonnie as Queen Ana's,' Aidan said. 'No one will miss the Antlered Crown, not when Elizabeth, the Outlaw Queen steps in the room.'

'*Outlaw?*' Bess said. 'By then I'd hope we'd be very much within the law.' The sky swayed, the moor disappeared from under them, and suddenly they were sprawled side by side in the heather. Bess rolled on her side and rested her head on her hand. 'So, what will Anndras think of this?'

Aidan shook his head and grinned. 'Dinna ken. He's not here.'

'I suppose what he doesn't know won't hurt him.'

Bess reached over and brushed something out of the beard Aidan had been attempting to grow.

'I love you,' Aidan said.

'More than Anndras?'

'Well ...'

'You rotten —'

Her sentence died and gave way to a giggle as he pulled her in closer, and finally drank up the taste of her lips. This was home, with Storran's stars spinning high above him, and his Queen of Heather in his arms. No crown could ever compare. No destiny was as grand as this one. Something cracked in the foliage nearby, and they froze. Aidan's heart lurched, thoughts immediately turning to Lealists.

'Look,' Bess whispered, and Aidan followed her gaze to a short distance away where a magnificent stag picked its way through the heather.

'Wow,' Aidan breathed, and Bess shushed him. They lay very still, hardly daring to breathe as they watched the creature move, moonlight dancing against its fur, antlers dowsed silver like the crown that once was. Aidan could understand now why the ancient Storrians revered the Great Stag so much. The stag was the kingliest animal he had ever laid eyes on, a great deal more elegant and powerful looking than any Afrenian boar. He longed to touch the stag, to feel its warm breath on his hands and the power beneath its bones. He wanted to loop a rope around its neck and take it back to Gowdstane, where he could watch it forever.

In the distance, something crashed. A flock of birds took to the sky, and the stag lifted its head, sniffed the air, and bounded out of sight. He shook away thoughts of domestication. A stag shouldn't be chained.

*

Aidan gently closed the door to Bess' room behind him and made his way down darkened, breezy passageways. The walls swayed slightly, and his head was cushiony and warm. He grinned as he rebuilt the draughty castle in his mind. The gilding on the outside walls had weathered and flaked, revealing the cracked, yellow paint beneath. Soon, he would restore it to its former glory, and the whole castle would shine gold and be seen for miles around. He'd deck the passageways in tapestries depicting the greatest moments in Storran's history. He'd commission one especially for Bess, depicting her as a valiant queen. The roof in the Great Hall would be repaired so rain would no longer pool at the far side, and it would be there that he and Bess would entertain rulers and politicians from all over. There would be a band with pipes and drums, and there would be dances every night. Lister's wine cellar would never be locked again. Bess would like that. She loved to dance. Gowdstane would be a sparkling symbol of Storran's resurrection.

He was passing the library when the sound of muffled voices caused him to pause and peer through the door. He heard Lister's voice, speaking softly, like footsteps creaking on slats. Aidan listened.

'It's not what we were hoping for,' came Lister's voice.

'No, but it's better than nothing. In fact, I'd say it was better.' That was the voice of one of the newcomers, Calan, the one Lister had accused of melting the crown.

'What do you think Aidan will think?' A wispy voice, the girl with the white hair. Cait, she had said her name was.

'My concern isn't Aidan. It's the Council of Five and the Queen.'

Aidan stepped into the room. As the door creaked open, the three newcomers and Lister stared at him. Anndras was there, too, stood invisible at the back of the room, solemn as ever.

'Good evening ... Your Grace,' Cait croaked. She dipped into a shaky curtsy, and Jamie, the Talasaire, thumped her on the arm with a hiss. Aidan had never received a handshake, let alone a curtsy, and he bowed straight back.

'Aidan,' Lister said through pursed lips. 'Why are you here?'

Aidan panicked, immediately regretting entering the room. He ran the back of his hand across his mouth to get rid of any evidence of the wine. He hoped Lister couldn't tell he was tipsy and had just left his daughter's room. 'I couldn't sleep,' he said. Lister only grunted, then his eyes fell to the table in front of him where a bundle was sat. 'What's that?' Aidan asked, stepping forward. All eyes in the room flicked towards Lister, who, after a moment began to gently unwrap a lump of distorted metal. Aidan stared at the shape. 'What is it?'

'How is anyone else going to know what it is if he doesn't?' Jamie said. Lister silenced her with a hand.

Aidan peered harder at the shape. The metal was cast in a vague circle that was indented and skewed. Aidan's heart lurched as he looked up at Lister. 'This is it?' It looked like it had been in a furnace. Lister gave a curt nod. Aidan reached out a hand but stopped short of the pewter, afraid that his touch would turn it to dust. The Antlered Crown. Anndras' crown. *His* crown. The crown that would bolster his claim to Storran. 'It's ...' Aidan whispered.

'Ruined,' Lister said.

But Aidan shook his head. Even in its garbled state, it took his breath away. It was perfect. He felt a pull to it, like they had been waiting for each other. 'Beautiful,' he said.

'It's not what it used to be,' Calan said quickly, 'but, if anything, it's better now.'

'Mr MacKenzie was just about to explain exactly why that is the case,' Lister said.

Calan nodded feverishly and pushed his glasses up his nose. 'Yes. Well, it's a statement, you see.' His mouth curved into a faint smile. 'The whole point of the crown was its history. Its legacy. The power it holds over people and over the state. It's also a powerful story. There's something symbolic about a long-lost artefact coming home, right? Can you imagine the story we can tell alongside *this*?' he waved his arms at the crown. 'The crown that couldn't be destroyed. The crown that they tried to kill, but survived, and chose its wearer regardless. The Lealists have given us a symbol, and they may as well have wrapped it up with a bow!' When Aidan had first seen him, Calan had been like an arrow trembling on a bow that was far too heavy for its archer. His energy had made *Aidan* nervous. Now, with a conspiratorial glint in his eye, Calan seemed like a completely different person; an arrow that had struck decisively into its mark. He started to pace slowly on the other side of the table. His hands made peculiar shapes as he talked. Lister watched him with a vague look of bemusement. 'We show it to the people in the state it's in, and they'll be livid. That's a score against Afren.'

'You forget, MacKenzie,' Lister drawled, 'that it was widely reported in the press today that a certain Separatist melted the crown.'

Calan shook his head, and Aidan couldn't tell if he was thinking on the spot or if he had smoothed this all out earlier. 'Not if we tell them how we were coerced, and how one of our own sacrificed her connection to the Cy to save it.' He paused, then the bolt of a new idea seemed to spark his adrenaline, and he was pacing all over again. He talked so fast that Aidan struggled to keep up. 'And Talasaire are pacifists, they're respected. When they see one — *two*, including Tavis — support us —'

Jamie scowled at him. 'Whoah, I'm not a pawn, Calan.'

He peered at her over his glasses. 'What if we were to be sure you were a valiant and selfless pawn?'

Jamie looked conflicted for merely a fraction of a second then leaned back in her chair. 'I could be swayed.'

Calan was such a dramatic change of pace from Lister that he left Aidan winded. The young man's energy made him feel like he was stood on the front lines of Anndras' small army. All sorts of stupid, hopeful thoughts crossed his mind. Victory. Freedom. Glory.

'We're not ready,' Lister said. 'I'm in the process of negotiating a number of valuable alliances that won't be over the line for months.'

'We don't have that long,' Calan said. 'We threw the Lealists in that bothy, but they're not done with us. Plus, the press doesn't have a good memory. We need to make a move while the crown is on everyone's minds.' Lister narrowed his eyes, thinking. Calan looked to Aidan imploringly.

You are not a strategist. You are not a politician. But he *was* the heir to

Anndras Àrdan. He *was* the rightful King of Storran. The crown was like a poorly rendered image from a dream, twisted and uncanny, snatched straight from an upside-down world where nothing made sense. And yet, it was *his*. It was familiar. It called to him. 'I want to do it,' Aidan said.

'This isn't your decision to make, boy,' Lister said, and Aidan almost shut up and obeyed when in the corner, he noticed Anndras do something he had never done before. He smiled. That smile was his endorsement of Calan's plan. Aidan felt sure of it.

'I'm done doing nothing,' Aidan said. 'I'm ready to stop hiding.'

He thought Lister might scold him, but the politician's eyes slid to Calan. 'How do you envisage this working?'

Calan rubbed his hands together like he had been waiting for this. 'I propose a small but public coronation. We don't want to attract the wrong type of attention, but we want to make it clear that we're not hiding.'

Lister nodded. 'Providing the news doesn't reach Hart Hall, we have a big enough force to defend against any unhappy locals.' He studied the ceiling as he pondered. 'And we'll need a respectable individual to conduct the ceremony.'

'I've got an idea,' Calan said. 'Leave it with me.'

'I trust I can leave you to organise the pomp of the occasion,' Lister drawled.

'Yes,' Calan said on a determined nod. 'Once it's done, we notify the rest of the Five Realms that we've crowned Anndras' heir, and the implications that has for Storran's autonomy. Then while we wait for news, we can get started on sweeping south with Aidan, gathering support, and the like.'

Lister nodded thoughtfully.

Aidan's eyes narrowed. 'What news would we be waiting on?'

'Whether or not Afren considers your appointment lawful,' Lister said bluntly.

'It *is* lawful!' Aidan said. 'They wrote the laws!'

'We know that,' Calan said. '*They* know that, but it's just how things work.'

'But it's no their decision to make.'

Lister pinned him with his stare. 'Know your enemy, Aidan, or this will never work.'

Trust my father, Bess had said. Aidan bit down his frustration. 'What if they don't recognise it?'

Lister looked to Calan. Their conspiring with each other made Aidan a little sick. Who was this boy to come here and explain how to run his campaign? 'If that happens, the people's anger will be our biggest weapon. Separatist or not, many of them will feel betrayed that Afren have blocked this, despite it being in written law,' Calan said.

'Which brings us to another matter,' Lister said. He and Calan exchanged a glance, then looked at Aidan. Lister indicated that Calan should continue, and Calan sighed.

'For the people to feel angry enough to side with you, they need to have been betrayed by Afren. Undoubtedly so. If Afren rejects your claim, it needs to be because they've disregarded their own laws in order to keep Storran under their thumb ...' he trailed off.

'As opposed to ...' Aidan prompted.

'Well.' Calan cleared his throat, then loosed a long, slow breath through his nose. 'Doubts about your legitimacy, per se.'

The words took the breath right from Aidan's lungs. He laughed. 'There's none. I know where I came from.'

'I'm sure you do,' Calan said carefully. 'But if there's any doubt —'

Aidan looked at Lister. '*You* found me. Tell him I'm who you say I am.'

Lister's gaze hardened under the order. 'This isn't personal, Aidan. This is insurance.'

'We can't give the Lealists any reason to doubt who you are,' Calan said. 'Do you have anything that could prove your heritage?'

The way Calan phrased the question made him bristle, but Aidan ignored it, slid the ring from his finger, and pushed it across the table. 'Just this.' His mother's ring, the Àrdan ring, had come from her father, who received it from his grandmother. The name Àrdan had been lost to family names like *Smith* and *Roberts,* but his blood was still Àrdan. His blood was the same that flowed through his mother's veins and every family member before her, until Anndras himself. The Lealists could take his crown, but they could not take his heritage.

'Last question,' Calan said, and he directed this one at Lister. 'Are there any documents in this castle that might have belonged to Anndras?'

Lister shook his head. 'No. We audited the contents of the castle when we arrived. The only items of historical significance are sealed in the crypts. Why?'

Calan's eyes slid sideways to Cait, who was worrying a strand of her white hair. She cleared her throat and placed the tips of her fingers down on the table. 'Yes, well. You're familiar with the *Ballad of Anndras and Cathal?*' she said. Aidan nodded, and Cait went on to tell him about her father, a scholar of the text who was working with the Lealists, and the line he believed could refer to a document that saw Anndras sign Storran away to the people.

'It's just one line,' Aidan said. 'You don't really think the Lealists will take that seriously?'

'Again, Aidan, *know your enemy,*' Calan said. 'We can't take anything for granted.' Lister cast him a look that might have resembled pride. Aidan felt sick.

The pair of them started to talk between themselves about the tombs and crypts far beneath Gowdstane, a place that Aidan hadn't been able to bring himself to visit. He'd tried once, but the spirit of Anndras seemed to grow too strong there, suffocating him. He looked across the room at the King who watched the crown with his chin lifted, his hand steady on his sword.

So, what will Anndras think of this? Bess had asked him.

I don't know. He's not here.

Anndras was here now, and though the King never spoke, Aidan knew how he felt. The feeling echoed in his bones. A distant memory, not his, but borrowed: the blazing morning sun that ruddied the battlefield; hundreds of eyes lifted to him in hope. He owed this crown to Anndras' bloodline.

Lister's voice broke through his thoughts. 'We'll begin preparations for a coronation, and hope this doesn't lead to civil war.'

War. Anndras had been a war leader. Sometimes Aidan forgot that. The ghost's tunic was marred with phantom bloodstains that showed the battle had been gruesome.

I'll be everything to you.

A soldier.

A queen.

Aidan couldn't picture Bess dressed for war. He couldn't see her with a rifle in her hand. 'Wait,' Aidan said, and all eyes in the room fell on him. He realised he hadn't known what to say, only that everything was moving so fast, and he needed to catch his breath.

'Speak, boy,' Lister said.

He looked back at Anndras. This is what he'd been waiting for, what he'd been begging Lister for. Action. A beginning to his tale.

He breathed. 'Okay. Let's do it.'

Lister gave him a fleeting look of approval, and out of the corner of his eye, Aidan saw Anndras' smile widen.

Chapter 27

The Second King of Storran

They set a date to inaugurate the Second King of Storran three days after the crown had been found. It was on that day the castle's physician told Cait that Aggie's health had taken a sharp decline. It was unlikely she would ever see King Aidan with her own eyes. Cait chose not to believe it. She knew it was silly, as her parents had raised her to face the truth head on, but those painful diagnoses had only ever been received by patients whose names and medical histories were the most intimate things she knew about them.

It seemed that every resident of Gowdstane had gathered for the event. The previous night, Cait asked Calan how many people he thought lived in the castle, and his estimate had been around one hundred. In reality, there must have been at least double that crammed into the Great Hall that morning. When the huge doors swung open, a May breeze snatched the hat from Cait's head. She spun to catch it and found herself face to face with a young girl with soft, black curls and a pretty, lilac dress.

'This is yours,' she said, passing the hat back to Cait. Cait thanked her as she placed it on her head. The girl smiled.

Cait thanked the girl with a grateful bob of the head. 'I like your dress.'

The girl laughed and swirled her skirts from side to side. 'Thank you.'

'I'm Cait, by the way.'

The girl leaned in with a canny grin on her lips and whispered, 'And I'm Storran's future Queen.' She was there and then gone, like a snowdrop, or the laughter of a fairy.

'Storran's future Queen?' Cait echoed.

'Lister's daughter, Elizabeth,' Calan said, but he wasn't paying attention. He gazed down the road that wound from the castle to the gatehouse, and out into the town below. A lumbering beast prowled at Gowdstane's threshold, its skin squirming and shifting and scraping.

'That's a lot of people,' Jamie said, and Cait realised it was not a beast at all, but a mob. The residents of Clackhatton looked on silently as the Separatists traipsed from the safety of the castle down to the gatehouse, and Cait tried her best to keep the sound of the rifle shot that had scattered the crowd in Thorterknock from her mind.

'How did they know?' Jamie said as they walked towards the crowd.

'Lister would have tactfully leaked it,' Calan said. 'We need an audience.'

'One this big?'

At some point, Elsie appeared at Calan's shoulder. Cait thought she saw some trepidation in the girl's bright eyes. 'How close are we going to get to them?'

'It's going to get quite cosy,' Calan said.

At the gates that marked the edge of Gowdstane's refuge, the Separatists paused their steady march. They eyed the spectators cautiously, and the spectators considered them in return. Cait could see their faces now, some craning their necks in neutral curiosity, and others glowering. As the Separatists passed, the crowd parted and flanked the road. If Cait reached out, she could touch them. They could touch her. They could rush the Separatists in a hungry throng and devour them in moments if they wanted to. Somewhere, a baby cried. The Separatists moved silently through the onlookers until they climbed a hill at the edge of the town. They assembled atop their grassy plinth for all to see. If Gowdstane's inhabitants had once been a secret, they certainly weren't anymore. Then the drumming started: two spurts of rattling beats accompanied by a strong baseline somewhere in the distance. The wheeze of a drone tugged the crowd's attention away from the Separatists gathered on the knoll, to the short procession advancing down the path from the castle.

Three days ago, Jamie had scanned through Calan's plan and snorted. 'Pipes and drums? Are you for real?'

Calan had only shrugged. 'It's the King of Storran's coronation. Lister wanted pomp.'

'Does anyone even play?' she'd asked.

Calan had cast her an uncharacteristically wry look across the desk. 'I thought the Talasaire were musicians. Are you telling me you didn't bring your pipes?'

Jamie had just rolled her eyes at him.

Some of the Separatists at Gowdstane did play, it turned out, and they formed a tiny band of two pipers and three drummers. The rattle and drone of their rehearsals had buzzed through the castle for three days straight, to the point where Cait thought she was going to lose her mind.

The small pipe band processed down to the grass knoll, followed by a handful of Separatists bearing mismatched rifles. Their only sign of uniformity was a navy sash strung from shoulder to hip, pressed tight against their hearts.

A day into preparations, Calan had tracked Cait down with a bundle of navy fabric and spools of gold thread.

'Ever stitched up a wound?' he had asked.

'Once,' Cait had admitted, 'with minimal success.'

Calan had cast the materials in front of her. 'Good enough. We need sashes. Enlist whoever you need.'

So, Cait had busied herself sewing. Elsie and Jamie had joined her, and Elsie had spent the time speculating about the coronation, and Aidan, and what kind of king he'd be. Cait hadn't minded her chatter, sinking comfortably into the meditation of sewing and enjoying the feeling of being useful. Calan had become something of a drill sergeant, and Cait had struggled to keep thoughts of Aggie far away, imagining how she would have reacted to him, and how it would be a glimpse into their time as schoolchildren. *She should be here.* Aidan practicing his vows under Lister's watchful gaze, the sound of pipes wafting through the halls, the energy, and chatter, and excitement that came with standing on the threshold of history. *She'd love this.*

Behind the pipes and riflemen advancing towards the knoll came a figure that Cait was delighted to see.

'*He's* here?' Jamie whispered.

'He arrived this morning,' Calan said with a knowing smile.

'No one thought t' tell me?'

The utility belt and earthy travelling clothes Tavis had worn on the trip into Eadwick were gone, replaced by a deep emerald robe adorned by swirling knotwork at the hems. He clasped his hands somewhere within his sleeves, the bottoms of which brushed the floor. His sombre expression flickered briefly into a smile when he caught sight of them in the crowd.

The only person that hadn't traipsed down the road from the castle, Cait realised, was Lister and his daughter. When she looked about, she caught sight of them at the other side of the knoll, packed discreetly among the other Separatists. *Sneaky,* she thought, but there wasn't time to dwell on it. Someone else was coming down the road. A murmur rushed through the crowds of Separatists and civilians alike. Elsie raised herself onto her tiptoes and Cait found her view obscured by the backs of a hundred hungry heads.

'Look at him!' someone gasped to Cait's right.

'Jings ...' breathed someone behind her.

'That's a statement and a half ...'

Elsie's hand lashed out and clutched Cait's sleeve. 'Shadielaunds,' she breathed, enraptured by what she saw. 'He's perfect.'

The whispers surrounded her, and Cait didn't understand what they were talking about until Aidan climbed the hill towards them.

Two weeks before Cait's eighteenth birthday, she had been helping her mother tidy the surgery. She was wrapping bandages into neat coils when her mother said, 'We'll need to get you a hoop for your skirts. We can have Maggie down the road put some boning in your clothes, too.'

'Do I have to?' Cait had asked, pulling the roll of bandage in her hand tighter with a firm *snap*. 'No one else does.'

'Well, I do. And your father wears his suits. And there are plenty of girls your age who dress well.'

Cait's fingers had fumbled and the bandage had slipped, the whole thing unfurling across the floor. 'What's wrong with how I dress?'

Her mother had cast her a well-meaning glance across the room from where she was changing the sheets on the patient bed. 'We're a respectable family. We should present ourselves that way.'

It seemed the mark of a proper and productive member of society lay in a sharp silhouette: tailored trousers with crisp edges, neutral-toned jackets with cleanly cut shoulders, gowns that cinched in all the right places. They no longer lived in a society where they needed to run, or hunt, or toil, so why should they dress like they had to?

'Oh my, you'll get one of those smart uniforms, won't you?' Cait's mother had gushed when Kenzie told them he'd been recruited in the city. 'You'll have to get a hoop now, Cait. You can't be looking like a scruff next to our Kenzie.' From slender boots, to smart jackets, wasn't the Queen's Watch the epitome of the ideal citizen? Whoever had chosen Aidan's outfit for his coronation had flouted each and every one of these apparent rules.

A kilt, woven in a bold pattern that Cait had only ever seen on picnic blankets and some Birkenweave scarves, hung about his knees. A heavy length of the same fabric slung from the kilt, across his chest, and draped elegantly over his shoulders like a pair of hefty, folded wings. Cait had heard people mock the style before, comparing it to a lady's skirt, but it made Aidan look formidable and strong. As he moved, the fabric shifted and breathed. The hem swished at his knees with each step. The cloth added mass to his body at his shoulders, giving the impression that the slender boy beneath was strapping and battle-hardened. The fabric's whites and golds and blues criss-crossed, as if Storran's flag had been cut into ribbons and stitched back together. Gazes trailed him as he went. This was the dress of an ancient song. It belonged to a time before the Five Realms and before Afren. It was not appropriate for civilised company, let alone a king.

When Aidan reached the front of the crowd, Tavis spread a flag bearing the crowned stag over the morning dew and signalled for Aidan to kneel upon it with a quiet word and pat on his shoulder. When Aidan took a single knee, his plaid garb fell in elegant drapes about his legs.

'Cauld knees?' a mocking voice piped up from the gathered onlookers. A chuckle followed.

Aidan craned his neck to investigate the crowd, but Tavis muttered something to him, and he cast his eyes determinedly up at the Talasaire's face. With a flurry of green sleeves, Tavis spread his arms. His entire demeanour changed, as though he had dropped a curtain and assumed an act. Where usually his long limbs seemed to hang from his shoulders, he now stood as tall and still as an oak.

'People of Storran!' he cried. Separatist or townfolk, every eye trained on him. Cait wondered if he could use the Cy to carry his words lightly through the air to each person, until she remembered he no longer had access to those abilities. 'I join you today from Prilwyn, Land of the First Groves. Today, we will witness an heir reclaim his ancient legacy. Today,' he paused and lowered his arms, considering the crowd. 'We will crown a king.' Cait held her breath while she waited for the heckling to begin. A cough from the crowd made her jump. Tavis continued, 'To proclaim a king is to claim Storran's autonomy by the laws laid out in the Council of Five.' He indicated Aidan with a sweeping arm. 'Before us sits the heir to the Àrdan legacy, once thought to have ended. We ask now that Storran's Great Stag claims the inheritor of his power, with the bestowing of his sacred and ancient antlers.'

A sharp murmur sliced through the crowd as undoubtedly the people questioned how they would do that when the Separatists had destroyed those ancient antlers. Lister stepped forward and passed Tavis a bundle wrapped in a fabric identical to Aidan's garb.

'I have here an artefact that was destroyed ...' Tavis called, lifting the bundle high. He swiped the covering away, and when it fell away and revealed the melted crown for all to see, the crowd gasped. '... And born anew.'

Silence. And then a scoff from somewhere in the crowd. 'Melt it doon and finish the joab!' A mutter of vague agreement passed through the crowd, but no shouts. No gunshots. Not yet.

Ignoring the heckler, Tavis raised a hand to Aidan. 'The Great Stag bestowed these antlers to King Anndras in exchange for a promise. That promise was that he'd serve the people of Storran and lead them to freedom. In accepting these antlers, you agree to uphold that promise.'

'Ye can shove those antlers up yer —'

Tavis fixed Aidan with a firm, yet reassuring, look that seemed to say *ignore them, lad*, and Aidan nodded quickly. 'I will.'

'Do you vow to serve none other than the people of this land?'

'I do.'

Aidan's voice was so quiet that Cait wasn't sure even the Separatists could hear his promises.

Another voice rose up. 'We dinna want yer outlaw king!'

'Pretender!' Another shouted.

'Pretender! Pretender!' One by one, other voices joined the chorus, until Tavis' words and Aidan's vows were drowned by the chant. 'Pretender! Pretender! Pretender!' As the chant grew to an unintelligible uproar, the onlookers inched forward, some with raised voices, others with raised fists. Cait seized Calan's sleeve as the Separatists shied from the frothing shoreline of the crowd.

'They need to get a move on and stick that thing on his head,' Jamie hissed.

Calan shook his head. 'If we can't even get the people of Clackhatton on board, we're stuffed.'

It looked like they wouldn't even get as far as crowning Aidan, as the crowd grew rapidly more agitated, and the Separatists' grips tightened on their rifles, eyes darting between each other, and Lister. Then slowly, Aidan rose to his feet. Tavis tried to keep him down with a hand on his shoulder, but Aidan shook his head and stepped past him. On the opposite side of the knoll, Lister's eyes narrowed.

'Stop!' Aidan cried, but his voice was carried away by the clamour. 'Listen to me!' He shouted louder. 'Oi!' The crowd paid no heed until the piper blew one sharp note that jolted them into a brittle silence. 'I ... uh ... I'm Aidan,' Aidan said, looking around at the crowd below. The drapes of plaid over his shoulders swelled with his heavy breaths. Somewhere, someone snickered. Aidan's cheeks reddened and his jaw clenched. 'I just thought, kneeling there,' he gestured back at the flag on the grass. 'I wanted to say something.'

Another mumble made its way through the crowd, this time with the trappings of ridicule, and Cait winced. She saw Aidan how the residents of Clackhatton saw him: a red-cheeked boy draped in old-fashioned clothes who thought himself their King. He was no Anndras. He didn't look like he could challenge Queen Ana and her Council of Five to cards, let alone war. This would be laughable back in Briddock, too.

'I'm gonnae —' He cleared his throat. '*Going* to be honest,' Aidan said.

'That's a first from you lot!' piped up a voice from the crowd.

Aidan blinked at him. 'If you've got questions, I'll answer them.' Lister took a step forward, but his daughter snatched his wrist.

'If you give two shites about Storran, why'd you do that to its crown?' Aidan opened his mouth and shut it again. 'Well —'

'Dinna, he'll just deny it,' another voice called.

'It's true,' Aidan said. 'I mean,' he signalled the Separatists gathered on the knoll. 'They did take the crown from the Treasury.' Then he added quickly, 'On my behalf.'

'He admits it!' the initial heckler called. 'They're guilty as owt!' A new chant broke across the morning. *Guilty. Guilty. Guilty.*

Cait thought Aidan might bolt. He glanced, clearly panic-stricken, at Lister, but then his eyes seemed to settle on something next to Lister that Cait couldn't see. Assuredness fell over him. He raised his chin and turned back to the crowd. 'You can chant when I'm done talking!' He shouted, and the crowd settled again. 'The Queen's Watch gave us an ultimatum, that either we melted the crown, or they executed one of our own. We complied and they shot anyway.'

A barely audible *tut* carried through the crowd and Cait wondered if they'd have the same reaction if they knew it was the Fox of Thorterknock who had been felled. There was silence, followed by a shout of, 'We're supposed to bow to a thief?'

Aidan scoffed. 'Stealing means something doesn't belong to you.' He shook his head and waved his hands. 'But that's not what I wanted to talk about. I know that an estate was built recently on local land that was set aside for a new school, aye? Just down the road?' An affirmative, and disgruntled, murmur moved through the crowd.

Calan made a sound at the back of his throat. 'He's done his homework.'

'And no one asked you about it?' Aidan continued. More affirmative noises from the crowd. 'Right. That's what I thought. And that decision came from the Council of Five?' More nodding. More shifting. 'See, so that's unfair, cause no one on the Council of Five actually lives here. *That's* stealing.'

At Cait's side, Calan made an unnerving sound that caused her to turn. He was *giggling*. 'Look,' he said, pointing to the opposite side of the knoll. 'Lister's absolutely spitting.' Lister, with his head held high and vacant frown, didn't look livid, but Cait got the sense that below those still waters was a creature poised to drag Aidan down and destroy even the memory of him.

'I dinna — *don't* ... want to steal from you,' Aidan continued. 'Especially not with a decision over who should lead you.' Aidan paused and took a breath. 'They say the crown chooses the worthy ruler.' He pointed to the crown, still weighed in Tavis' hands. 'But I won't put that crown on my head unless you say I can. It's Storran's choice. It's Clackhatton's choice.'

At the Fest of Hawthorne five years earlier, a girl from Cait's village had been among the choices for Queen of the May, but Briddock was small, and when the public had cast their votes it was a lass from the bigger, neighbouring town of Stob Head that won the crown of blossoms for her pretty head.

Election day, three years ago. Cait had asked Kenzie if it annoyed him that the candidate he voted for never became Chancellor of the Five Realms. He had shrugged and said, 'That's democracy, little dove.'

Around the knoll, silence fell. Cait watched the crowd as they contended with a choice they'd never had to make before. Ripples formed through the crowd where first a couple, then a dozen people turned to leave. Many who didn't crossed their arms and shook their heads. Others looked about at their neighbours. Then, from the centre of the crowd, a shout. Cait flinched at first, expecting another heckle, then realised the word formed had been *Aye!*

'The laddie's speaking sense!' the man shouted. 'Have a bash, son. Show us what you've got.'

Deathly silence followed. Cait saw the shapes of figures leaning away from the source of the shout. Then someone clapped. Once. Twice. Slowly, they built into a strong and decisive pulse. It caught slowly, hesitant hands joining in, one by one, until those who clapped outnumbered those who didn't. Something long thought to be dead stirred on that knoll in the shadow of Gowdstane's ancient walls. To those gathered there, Aidan was no longer a stranger put before them by a group of renegades, he was no longer an outlaw and a pretender, but myth breathed fully and vividly to life. As Cait watched him, her golden-haired image of Anndras changed, and she wondered if the other spectators were rewriting their own folklore to make way for him, too. Aidan was one of them. Aidan was hope. Aidan was their choice.

'King Aidan!' someone cried, and the Separatist drums struck up along with the applause, thunderous beneath the grey sky. Cait hoped that down in the surgery, Aggie could hear them. She hoped the drums shook her bed and rattled the windowpane, and cheers for King Aidan roused her from her sickness, ready to fight again.

'Lealtie Ayebidin!' Aidan cried, and the Separatist phrase was hollered right back from the mouths of regular folk.

Aidan knelt back before Tavis, and when silence fell, Tavis laid a hand upon Aidan's head and said, 'By the ancient laws laid by the Five Realms, and the sacred neutrality of the Talasaire Groves,' — Jamie snorted at that — 'I declare thee, Aidan of the Ancient House of Àrdan, Second King of Storran.' Tavis lowered the crown onto Aidan's head, and with his head bowed, Aidan rose as orphan boy no longer, but anointed member of the House of Àrdan, and King of Storran. The melted pewter antlers streamed past the King's temples and down past his cheek bones. Frozen droplets of pewter formed jewels along his brow. Somehow, it looked even more majestic sat upon his head than when it had been whole.

The applause was slow to come, as if Storran had been waiting for this moment for so long, and now that it was here, it did not know how to react. Then the sun shattered through the clouds, and when one soul cheered, the rest followed close behind. The air trembled with the first breaths of a nation reborn as the people of Storran found their voices once more. Standing above them, the golden light illuminated Aidan's outline, like

Anndras when he hurtled towards the Afren forces all those many years ago. At Cait's side, tears streamed down Elsie's face as though she'd been waiting for this moment all her short life. Cait joined the jubilant cries and felt the squeeze of pride in her chest. She might also have felt relieved, or energised, or hopeful for what was to come, but her past experience had taught her well. She steeled herself for what lay ahead, for she knew that walking out of a cage was never as easy as it appeared.

Chapter 28

Sheep's Clothing

The fires in the Great Hall were lit that night, and the door to Lister's wine cellar was flung open. Gowdstane was no longer a shivering secret, but a great stag high upon the mountains, bellowing to the moon. *At long last, I am alive.*

Cait's cup was never empty. Her feet ached as she danced reel, after reel, to the strains of fiddles and pipes. The music jigged around the hall in repetitive, light-footed beats that had everyone tapping their toes and clapping their hands. Tables were littered with bottles, and the air was musky with the taste of a good night. The revery took Cait's mind off Aggie. The King himself, however, was mysteriously absent from the celebrations, as was Lister Burke.

'How much of a rollicking do you think he's getting?' Jamie said, her cup swinging in the air as her elbow rested on the table. 'You just know Lister's right fuming he went off-script.'

Calan sipped his whisky, grimaced, then poured a glug of water into it. 'The roof hasn't come down.'

'Yet,' Jamie said.

Calan sighed. 'Lister should be praising him. He turned around an entire village. It's more than anyone's done in years.'

Cait glanced around the hall and spotted Elizabeth moving across the room towards them. Her purple skirts billowed about her and somehow, she had acquired a ring of flowers in her hair. She breezed over to them and pulled out the empty chair beside Cait — the chair that should have been Aggie's — and sat down.

'How's the wine?' she asked, reaching for a jug in the centre of the table. The ring of flowers on her head slipped as she moved.

'Where did that come from?' Jamie said, nodding at the crown on Elizabeth's head as she sat down.

Elizabeth filled her cup and rolled her eyes, but behind her exasperated look was a fond glow. 'Aidan was worried I'd feel left out.'

'I didn't realise we were sat in the presence of the Queen of Storran,' Jamie said on a wink.

Elizabeth laughed. 'Please, I'm already losing petals.' As if to prove a point, she brushed one from her shoulder, and it twirled elegantly to the floor where it was swept into the dancing. 'Alas, I'm only Queen of the May.'

'You're Elizabeth Burke?' Cait asked.

Bess' eyes widened behind her raised cup. 'Please, call me Bess. I'm Aidan's betrothed.'

Jamie coughed. '*Betrothed?* You're, like, twelve.'

'Seventeen, actually,' Bess said, then she put her cup down and sat forward. 'I'm older than Aidan though. I'll be eighteen in November, and he doesn't turn eighteen until January. He sometimes *acts* twelve but ...' Cait watched the hazy joy across Bess' face as she spoke and Cait wondered if she had ever looked that way when she talked about Kenzie. Perhaps when she, too, was seventeen, when he was her prince and Briddock was their kingdom.

Something by the door at the end of the room stole Bess' attention and Cait followed her gaze to where Aidan was entering the Great Hall. Lister appeared behind him, and his glower flicked instantly into a paper-thin smile as eyes fell upon him.

'How did it go?' Bess asked Aidan when he reached their table.

'Eh,' Aidan shrugged as he took her hands and kissed her. 'Let's dance!' He dragged her off to the dance floor where a vigorous reel was underway. Cait's heart gave a jealous pang, and she glugged down a swig of wine.

'Come on,' Elsie said, pulling Cait to her feet. 'Let's dance, too.'

As night inched on, the chatter and the pipes battled for volume, and dancing grew languid as alcohol seeped into the bloodstream. Cait was about to retreat to bed to rest her feet and soothe her throat when she was burled mid-reel into Aidan as her next dance partner.

'And where are you aff tae?' he asked as she made to move off.

'To bed,' she laughed. 'I'm shattered.'

Aidan's face opened like a boy begging for sweets. 'Just to the end of this dance.' Cait hesitated. She worried that if she stayed, she would never go to bed, much like the stories about people who danced under fairy hills until the world they knew had long gone. Aidan gave her a jab in the ribs. 'You can't turn down a royal invitation.'

Cait rolled her eyes but laughed and took Aidan's hands. He pranced greenly ahead of the music and mixed up the steps on more than one occasion.

'You're not good at this,' Cait said as he tried to spin her instead of stepping sideways and clapping.

'Treason,' Aidan laughed. 'Immediate death.' He then proceeded to trip up on Cait's feet.

'Any chance I can see the crypts at some point?' Cait asked.

'That's a cheery thought for a party,' Aidan said as he spun her to the music once, twice, three times.

'I need to see if —'

'That document, I know.'

Cait grasped the front of her skirt as they faced each other and jigged on the spot for two beats. 'Just tell me where to go,' she said breathlessly.

Aidan wiped a hand along his sweating brow as the strings finally thrummed to a stop. He glanced thoughtfully over his shoulder at Lister, and then back at Cait. He looked up at the band who were gulping down cups of water. 'Band's taking a break. Let's go now.'

*

They left the warmth of the Great Hall and crossed the castle's central courtyard to a little building Cait quickly realised was a chapel. The inside was dust-coated, the stained glass dulled, and the once-glimmering golden adornments faded from time. The altar was guarded by the statue of a long-forgotten god who gazed sadly through petrified, sullen eyes at the emptiness that was once her church. They slipped behind her, and Aidan pulled open a little wooden door and struck up a lamp. As they descended the slippery steps into the underbelly of Gowdstane, Cait clutched the damp wall to keep her footing. The stairs seemed to descend into nothingness. Occasionally, an opening branched off on their left or right, no brighter than the path in front of them, but Aidan kept up his steady descent. She didn't need to see with her own eyes to know what the openings housed. They were like the dark little doors into the buried houses of the Unnertoun, but she knew that none of these openings housed anyone living.

Cait glanced over her shoulder as the weak light from the wooden door dipped behind a corner. 'We don't need to do this right now,' Cait said. 'We can wait until morning.' A strange noise from one of the supposedly empty rooms made her jump. 'Maybe bring Calan and Jamie.'

'I need tae see it,' Aidan said.

'Shouldn't you be dancing with your Queen of the May?' Cait said. She only realised her voice had twisted cruelly when Aidan cast her a strange look over his shoulder. She told herself she wasn't jealous of him, but she knew she was lying. She pined for something like he and Bess had. She'd had it once, but not for a long time.

'The family trees of kings are inscribed on plenty of their tombs,' Aidan said without looking around. 'It's been done for hunners — sorry, *hundreds* of years. I'm trying to speak more proper. For, y'know, respect and aw that. *All* that.'

Eventually, Aidan veered left into one of the dark chambers, and Cait gulped in a lungful of stale underground air before following him. The light from his lamp caught dully on a vaulted ceiling only a few feet above their heads. Behind them was the gloomy corridor they had come from; before them, an enormous stone door.

'This is it,' Aidan whispered, looking up at the door. 'Anndras is buried behind this door.'

Slowly, Cait walked past him and ran her fingers across the stone's cool surface. Aidan had been right, there were engravings on the stone, but no names. Instead, Anndras' story was immortalised in twisting knotwork and abstract figures: his first encounter with Cathal; his flight north from Afren's court; meeting Cathal at Oathlaw; the encampment at Gowdstane; Cathal's severed head; the dawn victory that freed them. It ended at the far end of the door with a distressed council of noblemen laying the heirless King to rest, a fearsome Afrenian boar lurking on their periphery.

'What does it say?' Aidan said.

'It's Anndras' story,' Cait said. 'Everything from the tale. Maybe a few extra bits that were left out.' When she looked back at Aidan, he wasn't looking back at her. His gaze stared off into a dark corner beside the door. 'Come and see this,' Cait said, and it stirred him from whatever daze he had been in. Slowly, he approached the door and traced a finger along the figure of Anndras lifting the crown to his head.

'They're not here, are they?' he said. Cait knew that he meant the names of his forefathers, the proof of his lineage, the name of his mother, set in stone.

'Just Anndras,' Cait said. She glanced at the ring on Aidan's finger. Could a simple band of gold really prove that king's blood ran through his veins? Could an heirloom really stand against the will of Afren? He may have received it from his mother, who may have received it from her father, and so on, but somewhere down that line, would it be so unrealistic that a farmer found it in his field and turned it into his own family's folklore?

'I'm going to put her name here,' Aidan said suddenly. His hand was still pressed against Anndras. 'She deserves to be remembered as a queen.'

'What was she like?'

'Fierce,' Aidan laughed. 'A battle-axe of a woman. You wouldn't want tae get on the wrong side of her. I certainly didn't.'

'And your father?'

'He was a brute. Took my mither from me.'

Cait's blood turned cold. 'Shadielaunds.'

'I think she knew. She dropped me at the orphanage the night before it happened.'

Cait stilled. 'I'm sorry.' She wished there could be justice for him and his mother. She wished her words were better.

Aidan traced a finger across the tomb and spoke quietly, though the stone amplified his voice all around. 'I can't help but wonder if things would be different if we weren't hungry all the time.' He turned to face her, and Cait saw the cold, hard determination of the ruler she had imagined. She saw a better future written across his face. 'When we take Storran back, no one will be hungry. No one will have to suffer like my mother did.'

Cait thought back to the writhing little waiting room in Thorterknock. How different could the world be if nobody wanted for anything? Aidan was not the image of Anndras that she would have painted, with his dark hair and deep brown eyes, but asking him to look the double of a relative that lived hundreds of years ago was a tall order. Descendant of Anndras or not, he cared for Storran, and that was all that mattered. And then there was that look again. He glanced over Cait's shoulder to the corner. His face paled.

'What is it?' Cait turned to look behind her. The corner was empty.

'Can you see him?' Aidan asked. 'He's different ... his sword ...' The sound of footsteps echoing down the passage startled him, and he turned enquiringly to Cait. 'Your friends?' he said.

Cait shook her head. She frowned. There was something about the pounding feet that gave her pause. She squeezed her eyes closed, listening, dipping beneath the echo until she heard it: a delicate jangle of chains. Her eyes flew open. 'Kenzie.'

'What?' She seized Aidan's wrist and dragged him out of Anndras' tomb. 'What's happening?' he asked. Cait hushed him.

They ran blindly into the darkness, deeper, and deeper into the crypts, putting as much distance between them and that mocking jingle as possible. They ran straight into a dead end, and when the glimmer of lamplight sniffed at their heels, she dragged Aidan into the tomb of a soul whose name she would never know.

'What's going on?' Aidan asked as she extinguished the lamp.

Why were they here? How many were there? What had happened to the others in the Great Hall? She hunted for impossible answers, but Cait had the sickening sense that Kenzie was here looking for her, and he'd blustered his way through the rest of the castle and its inhabitants to get to her.

'Cait.' Hands on her shoulders. Aidan whispering in the dark. Cait fought to catch her breath. 'Talk to me.'

'It's the Watch,' Cait whispered.

Through the dark, she saw his face fall. His hands dropped from her shoulders. 'You're joking.'

'No,' she whispered. Her hands trembled. He was here for her. He was sniffing her out.

'What? Why?'

Cait opened her mouth to tell him that she didn't know when voices reached her through the dark and her breath caught in her throat.

'Take everything,' Kenzie's voice said, echoing down the passageway. 'It could all be useful to Hardie.'

Hardie. Cait's heart lifted ever so slightly. It meant her father was still working with Kenzie, which meant he was unharmed from the fire.

'We should do something,' Aidan said. He made to brush past her, but she seized his arm with both of her hands.

'No!' she said, then snapped her jaw shut. Too loud. They'd heard her. Except they hadn't, because her voice was drowned by a loud rumble. Cait and Aidan staggered as the floor shivered. They cast their eyes upwards as flecks of dust spun down from the low ceiling.

'What are they doing?' Aidan hissed.

'I don't know.'

A second rumble. This time, deafening. It knocked them to their knees. Cait pressed her hands over her ears. She felt the sprinkle of stone across her back. *We're going to be buried alive,* she thought. *I'm going to be buried with Anndras.*

'This is bad,' Aidan said, fear buried into his features. 'Isn't it?'

It was silent again, and Cait pressed a finger to her lips. As the dust settled, an unfamiliar voice spoke through the darkness.

'Shame to disturb Lister's party.'

'Ha! That rat,' another spat. 'Always had a bad feeling about him.'

'His daughter's bonnie. I almost feel bad — jings!'

A third rumble cut him off. When Cait glanced at Aidan, his skin had paled. He breathed heavily, staring at the opening where the voices were slipping through to them. 'What are they talking about?' Aidan asked, voice trembling.

'They'll hear us in Witteneuk,' the first voice said.

'Ross! Shut it and get to work!' barked Kenzie. Cait winced.

A hand snatched Cait's wrist and she almost yelped. She turned to find Aidan staring at her. 'Bess is up there. What have they done?'

'I don't know,' she whispered, but his grip tightened.

'If they've hurt her …' his words and the awful images that were no doubt attached to them seemed to catch up with Aidan, and he dropped her wrist. His breath sped up, ragged and uncontrollable. 'Shadielaunds, Bess.' He paced away from Cait, one fist snatching the crown from his head in an angry fist.

She stretched out her hands, afraid he would throw the crown to the ground and alert the Watchmen to their presence. 'Aidan, stop.'

He didn't. 'I need to go up there.'

'We can't.' There was nothing they could do while the Watch was in their way.

'I have to!' Aidan cried.

The voices in the passage stilled. Cait clasped a hand over her mouth to stifle her whimper. *They're going to find us.*

'Spooky down here, innit,' one of the voices said, and they got back to work.

Cait stepped forward and took Aidan's cold hands. There were no words of warning that could cut through the panicky snare closing around his neck. 'Listen,' she whispered. 'We are going to find her.'

Never make a promise to a patient you can't keep, her mother chided in her ear. Cait ignored her. 'We are going to find Bess.' She guided Aidan to the floor where she crouched in front of him and let him cling to her hand until it was numb. 'We will find her, but we need to stay here for a little while.' Aidan nodded, but his breathing was still jittery and far too loud. 'Breathe with me,' Cait said, sucking a breath in, holding it, and letting it go. Aidan copied, shaky at first, but he slowly eased into the rhythm of it. She felt his ebbing panic cover them like a dark sheet that concealed them from the Watchmen. 'Just keep counting,' Cait said. The Watchmen continued working. Kenzie's voice bayed above the others, and Cait panted like a rabbit in the dark. One, two, three, four. How many breaths did she have left before he found her?

Eventually, the Watchmen finished their work, and their sounds grew more and more faint. Cait continued to crouch in the silence, before finally plucking up the courage to check the passage. The Watch were gone. The crypts were dark and slept again.

When she returned to Aidan's side, he looked up at her, looking very much like a child curled into a ball. 'Are they gone?' he said, voice too much like a whimper for a king.

'I think so,' she said, and put a hand down for him. 'Let's go up.'

She'd rather stay where she was, because the Watchmen were finished here and they wouldn't be coming back, but she needed to get Aidan out of this necropolis. She held his shaking hand tight as they hurried towards the surface and prepared herself for what they might be met with. The chapel, however, lay peaceful. They inched out the door into the courtyard and Cait squeezed her eyes shut, bracing for the Watchmen to fall on them, readying for the thrum of adrenaline as she tried to escape, but the courtyard didn't stir. Light and music slunk under the windows and doors of the Great Hall. She could hear laughter.

'I don't understand,' she said.

Aidan wasted no time in hurrying towards the doors of the Great Hall, and inside, Cait lost him to the reels and revelry as he strode off to find Bess. She stood in the doorway with the chill of the dark at her back and watched the celebrations blankly. The Watchmen had been in Gowdstane. She was certain she hadn't made any of it up. She had felt her fear strangling her when she heard Kenzie's voice.

'Cait?' Calan asked, appearing at her side. 'Are you okay?'

Cait blinked. 'The Watch ... they were ...' she stared at the dancing. The music felt too loud. She couldn't understand. The Separatists were drunk. They were distracted. The Watch had discovered their base and held every advantage, and yet ... Then her thoughts shifted to someone else they held every advantage over.

'Aggie!' Cait blurted. She turned and ran from the Great Hall.

*

'An fit's a this aboot?' The doctor squawked as they burst through the door to the infirmary. The rest of the castle had been as untouched as the Great Hall.

'I just wanted to check on Aggie,' Cait said.

The doctor bustled about her business as usual. 'Weel, she's no ony better than the last time ye looked in. I widna be surprised if the pair quine's hairt had given out aifter that intrusion.'

'There were Lealists in the castle,' Calan said. 'Apparently.'

The doctor shook her head. 'Weel, furst ah've heard o it.' When Cait and Calan hovered on the stairs, the doctor *tsked* and waved at the bed. 'Sit ben.' They sat either side of Aggie, and Cait watched as Calan looked out the window, or at the ceiling, or his hands. Then the door opened, and Jamie barrelled through. The doctor gave an exasperated sigh. 'Fin wis knocking ootlawed?'

'Sorry,' Jamie muttered, dipping her head as she descended the stairs to join them. 'Castle's clear. Whatever they were here for, they've left.'

The doctor sighed. 'Weel, thank the Shadielaunds for that. Now you're here ah may as well get a drink. You lot git tae hae yer drinks and dances, aye but *someone* needs tae stay here and look efter the ill.' She bustled past Jamie and the door swung shut behind her. Jamie raised her eyebrows and tucked her thumbs into her braces.

Calan slumped. Cait wished she could relax. She could still feel Kenzie's presence. His voice clung to her skin. She felt him around each corner and in every gloomy doorway.

'They were definitely here?' Calan said after a long, bewildered silence. 'Are you sure?'

'I heard them,' Cait said.

'They were here, and they did ... nothing.' Perhaps for the first time since they arrived at Gowdstane, Calan looked at Aggie. He was looking to her for an answer, perhaps, but her only answer was her pallid face.

'Why would they do that?'

'I think they were trying to get into Anndras' tomb,' Cait said. 'Didn't you feel it?'

Jamie's eyes widened. '*That's* what that was? Didn't feel like much, most just laughed it off as the dancing.'

'A particularly energised *Drops of Brandy*,' Calan muttered. He rubbed his shoulder and winced.

'Kenzie was with them,' Cait said. 'He told them to take everything inside the tomb.' Kenzie wasn't one to just vanish. He wasn't one to just leave Separatists to get on with what they were doing. He'd continued to push even when Mr Blaine was proven innocent.

Calan sighed. 'I somehow doubt they just wanted to pilfer some jewels.'

'He mentioned my da's name. Whatever they were collecting, it was for him. The line of the ballad he's been studying mentions a charge being *enshrined*. Maybe that means a tomb. I'm worried they've got it.'

'That's troubling,' Calan said.

Jamie shook her head. 'I don't get it. They were here, they had the upper hand. Why not just kill us all and save themselves some time?'

'They're trying to discredit Aidan,' Calan said. 'If they just stormed in here and killed the lot of us, he'd become a martyr. I reckon they're trying to spin something in his past to turn people away. It'll be easier to topple him that way.'

It seemed Kenzie had moved his attention away from Cait. Perhaps he was focused on his ambition, or perhaps he thought she was far too feral to control any longer. Regardless, she needed to force his attention back to her.

'I'll go to him,' Cait said, and suddenly all eyes were on her.

Calan frowned. 'What?'

She spoke slowly, trying to convince herself it was a good idea more than anyone else. 'There's nothing Kenzie wants more than to bring an end to separatism. Except maybe one thing.'

Calan watched her carefully. 'You.'

Not just Cait. If all he had wanted was Cait, he would have let her go home at the first sign of trouble. Kenzie didn't only want Cait; he wanted Cait inside a pretty, golden cage. 'I'll go to Hart Hall and tell him everything he wants to hear. I'll find out what they're planning, and I'll get that information back to you.' It was easier said than done. Hart Hall was a fortress.

'Let me come with you,' Jamie said.

'No,' Cait said. 'If he's going to trust me, I need to be alone.'

Calan studied her. 'I don't think it's wise.'

Cait had to pretend that there wasn't a part of her that would find it easy to go back to Kenzie. It was the part that stayed awake at night and dreamt about sneaking out and feeling numb, of prostrating herself before him and claiming his proud forgiveness. But the part of her that made this decision had thawed right down to the bone.

'What's the alternative?' Cait asked.

Calan stared blankly at Aggie. He knew as well as she did that the alternative would be to let Kenzie take whatever he had been searching for and use it to crush Aidan. If Cait couldn't stop him, she could at least warn her friends.

'I'll go in a few days. I'll wait until ...' She glanced down at Aggie. 'Until we know more.'

Calan shook his head. 'If you're going to do this, it needs to be soon. The information needs to be stopped before it spreads further. And if it is that treaty, we need it back before it can be destroyed.'

'But what about Aggie? I can't —'

Calan's voice trembled as he looked up at her. 'I'm worried about her, too.' He righted himself. 'But she wouldn't want you sitting here while the movement was at stake.'

Cait nodded. *Hang on until I get back,* she silently begged Aggie's still frame. *Please.* She was only starting to know the Fox of Thorterknock. She couldn't fade now.

'We can't tell Lister,' Calan said. 'After what happened with the crown, he won't trust you.' He looked away, and Cait felt like she was back on the train as they hurtled home from Eadwick all over again.

'Calan,' she said firmly. 'Do *you* trust me?'

He looked up and met her gaze. 'Of course I do.'

*

Cait's sky-blue dress breezed about the top of her boots as she waited at the gates to Gowdstane. The dress smelled awful, and the sole of her right boot was practically falling off, but she had to look the part. She needed to return to Kenzie as she had been, not as what she had become. But she didn't want to resemble the girl on the missing poster just yet. She scooped her hair up inside her hat. When Calan walked up to the gates at a brisk pace, Cait foolishly hoped he was coming to tell her that Aggie had taken a miraculous turn for the better.

'The tomb's empty,' was all he said when he reached her. 'We don't have any way of knowing what was in there before, but we know for certain that one thing in particular was taken.'

'What was it?'

'They broke into his casket. His remains, at least what was left of them, are all gone.'

Cait nodded. 'So, I'm on the lookout for a skeleton.'

'I managed to find out that Gowdstane has a secret telegraph line to Hart Hall, so we receive all their messages,' Calan started to explain.

'They do? What do they say?'

He batted the question away. 'Nothing useful. Lister's codebreakers seem mostly clueless. The point is, anything sent from Hart Hall comes here, so if you find anything, try to get it to us in a telegram. Make it cryptic.'

Cait nodded several times over. 'Okay, yes.' A long silence stretched out between them. 'Look after Aggie,' Cait said. 'If she's not —'

'She will be.' But Calan didn't look as certain as he sounded. 'Keep yourself safe.'

She was about to nod and wave and hurry off down into town, but before she could, Calan fished something from his pocket and passed it to Cait. His lock picks clinked gently into her hands.

'I hope I won't need these,' she said.

'You never know with Hart Hall.'

She hesitated, then pulled Calan into a tight embrace. 'Thank you.' *I won't let you down, not this time.* It took a moment, but she felt the press of his arms on her back.

When Cait reached Clackhatton's train station, she paused at a noticeboard plastered with posters: local events, items for sale, missing pets, missing people. She found the poster with her likeness and ripped it down, folding it carefully into her pocket.

She was barely mindful of the steward pacing back and forth as she slipped into the luggage car of the last train to Thorterknock and sped into the night, a wolf in a sheep's sky-blue dress.

Chapter 29

A Gilded Cage

Four hours later, Cait stood before the gates of Hart Hall.

'Business?' one of the two officers on duty said, his expression bored and unamused.

'I'm here to see someone,' Cait said. 'He's family.'

The Watchmen exchanged a quizzical glance, and when they looked back at Cait their faces were set with renewed stoicism. 'I can only let you in if you're with an officer.'

Cait removed the poster from her pocket and held it out to them. 'I am.'

As they studied the image, she removed her hat and her hair fell about her shoulders. The officers peered at the poster, and then at Cait. The second officer murmured, 'Jings, it's Kenzie's lass.'

Kenzie's lass. As if she were his dog.

'Where is he?' she threw a cursory, panicked glance over her shoulder. 'I need to see him.'

They let her through. Someone was called to escort her, and they explained that Kenzie was tied up in a meeting, but he would be notified the moment he was free. Cait expected to be taken to the barracks, the tall block on the castle's centre courtyard, but she was marched up the cobblestone road that curved through the castle's middle ward and up to a square set of buildings above the courtyard. She was led through a door into a dark corridor and followed her escort into a warm and trim room with dimpled leather sofas.

'Make yourself comfortable,' the officer said, and bobbed out of the room. The door closed behind him, but Cait could still feel his presence on the other side, muscles tensed, gun resting on his arm. She couldn't bring herself to get comfortable, so instead she stood in the centre of the room and waited. Oil paintings of nameless, uniformed officers stared blankly from their golden frames. The fire in the hearth made her skin clammy despite the cool night air. She clenched and unclenched her fists. She thought about pacing, but the floorboards beneath the plush red carpet groaned at the slightest shift in weight. She rehearsed the moment she'd see Kenzie again: the sob that would burst from her throat, and how the floorboards would cry out as she ran to him. Her words would be nothing but the apologies of the stupid and terrified girl he needed to see.

But when the door opened and he strode in, Cait froze.

Kenzie looked cleaner than he had in the bothy, less road weary. Otherwise, he was the same, only now his cloak was clasped with a neat golden chain where it had been empty before.

'Kenzie,' she whimpered. He stood by the door, watching her. She couldn't make out the expression on his face. 'Don't be angry.' He watched her for a moment longer, then slowly began to approach. His boots creaked on the carpet; his chain clinked with each step. 'I — I'm sorry.' Her fear was palpable. It was real. These words she meant, every single one of them. She couldn't face his anger, his disappointment, his raised palm.

He stopped by the sofa, a good six feet between them, and stared.

'I escaped as soon as I could,' she said.

'I came for you,' Kenzie said, his voice drained of all emotion. 'You chose them.' No, his eyes weren't emotionless. They were wounded.

'I know, I know, but they got to me.' She tapped a finger to her temple, like Kenzie had done back in Thorterknock. 'They were in my head. You were right.' Then, when he didn't seem to stir, she added, 'They threatened me.'

'What could they possibly have over you with me there?'

Cait hesitated. The tears that sprung into her eyes were perfectly real, and the crack in her voice unplanned. 'I don't know.'

Kenzie's jaw grated from side to side as he watched her. For a long time, she didn't think he would speak, until he asked, 'Why now?'

'I wanted to come home. I wanted you.'

'Why now?' he repeated. 'Why not when I first found you?'

'I told you, they —'

'The truth, Cait,' he snapped, voice whip-like.

She realised then that her worst-case scenario was coming true, and she had already taken Kenzie's trust and crushed it. It only occurred to her as she stood there, in the centre of Hart Hall with all its soldiers, that

Kenzie may only see her for what she was now: a Separatist. A scheming, lying, Separatist. A soldier of the Queen's Watch stood before her, but Cait could only see the boy beneath the uniform. He wasn't Kenzie the Lealist, or Kenzie the man who had lied to her and hurt her friends, but Kenzie the hard-working and ambitious borders lad. That boy had been innocent once. That boy's parents had been ripped from him. Now, that boy was watching the only person he had left in the world side with those who made him an orphan. He didn't look at her with anger, but with agonising betrayal.

'I was stupid,' she said, her composure finally crumbling. 'Please. I don't know what to do. I'm scared.' And she was. Hot tears spilled down her cheeks. She wanted Kenzie to be near her. Numbness was better than this crushing dread. 'I'm so sorry,' she sobbed, again, and again, and again. She needed his forgiveness like a drug, his sympathetic smile, his cock of the head, and his sweetly patronising voice as he stroked her hair and told her everything was okay.

Across the room, Kenzie watched her. His stony expression held fast until his shoulders sagged, and he seemed to shrink within his uniform to an echo of the boy he had been, coltish and steadfast all at once. He shook his head. 'I can't do this.' His expression fractured and he hurried to close the space between them. He pulled Cait into trembling arms. She buried her head in his shoulder, and even when his hand brushed her head and her skin crawled, she didn't care. This was safety. She had missed it. 'It's okay, little dove.' His voice was tender.

'Where's da?' she asked.

'He's back in Briddock. We all escaped your friend's ... outburst.'

'She's not my friend,' Cait said quickly. 'None of them are.' A new sob wrenched from her throat as a memory hit her out of nowhere. Her picture in the paper. *Missing.* Not *Wanted.*

Missing.

'You covered for me. You ... and I —' she cried into his shoulder all over again. Her head spun. 'I was being selfish.'

'You were.'

'Forgive me.'

'I do.'

'I just ... I just thought ...'

He hushed her, and as she clung to him, she felt herself sinking. 'I know,' he whispered. 'I know you.'

He did know her. Far more than the Separatists ever would. They had known each other a lifetime. Was she really prepared to throw that away? They always said that once the water had rushed into your lungs and scorched your breath, that drowning was easy. Here, in Kenzie's arms, she felt ready to let go.

Calan, do you trust me?
Of course I do.
Enough.

Cait took a gulp of hot air and let it burn through her weakness. She swallowed her sobs. She steeled her mind against Kenzie's words. She straightened and looked up at him, wiping her eyes, sniffing. Kenzie lifted a hand and wiped a tear away from her cheek, then dropped his hand. That wounded look fell over his face again.

'Kenzie?' Cait asked.

'You ran to her,' he said quietly.

Cait didn't need to ask who he was talking about. 'I would run to anyone who needed help.'

'You ran to her,' he said again, this time looking at his feet, talking to himself, trying to convince himself he hadn't seen what he had. 'And you stayed with her ...' He looked up again, sheer uncertainty in his eyes. 'Why did you come back?'

She opened her mouth to tell him the lies: that she missed him, that she had it all wrong, but now that she had been mentioned, Cait thought about Aggie. She'd fought so hard not to think of her, how her wound festered more with every passing moment. How her voice was silenced, spirit faded. It was almost dawn. Aggie may already be a shadow. 'I lost my patient.'

Kenzie straightened ever so slightly. The corners of his mouth fought to turn up, his eyes widened. She could tell he was fighting his delight. 'The Fox is dead?'

Cait wanted more than anything to tell Kenzie that the Fox had a name. She wanted to tell him that she wasn't just the Fox; she was a lover of stories, a skilled debater, a loyal friend. Cait wanted to tell him all the things about Aggie that he would never know because he would only ever see her as the Fox of Thorterknock. She held her tongue. Aggie was all these things, but she was also mortal, and Cait knew she would never see her again. 'Yes,' she said at last. 'She's dead.'

For the briefest moment, Kenzie's face trembled between delight and pity, then at last, it crumbled. Something inside him gave. He dropped to his knees and wrapped his arms around her, clinging tighter than he ever had before. 'I thought I lost you,' he mumbled. 'I only stopped because I thought I'd lost you.'

'I was scared,' Cait whispered. She was surprised at how steady her voice had become. 'You told me you wouldn't hurt them. You ... lied to me.'

She braced for him to balk, but he only muttered, 'I know.'

'And seeing you with ... with that gun ...'

'Cait.' Kenzie looked up and his eyes were full of tears. They turned his irises the most electric blue. 'Can you ever forgive me?'

Cait hesitated, enraptured by his gaze. She was back in Briddock with a boy she once knew. It was a Sunday afternoon. She'd been up in the hills, just wandering, when word reached Briddock that a civilian had been caught in the crossfire of the weekly hunt. Cait had been none the wiser, and when she'd returned to the village that evening, Kenzie had held her and would not let her go. And here he was, once again that frightened boy who didn't want to lose his little dove.

'Cait, please,' Kenzie begged. He was begging *her*. 'Forgive me.'

Deep in Hart Hall, so far from Gowdstane, and King Aidan, and the Fox of Thorterknock, it all felt like an obscure dream. Cait wondered, if she were to just stay here, maybe she could have that boy from the village back. Perhaps it was time to let noble causes go. 'Okay,' Cait whispered, and she sank to his level, and let him bury his face into her shoulder. They held each other forever, and she ran her fingers through his hair, and whispered affirmations in his ear. 'It's okay. I'm here. I won't go away again.' She wasn't sure if she was lying. She didn't know what the future held, but all she knew was that it felt good to be here with him, pretending nothing had changed and they were back in Briddock.

At long last, he raised his head. 'Come on,' he said, standing. 'It's late. You must be exhausted.' He kissed her. He helped her to her feet. He held doors for her as they moved through the castle. His fingers twisted around hers.

'Do you need to tell someone I'm here?' she asked him.

'Tomorrow,' he said.

When they returned to the barracks, Cait was surprised to find the room she had stayed in the last time was just as she had left it, with her suitcase at the foot of the bed, all her things still inside. She readied for bed and curled up on the narrow cot. Kenzie crouched at her side and watched her as his thumb brushed absently along her arm.

'Stay with me,' she murmured, already tumbling into sleep.

He squeezed into the bed beside her. She felt his breath on the back of her neck, his arms around her waist. When she closed her eyes, she was home, and it was five years ago, and everything was right, and their future surrounded them.

*

When Cait awoke the next morning to the sun streaking through the windows, forming aching sunspots behind her eyelids, Kenzie was still at her side. His body was warm, and she was disappointed when he rose and cold swept in under the thin blanket.

'Don't go,' Cait mumbled. If Kenzie was getting up, that would mean she would have to soon as well, and she would need to start the day and help ready the surgery for the patients. And today, she really didn't feel like it.

Kenzie chuckled from across the room. 'I have to, little dove. Duty calls.' A jangling sound snagged at the edges of Cait's wakefulness, and she followed it out of her dreamy bedroom in Briddock, and into the barracks of Hart Hall. The chain on Kenzie's cloak clinked as he threw it over his shoulders. 'I'll come straight back after work,' Kenzie said, bending down and planting a kiss on Cait's head. His eyes brightened suddenly. 'Oh, look what I found in your case!' He reached into the case and fished out a book with familiar emerald binding and golden lettering. Kenzie passed it to her, grinning like a schoolboy. Cait opened her own copy of *Songs of Storran* and flicked through it, smiling when she noticed the dog-eared pages and her father's illegible annotations. Aggie would be mortified.

'What is it?' Kenzie asked.

Cait closed the book and looked up at him. 'Just happy memories.'

Kenzie smiled. 'They are.'

She watched him close the door gently behind him, and the simple *click* of the lock slipping into place was enough to shake her from the foolish dream she had drifted into last night. This was not home. Kenzie was not the boy he once was. The Separatists were counting on her, and she would not fail them this time. She shivered as she climbed out of bed and peered out of the window, watching the blurry outline of Kenzie striding across the courtyard and moving off into the city with a group of other officers. Cait pulled on her boots and seized the lock picks from her pocket, suddenly glad that Calan had the foresight to give them to her. *You never know with Hart Hall.*

Even as she started working on the lock, Cait wondered if Kenzie could be different now that she was back, and he had tasted her defiance. Maybe now that the Fox was out of their lives, things could go back to the way they were. Maybe he'd changed. Part of her didn't want to throw that possibility away. She shook the thought off. He'd locked her in. She knew the truth: he would stay, and so would she, and she would die here in Hart Hall before she could feel the border hills beneath her feet again.

Calan had made it look easy when he sprung the office lock back in the Treasury, but it took Cait most of the morning and into the afternoon to get at least the slightest grasp on the mechanism. She struggled with the intricate movements, her vision making it hard for her to consistently put the picks into the lock. Finally, just when she expected the lock to spring open, the picks bent in her hands, and she cursed. She rattled the door, but it was locked fast, and she paced to the window. She stayed there for hours watching shapes in soldiers' uniforms flit back and forth across the courtyard, listening to their muffled camaraderie behind the glass windowpane. As the daylight started to tarnish with evening, Cait heard that mocking *click* of the lock and sprung to her feet.

'Kenzie!' she gasped, dancing towards the door on her toes as she had planned. 'You're back!'

Kenzie gave a dashing grin but blocked her exit with his body. 'It's nice to see you, too.'

'The door was locked. All day,' Cait said, bouncing on the balls of her feet. 'I need to use the lav.'

Kenzie's face fell into understanding. 'This way,' he said, and beckoned her out of the room.

*

Back in Cait's room, Kenzie lay on the bed and pulled her towards him. She lay with her back to him, his body curled around her own. Her skin prickled with every breath of his that kissed her neck. She lay there in his arms, staring vacantly at the next cot over, as the shadows of the windowpane stretched into bars across its thin white sheets.

'Tell me how it happened,' Kenzie murmured into her neck.

'How what happened?' Cait asked.

Kenzie stroked her hand with his thumb, slowly, over, and over and over. His voice pitched low and lazy. 'Tell me how the Fox died.'

Cait hoped he couldn't feel her heart racing in her chest. 'You were there.'

'No.' Longing dripped from the word. 'Tell me everything. What happened after?'

Cait hesitated, then said slowly, 'Her wound was infected.'

'Which one?'

'Her shoulder.'

'I see. How long did she last?'

How long had it been? 'Um ... a couple of days? I'm not sure.'

'And did she say anything?'

'No.'

'Did she say anything about me?'

Disgust crept up Cait's throat. 'No, she fell unconscious.'

'And where did she —'

Before he could press her for any more details, Kenzie's stomach grumbled against her back. 'You're hungry,' Cait said quickly.

Kenzie ignored her. 'Where did she die?'

Cait pushed herself up and shook his arm from her. She smiled sweetly at him. 'You need to eat.' She gently tugged at the fine tailoring on his jacket and ran her fingers around the buttons. 'How are you supposed to protect the Five Realms if you don't keep your strength up?'

He smiled lazily at her, putting his arms around her, and scooping her down onto the bed again. 'I'd rather stay with you.'

Cait tilted herself up on her elbows and raised an eyebrow. 'Go and eat.'

He sighed, pouting a lip like a petulant child, then jerked his head towards the door. 'Fine. Let's go.'

'I'm not hungry,' Cait said, sitting up. She fiddled with the thin bedsheet to hide the lie in her eyes, and to distract her stomach from betraying her.

'You've been in here all day.'

She let her voice weaken. She let herself sound like he made her feel. 'I just ... don't feel up to it.'

'Are you sure?' Kenzie said, hesitating by the door.

Cait nodded, and when he still didn't make to leave, she muttered without looking up at him, 'The Fox did wake up … once.' Out of her periphery she saw Kenzie tilt his head. 'She was in a lot of pain. She did say something.'

'What was it?' Kenzie asked.

'I'll tell you if you go and eat something,' Cait chided.

Kenzie laughed. 'Very well, little dove. You're a tough mistress.' He pulled a set of keys from his pocket as he reached for the door.

'Don't lock it!' Cait's words left her mouth too quickly and Kenzie frowned. She added with a sheepish grin, 'Do you really want me to have an accident?'

This seemed to satisfy him, and Kenzie gently closed the door behind him. Cait watched his shape striding across the courtyard. She waited five seconds after he had turned the corner, then sprung for the exit.

*

She collected sideways glances and whispers as she moved through Hart Hall's seemingly endless passageways that all smelled of warm fabric and polish. She had been careful not to use the same door Kenzie had, and instead chose one that looked as though it would lead her down, but somehow, she still ended up outside the door to the dining hall, the sound of cutlery and chatter coming from within. As she hurried by with her head bowed, she locked eyes with a familiar face.

'Cait!' Innes cried, rushing over, and leaving the group of Watchmen he had been standing with. She cringed at the volume of his voice, her head jerking involuntarily over her shoulder to look at the dining room door.

'I can't believe you're here!' he said. Then his grin faded, and his eyes roved up and down. 'Are you okay? Did they hurt you?' He looked taller, somehow. He seemed to fit his uniform more, and a single gold chain adorned the fastening of his cloak.

'Thanks, Innes. They didn't hurt me. I'm fine.' She remembered the night on the pier with a stab of guilt. 'What about you?' She looked at her boots. 'I'm sorry about what happened in Eadwick.' They walked side by side and Cait was glad to leave the peering eyes of his friends and the entrance to the dining hall behind.

'I'm grand,' Innes said dismissively. 'If anything, just a bit bored right now.'

Cait fixed him with a look of disbelief. 'Bored? A high-flying decorated

Queen's Watchman?'

'What they don't tell you about earning your chains is that the more important responsibilities are the worst ones.'

'Like what? Polishing the Brigadier's boots?' Cait said, managing a laugh.

Innes' expression remained deadpan as he said, 'Cleaning up after executions.'

Cait almost stopped in her tracks. 'Oh.'

'It's not exactly the type of work I signed up for, but all service is good service.'

'What about Kenzie?' Cait asked. 'Can he not give you something better to do?'

Innes ran a hand through his short hair. 'Honestly, I've hardly seen him since we got back from Gowdstane.'

Cait raised her eyebrows in authentic surprise. 'Gowdstane? You've been there?'

'Um, yeah. Once. Just to look. Kenzie has had a lot of meetings with the Brigadier since then.' He added the second part quickly, clearly realising he'd said too much.

'Really? What do they talk about?'

'Dunno.'

'What were you doing at Gowdstane?'

'Can't say.'

'Oh, go on,' Cait said with a laugh. 'You know you want to.' It had always worked on Aggie.

But Innes' face held no warmth. He stopped walking. His voice lowered to a frantic whisper. 'Cait, please. Do you want me cleaning up after *myself* on the gallows?' Cait felt a twinge of pity for him. He'd spent his time in the Watch chasing after Kenzie, and now that he had played his part, he had been flung to the side while Kenzie lorded it up with the Brigadier. 'Ah, is that the time?' Innes said, peering at a watch. 'I've got … stuff to do.' He gave Cait a close-lipped smile. 'Good to see you, Cait.'

For a moment, Cait considered asking him where the Watch might hide their skeletons, but she didn't want to push her luck. It was clear Innes didn't fully trust her either. 'See you later,' she said.

She continued walking down the corridor, putting space between herself and the dining hall while trying to mentally deduce how long she had been out of her room, and how long it would take Kenzie to eat. She had to be running out of time. Maybe it was safer to go back to the room and try again later. Kenzie was bound to be on duty tomorrow, she'd have plenty time then. She was walking back across the courtyard, towards the dormitories, when she passed a couple of Watchmen in the courtyard outside, and overheard their conversation.

'You're having laugh.'

'No, dead serious! They put it down in the old vaults.'

'What vaults?'

'Ach, I'll show you.'

As their voices faded across the courtyard, Cait turned and slunk after them. She trailed them into the quieter parts of the castle, and eventually, through a rickety wooden door and down into the vaults. Where once ammunition or food or critical supplies may have been stored, it now just seemed to be the home of broken furniture and empty storage boxes.

'This way,' the leader of the pair said, and from her hiding place behind an old bookshelf, Cait watched them stop at a closed door. The leader pulled the door ajar, and the pair hissed as it creaked at them.

'They don't lock it?' the follower said.

'They did, until Harry broke the lock trying tae get a keek. No one knows yet, so wheesht.' He pulled the door open further and pushed his companion's head into the dark space. 'You see it?'

'It's too dark. Wait … shite. You're right. He was bloody tall, wasn't he?'

'Want to go closer?'

'As if. Come on, this is spooky, like.'

'Aw, dinna be a woose.'

'I'll be a woose if I want to be. Let's go.'

Cait crouched in the dark as the pair's voices faded into the world above, then she treaded softly towards the door. She placed trembling fingers around the handle and took one steadying breath. *Please be Anndras,* she thought. She pushed the door open.

The bones were laid out on a trestle table at the centre of the room, like an offering upon an altar. They were worn, and brittle, and none of them attached to each other, but someone had taken great care to lay them out in the familiar shape of a human being. Cait lingered by the door, struggling to summon the courage to approach the table and the ancient King that lay upon it.

Anndras *was* tall, even as a dislocated skeleton on a table. In life he must have been close to seven feet. What could these bones possibly do to patch the hole in the tale her father was trying to fill? What could they say about the declaration he was so sure existed? Slowly, she approached Anndras' frame. Her father's argument for the treaty had hinged on a line from the ballad that spoke of a charge, an oath, that gave Storran's freedom to its people. That was a dead end. There was nothing else in here other than the lonely skeleton, no documents, or memorabilia, or anything.

'What do they want with you?' she muttered, perching her fingers on the wooden table, daring them to be within an inch of Anndras' bones. She looked at his ribs, which would have once arched into a breastplate for his royal heart, now flattened in neat little rows. Aidan hadn't looked a thing like the image of Anndras she had been fed, but neither did this skeleton. The diary in the Treasury had said how Anndras had shown no mercy to an Afrenian spy and taken his head. She was quickly coming to realise that hanging the politics of a land on an elusive figure from the mists of history wasn't a very wise idea. Anndras couldn't even seem to know who he was. The historical version was too brutal, the imaginary too ideal. It only reminded her that Cathal didn't exactly know who he was either. What kind of a shrewd strategist would walk into the Queen's trap?

Unless. Cait glanced at the bones as an impossible thought occurred to her, then she shook it off. *There's no time for stupid theories,* she scolded herself, beginning to pace before the bones. *You're running out of time.*

'*A chairge enshrined within the law*
Fur freedom jointly owned.'

She recited the lines again, and again, until her jaw ached. She was missing something. She had to be. There must be a reason they needed these bones. When her mind had run itself in too many circles, she took to desperately hunting among the bones, carefully lifting them up and studying the underside of them for something, *anything,* that might be inexplicably attached to them. She thought of how Aggie would cringe that she wasn't wearing gloves.

'I'm trying to help your stupid country!' she groaned, kicking the leg of the table in frustration. She immediately regretted it as the table trembled and the bones quivered in their place. Cait studied the long, yellow bones. It was a long table, and they stretched out across the whole surface, end to end. Cathal had always been described as the tallest of the two.

Cathal was the tallest. Cathal was more likely to strike down a traitor.
So Anndrus called his men tae airms
And took up Cathal's sword.

The impossible thought returned to her, and this time Cait couldn't put it down. She moved slowly towards the skull with its gaping eyes and toothy grin. It sneered at her. It knew. It had known all along.

She heard Bram, chatting over a hearty broth in The Crabbit Corbie.

'Ye know, I never understood Cathal's death in that story.'

Cait had laughed. *'I always thought the same thing.'*

'Yi'd think a tactician like Cathal would see richt through that. Makes you wonder why.'

Folklore is fluid. That's what her father would say. Some people would want to give Cathal a moment of weakness. Some would want to give Anndras a brutal edge. Cait had a feeling it went beyond stories this time.

Did yir faither ever tell yi the tale o how Cathal slipped and cracked his heed half open on rock while runnin from the Queen's sodjers? Bram had asked.

She reached down and put her hands around the King's skull. 'Sorry,' she whispered as she lifted it carefully. She held it at arm's length for just a moment, then slowly turned it so she could see the back of the head. A jagged fracture stretched down the bone. Cait ran a finger over it. It was so faint, and yet it felt to Cait like the deepest gash. It was a wound that had gone untreated. A young man, slipping and striking his head on a rock. He'd be concussed for a while, but a hardy mercenary like Cathal wouldn't dwell too much on it. As he aged, the injury may have complicated things, but Cathal had never lived that long. He had lifted the Antlered Crown to his head in the moments following victory, king for a moment, and then gone. Somehow, he had taken Anndras' place in the story. Cait didn't know how or why, she only knew that this thin fracture had more repercussions than Cathal ever could have imagined.

Cait turned the skull over again and looked Cathal, the First and Last King of Storran, in the eye.

Chapter 30

Kenzie's Lass

Cait made it back to her room just moments before Kenzie opened the door.

'Sorry I took so long,' he said. 'Got caught up with something.' He sat down on the bed and placed his hand on Cait's thigh. 'I missed you.' He kissed her head, and Cait knew the moment he pulled away he would demand to hear about the way Aggie used her final breath to curse the name of Kenzie Bell. She needed to get out of this room before he asked.

'Actually,' she said on a laugh, taking his hand so it no longer burned against her leg. 'I could do with something to eat.'

Kenzie frowned. 'What? You just said you weren't hungry.'

'You were gone *ages*, Kenzie. I would've come to meet you, but I didn't know if that was allowed, and —'

Kenzie gave an exasperated sigh. 'What are you like?'

'Hungry,' Cait said.

Reluctantly, Kenzie led her from the barracks, bemoaning her finicky nature the entire way to the dining hall. Cait put on the act of his gracious and embarrassed little pet. It was easy. It fit like a glove.

The dining hall was stuffy and rang with conversation from six long tables. The food wasn't half bad either, with juicy, tender lumps of mutton, and a dollop of creamy potatoes slapped onto Cait's plate. A roof over their head, a salary, and good food. Cait was starting to understand why becoming a Watchman was so coveted. As they walked towards a table, heads turned their way and whispers trailed them.

'Ignore them,' Kenzie said, though there was a furious impatience in his eyes, like this had been going on for a while now.

'How was your day?' he asked once they sat down.

'Quiet. I read a lot,' she said. 'What about you?' She tried to recall the way she once would have asked the question, when she wasn't searching for information, but genuinely ready to drink up every detail of his day.

Kenzie shrugged at the question. 'Couple of meetings. Nothing exciting.' She watched him looking around the room, deflecting. Once, that question would have triggered hours of narrative about his day and the conversations he'd had. Cait chewed her food slowly, trying not to let the suspicion show on her face. She swallowed. 'Meetings? Didn't think the heroic Watchmen would waste their time with that.'

Kenzie chuckled. 'Unlike the Separatists, we understand the value of strategy.'

'Are you planning something?'

'We're always planning something, Cait. That's how we stay on top.' Out of the corner of her eye, she saw Kenzie glance at her. 'I think that's enough talk about me.' She ate in silence while Kenzie watched her closely. He may have taken her back, but he certainly didn't trust her.

'It would be good to send a message to Briddock,' she said at last.

'We only send military communications from here,' Kenzie said simply.

'Mam and Da need to know I'm okay.'

Kenzie smiled. 'I'll make sure they know.'

After another few moments of painful silence, Kenzie turned to Cait again and cocked his head. 'What did you think of the north?'

Cait turned her fork slowly through her potatoes. 'It was nice.'

'Not as nice as the borders though, I bet. It's colder up there.' He paused, and Cait thought he was ready to let it lie, when he added, 'Gowdstane is a fine fortress, isn't it?' Cait swallowed and nodded once. 'Is it particularly busy?'

'It's a ruin.'

'Hmm,' Kenzie furrowed his brow and looked up thoughtfully. 'I wouldn't have thought many people would be there in its condition, but the rabble I heard suggests otherwise.' He looked at her expectantly. 'Was it a good party?'

'It was fine,' Cait said.

Kenzie bellowed a laugh. 'Just "fine"? Remind me not to try to impress you any time soon.' Cait swallowed another forkful of food. It clung to her throat as it went down. 'It sounded fun to me,' he said. 'The Separatists certainly know how to throw a knees-up. Though I suppose a good crowd makes all the difference.'

'And alcohol,' Cait said.

Kenzie chuckled. 'Very true. How many people were there?'

'Some. Not a lot.'

'Anyone I'd know?'

'I don't think so,' Cait said, stuffing more food in her mouth. She wasn't hungry anymore, but the more she ate, the less she could say.

Kenzie made a musing noise in the back of his throat. 'Lister Burke was there. That was a surprise. Were there any other important names thrown around?'

'None that I recognised,' Cait said.

'Did you speak to many people?'

'No.'

Kenzie raised his eyebrows. 'I don't know why you're being so defensive. I just want to know what you got up to.' He chuckled to himself. 'It could be worse. I could take you to the interrogation rooms.'

Cait didn't find that so funny. She tried to think like Calan. She tried to plan her moves like the pieces in a game, but she just couldn't see that far ahead. All she saw was gaining Kenzie's trust, and she knew she couldn't do that without spilling Separatist secrets.

'Tell me about your new friends.'

'They're not my friends.'

Kenzie waved a hand dismissively. 'Details. You must have thought to find out *something* about them while you were there.'

'They didn't tell me.'

Kenzie reached across the table and took her hand. He held it firm, a gentle squeeze to onlookers, but Cait felt pinned. 'Don't be silly, Cait,' he said softly. 'You don't need to pretend anymore. I'm here.'

Beneath his hand, Cait gripped her knife. 'I don't know what their plans are.'

Perhaps her voice rose too high, or perhaps Kenzie detected it quiver, because he squeezed her hand tighter, and Cait almost cried out. 'I don't want to lose you ever again,' he said. The tenderness of the previous night was gone, and Cait wondered if she stayed at his side how long it would be before tight squeezes and locked doors became something worse. Before Cait had a chance to answer, a soldier with her hair scraped back into a tight bun appeared at the table and snatched Kenzie's attention away.

'Bruce is here to see you, Bell,' the woman said in a hushed voice. She had a couple of chains on her cloak, and Cait had the impression that Kenzie should be taking orders from her as opposed to the opposite way around.

Kenzie frowned. 'Tonight? She's not supposed to be here until the morning.'

'Aye, she's being held outside.'

Kenzie sighed and rose to his feet, placing a hand on Cait's shoulder. 'Come on, little dove. I'll walk you to the barracks.'

They followed the officer out of the mess hall and across the courtyard, and Cait caught sight of a young woman in a tweed suit with a neat, blonde bob. As Kenzie steered Cait towards the barracks, the woman who had come to fetch him muttered, 'Don't keep her waiting.'

'Who's that?' Cait asked, peering over Kenzie's shoulder as he shepherded her into the barracks.

'Just a journalist,' Kenzie said. He glanced over his shoulder and then back to Cait. Heather was staring at them. 'Impatient bitch. You know the way?'

Cait nodded. 'It's just upstairs.'

'See you later.' Kenzie kissed her on the head and turned back into the courtyard, leaving Cait alone on the staircase. She pressed her eye to the crack in the door and squinted, watching the figures of Kenzie and the blonde woman disappear into one of the buildings off the middle ward.

A journalist. The Watchmen certainly had a story worth reporting on their hands.

*

It took her far longer than she would have liked, but eventually Cait found the communications room. She took the stairs to the door two at a time, and the officer yelped when she barrelled through.

'Can I help you?' he asked, blinking quickly. He was a mole of a man, with small eyes and thinning hair. He looked like he hadn't left the room in a very long time.

'I need to send a message to my family.'

The man shook his head once. 'Military communications only.'

'Please,' Cait said, taking a couple of steps towards the table. The man leaned backwards. 'No one needs to know. I just need to tell them I'm alright.'

'Can't allow it.'

She removed the little slip of paper from her pocket and held it up to him before reading, 'At Hart Hall. All is well.'

'Stop.'

'Good food, disappointed rumours about venison aren't true. Stew filled with mutton. Kitchens must have swapped meat. Shall have to write to papers. Hope you are well. All my love, Cait.' It was the best she could come up with, and she only hoped Calan would understand.

The communications officer bleated a laugh. 'You think I don't know you're Kenzie's lass?' There was that phrase again. 'You mix with the wrong crowd, girlie.'

'I was kidnapped.'

'Aye, so she says,' the officer said, sifting through a pile of papers on his desk with an incredulous expression across his face.

Cait heaved a sigh. 'Please, I don't know when I'll get to see them again.'

The communications officer looked up at her. 'I'm not going to send your message, and I'll be telling Kenzie about this.' He punctuated the sentence by giving the papers one swift *bang* against the table.

Fine, she thought. *Tell him. I'll be long gone.* Instead, she said. 'Okay. Tell him how you wouldn't send the message to my family after he specifically said I could.' She watched the cogs turning in the officer's mind as he stared at her through narrowed eyes, trying to weigh up whether she was bluffing or not, weighing up whether the risk was worth angering Kenzie, whose name clearly carried power in Hart Hall. 'I'm sure you wouldn't like it if he dropped your name in his next meeting with the Brigadier,' Cait said pointedly.

The officer watched her carefully, eyes narrowed. Cait prepared for his rebuttal. She clutched her right forearm, where the knife from the dinner table was tucked up her sleeve. She didn't want to use it, but if she had to take a leaf out of Aggie's book …

Finally, the officer breathed out slowly through his nose, and then swivelled his chair to the telegraph at his side. 'The message,' he said, holding out a hand, but avoiding Cait's eye. She handed him the slip of paper, her fingers gripping it as he pulled it away from her. 'Where's this going?'

'Brid — Stob Head,' Cait corrected herself. As much as she wanted to send a message to her parents, she didn't want them receiving this one, especially if her father knew the truth about Anndras.

Without a word, the Officer started to tap away at his device. Cait imagined the dots and dashes spinning off across the wires and up to

Gowdstane. Calan would know what to do. Then the officer stopped, folded his hands, and said, 'That's it.'

'That's it?'

He nodded once. 'Sent.'

Cait almost wept. 'Thank you.' She went to take the paper from the desk, but the communications officer snatched it up and placed it in a divider in his drawer. 'We need this for our records,' he said.

Cait managed a nod, then turned on her heel and ran back to the barracks.

*

Cait changed quickly, shoving the blue dress to the bottom of her bag, and throwing on her darkest clothes. She was pulling her hat over her head and tucking her hair in when a sharp rap came at the door.

'Miss Hardie,' came a voice, hard as Hart Hall's walls. 'Open up.'

She had barely taken a step towards the door when it sprung open, and three Watchmen strode into the room.

'You're to come with us,' said a muscular man with four or five chains on his cloak.

Cait took a step backwards. 'Why? Has Kenzie sent for me?'

The Watchman's expression remained stony as he waved his two companions into the room. They marched towards her. Cait scuttled backwards and braced herself on the other side of the bed, but the Watchmen grabbed her from either side and hauled her out of the room with bruising grips.

'What's going on?' Cait's voice rose in a panic that she tried to contain. 'Does Kenzie know about this?'

They ignored her, faces blank, as she was marched down from the barracks and across the courtyard, impervious to threats about Kenzie's wrath, unlike the communications officer. They led her around a sharp corner off the main courtyard and into a dark little doorway the officers had to duck under to get through. She slipped as the ground disappeared beneath her feet, and her knees struck stony steps. The Watchmen wasted no time waiting for her to regain her footing, and practically dragged her down. At the bottom, in the darkness, she heard the scream of a metal door being flung open, and the next thing she knew she was thrown forward and hit the ground with a painful crack. Immediately, moisture seeped through her clothes at her knees. The door clanged shut. When her eyes adjusted, she was in a cell.

Cait flung herself against the bars. 'Get Kenzie! Kenzie Bell!' she shouted. The Watchmen didn't acknowledge her, and their footsteps rung up the stairs and faded into silence. Somewhere upstairs, a metal gate groaned shut. In the cell opposite her, she saw the eyes of the communications officer blink, then slowly look away.

Chapter 31

First and Fairest

The news arrived in two quick blows. First, that Afren refused to recognise Aidan's claim, and second, that the remains robbed from Anndras' tomb belonged to Cathal.

Aidan had barely finished reading the public statement signed by Queen Ana and Chancellor Borden that branded Aidan a pretender, when Calan received a telegram from Hart Hall. After Calan had decoded the erratic symbols and cracked the code within Cait's words, he sat back, removed his glasses, and slowly wiped the lenses on his jacket. It took five minutes for Aidan to get an answer out of him.

Cathal's remains had been unearthed from Anndras' tomb, meaning that somewhere in their mist-cloaked history, Anndras and Cathal had swapped places. It meant that Anndras, Aidan's ancestor, died walking into the Queen's trap. It meant that Cathal had defeated the Afrenian army and been crowned King. It meant Aidan was nothing but the descendant of a rebel nobleman. When Calan finished explaining, Aidan stormed from the tower and prowled the grounds in search of Anndras, but the ghost was nowhere to be found. He watched the rumour break and spread through his people like an illness. They bowed their heads as they passed him by on their way to town, clutching their belongings close.

Let them go, Aidan thought. *It's only a rumour.* Cait might well have been telling her parents about the food on offer at Hart Hall, or Calan may have misunderstood her meaning. Still, no matter how hard he looked, he could not find the ghost of the King anywhere.

*

Hours later, Aidan's search led him somewhere he had never been before: to the door of Lister's office in the west wing. He knocked twice, and following a few moments of silence, Lister called for him to enter. Aidan lingered in the doorway. 'Mr Burke,' he said.

Lister glanced over, then put his pen back to the letter in front of him. 'Take a seat, and close the door,' Lister said when Aidan hadn't moved. 'You're letting the heat out.'

Aidan sank into the armchair adjacent to Lister's desk and watched him write in pleasant cursive. The office was a far cry from the rest of Gowdstane. There were no draughty holes or noisy leaks. It was cosy and well-maintained, and the walls were adorned by oil paintings depicting religious iconography from Afren: a dark-eyed girl with shadows spilling from her hands, a blonde-haired woman with a crystal chalice, a man in robes of black and white. Aidan couldn't quite remember the names of the characters, but they all had the same lofty, absent look in their eye, each elegant limb languid even in battle.

When Aidan could no longer stand Lister's pen scratching at the silence between them, he said, 'I'm going to Thorterknock.' Lister offered no reaction. 'We're going to take the city.'

Lister didn't look up as he said, 'We?'

'Those who have stayed,' Aidan said. 'They're willing to fight.' There were around a hundred and forty who remained at Gowdstane. The numbers weren't great, but it was a start. Besides, the underdogs always won the day in ancient epics. Lister only grunted. Aidan leaned forward on his knees. 'Afren betrayed their own laws, and Storran should be free right now. Some of us aren't willing to let them get away wi — with ... it.'

Lister slowly, carefully, laid his pen down on the desk. 'No laws have been broken. You are not Storran's true heir,' he muttered, lifting the page before him, and inspecting the words he had just penned.

Aidan bristled. 'The people *chose* me.'

'Don't get cocky.' Lister laid the paper down and picked up his pen again. He opened the lid with a pointed *pop*. 'A few hundred residents of a small town chose you. But will they support you when they find out that you're a pretender?'

'I'm *not* a pretender.'

Lister continued writing. 'We'll see what the people think when they read tomorrow's paper.'

'But journalists lie.'

'Kings lie, too.'

'So do politicians.'

The nib of Lister's pen cracked against the page and his jaw clenched.

Dark ink pooled across the paper. 'If you have only come to antagonise me, I suggest you run along and play revolution.' Aidan watched Lister fold the paper and dispose of it. He mopped the spilled ink, selected a new page, and addressed the letter, with all the grace and precision of a conductor.

Lister had given him the permission he needed, but Aidan couldn't bring himself to leave the warm office. He wanted to stay in this comfortable chair, watching the ink trail from Lister's nice pen as it looped across the page. He wanted to feel the security of a man whose station was secure. He wanted to feel *safe*. 'What should I do?' The words scraped by his throat.

Lister's eyebrows lifted. 'So, now you want my advice, boy?'

He didn't, but Anndras was gone, and Lister was the cleverest man he knew. It was Lister who had built the Separatists from the ground up. He saw himself as Lister must see him: a child kicking his legs against a writhing sea, clinging to a splinter of driftwood. Lister was a ship, and Aidan had been kicking against the wake for so long.

Trust my father, Bess had said.

'I don't know what to do,' Aidan said, voice pathetic and small.

Lister stopped. He laid his pen on the desk and swivelled in his chair. 'What is it you *want* to do?' He looked at Aidan with an inquisitive tilt of the head.

He wanted Storran to be free. He didn't want to be ruled by a land that forced them to live cap in hand, twisting their own laws when it suited them. He didn't believe for a moment that Afren knew the truth about Anndras when they initially denied his right to rule. Most of all, he wanted to be someone, just not the rootless boy from the orphanage he was all those years ago.

In one of his earliest memories, he sat on his mother's knee and twisted a strand of her dark hair around his finger. 'I've got something important to tell you,' his mother had said. 'You can't visit Mr Smith for a while.'

Aidan had blinked innocently up at her. 'Why?' Mr Smith had the biggest collection of novels Aidan had ever seen.

'He's had to move away,' his mother had said. It was the way she'd skirted around the issue that cemented the memory in Aidan's mind. He remembered so distinctly thinking that getting the truth out of her would be a fun game.

'Where did he go?' Aidan had asked.

His mother had paused, clearly choosing a combination of words that were both gentle and true. 'He's not able to live in his own house anymore. He needs to live in a workhouse for a while.'

'Why?' Aidan had asked.

Again, she had paused, then seemed to choose truth. 'Sometimes, money is hard to come by.'

Little Aidan had heard his father shouting about money before. Fear gripped him. He liked his home, and the vegetable patch, and the neighbours. 'Will *we* need to move to a workhouse?' he had asked.

'Oh, duck,' his mother had said, pulling him close. 'No. We'll be alright.'

Aidan had sat quietly for a moment, though he couldn't remember what thoughts passed through his mind in that time. 'Are there a lot of people in workhouses?' he'd asked.

His mother had sighed. 'Yes, duck. Quite a few.'

'Are they stuck there?' he'd asked innocently.

His mother had smiled sadly, though he hadn't realised it was sad at the time. 'Yes, they're stuck there.'

He'd burrowed in closer to her and continued wrapping her hair around his finger. 'Well, I'm not stuck. When I'm bigger, I'll get them out.'

His mother had laughed and drawn her arms around him. 'Yes, my little hero, you will.'

Aidan glanced at the portraits on Lister's wall and wondered if they had ever doubted the path laid out for them. 'I want to fight,' he said.

'Then there you have it,' Lister said.

'No, but ... is that right? What's the best course of action?' *You are not a strategist. You are not a politician.* You are not a king.

'I'm going to give you some advice that was given to me at the start of my political career,' Lister said, leaning in. Aidan had never been so close to him, and he realised Lister smelled of oaky musk. His skin was marked like aged tree bark. 'You will have many stances in your life, and they will change. Sometimes, they will change quicker than you imagined.' He gave a wry grin at that. Aidan wondered what causes Lister had abandoned on his way to the top. 'But every leader has their truth. Don't betray that.' There was a vulnerability in Lister's eyes that Aidan had never seen before, but he recognised it from Bess' round and honest face. Before Aidan's eyes, Lister Burke seemed to shift from a stone monument, into a mortal man.

'Your truth's Storran, isn't it?' Aidan asked. What else would push a successful politician into this hovel of a fortress?'

Lister chuckled darkly and closed off again. 'My truth is my family. My truth is whatever will keep them fed and warm.'

Maybe we have more in common than I realised, Aidan thought. Aidan's truth was Bess, and his mother's memory. Aidan's truth was building a world that wouldn't hurt the people he loved. And he was so, so close.

Pretender. That was what Afren saw him as, but Anndras had been a pretender all this time, too. Aidan was unsure why he and Cathal had swapped places, but it was Anndras who had led his people to the doorstep of freedom. It was Anndras who had built the army and inspired the troops. It was Anndras that the people had looked up to. Aidan would lead them across that line now and do what Anndras never had the chance to.

'Thank you,' Aidan said, standing.

'You'll make the right decision,' Lister said, engrossed in his letter writing once more. He flashed one brief glance at Aidan and added, 'Little king.'

Aidan hovered at the open door. There were words that he should say, like *thank you for always guiding me,* or *you're like the father I never had.* But it was a little too late for that, and Aidan was letting the heat out.

*

Aidan informed his force of one hundred and forty that they would set off for Thorterknock the following day. He then retreated to the ramparts, where he watched one hundred and forty become one hundred and ten. People who had just promised him their sword threw guilty glances over their shoulders as they disappeared into the night. They didn't think he saw them leave, but he did. He saw every single one of them.

'Don't watch, Aidan,' a quiet voice said behind him, and a breath later, Bess was at his side. She wrapped an arm around his and laid her head on his shoulder. How did she always know where to find him? 'Come inside.'

Aidan shook his head. 'They never believed in me. They only believed in Anndras.' He gave a defeated laugh. 'They're calling me a pretender.'

Bess threaded her thin, cold fingers through his and sighed. 'Maybe we're all just pretending.'

'Do you agree with them?' Aidan asked, too quickly, the flash of hurt in his chest speaking for him.

She looked up at him. 'I don't believe in Anndras,' Bess said with a smile. 'I believe in you.'

Her sparkling eyes were worth a hundred Separatists. He'd let them all leave if it meant Bess would be at his side. They'd take on Afren. They'd take on the world. He told her of his plan, of the ship one of his men had secured that was currently waiting in Carse's harbour. He told her of the route they'd sail from Carse in the dead of night, sneaking around the islands and peninsulas of Storran's Northern Prongs, down the west, and into Thorterknock's port. He told her that, in two weeks' time, they would take the city of Thorterknock for the people of Storran.

When he finished, she blinked at him. 'I don't understand.'

'We're going to stand up to Afren,' he said. The rush of it stretched his cheeks into a grin. The plans had been set in frantic, rushed whispers, but now that he unleashed them into the night air, his heart pounded. This was his destiny. He had no doubt that it would be hard, but once they won, it would be the happiest day in Storran's long history. So why did Bess look so incredibly sad?

'You're going to fight?'

'That was always the plan.'

'N — no. No, it wasn't,' Bess stammered. He wasn't sure he'd ever heard her stammer before. 'My father's plan was to move south as peacefully as possible. Not to march straight on Thorterknock —'

Aidan grinned and took her hands. 'It's okay. Lister agreed.'

'Aidan —'

'And our numbers aren't bad.' Silence lapsed between them, and treading in it, Aidan clung tighter. 'Don't be scared. We've got weapons, and *Calan*. You saw how he pulled together that coronation.'

A cold laugh escaped her lips. 'I've never been more scared.'

'Anndras', well, Cathal's forces were three to one when he beat Afren. We can do the same.'

'That's a *story*.'

'It's history.' He thought Lister would be hard to convince, he never even considered that Bess would be so frightened. 'Your father —'

'My father has arranged to leave for Witteneuk tomorrow. He's written to Enlighten and resigned,' Bess said. *Hypocrite,* Aidan thought, but he bit the word back for Bess' sake. Her next words struck him in the heart.

'I'm going with him.'

Aidan's chest numbed. His mouth hung open. 'What?'

'I'm going to Witteneuk.' Her words sounded so strained.

'You're leaving?'

Bess stepped closer to Aidan, a hazy wistfulness across her face. Or was it desperation? 'Come with me,' she said.

'To Witteneuk?'

'We'll change our names, take up fishing —'

'You said you'd stand with me.' Aidan stepped back. 'We ...' He felt his voice crack and fought to regain control. 'The heather.'

'That was before.'

'Before what?' Aidan snapped. 'Before you found out I'm not royalty?'

Bess' expression hardened. 'You know that has nothing to do with it.' He stepped towards her again. 'We can win this.'

Bess shook her head. 'Not this way.' Her eyes travelled to the path that led from the castle and up to the Cronachs, where not long ago he had thought about running away with her. 'You could lay low. In time, you could advocate for Storran.'

But he didn't want to advocate or petition. It wasn't what Anndras would have done. 'I'm still King of Storran. I can't just run away when there are people willing to put up a fight,' Aidan said, perhaps too abruptly. He ran his fingers through his hair. 'There are people suffering every day, and that's not going to stop. Not until *someone* does something, and I've been waiting to do something *my whole life*.'

Bess' expression darkened. 'You're not their saviour.'

'Someone has to be.'

'Aidan, I'm begging you.' He hated the way her voice wobbled, he hated the desperation burning in her gaze, and he hated that he didn't know how to soothe it without saying words he knew he didn't mean. 'I will lose you,' she said. 'If you try to face Afren, I will lose you. In one way or another.' Her voice cracked, and Aidan's heart with it. He pulled her in, holding her trembling frame.

'It's okay,' he whispered.

'No, it's not.'

Their hearts raced side by side as he held her close. 'Don't cry,' he said, wiping the tears from her pretty face. 'I'll outlaw crying, right here and now, and then I'll have no choice but to execute you, and neither of us want that. I've got the power to do that.'

Bess groaned into his chest. 'I love you,' she moaned, then gasped out a sob.

He tilted her face to his and smiled reassuringly. 'Trust me.'

'You don't need to be the hero,' Bess said after a pause.

'Who else can I be?'

'You could be mine,' she said. 'Unless that's not enough.'

Shadielaunds, that was so far from the truth. Elizabeth Burke was far more than he deserved. 'You know that's not true.' He pulled her close again, wrapping his arms around her waist. Her hands slid up his chest and clung to his shirt, as if he would dissipate into the night. With their foreheads pressed together, her hair brushed his skin.

'Then run,' she whispered.

For a moment, Aidan saw that future, and for a moment, he wanted it. A simple life, a little family. Growing old by the wind-battered coast. 'I will give you the life you want, Bess. I promise you.' He could be happy, but he would always regret it. Anndras would fade, and Aidan would slowly lose himself by the coast. 'But let me do what I was born for first.' The last of the hope that had been in her eyes shattered. She didn't say anything, and just traced a finger around one of the buttons on his shirt. 'Bess,' he said, longing for the warmth of her amber eyes and the hazy grin of wine-stained lips. 'Bess.' Her gaze lifted. His heart leapt. 'I love you.'

'I know,' Bess said. 'I love you, too.'

'I'll come back for you,' Aidan said. 'When it's all over, I'll come to Witteneuk. We'll live the life you want.' Even as he said the words, he wasn't sure if he meant them, but if they took away some of her pain for now, he could work out what to do once the battle was over.

Her features hardened into stoic determination. '*Lealtie Ayebidin,* ma jo.' She used the Old Storrian term of endearment. *My darling.* Then her lips were pressed to his, her hands in his hair, his in hers. They pulled into each other, hands grasping, and clinging, and remembering. For that moment, he threw himself headlong into the life that she dreamed of, fish, and wind, and all. 'See you when we're free,' she whispered.

And then she was gone. His hands were left cold and empty. Her words lingered on the breeze, and the salty taste of a different life on his lips. When Aidan opened his eyes, Anndras was still nowhere to be found.

Chapter 32

Sever

The window in Cait's cell looked down onto a little courtyard with a whitewashed wall on one side, and a tiny wooden door on the other. A bloody sunset spilled across the cobbles. The communications officer had refused to speak to her at first, but after some time, she'd learned that his name was Fraser. Sat cross-legged at the bars of her cell, she managed to coax from him increasingly detailed stories about his life back home in Carse: his prior job in the mills, his love for the tin whistle, the little sailboat he liked to sail down the River Garbh, but only ever in the summer because otherwise it was simply too treacherous.

'So, is it busy work?' Cait asked off the back of a story about how he came to work in the communications office.

'Oh, awful busy,' Fraser said. 'You need a steady hand, too. One dash too many and instead of oats for breakfast you're having goats.' He chuckled to himself.

'What's the most important message you've ever sent?' Cait asked out of genuine curiosity.

Fraser laughed. 'Nice try, pet.'

Pet. Her heart gave a longing twinge. The silence that followed was like every other that lapsed between them, filled only with the water dripping from the ceiling and the distant clatter of a busy military barracks above. After a while, Cait would usually plug this silence with a new question for Fraser, but this time she took a deep breath and asked him the one they had both been exhaustively dodging. 'What do you think happens now?'

'Cannae speak for you, but I imagine there's a hefty slap on the wrist coming my way,' Fraser said, arranging himself on the floor of his cell with one leg draped over the other. 'Or maybe they'll ship us both off with the refugees.'

Cait grimaced. 'That's not funny.'

Fraser turned his head to face her. 'Oh, I can assure you it won't be. You think Thorterknock's bad? You've got another thing coming when you get to Iffega. Sorry bastards.'

'They can't actually ship people out of the country,' Cait scoffed. She'd grown up with rhetoric about Iffegan refugees, about how they stole resources and jobs, and that was the reason so many people from Storran were struggling. She'd heard her mother suggest shipping them off countless times before. Fraser's bigotry was no different to that of her mother's.

'They certainly can, and certainly will,' Fraser said, then added quickly, 'but that's strictly embargoed information that you didn't hear from me.'

'What do you mean?' Cait pressed. Fraser ignored her, draping an arm over his eyes. 'Fraser!'

He seemed to weigh up the fact he was sat in a dark cell with nothing else to do, so flipped onto his side. Cait scooted closer to the bars as he spoke in a hushed voice. 'I got a telegram from Chancellor Borden for the attention of the Brigadier, what, two days ago? It was instructing us that while the duties of the Queen's Watch haven't changed in the wake of the Council's decision, we're to be on the lookout for —'

'*What* decision?'

Even in the shady prison, Cait saw Fraser's expression darken. 'Afren have torn up the Iffega Agreement. The refugees have no right to live in the Five Realms anymore. Documented or not, they're sending them home. It comes down to the usual rubbish. Job stealing, and resource leaching, and all that tripe. A lot of people in Afren are in favour.'

His rhetoric wasn't just rhetoric, then. It was the truth. 'But what about here? Surely not here?' Cait said, voice rising. It didn't matter what land had birthed him, Calan was Storrian through and through.

Fraser shrugged. 'Doesn't matter, realm-wide legislation, so it is. The news goes to print Monday,' he said, then added quickly, as though she were in any position to spread the word, 'But don't be telling anyone, or I'll get double the smacking.'

Monday. Could this have been what Kenzie was meeting the journalist about? If he hadn't been discussing Cathal's remains with her, maybe they hadn't worked out the truth yet.

Somewhere above, a door blustered open and cool evening air swept into the cells. Cait scrambled to her feet just in time for Kenzie to appear and stalk down the passageway towards her. She lunged forward, gripping the bars tight.

'Kenzie, there's been a mistake.'

'I should've known,' he spat. 'You made me trust you.'

'I don't know why I'm here!'

Kenzie fished in his pocket, and when he removed his hand, a little card bearing Cait's message had appeared between his fingers. Cait's hands dropped from the bars. 'This was not sent to Briddock,' he said, brandishing it closer to her face. 'Who was this meant for?'

Cait glanced past Kenzie and over to Fraser, who watched them from the shadows. 'Did you send it?' Cait's voice trembled. 'Tell me you sent it.' Kenzie plunged his hand through the bars, and he caught the cuff of her sleeve, pulling her hand towards him as she twisted to get free. 'Kenzie, let me *go*.'

'Tell me who is in Stob Head!' he shouted.

'There's no one!' she shouted right back. The volume of her own voice almost sent her to her knees. He released her. An incredible sense of giddiness washed over her. She wanted to shout until her throat was raw and her lungs burned. She almost laughed.

Kenzie's lips drew into a thin line, wetted with rage. 'Lying little bitch!' he hissed, hammering his fists on the bars of the cell and they rung, shivering.

Cait stumbled backwards and landed on the floor. 'What are you going to do? Are you going to let them shoot me?'

'That's the punishment for Separatists,' he said cooly, studying the message in his hand.

He was bluffing. He wouldn't let her come to harm. But when Kenzie raised his hands to the bars, Cait saw a flash of his white palms and realised that wasn't true. She let herself laugh now. He would have hurt her a long time ago if duty hadn't called. 'Then make sure I'm unhooded, so I can look right at you when —'

'Why, Cait?' Kenzie roared at her through the bars. She stilled. Shouting wasn't so fun anymore. 'Why have you done this to me?' He started pacing like a frothing, maddened animal. Despite the fact she was in a cell, she felt like she was watching a tortured bear pacing back and forth in a cage.

'It was the right thing,' Cait said, the pace of her speech quickening. 'They're going to send away the refugees, they —'

'Oh, shut it,' Kenzie snapped.

'No!' The word ripped out of her hard, and fast, and loud, and she watched it lash him. She watched him reel for moment.

'I loved you, Cait,' Kenzie hissed through gritted teeth.

You took me from my home. You left me, you lied to me, you murdered a man behind my back. You convinced me I couldn't breathe without you. You locked me away. You never listen. She almost said it all, but the way the dim light from her cell's window caught his twisted face conjured a memory that hit her so staggeringly bright and vivid, it snatched her mustered breath. She and Kenzie in a field of sheep on the cusp of night, ages eight and eleven, stalking the lambs together so Cait could stroke their wool. They had never gotten close, their laughter scaring the animals away. 'You did love me,' she said quietly, still half in the memory. 'Maybe once, when we were little.' Another memory came to her, when Cait had learned in school that the ancients used to leap over fires at their weddings, and so they took it upon themselves to try. 'You singed your trousers,' Cait said to herself, remembering the panic that had crossed his golden face when he realised.

Kenzie looked at her, bewildered for a moment, then seemed to catch her in that field that only they could see. His anger faded, and he laughed weakly. 'They were your da's, actually. He almost had my head.' Cait smiled. They *were* happy. She had spent so much time recently wondering if they ever had been. Sometime long ago, she had looked at Kenzie with the same drunken gaze Bess wore when she looked at Aidan. Slowly, as though he were approaching the cage of beast, Kenzie walked to the bars and crouched down. 'Cait ...' he said, his voice fracturing. A tear streaked down his face, and he hurriedly brushed it away. He grasped the bars of the cell. Cait pulled herself closer and lay her hands over his. He flinched at her touch. 'I love you,' he said, and on the words an ugly sob burst from his throat. His nose snotted. His eyes reddened. 'I love you, Cait. Please.'

But it didn't matter how many times he said it now. Those words felt tainted by the desperation that drove him to speak them. 'You did love me. And I loved you.' As she watched him, she felt herself cry, too, missing the carefree boy he had been before his parents were taken, and before the weight of the world clung to his cloak in delicate, golden chains. 'But at some point, it became a prison. I need my freedom.'

Some clarity seemed to come over him, and he looked at her, wide-eyed. He shifted his grip on the bars, so his hands covered hers. 'Then deny it all. Stay here with me.'

'That won't work.'

'I'll vouch for you. We'll work something out.'

Conspiring with him in the dark like they were children again felt good, the warm rush of nostalgia that she realised she hadn't felt in years as their love had slowly curdled. 'I can't do that,' she said before that familiar and comforting feeling could choke the sense from her.

Kenzie's face glowed with a hopeful determination. 'Trust me, Cait.' He'd normally call her *little dove* there. Her name was only for lashings and ridicule. It felt odd for it to fit her so nicely.

'No,' she said, her voice breaking. 'I won't.'

He tried to reach through the bars for her face, but Cait pulled away. On trembling legs, she stood, and watched the hurt flash across Kenzie's face as the knotted thread that linked their lives finally severed. He stood, wiped his face, and his cool mask fell across his features once more. He turned his back on her and delivered the sentence to the communications officer calmly. 'You will be executed by firing squad.' Then he turned to look at Cait. 'Both of you.' Cait realised that this was his goodbye. There would be no secret plot to break her out, no last-minute turnaround. Kenzie never intended to see her again.

When he swept from the cells, Cait sank to the ground, but she was finished crying. She heard a whimper through the silence and found Fraser crouched on the floor of his cell with his head in his hands.

'I'm sorry,' she said.

He looked up at her slowly, his eyes blazing with what could only be hatred. She saw in him a reflection of her past self: the girl who had turned to Kenzie and told him about a suspicious innkeeper; the girl who had craved Kenzie's approval and thrown someone else to the dogs in order to get it; the girl who cried in a darkened pub with the ghost of Kenzie's ire forever hanging over her head.

*

Cait realised that the little courtyard outside, with its whitewashed wall, was to be the site of her execution. She would have expected to see blood up the walls and over the cobbles, but it looked clinical in the dying light. Like a hospital. What did it feel like to have a bullet enter your heart? She had watched her mother slice into someone's abdomen once, but they were under so many painkillers they had no idea what was happening, and it was neatly stitched up afterwards. Surgery was careful and exact. Gunshot wounds were messy, and they could only feel messy. She couldn't soothe herself by pretending she could fix herself. She sank down the wall and began unspooling her thoughts from their dark spiral for the umpteenth time. When footsteps came clattering down towards her, perhaps on the first night, perhaps the second, Cait stumbled to her feet. *Not now. Please not now.*

It was Innes. He appeared at the bars of her cell with a little plate of shortbread. 'I took these from the mess,' he said breathlessly, sliding the plate under the bars. 'I thought you might be hungry.' He hesitantly returned her smile then added quickly, 'It's not a last meal. You've just been in here a long time, and prison food isn't great. I've seen it, when —'

'When executions happen?' Cait said.

'No, no, not that!'

'It's okay,' Cait said with a laugh that was exhausting to muster. Food was the last thing on Cait's mind, but she gratefully picked up the plate. Her eyes hunted for the note, the key, the glimmer of salvation secretly slipped to her like it happened in the books, but there was nothing there other than a crumbly pile of shortbread. 'Thanks, Innes. Though I fear it might be my last, after all.'

Innes shook his head vigorously. 'No, he'll get you out.'

Cait studied him. 'Who will?'

'Kenzie. He won't just leave you here, he'll speak to someone.'

Cait sighed. 'I wish you were right.'

Innes searched her face, perhaps trying to find the lie, the hint that Kenzie had revealed a secret plan to her. Then he lifted his chin slightly. 'Then I will. I'll speak to the Brigadier, or I'll steal the key, or —'

'Innes, no.' She needed him to be quiet before the wrong person overheard. 'Listen, what I need you to do is go back upstairs. Go to bed, get some rest, and don't think about me.'

'Yeah but, I can't just —'

She spoke firmly, with a lot more confidence than she felt. 'If Kenzie can, so can you.'

He stood there in silence for a moment, then his eyes darted up the passageway and he stepped closer to her. 'Cait.' He kept his voice low as he said, 'I ...' He shook his head, running a hand through his hair. 'Doesn't matter.'

'No, go on,' Cait said.

Innes threw a quick glance over his shoulder, but Fraser appeared to be asleep. 'How did you ... how do you know the Separatists are right?'

'The Separatists?' Cait asked, surprised. 'I mean, I don't agree with a lot of their methods, but I think they have Storran's best interests in mind. Their goals sit right with me.'

'Okay,' Innes said, nodding to himself.

'Why?' Cait asked.

He hesitated, then said, 'Sometimes ... sometimes the Watch's goals don't sit right with me.'

Cait's heart broke for him. When she first met him, he was a proud boy in uniform who wanted to do what he thought was best for the country. The man before her was decorated, but scarred, and deeply, deeply confused.

'What makes you say that?' she asked.

Innes looked conflicted for a moment. His eyes traced a path to the stairs, and he took another step closer, so his nose was almost pressed up against the bars. 'Just the way they do things. I understand *why* we do them but there's so many secrets.'

'What secrets do they make you keep, Innes?' Innes opened his mouth, then closed it again. He gave a breathy laugh and shook his head. 'Don't worry,' Cait said, then added with a coy smile, 'I'm a dead woman.'

Innes fidgeted with the buttons on his sleeves. 'Sometimes they twist things, or cover things up.' He took a shuddering breath. 'I shot a man that was completely innocent. He died.'

'Oh, Innes.'

'Kenzie told me to do it. He said that he was a dangerous Separatist, so I did it, but I had to go around the back to throw up after. That's when I saw him looking for evidence.' Innes shook his head. 'He made it up. The man was never a Separatist, and Kenzie lied to cover it up.'

Cait's heart faltered. 'Where did this happen?' She almost didn't want to know.

'An inn.' Realisation dawned on Innes' face as he said the words. 'The one you were staying in.' So, Bram died by Innes' trusting hand. 'I can't sleep. I think about him all the time. When I told the truth, they just told me that these things happen, and to get on with it.' Innes spoke in short, sharp gasps. 'He looked so confused. He was really scared, and I just panicked and —'

'Innes, listen,' Cait said, holding the bars of the cell, mostly for her own support. 'It's not your fault.'

'It is.'

'Kenzie should never have covered it up. He should never have been there in the first place.' She understood what Innes was going through. There was rarely a night that Bram didn't appear in her dreams, but her own words granted her slight reprieve, permission to maybe one day forgive herself.

'But —'

'And I'm going to be honest with you. I think the Separatists and the Lealists are just as bad as each other.'

A look of horror ghosted across Innes' features, and Cait realised she had used the word *Lealist*. After a moment, he said, 'Then what's the point in all of it?'

Cait sighed. She had thought the same thing over and over, when Bram was murdered, when she stood on the pier in Eadwick, when Aggie almost spilled blood in the Dorcha Pass. But when Aidan was crowned and she watched the reactions of the people of Clackhatton, she saw an expression form on their faces she hadn't seen since she set the injured woman's arm in Thorterknock: hope. It was the same expression that had been on Innes' face when she first met him, and the same one that fell upon a patient's face when they were passed a concoction that promised to cure them. A smile tugged at Cait's lips. 'To do what's best for our people, what's best for Storran,' she said. 'We all have a lot more in common than we realise.'

Innes nodded. 'I do want what's best for Storran.'

'There you have it.'

'I'll get you out,' Innes said, this time quieter.

'No, no, listen. You know what you *can* do for me?' He leaned in expectantly. Cait fixed him with a hard look. She needed him to remember this. There were good people out there, people like Calan, and Jamie, and even Aggie. People who cared. Innes was one of them, regardless of the uniform on his shoulders. 'Keep fighting. Do what *you* think is best for Storran, not Kenzie, not the Watch or the Separatists, and never, ever stop. The moment people who care stop caring, we have nothing. Okay?'

She saw a glimmer of renewed steeliness enter his frightened eyes. 'For Storran,' he echoed. He glanced up the passage and straightened as if to leave, then hesitated. His voice rose in fear. 'I don't want you to die.' Where Kenzie's emotionless death sentence hadn't shaken her, Innes' words crept under her skin, and the reality struck her cold and hard. She didn't want to die either. Her vision blurred and Innes' eyes widened. 'I've upset you.'

'No, it's not you.'

Innes took her hand and pulled her to the ground, sitting cross-legged at the other side of the bars. 'Tell me a story. Your favourite.'

Cait tilted her head and narrowed her eyes. 'Did Kenzie tell you I like stories?' she asked.

A smile flickered on Innes' lips. 'No. Your da did.'

Cait breathed deeply, trying to arrange her thoughts. Through quivering breaths, she told Innes the story of the doo in the golden cage. Just as the bird was about to make her first bid for freedom, a voice from above called for Innes. He hesitated, staring at her with fearful eyes. 'Go,' Cait said, and gave him a smile that she hoped was reassuring. It took him a moment, but he did. He stood, and his footsteps echoed on the steps as he vanished, leaving the cells in silence once more.

Chapter 33

Shadow of the Fox

Through the dark, the interior of a little house came into focus. Aggie stood at the centre of a small room, but her surroundings were veiled in gossamer. The walls rippled. The floor swayed. A blond man in uniform stood before her. *Kenzie.* She didn't know why she knew that name, but it rattled around her chest. When she looked around, there were other figures in the room all with Kenzie's face. Their eyes flashed at her, hungry.

There was a loud *crack,* and Aggie fell to her knees. When she glanced down, a white lance throbbed through her gut. *Crack.* Her shoulders jarred backwards. A second lance protruded from her right shoulder. She screamed against the white pain and dropped forward onto her hands. Kenzie's faces leered down at her, all swimming in and out of focus. She'd kill him. If she couldn't work out which one was real, she'd kill them all. As she tried to stand, her limbs deadened, and a crushing weight pressed down on her shoulders. The figures above her closed in, then duplicated and swayed. Aggie looked down at her hands and realised she was seeing double. Shadows stretched out across the floor towards her, and a smoky haze settled across her vision. A moment later, the room gave way to pitch darkness, and Aggie was falling.

When her eyes flew open, she was on a bed. The ghost of the fall lingered in the air around her. Her limbs were pinned, her muscles frozen, and darkness leached into the edges of her vision. Through the haze, she heard mumblings. At first, they had no form, but every now and again, full phrases reached her.

Infection's spreading.
She'll lik be dead the morn.
Ah ken a doc up the Prongs who kens a hing or twa. I'll call in some favours, but I wilna mak ony promises, lik.

And there were images, too: a beautiful warrior and a strong blacksmith;

a white doo in a golden cage.

Pinned to the bed, Aggie could only look on as her vision divided and one room became two: one vibrant, the other built of shadow. *This is it,* she realised. *These are the Shadielaunds.* Soon, the vibrant world would fade, and she would be reduced to a shade stumbling through a dark labyrinth. If she was lucky, which she never had been, she'd reach the land of eternal gloaming on the other side.

There were other images: an antlered crown and a royal stag; a boy who frowned behind a pair of round glasses. They were familiar. She was certain of it. The darkness had almost taken her when she finally managed to push herself to her feet. This time, she felt light, as though she were made of breath. When she looked down, she saw her body lying on the bed. Her lips were blue, her face grey. *Not yet,* she thought, and put her hand to the lance in her stomach, and pulled. She screamed with the effort as pain bloomed across her torso, and when the lance came free, she buckled. She watched as the light dissipated into little sparks, swallowed up by the shadows one by one, blinking out. Then the world trembled. The bed, and her body upon it, doubled, and tripled, and fractured into a thousand transparent slides, one atop the other. As quick as it had changed, it returned to normal, only darker than it had been before.

I'm fading.

She pulled at the lance in her shoulder, but it stung her hands and burrowed deeper. She cried out. The shadows looped around her, their frigid tendrils snaking at her ankles. When she tried to swat them away, they clung tighter, inching up her legs. Aggie looked up and found herself face to face with a figure she quickly recognised. Its red hair hung limp at its cheeks, which were hollow, and pooled with darkness. Its eyes blazed. It bared its teeth in a maniacal grin.

'You…' Aggie breathed. The Fox of Thorterknock stalked towards Aggie, who shuffled pathetically backwards. Each agonising movement made the world tremble and darken some more. 'What are you going to do?' Aggie spat. 'Are going to kill me like you tried to kill that girl? Or that politician with the fireworks? I know you wanted to.' The Fox halted. Its long, dark figure loomed over Aggie, who couldn't remember how to stand. 'Go on,' she whispered, taunting the Fox.

The Fox's grin stayed put as it lifted its hand, and Aggie braced for the final blow, but instead of cutting her down as she might have deserved, the Fox offered a hand to Aggie. Its nails were caked in blood. Aggie understood.

Come with me.

The Fox was giving her a way out: a path back to the world of the living.

Aggie glanced at the pale figure on the bed beside her. Felled by a Lealist and barely clinging to life; Aggie wanted nothing to do with her. She looked back to the Fox, who flickered before her with a lifeline extended. The Fox would never let itself be destroyed by the likes of Kenzie; it would be his hunter, his foe, his sorry undoing. It took every ounce of her strength, but slowly, Aggie lifted her hand towards the Fox. As their fingers brushed, another image cut through her memories: a scuffle, a knife, blood streaked through white hair, ever-changing eyes that stared at Aggie in a hundred shades of fear. In those eyes, the Fox grinned back at her.

The shadows curled around Aggie's shoulders and up her neck. She raised her chin as her vision doubled again. The Fox turned its palm upwards towards Aggie.

Take it or become a shadow.

Aggie didn't know to whom those pretty eyes belonged, but she knew she would never rest in eternal dusk until she'd taken away their fear. The Fox's figure shivered as the world began to fracture.

Take it.

'Next time,' Aggie said, then with a scream, wrapped her hands around the lance in her shoulder, and heaved. The Fox lunged for her. Fire surged through Aggie's veins. She pulled the lance free, and the ground disappeared beneath her, and she fell through darkness once more.

*

Aggie screamed, but she couldn't remember why. Hands touched her. Cool liquid touched her lips. Hot pain abated.

'Lie back, lass. It's too soon.'

Aggie lay back and allowed the darkness to take her.

Chapter 34

The White Doo

The next time Aggie opened her eyes, the world was clearer. She lifted herself onto her elbows and looked around. She lay on a bed in a dim surgery, one that she felt like she had seen in a dream. The only shadows in the room were pinned in the corners by several low-burning candles. Calan slouched on a chair by her bed. His breath filled up the room with a steady snore, and his glasses lay crooked across his face. Aggie laughed, but the effort snatched her breath and made her chest hurt. Her torso and right shoulder throbbed under clean bandages, and she studied her hands to check she was no longer seeing double. She remembered now: the Lealists in the cottage, and the gun that Kenzie fired into her. She smarted with the effort of pulling herself out of bed and hobbled across the empty room to the door. She considered waking Calan, but she couldn't remember the last time he had looked so peaceful.

It was night outside, and every passageway she staggered down was silent. If it hadn't been for one tower glowing like a beacon in the dark, she might have thought she and Calan were the only living things there. She dragged herself up the winding stairs to the top of the tower and almost fell through the door. Jamie gave a start on the other side.

'Shadowlands,' Jamie hissed, scrambling to her feet. Her hair was bedraggled, and dark circles hung beneath her eyes.

Aggie fought to catch her breath, leaning against the door for support. 'You look shite,' she gasped. Jamie helped her across the room to the table she had been sitting at. Between them sat a telegraph and pad of paper covered in messy doodles. 'Not a lot going on?' Aggie said, nodding to it.

Jamie ignored her. 'You were all but dead yesterday.' There was a suspicious edge to her voice, as though she didn't quite believe Aggie was real. Aggie still wasn't so sure either.

Aggie shifted uncomfortably in the chair. She'd vastly underestimated the toll the climb would take on her. Everything hurt. 'I think I'd be better aff,' she said. Jamie looked horrified, unsure what to say, then they laughed. The laughter ended with Aggie spluttering. Outside the door, hurried footsteps pounded up the stairs towards them, and moments later, a panic-stricken Calan burst through. When his eyes settled on Aggie, he sighed and clutched his chest.

Aggie snorted a laugh. 'Sleep well?'

Calan glared at her for a moment. 'You are something else.'

'Fill me in,' Aggie said.

'It can wait,' Calan said. 'How do you feel?'

'Perfect. Braw.' She wriggled slowly to get comfortable in the chair, but her bones screamed to be horizontal, and the wood gnawed into her aching muscles. 'Go on.' Calan and Jamie exchanged a long look.

'You don't remember,' Calan said slowly, moving towards the table.

'Remember what?'

Calan pushed his glasses up his nose as he sat down. He twisted a braid around his finger. He clasped his hands together. That meant bad news. He was stalling, she'd seen him do it countless times before. 'You were shot,' he said.

Aggie laughed, then winced. 'Funnily enough, I do mind that.'

'And then, after —'

Before he could finish, it all came crashing back to her in a white-hot lance. The crown in Calan's hand. The gluttonous flames. She stared at Calan. 'You did it,' she whispered.

'He was going to shoot you.'

'He *did* shoot me!' Aggie cried. In better circumstances, she'd fight him tooth and nail on this, but her body was too tired. She slumped back in the chair and waved a resigned hand at him to continue. 'So, what happened?'

Between them, Calan and Jamie explained it all. Gowdstane had been home to a small force of Separatists. The crown was melted, but they used it anyway. The crowds cheered for Aidan, the boy king. When Aggie inquired why the castle was so empty, they dodged the question.

'How long was I out for, like?' Aggie asked when they were done.

'About a week,' Calan said. 'By all rights, you shouldn't be sat here. If it hadn't been for that doctor from Witteneuk and Cait —'

Aggie's hand went to her wrist absent-mindedly. 'Where is Cait?'

'She's in Hart Hall,' Calan said. 'She's —'

Aggie tensed. 'Kenzie.'

'No, she went willingly.'

He was only the messenger, but Aggie felt like Calan had just reached out and smacked her across the face. Cait returning to Kenzie didn't just jeopardise their confidentiality, it made Aggie's chest ache. 'Why?' Aggie said. Shadielaunds, her injuries were making her voice so weak. Calan explained why she had gone and what she had discovered. He showed her Cait's message, and Aggie read the words over and over. She knew the words spelled trouble for their movement, but all Aggie could focus on was the sweet image in Cait's code, an echo of her biscuit-tin life.

'Aidan is not legitimately heir to the throne of Storran,' Calan said conclusively, as though summing up an argument.

Aggie laid the message on the table and slumped back on her chair. 'So that's why this place is a ghost town.'

Calan nodded. 'Lister and his daughter went north. His allies have all dispersed across Storran.'

'Cowarts.'

'A lot of the Separatists that were here have gone home. The others …' Jamie hesitated.

'The others what?' Aggie pressed. 'What about Aidan?' The King of Storran wouldn't just abandon the cause. Heir to Anndras or not, she had to believe that.

Calan and Jamie exchanged another loaded look, and Calan's next words hulked reluctantly from his mouth. 'Those who didn't flee are with Aidan. They're sailing to Thorterknock as we speak.'

Aggie's head snapped up to look at them. 'They're going to fight?' Calan gave one reluctant nod. *Then it's not over.* The Lealists might have the information against Aidan, but that didn't mean they were beat, not if Aidan had won the people round. 'Then what are we doing here?' she said.

'Aggie,' Calan started.

She shook her head at him. 'Save is your spiel, MacKenzie.'

'It's not wise,' he said.

'You said yourself, the people chose him.'

'Yes, a town's worth.'

'It's a start.'

Calan straightened in his chair and cast her a warning glare. 'Aggie.'

'Better to strike before the Lealists get the edge on us.'

'He's just a boy,' Calan said.

Aggie spat out a laugh as she stared at him. 'Lister promised us a king. We got one.'

'What we got was a seventeen-year-old boy who doesn't know anything except that he needs to live up to a fantasy legacy.'

Seventeen. It was young. Hardly the powerful and steady figurehead she would have chosen, but if he was for Storran, she'd back him. He was her King. And besides — 'Sounds like another seventeen-year-old I once knew.'

Calan opened his mouth to retort just as the telegraph whirred to life. The device spat out a frantic series of high-pitched *beeps* followed by a little slip of paper, and Calan, looking surprised, tore it off. 'Seems late for Hart Hall to be sending anything,' he muttered.

'It's from Hart Hall?' Aggie said. She reached over to seize the paper from him, which earned her an over-the-glasses glare. Calan's frown deepened as he scanned the little note, which didn't necessarily indicate bad news, but Jamie and Aggie exchanged a glance regardless. 'Little dove caged,' Calan read aloud. He shook his head. 'I don't understand.'

'It's probably not meant for us,' Jamie said. But Aggie stilled. A memory from her time in the darkness stirred. 'Maybe —'

'Shh,' Aggie said, cutting Jamie off. She screwed her eyes closed. *Little dove.* The phrase raked at the edge of her memory. It set her teeth on edge. *Caged.* A golden cage came to mind, with a white doo inside it. 'I think it's a reference to a story,' she said. And then, though she didn't know what compelled her to, added, 'It's Cait's favourite.'

Little dove caged.

Aggie flew to her feet with the realisation, then doubled over on the table, spluttering and groaning.

'Watch it!' Jamie cried, already at her shoulder.

'We need to go to Thorterknock,' Aggie said through a grimace.

Calan walked round the table towards her. 'What does it mean?'

Gasping for breath, Aggie looked up at him through the greasy strands of her hair. She didn't know who had sent the message, or what their intentions were, but there was one thing she was absolutely certain about. 'Cait's in trouble.'

Chapter 35

Born to be King

Thorterknock's skyline grew closer with every wave the ship crested. The deck was mostly empty, and Aidan watched the city's dark outline grow in the daybreak. He could pick out the rounded back of Oathlaw curving high above the tenements in the heart of the Old Town, and Hart Hall in the west, roosting like a beast, waiting for Aidan and his people to strike. As the shore inched closer, an uninvited thought crossed his mind time and again. *Turn around.* It spoke in Bess' voice, which made it all the more difficult for Aidan to set aside. His fingers brushed the sprig of heather in his pocket. *Soon.*

He was grateful that his people slumbered below the deck, because he had started to dread the way their eyes filled with hope when they looked at him. They were mostly young, and from the lands around Gowdstane. Some had walked paths like Aidan's, in orphanages, and workhouses, or cold homes with bare cupboards. Every single one of them had had enough.

Turn around.

Aidan turned his eyes from the city and made to cross the deck, but standing at the bow of the ship he spotted a figure he had not seen there moments before, silhouetted against the rising sun. The figure's back was turned, fair hair and golden tabard billowing on the salt wind. As always, his right hand rested on the pommel of his blade.

'Where have you been?' Aidan shouted over the wind, taking two steps towards the ghostly King. When Anndras did not do so much as stir, Aidan shouted louder. 'Is it true?' The wind tore at his words like the Great Stag standard on their mast. 'Were you never King?'

Still, Anndras did nothing.

Anger thrummed in Aidan's chest as he took another step towards Anndras. 'Talk to me, you bastard!' He cried, uncaring if the crew heard, uncaring if they thought he was mad. 'If you were never King, and I'm not the heir to Storran, why have you been following me around? What do you want from me?' His voice faltered, and he almost cried. After years of Lister Burke telling him what his life would mean, he felt like a very small boat adrift on a very large ocean. 'Why me?'

Then Anndras did something he had never done before. Slowly, he pivoted to face Aidan. His eyes, a vibrant seaweed green, pinned Aidan in place.

'Shadielaunds,' Aidan whispered, body going cold.

Anndras regarded him for a long moment, assessing him under the cold light of morning. Then he started to walk. Each step took an age, and though he was merely an apparition, Aidan felt each one tremor through the deck. He tried to back away, but his boot slipped on the wet deck, and he stumbled backwards to the floor. 'Wait!' he cried, as Anndras stood over him and raised his blade. He swung.

Aidan closed his eyes. Images washed through his mind. There were people singing in the streets, hundreds upon thousands of people, led by Anndras himself. They carried flags and beat drums, and a sense of joy and hope hung in the air. They sang songs long forgotten, and spoke in a tongue that was familiar to Aidan's bones. They were unashamed. They were free.

When he opened his eyes, gasping, the deck was clear, and Anndras was gone. The sea spray freckled Aidan's cheeks, and the wind whipped his hair from his face. The water from the deck seeped through to his skin. He pushed himself up to a sitting position, and stared at the slick planks of wood beneath him. The images Anndras had showed him played through his mind. He could almost hear the songs still lilting through the sea wind. Something had happened at his coronation that everyone had been quick to dismiss as soon as the article was published: the people had chosen him. They may have been small in number, but they had thrown their support behind him. If he could turn the loyalties of a small town, what was to stop him turning the loyalties of a city, or a nation? Even an entire peninsula? Anndras and Cathal hadn't been of royal blood either. It hadn't mattered. They had stepped up to fight for the people, and the people had followed them. They had been *chosen* to be Kings. Anndras may never have been King himself, but he had served Storran nonetheless. He had appeared to Aidan because he knew that Aidan had it in him to do the same.

As the ship started to come to life around him, Aidan remained sat on the deck until Elsie appeared at his side. 'Everything alright, sire?'

Aidan shook himself from his haze and rose to his feet. His blood was not royal, but his people had chosen him, and Aidan had no intention of letting them down. They would see that joyful dawn. 'Find anyone on board who knows the way to the Unnertoun.'

Without another word, Elsie dipped her head and disappeared. Aidan paced to the front of the ship, where he watched Thorterknock draw ever nearer, his ship riding the swell of history.

Chapter 36

Tragic Songs

On her seventh night in the cells, Cait slept fitfully. Her eyes were closed, but her mind scrambled from dream to dream. In one, the firing squad missed their mark and struck her in the arm, and she bled out. In another, which repeated itself in a torturous loop, there had been some confusion, and she was put to the gun only for the procedure to be halted, and she was marched straight back into the cells. In one dream, Aggie was in the cell with her. She told her that death was okay, really. It was a bit dark, but at least there were no Lealists. Cait wasn't sure if she believed in the Shadielaunds, but she wondered if Aggie was waiting for her, wherever she was heading.

She jolted awake to the sound of feet tramping down the stairs. She scurried backwards across the floor as four Lealists appeared and threw open the doors to her and Fraser's cells. The shadows cast by their caps made them appear faceless, and Cait let her limbs go slack as they wrestled her to her feet and plunged a rough jute bag over her head.

She only had time to sob, 'Wait!' before darkness snapped across her vision, and her uneven gasps filled the space around her. The sound of a scuffle came from Fraser's direction, followed by the crack of fist greeting bone, and a whimper. Rope bit into her wrists. She had been wrong, none of this was clinical.

'Please,' she gasped as she was led from the cell. 'Just get Kenzie. Please.'

Stop pleading for him, she chided herself, but as the cold morning air hit her and she felt the looming presence of that whitewashed wall, she found herself praying to any god who would listen that Kenzie had plotted her escape. A gentle hand found her shoulder and offered some hope, but the next thing she knew her back was pressed against the wall. She didn't want her last memory to be her tears misting the inside of a jute bag, so she tried to recite *The Ballad of Anndras and Cathal* under her breath, but she couldn't get past the first verse.

Fair Anndras was a rich man's son
Nae worries did he ken
And Cathal jist a weaver's lad
From doon the emerant glen

What came after? Cathal's beheading? Anndras with an arrow in his heart? The songs were always tragic. No one ever got a happy ending. Somewhere in front came a series of quiet *clicks* and Cait screwed her eyes closed as she recognised the sound of guns being loaded.

'This is wrong!' Fraser cried. 'I handed the witch in, didn't I?'

'Ready,' came a voice with an accent from the north of Afren.

Please aim well, she begged silently. *Don't let me be in pain.*

The shots shattered the morning peace. A flock of birds took to the sky, screaming. Cait swayed and stepped back against the cold wall. Her world rung. Gunpowder brushed her lips. In the haze, she heard Aggie saying her name. Cait felt her body tilt forward, and as she waited for the ground to strike, she wondered when she would feel pain. She blinked as light bombarded her eyes. Her hands fell free. Someone grasped her shoulders, steadying her.

The first thing she saw when her eyes adjusted was hair. Red hair.

Cait found herself in the courtyard, a blue sky dappled with pink high above. Aggie stood before her, grasping her shoulders, grinning out from under the peak of a Watchman's hat. Only one coherent thought entered Cait's mind and that was that this afterlife didn't make one bit of sense. 'Why on earth are you wearing that?' she said.

Aggie threw her head back and laughed. 'Did you get a fleg?'

'Just a bit.'

'Sorry. It had to sound real.'

Real. Cait caught sight of Calan and Jamie releasing Fraser's bonds, also dressed in the uniform of the Watch. They were real: the courtyard, the morning breeze, Cait's quickening heart and trembling hands. It was all real. Not some twisted dream pulled from her anxious mind. *Real.* The rosy flush in Aggie's cheeks meant that she was real, and not only that — she was *alive.*

'You ... *fool*, I was so worried about you!' Cait said, throwing her arms around Aggie and pulling her into a tight embrace. She smelled of hay, and her heart beat quietly, stubbornly, away under the uniform. She gave a sharp wince, and Cait quickly released her. 'Sorry.'

'Still a bit fragile,' she said. Now Cait could see her cheeks were hollowed and her skin pale, but there was fire in her eyes. There was life.

Jamie tossed Cait her Watchman cap which proved a welcome relief from the low sun. 'Don't get too comfy, I want that back,' she said.

'How did you do it?' Cait asked.

Calan gave his rifle a little shake and grinned. 'Blanks.'

Aggie rolled her eyes. 'He's never going to come down from this.' Then she nodded at the fourth officer who held open a door at the far end of courtyard, exposing a narrow street outside. 'We had a tip-off.'

'You need to go,' the young soldier said as he turned to them. 'Quickly.'

For a foolish moment, Cait hoped it was Kenzie, but when the boy turned and grinned at her, she only felt relieved it wasn't. 'Innes,' she breathed.

As they hurried to the door, Fraser looked none too pleased about being smuggled out of Hart Hall by a group of Separatists, especially ones that had just given him a black eye, but he didn't complain. Perhaps the feeling of breath in his lungs far outweighed any moral qualms he had.

'You didn't have to do that,' Cait said, pausing by Innes. 'Thank you.'

He gave a shaky nod and a weak laugh. 'For Storran.' Then he glanced back at the cells and pushed her through the door. 'Hurry.'

Be safe, Cait thought as she heard the bolt slide into place, locking them out of Hart Hall.

*

'I don't know why we didn't try this before,' Jamie said as they breezed easily past a group of Watchmen on the early patrol.

Aggie made a face. 'Because we look daft.'

'Ahm keeping this outfit,' Jamie said, dramatically swishing the cloak. 'Just try and take it off me.'

Aggie looked unimpressed. 'I'm burning it the first chance I get.'

They moved through the streets with far more caution than was necessary. Calan set a steady pace and paused at every corner, taking his time to peer left and right, and left again, even when the coast was already clear. Cait quickly realised he was doing it for Aggie's sake. Despite the valiant effort she put into her effortless stride, she moved slowly.

'You read to me,' Aggie said through shallow breaths as Cait fell into step with her.

'No, I didn't,' Cait said, far too quickly.

'When I was sick.'

'You're *still* sick.'

'You read me the story about the doo in the cage. You said it was your favourite. I can't think why. It's bloody grim.'

'I don't remember.'

Aggie raised an eyebrow. 'Aye, right. And you're not blushing either.'

Cait looped Aggie's arm over her shoulder and supported her weight. When Aggie looked like she might protest, Cait said, 'Now *you're* blushing.'

'I can manage fine.'

Cait raised her eyebrows at Aggie's sulking pout, but it made her laugh. 'Just accept the help.'

'The city's too big,' Aggie muttered. It was good to see her this way again. Cait hoped she never stopped fighting.

When they reached Barter Bridge, Calan came to a halt and nodded across at the New Town. 'We can catch the eight o'clock train if we're quick.'

'Where are we going?' Cait asked.

Aggie shook herself free. A hint of that familiar and savage air fell over her. 'More importantly, why?'

Calan turned to Cait. 'Aidan's on his way with a group of Separatists from Gowdstane. He plans to take the city.'

Cait frowned. 'Take the city. Can he do that?'

Calan threw his hands up in a bewildered shrug and threw a pointed look at Aggie.

'I'm not running away,' Aggie said, folding her arms.

Calan sighed and closed his eyes. 'Do you really think a seventeen-year-old boy is going to be able to single-handedly overthrow the military might of Afren?'

'Yes.'

'In fact, it probably won't even come to that, because the Lealists will have his head on the city gates by lunchtime!'

'I reckon he's right,' Jamie muttered.

Aggie's eyes flared. For a moment, it was like she had never even glanced at death. 'That's all the more reason to stay.'

'This isn't about pride anymore,' Calan said.

'I'm not saying you need to stay with me,' she said. 'Gaun.' She waved across the bridge. 'Take the coward's road.'

'You're still weak,' Cait said quietly, feeling exposed as she waded into the fray.

Aggie threw her eyes to the sky. 'I don't believe this.'

'Look,' Calan said. 'We'll go to Witteneuk, or one of the islands in the Prongs. Maybe even Afren. Just anywhere we can lie low for a while, and wait until this all blows over.' Aggie didn't answer. She just cast him a sideways glare. 'Anywhere is safer than Thorterknock right now,' Calan said.

Cait stilled, remembering what Fraser had told her in the cells. 'Not anywhere.' *Not for you.*

Calan turned to her. 'What do you mean?'

Cait glanced at Fraser, who had been stood at the side, silently watching his rescuers argue. 'Tell him what you told me,' Cait said. 'About the ships.'

The fight that had coursed through Aggie moments before ebbed from her as Fraser explained Afren's new policy. Cait watched Calan carefully. His face was perfect marble.

'Okay,' was all he said when Fraser finished. Cait stepped forward and made to touch his shoulder. He shrugged her off. 'So, they're tearing up the agreement. I knew they would. It was only a matter of time.' He stared at the ground.

'We won't let them take you,' Aggie said.

'No point,' Calan said simply. 'I know how they are. They'll find me eventually.' He stared at the ground a moment longer, and then without warning, turned on his heel and marched back into the Old Town.

'Where are you going?' Jamie called after him.

Calan didn't so much as glance over his shoulder as he said, 'To show Afren how we do things in Iffega.'

Chapter 37

Bought and Sold

By the time Calan's watch read half past seven in the morning, the Unnertoun was busier than he had ever seen it. Separatists from Gowdstane filled every little underground flat, and throughout the morning a steady stream of weapons and supplies taken from Gowdstane were smuggled from Aidan's ship through the streets and into the shadows of the Unnertoun. Calan had been surprised to discover that Tavis had sailed with them. He wondered if the Talasaire was here because he wanted to be, or because he had nowhere else to go. Both options were fairly bleak.

The Separatists gathered in the largest room. Aidan was already there when Calan and Aggie arrived, and Aggie faltered at the doorway.

'Are you okay?' Calan asked her, taking hold of her elbow.

She didn't respond, but stared across the room where Aidan was making conversation with an enamoured-looking Elsie. He was still wearing his crown.

'That's him,' Aggie whispered.

'Yes,' Calan said. He waited for her to say something else, perhaps remark how young he was, but she merely nodded once and let Calan lead her to a chair.

One hundred and ten had travelled from Gowdstane, and there were around another sixty or so crammed into the Unnertoun. How many would remain once Jamie returned with the day's newspaper? When she did at last appear, Jamie dropped not just one paper, but a whole stack on the table in front of him. Calan flicked through the pile, noting all the recognisable local and national names.

'Jings, Jamie, did you buy every paper in Storran?' Aggie asked.

'More or less.' Jamie tossed her one of the papers and Aggie clumsily caught it. 'It's on every front page.'

Calan's cheeks puffed as he scanned down the front page of *The*

Storran Gazette. It was a well-respected broadsheet that provided expert analysis on business and politics, so Calan was surprised to see Heather Bruce's name stamped across the by-line of the cover piece.

Aggie frowned down at *The Thorterknock Herald*. 'Who's this Heather Bruce character?'

'She wrote this one, too,' Cait said, holding up *Lowlands Weekly*.

Calan shuffled the monochromatic splash of newspapers across the table, his eyes skirting the by-lines, and headlines, and every tight column of text in between. They were identical. 'It's the same story. They've put it in every paper.' How much had Afren shelled out for this? How much had Bruce accepted to do the task? Calan struggled to believe she would still be holed up in her pokey little office now.

The article laid it all out: the findings uncovered by the Lealists, a sketch of Cathal's fractured skull, and even a dubious source that proved the historic figure had sustained a similar injury. The quote from Dr Hardie gave a plausible explanation for the findings: it was never Cathal who received the summons from the Queen of Afren, but Anndras. Sensing a trap and reluctant to leave his people without a leader, he went to meet the Queen in the guise of Cathal, and left the outlaw in his place. The article slandered Aidan as a pretender who had usurped one of Storran's greatest legends in order to gain power. They sat in silence, and Calan knew they were all thinking the same thing: long-lost crowns returned home were poetic, and kings chosen by the people sparked hope; liars who exploited the nation's heart would never inspire a following.

In the middle of the article was a simple little paragraph that stood out against the slander. Afren promised, in spite of the unsavoury criminals and their outlaw king, that they would show their appreciation to the law-abiding people of Storran. Queen Ana would generously gift new powers to Storran's shell of a parliament, all the Separatists had to do was turn in their King. With her words, Heather Bruce placed the ball firmly in the Separatists' hands, and Calan loathed himself for the temptation in his gut.

The room remained quiet until Aggie said, 'It's clearly a lie.' And her words seemed to unblock a dam.

'Now, we shouldn't immediately dismiss this,' Tavis said.

'Seems too good t'be true,' Jamie said.

'It's a trap, we all know what happened to Cathal!' Elsie piped up.

'Anndras, actually,' someone Calan didn't know helpfully corrected her.

Amidst the hum and debate, Calan silently flipped through the pages of the paper. Folded carefully between stories of crimes, successes, births, deaths, and local events, buried by the goings-on of a busy city, was a quiet article that snatched no attention. It spoke of the so-called Iffegan Refugee Crisis. The hordes of refugees crossing into the Afrenian Peninsula to pursue a new life were simply becoming too much of a burden, and something had to be done. The Council of Five would tear up the Iffega Agreement. Where previously people like Calan enjoyed free passage into the Five Realms and opportunities to set up a life, now they could be turned away or sent packing. There was no information for Iffegans who might be reading, no reassurance, or appeals, or procedures that could be followed, as though it was expected that people like him couldn't possibly be reading the article. It described his people's plight like just another affair, like an unnecessary weight on the budget that needed to be shifted. Calan wondered how long they had been preparing this behind the scenes, and how long they had waited for a story sensational enough to cover it up. His thoughts turned to his family, currently in some unknown town in central Storran. He longed to hold them. *I won't let them take you,* he'd tell his little sister.

'They're gonnae kill me, aren't they?' Aidan said, and for a moment the words, *don't be silly, you're not a refugee,* came to Calan's lips, until he looked up, and the sight of Aidan's round, frightened eyes told him he was still speaking about the article that had been penned about him.

Calan shook himself and turned his paper back to the front page. 'We can't know for sure,' he said carefully, but he knew. *If they get their hands on you, they will kill you. They'll hoist your corpse above the gates of Eadwick, and I'll be able to wave at you as they ship me off home.*

'It hasn't clarified what the extra powers are,' Cait pointed out.

'We would need to negotiate,' Calan muttered.

Aggie gave a disbelieving laugh. 'We're not actually talking about this, are we?'

'I think it would be remiss not to,' Calan said.

Aggie's mouth hung open. 'I think it would be *remiss* to suddenly trust Afren at their word.'

Tavis laid his hands on the table. 'It certainly would benefit Afren to give us a good deal. It saves them a lot of trouble. They'd be able to drastically reduce funding on the Watch, and giving us what we want without being pressured into it leaves them looking terribly valiant, so it does.'

Aidan blinked around at them as though they were discussing the intricacies of the stock market rather than his own martyrdom.

'With this article, they won't expect us to do anything at all. We might well be in the best position we could be to strike,' Aggie said. 'We could have a fully functional Parliament in a matter of days.'

Calan ignored her. 'Tavis is right,' he said. 'It's not what we wanted but it's a starting point.'

Aggie banged a hand on the table. 'You're *not* considering this.'

'What other choice do we have?' Calan asked, gritting his teeth.

'It doesn't matter what meagre power they throw at us. We'll still be under their thumb. They'll still have ultimate control, and that's if they even deliver,' she said. 'They never keep their word, and it would be the height of stupidity to assume they would now.'

'Examples,' Calan prompted, flat-toned. He wasn't trying to say she was wrong — she wasn't — but he wasn't about to let her win on rhetoric alone.

'That they'd replace the jobs when they closed the shipyards, that they'd improve wages, that Storran would get a better grant.' She counted the instances out on her fingers. 'Let's not forget that they promised not to occupy us when they offered to help fill the power vacuum that, well, Cathal now, I suppose, left behind. How did we end up under Afren's thumb again, Calan? Oh, because. Afren. Lies.'

'You've made your point,' Calan muttered.

'Is the best alternative fighting them?' Cait asked.

'Aye! It's the right thing to do. They've had it coming.'

'What's "right"?' Calan snapped. 'Do you actually want what's best for Storran, or do you just want a revolution?'

'Stop it!' Aidan shouted. It made Calan jump, and judging by the startled looks around the room, it shocked everyone else, too. Calan hadn't noticed him stand up. He looked taller among the low ceilings of the Unnertoun. 'Aggie's right,' he said. 'It was a bargain with Afren that got us here in the first place.' His eyes wove around the room, meeting each Separatist individually. 'We'd still be free if Afren hadn't taken advantage of Storran after Anndras — sorry —*Cathal* died.' It was true. Storran's nobility well and truly sold them out in those early days of heirless instability. 'I wilna — I *won't* be bought and sold,' Aidan said. He balled his fists against the table, and Calan, despite the dread in his gut, had to admit that Aidan *looked* like a king with the melted crown upon his head. 'I know you're all disappointed about the news. I am, too, but you all saw what we did in Clackhatton. We can do the same again. I'm sure of it.' He paused and nodded, as if to himself. 'I'm standing against Afren tomorrow. Join is if you want.'

*

Calan needed air, fresh air, not just the stale stuff in the Unnertoun. It was midday in Thorterknock, and the city went about its business. Calan stood near the grate entrance to the Unnertoun at Aist Bridge, watching people wander to and fro. People shouted to each other across the street, children played carelessly, skirting out of the way of clattering hooves just in time. He loved every crooked cobble of this city, even down to the bloodstained Skemmels that would always smell of meat. After leaving Iffega, he never thought he'd love a home again. His heart broke as he wondered what Aidan would turn these streets into tomorrow.

Behind him, he heard the sound of the grate sliding open.

'Where are you gan?' It was Aggie. She was angry. He could hear it in the timbre of her voice. He turned to face her, and she glared up at him as she struggled to clamber out of the hole. When Calan knelt to help her, she shook him off and climbed, shaking, to her feet.

'I just need some air,' he said, turning away. The back of his head tingled with her glare.

'You're leaving.'

'I'm not leaving.'

'After everything? You're really just going to abandon ship?'

He was growing impatient. 'I told you, I'm not leaving.'

'Why are you always so spineless?' Aggie pressed.

'*Spineless*? Why are you always so pig-headed?'

Aggie scoffed. 'Fair enough.'

Truthfully, Calan didn't know why he had come outside. Perhaps getting air was only an excuse. He couldn't pretend that he hadn't thought about going north. There could be an island up in the Prongs with his name all over it. A little bothy. A lot of books. Peace and quiet for the rest of his days. The day of the Separatist was quickly coming to an end, and Aidan and Aggie were clinging to it with all their might. He could enjoy a peaceful life until Afren tracked him down and sent him away.

When Aggie looked at him, her expression was all challenge. 'You're considering taking that deal.'

'Unlike you, I don't have a death wish.'

Aggie's glare hardened. 'Fine. Hand the boy in. Do what Afren wants. In the end, they won't keep their promises. They'll still come for your family. They'll still come for you.'

'And if we fight, my family will still be deported, only I'll be dead.'

Her gaze snared Calan with the usual bright intensity that meant she was painting him a picture. 'Not if you free Storran. We make our own rules. No one needs to be sent away.' An image flashed through his mind: Storran as a safe space for refugees, and not only those from Iffega. Damn, she was good at this.

'We win and get everything we ever dreamed of. Or we fail, and lose it all,' he murmured, mostly to himself.

'I like thae odds,' said Aggie.

'You're insane,' Calan grumbled. This earned him a thin smile from Aggie. They stood in silence for a moment watching the people go by. 'I really love this city,' Calan said, feeling like he needed to get it out in the open before he helped tear it apart tomorrow.

'Me, too,' Aggie said.

Calan glanced at her. 'Do you ever wish you just stayed in school?'

Aggie pondered this for a moment. 'Sometimes,' she said. 'When you talk about your family, or when the Storrian Schools' Debating Championship comes to the city. I'd thrash them.' Calan laughed. 'But Storran is in my bones,' Aggie said. 'These people are my people, and I can't just sit back and let them be lied to and stolen from. They're good people. They deserve more than what Afren gives them. *You* deserve more.'

'And what if we lose? They'll be left with nothing.'

Aggie pushed her hands deeper into her pockets and chewed her lip, and Calan could tell that despite herself, she was nervous. 'That all depends, doesn't it?'

He remembered the first debating contest they took part in. They were twelve years old, and Aggie had convinced Calan to go for it. He'd refused, still not entirely confident in the Afrenian tongue, afraid that what remained of his Iffegan accent would alienate him from his peers. She had signed up with him, and though she'd talked with bravado about crushing the opposition, she'd chewed her lip to shreds before she took the stand. They'd won. She'd signed straight up for the next one. Calan supposed that was the moment Aggie realised she had a talent for being incessant. Calan looked back out at the crowd. He sighed. 'Aidan's just a boy, and with Lister gone —'

'Lister's a fud.'

Calan looked at her sideways. 'Aggie …'

'You don't need him, or his fancy pals,' Aggie said.

'It's much easier to be lifted by someone who's already up there.'

'We're outlaws, Calan,' Aggie said, smiling. 'We're used to hoisting ourselves up.' She clapped him on the shoulder. 'Don't worry, I'm sure you'll think up something brilliant.'

Calan frowned at her. 'Excuse me?'

She shoved open the grate with a painful grunt and threw a grin over her shoulder. 'Your grand plan for taking back Storran. I can't wait to hear it.' Then she hopped down, disappearing into the dark.

Calan shook his head and looked back at the afternoon revellers. 'Thanks, Fox,' he muttered to himself. He had long toyed with the idea of some kind of civil uprising, like the hunger strikes in Leja, or the wool blockade in Norra, both events that earned the participants rights they didn't have before, but the Separatists didn't have people power on their side. The news about Aidan's lineage would have travelled fast. By now, every household would know, and it would be their truth because it was told to them by a source they trusted.

What if they were told Storran was free? Would they accept that so easily?

He thought about the squirrelly little communications officer from Hart Hall and an idea started to form in his mind.

Aggie would never fill a coward's grave, but he could see himself fitting quite nicely into one. If Calan ran north, his days would be peaceful. His days would be peaceful, but Afren would continue to abuse Storran, and one day, that peace would end for him. Instead, he could put his gifts to use, for himself, for his family, and for everyone who called Storran their home while their motherland burned.

*

It had been a struggle at first, but Calan finally convinced Fraser to tell him everything about the Hart Hall communications system, and how it might look in the Parliament. Calan knew the basics of how to work a telegraph. He knew how to decipher a code, and he knew how to tap it out and send it skirting down the wires, but he needed more. He needed expertise. By evening, he had his most trusted gathered around a table in the Unnertoun, plus a gaggle of other inquisitive Separatists who craned their necks over his crude map that depicted the bridges between the Old Town and New Town. Calan called the room to attention, and when the chatter died, he tapped the map.

'We can take Thorterknock, at least I think we can.' He saw Aggie grin, and he knew she was imagining a grand revolution. He looked at her when he added, 'Without fighting.' Her face fell. 'We're going to start with the Parliament. It's vastly easier to target than Hart Hall.' For a start, it was mostly empty. 'First thing tomorrow morning, before Barter Bridge is open, and before anyone is even thinking about going to work, at the absolute crack of dawn, I need barricades on key points in the city.' He pointed at the map as he rattled them off. 'All of the bridges: Wast, Aist, Grace, Barter, and Daibh's Airch. These stations will prevent anyone moving from the Old Town to the New Town, mostly civilians, but especially Lealists.' Then he pointed to the station. 'We also need a group at the train station to keep people from entering the New Town from there. It is vital we maintain the moral high ground. That means no violence.'

'We have plenty of guns from Gowdstane,' Aidan said. His eyes cast about the small number gathered in the room. 'Not enough for awbody but —'

'No,' Calan said shortly. He would not fill the streets with gunpowder.

'The Lealists won't play nice,' Aggie said, eyebrow raised, arms crossed. She tilted back in her chair. 'We'll need to defend ourselves when they start scrapping.'

'It won't come to that,' Calan said. 'The minute we put guns out there, we cloud our intentions, and worse still, we set ourselves up for violence. It only takes one person.'

'And that person won't be one of us,' Aidan said. 'We'll only use them if the Lealists shoot.'

Calan took a breath and pushed his glasses up his nose. Giving their people guns made sense, but it was only one step away from an all-out revolution, from civilians being caught in the crossfire. From a war zone. But he knew Aidan and Aggie were right. What would be the point in an honourable martyrdom if there were no Separatists left to finish the job?

'Fine,' he said. He swiped a hand across his brow. Shadielaunds, was it always so hot down here? 'Those on the barricade will have rifles to hand, but they're only to be used if *absolutely necessary.*' He looked first at Aidan, and then Aggie. 'Do you understand?'

Hesitant nods met him. He sighed and continued.

'Once the streets are secure, we take the communications. We can take control of the trains, or Barter Bridge, or the City Square, but we'll get nowhere without the comms. Once we have control over the telegraph, we can spread word to Carse, Witteneuk, Afren, and potential allies throughout the Continent. Once we tell them from official government stations that we are in control, we might just get away with it. Fraser and I, plus a few others for backup, will head to the Parliament once each bridge is secured.'

'Fraser?' Aidan said. 'Can we trust him? He's a Lealist.'

'I need him,' Calan said simply.

'And where will I be?' Aidan asked.

'Parliament,' Calan said. 'With us.'

'I'm not at the barricade?' Aidan said, pointing at the map.

'No,' Calan said.

Aidan shook his head. 'I need to be out there.' He gestured to the streets. 'The people need to see me.'

'What the people need is a king and not a power vacuum,' Calan said. 'The Parliament is the centre of power. That's where you belong. You'll be kept safe until you become most useful.'

'When will that be?'

'Towards the end, most likely.'

'But I can inspire the people.'

'We don't know how they'd respond to you.'

'They'll think I'm hiding.'

'You'll be the least of anyone's concerns.'

'How can they choose me if they canna see me?'

'*Aidan*!' Calan hadn't meant to shout, but the room snapped to attention like an electrical current had shot through. Aidan stared at Calan with a look as though he'd been slapped. Then defeat took him, the simmering, sulking kind. Calan didn't have the heart to tell him that it didn't matter where he lay on the board. It didn't matter that a small northern town had backed him, it didn't matter that he wore the Antlered Crown. All influence he might have held melted away with the publication of the truth. Front line or back bench, the boy king was an empty symbol. At least if he was nearby, the opportunity to take Afren's deal was still on the table. He shook the thought away and picked up where he left off. 'The Parliament, yes. Once I'm in there, I'll start communication with Afren and any other public bodies and governments on the Continent, to advise that Storran is free and ask for international support. I'll be communicating with Hart Hall, too, to try and secure some kind of deal. Tavis, is there any truth in what you were saying about Afren wanting to reduce Lealist funding?'

Tavis shook his head. 'Truthfully, it's just speculation, lad.'

'That's fine,' Calan said. Speculation would do. Speculation could give rise to paranoia, and paranoia to action, and legislation, and change. Speculation could force Hart Hall to turn a blind eye.

'What are the numbers like?' Aggie asked.

'They're ... not great,' Calan said. 'We have one hundred and seventy.'

'And the Lealists?' she prompted.

He swallowed the knot of dread in his throat. It had been the first thing he asked Fraser. 'Three hundred.'

Silence dropped like a stone through the room, until Cait said, 'What happens afterwards?'

Calan sighed. Telling a lie was easy, but maintaining that lie was difficult. 'We hold out for support. The only given is that Afren won't accept the result of...' — he paused, mustering courage through memories of bloodshed to say the next word — '... a coup. Our next hope comes from allies overseas putting pressure on Afren. If we can hold out until then, we might manage this.'

Aggie clapped her hands together. 'I'll take the lead on Aist Bridge.'

Calan shook his head. 'You won't be out there.'

'Aye, I will.'

'You're still recovering. I haven't factored you into these plans, and including you now would only confuse things.'

'But —'

'It's done, Aggie.'

This time, she didn't argue.

'There's a whole city out there,' Aidan said. 'I bet we can get civilians on our side to bulk up our numbers. We can convince them to fight.'

'I agree,' Elsie said. 'If Aidan speaks to them, we can do what we did at Clackhatton.'

Calan shook his head adamantly. There were terms he wasn't willing to negotiate on. 'I'm not involving the civilians in this, not beyond regular civic processes.' He expected Aidan to argue, but he didn't. Calan looked to him for approval on the final plan. Pretender and boy he may be, he was still their King, and the final call was his alone. Aidan considered for a moment, nodded absently to himself, and then affirmatively to the room.

'It sounds good,' he finally said. 'I'm sure the people will support us.'

Calan sucked in a breath. 'We can only hope.'

'Lealtie Ayebidin,' Aidan said.

'Lealtie Ayebidin,' a chorus echoed back at him.

Chapter 38

For the Love of an Outlaw

Cait eventually found Aggie in what must have been the only quiet corner of the Unnertoun. She leafed through a navy tome, seemingly unaware of Cait's presence. 'What're you reading?' Cait asked, ducking as she entered the squat room.

Aggie's eyes snatched up to her, and then fell back to the page. 'Something about a maid in a manor house. Scandalous affair. Something about a ghost. I'm not really paying attention.'

Cait removed Aggie's copy of *Songs of Storran* from her bag and held it out to her. 'It's about time I gave you this back,' she said.

Aggie set the tome aside and cautiously took the book from Cait. She turned it over, examining the front and back covers carefully, then peered up at Cait. 'Nae bent pages?'

'It's in perfect condition.'

Aggie studied the book for a moment longer, then gave a satisfied nod. 'I've taught you well.'

'It's seen a lot of the places mentioned in it now,' Cait said. 'It's been to Loch Cath, and Gowdstane, and it's even met a king.'

Aggie considered for a moment, her fingers dancing idly through the pages. 'Do you think it was everything it hoped?'

Under Aggie's gaze, Cait became overly aware of her limbs. Her arms hung awkwardly at her side. 'Well, I suppose it's not seen everything yet,' she said quickly. 'There's still the selkie of Witteneuk, the borders goblins, and it didn't get a chance to meet the Crone of the Cruin.'

Aggie laughed, placing the book next to her. 'How about we take it to all those places once this is over?'

Cait smiled. She liked the sound of *we*. 'I think it would like that.'

In the brief silence that followed, Cait pulled her arms to her chest and mustered up the courage to ask what she had come here for. 'I need to go up top.'

Aggie's eyes narrowed. 'You're —'

'Not running,' Cait said quickly. 'I just ... There's somewhere I need to go.' Her voice quivered as she whispered her plea. 'Come with me.'

*

The Crabbit Corbie lay like a corpse. Cait was certain that the crow on the signage had once looked a bit silly, but the night sent a scowl across its face. She shivered.

'I'm not sure getting hammered is the wisest choice,' Aggie said.

Cait managed a weak laugh. 'This is where I stayed when I first arrived in Thorterknock.' The door waited, but she couldn't bring herself to walk towards it.

Aggie looked up at the building. 'It had a good name.' When Cait did nothing but continue to stare at the building in silence, she said, 'Why are we here?'

It took a moment for Cait to find the words. 'Do you remember that night in the bothy?'

'Vaguely,' Aggie said. 'Had a lot going on.'

'Right,' Cait said. Kenzie's words from that night still spun around her mind.

You mustn't feel guilty.

Surely you knew what would happen when you turned him in?

Kenzie didn't know her at all. Of course, she felt guilty. Even when she thought Bram would be subject to an invasive investigation, she felt guilty. 'I turned the innkeeper in for being a Separatist,' she said at last, in one flat breath. 'He wasn't.'

Cait waited for Aggie to balk, and point fingers, and call her a filthy traitor, but all she said was, 'Do you want to go inside?'

'It's probably locked.'

Aggie's grin flashed in the moonlight, as she paced backwards towards the building with her hands in her pockets. 'Nae bother.' She bent her torso in a weak bow and winked. 'I'm more than a pretty face, hen.'

They tried the door first, but when it indeed proved to be locked, Aggie moved aside the window box with its cheery flowers and slipped the blade of her penknife under the crack between the bottom of the window and the frame. She hammered her fist against it a couple of times, and the window sprung open with a crack. She stepped aside. 'After you.'

Cait scrambled through the window, and then helped Aggie through. She almost expected Bram to be stood behind the bar with a pot of hot soup and a kind word, but when she looked around, the inn lay empty.

'Eugh,' Aggie said, and Cait turned to find her stood by one of the tables. She held up a sticky, half-finished pint before placing it back on the table and wiped her fingers on her coat. 'Typical of the Lealists not to clean up after themselves.'

Cait wondered what had happened to the regulars. Had they been here when the soldiers arrived? Cait doubted they had been given time to drink up. She struggled to imagine Kenzie taking the time to ring the bell for last orders on his crusade. Cait wandered slowly towards the bar, and behind it, Aggie helped her hoist open the trap door. When they descended into the dark, Aggie produced a lighter from one of her pockets and snapped the flame to life. 'I turned the innkeeper in to the Watchmen because I thought it would impress Kenzie. I thought he'd get a trial.' Cait whispered, afraid of rousing ghosts. Again, she tensed, afraid that Aggie's claws would show.

'We've all done things we regret.' Aggie's voice carried delicately through the dark. 'What was his name?'

Cait walked alongside the barrels that were still heavy with the promise of revellers. 'His name was Bram.' When she reached the spot on the floor where Bram had lay, she faltered. 'He was just making his own whisky, that's all.'

'Bram,' Aggie echoed. Cait flinched. She wasn't sure she had ever heard his name from anyone else's lips before. 'He wouldn't be the first innocent man to become tangled in this.'

Cait hunted the flickering shadows for Bram's ghost. She wasn't sure what she'd say if he appeared.

I'm sorry I accused you. I'm sorry you had to die.

His eyes would crinkle, and he'd probably say, *That's okay, young Cait. Ye did yer best. Now, I've put a pot of soup oan.*

When tears filled her eyes, she turned and climbed the creaking stairs and let the trap door to the past fall shut for the last time. She wasn't sure what she expected to find coming here. Maybe she hoped for a sense of clarity, or some certainty that the coming days would be worth it, but Cait just felt more lost. She made her way upstairs and found her old bedroom. The door was unlocked, and it still caught on the carpet as it opened. She half expected to find something she had left behind, but the room was spotless. She imagined Bram tidying it up for the next tenant, wondering why the last had left in such a rush.

'Look at this,' Aggie said. Cait turned to find Aggie poking around the door built into the wall at the end of the room. She'd always assumed it was a cupboard and never opened it, because opening cupboards meant unpacking, and unpacking made Thorterknock permanent. As Aggie slowly opened the door, it revealed a dark entrance. The shadows soon revealed a set of metal stairs that spiralled through a narrow brick passageway. Aggie started to climb without hesitation, and Cait hurried after her, careful to wedge the door open at the bottom. The passage was so narrow that Cait felt trapped. She wondered if this had once been a chimney, and the thought made her stomach churn. At last, Aggie heaved a trapdoor that opened out into the night air.

'Nice view, eh?' Aggie said as they stepped out onto the roof of The Crabbit Corbie.

Cait turned where she stood, drinking in the sights. It was beautiful. She could see the hulking mess of Old Town brick as it lurched across the Cath into the New Town. 'Best view in the hoose,' Cait breathed. *Jist for you.*

Aggie pointed to a dark shape rising out of the Old Town. 'Do you see that?' Her voice was so thin. Cait noticed the way she crippled to one side.

'I'll guess when you sit down,' Cait said.

When Aggie didn't listen, Cait took her by the shoulders and steered her to the low wall at the edge of the roof. Aggie threw her legs over the side, and Cait's heart leapt into her mouth as she carefully followed suit. Her boots dangled above the cobbles far below, and she was glad the night was still.

'Well?' Aggie urged.

'It's a hill,' Cait offered. She had seen it looming like set dressing to the city.

'No, it's a *law*,' Aggie countered.

'What's the difference?' Cait asked.

Aggie shrugged. 'Nothing. It's just the Old Storrian word for hill. But *that* law,' she lifted a hand and pointed at the dark shape. 'That's Oathlaw. Where Anndras first pledged allegiance to Cathal.'

Cait's breath hitched in her throat. 'Oh …' It was where Anndras first ran to after abandoning the Queen of Afren's allegiance. It was, arguably, where Storran's legendary history began.

"*'They found him high upon Oathlaw and kneelt before his baund.'*"
"*'And Anndras to the north he pledged his sword, his life, his haund,'*" Cait said, finishing the line. 'Imagine running all the way from Eadwick only to have to climb a big hill when you got here. Cathal could at least have come down to meet him.'

Aggie chuckled. 'He never did treat Anndras with much courtesy. I wonder why they even liked each other.'

Cait glanced sideways at Aggie. She still seemed like a restless flame, even if her light was a little dimmed now, like the wick had got stuck in the pool of wax. 'Your theory was right.'

Aggie frowned at her. 'What theory's that?'

'You said you believed that Cathal sacrificed himself for love of Anndras. The truth's the opposite way around, but the point still stands.'

Aggie pursed her lips. 'Rubbish. I wouldn't say that.'

'You did.'

'Must've been Jamie. That's the sort of shite the Talasaire would come up wi.'

'*You* said it!' Cait laughed. 'Besides, you were right, weren't you? Anndras put Cathal in his place to save him.' She looked back out at the city, where the River Cath meandered between the Old and New Towns. 'Maybe he knew Cathal would do the same for him, and he didn't want to give him the chance.' Aggie didn't respond. She looked out over the city, brow creased. 'What are you thinking?' Cait asked.

Aggie's head tilted as she considered the view. 'It should be called the *Anndras*.'

'What?'

'The river,' Aggie said. 'It's not Cathal's blood at all, it's Anndras',' Cait snorted, and Aggie smiled to herself. 'I'll rename it, you know,' she said. 'When Storran's free, I'll petition to have it renamed the River Anndras.'

Cait shook her head. 'You should have led with that argument. We'd have plenty of support by now.'

Aggie turned to her with eyebrows raised in goading. 'Listen to you saying "we." I knew we'd make a Separatist out of you eventually.'

'I'll never be able to show my face in Briddock again.'

'Ach, you're better off without them. They're basically Afrenian.' Cait cast Aggie a warning glare, and she threw her head back in a raucous laugh. 'Aye okay, enough of that. Promise.'

'Good,' Cait said. 'Because I'd hate to point out that your accent isn't as pronounced as you think it is.'

'Eh?' Aggie said, her voice rising as she accentuated the Storrian bite on her words.

'Compared to a lot of people, you sound almost like you're from Afren.'

Aggie's mouth fell open, aghast. 'It's beat oot o us! It's Afrenian imperialism an —' her words died in the air when she saw Cait's mocking grin. 'Get tae fuck.'

It was Cait's turn to laugh, and as the laughter died, she felt her thoughts turn to the future. She found herself wondering what she would see when the dust settled. When she pictured it in her mind's eye, it wasn't border hills and blond boys that she saw, but crooked buildings, and smog, and a crosshatch of washing lines; it was dark tunnels, and hard work, and change; it was learning more about the woman behind Thorterknock's least favourite urban legend; it was finding a place in this new world. Somehow, the unknown prospect of their winning frightened her more than their losing, in the most refreshing and wonderful way.

'I never thanked you for saving me,' Aggie said.

Cait blinked, and she realised she was staring. 'The doctor did the hard work.'

Aggie looked at her hands. 'I saw the Shadielaunds, Cait. I was almost there. If you hadn't — I just think —' She screwed her eyes closed and exhaled, then looked directly at Cait. 'It was terrifying. And ... for a moment ... for a moment I *wanted* to go.'

There was a strange and scared look in Aggie's eyes, and Cait wasn't sure what to do with it or what to say. 'What did you see?'

Aggie blinked about in confusion, but she said nothing. At last, a strange look passed over her face. 'Do you believe in ghosts?'

Cait had done, until she stepped into that empty inn. 'I don't know. Why?'

'I saw ... no ... It wis more of a ... a shadow. Like, a shadow of myself ...' Aggie's hands moved in the air as if she were trying to grasp something invisible, and Cait realised she had never seen her speechless before.

'What happened?' Cait said. 'What was it?'

Then, as quickly as the cracks had formed, all traces of vulnerability disappeared. 'I need you to do something for me,' Aggie said, the familiar and soft determination set back into her features.

'Anything.'

'I need to be out there tomorrow. Calan won't understand, so I need you to cover for me.'

Cait hunted for the joke, but when she realised Aggie spoke with complete sincerity, she shook her head. 'No.'

'You *just* said you'd do anything.'

'You've not recovered!' Cait couldn't stop the frantic huffs of laughter escaping between her words. 'You're far too weak to be on a barricade.'

'Calan said there would be no fighting.'

Cait fought to stop her voice rising, even if just to fool herself into thinking she cared less than she did. 'We don't know what's going to happen tomorrow.'

Aggie's voice dropped to a sigh. 'I've been fighting this fight for ten years. It would break me to sit this last one out.'

And it would break me if you were hurt again, Cait thought, but instead, she spoke without thinking. 'Then I'll go, too.' She had never used a gun, but she could learn, and she could keep Aggie safe. She could be there to hold her wrist and pull her back from the brink if something went wrong.

She jumped as Aggie leaned towards her and laid a hand over hers. 'They'll need you in the Unnertoun when it's all over,' she said.

Cait searched Aggie's face. She tried to meet her eyes, but her gaze kept settling on Aggie's lips, practically scarlet against her pale skin. 'That doesn't fill me with confidence,' Cait whispered.

Aggie smirked. 'Just a couple of scraped knees, nothing too serious.' She retracted her hand. The night air swept in, and Cait tucked her hands under her thighs. 'Do you understand?' Aggie asked.

Cait could understand, but that didn't stop her worrying. There was a pull in Cait that drove her to fix things, whether it was a patient, or a lover, or a broken country. She wanted to take the battered pieces and put them back stronger. She always had. It was the one thing she had complete confidence in. She suspected the pull Aggie felt towards Storran was much the same, and Cait knew how painful it was to resist. 'You don't need to fight,' Cait said softly.

'I do.'

'That's not what I meant.' She looked at Aggie. The Fox of Thorterknock was mostly an urban legend, but Aggie had breathed it to life. 'You have power in your words. Hearing you speak is the reason I'm here now.'

That afternoon seemed like an age ago. 'There was a boy talking to a crowd, and the Fox of Thorterknock was there, too. She pushed him off his podium because she thought they needed a better speaker.'

A faint smile appeared on Aggie's face. 'I do mind that, and I was right.'

'It wasn't any of the stunts the Separatists pulled that made me come with you to Gowdstane. It was the things you said, the thoughts you put in my head. They made me believe we could do better.'

'They call me a firebrand,' Aggie said without looking at her. 'A heretic. A terrorist.' She turned and fixed Cait with a curious look. 'What makes you so sure I'm not manipulating you? What makes you certain you're not just yet another radicalised pawn in a bigger game?'

The question made Cait squirm, bringing back half-wilted memories of thorny conversations in the rose garden. Still, she was certain, and she answered without hesitation. 'I know manipulation. This isn't it.'

'How do you know?'

'Because I made up my own mind. I started to see things for myself. I realised the only one telling us that Storran couldn't survive alone was Afren.' *Little dove, you'd be hopeless without me.* 'And the voice that said all that was mine. No one else's.'

Mine.

She was keenly aware of Aggie staring at her, and Cait's cheeks heated. 'That sounded silly,' she said with a dismissive laugh.

Aggie shook her head. 'No,' she said quietly. 'It's not.' A long moment of silence stretched out, then Aggie said, 'The voice in my head is also my own, and that terrifies me more than any brush with the Shadielaunds. Whether I like it or not, the Fox is a part of me. Its thoughts are my thoughts.' But when she looked at Cait then, all hints of the Fox were gone, and Cait felt she was looking at Aggie exactly as she truly was: a twenty-five-year-old who hadn't healed from the wounds of her youth. A young woman whom the system had betrayed and turned into something savage. Beautiful. But savage. Cait wondered what the voice in her head would say to her if she sat tomorrow out, and maybe that was exactly why she was so bent on fighting.

'It was your voice that gave me mine,' Cait said. Aggie's eyes glistened. 'Speak to the people on their level and they *will* listen to you.' When the fragile look on Aggie's face became too much, Cait looked away and added blithely, 'If you can talk someone who's basically Afrenian into becoming a Separatist, you can convince the whole of Storran.'

Aggie sniffed, quickly looking away. 'Thank you,' she whispered.

Cait noticed Aggie was shivering and climbed back onto the safety of the roof. 'Come on, before Calan notices we're gone and has a heart attack.'

'Can't you restart hearts?' Aggie asked.

'I'm good. I'm not *that* good.'

Cait reached down to grasp her wrist and help her up, but Aggie took her hand. When she stood, she looked at Cait, and Cait could pick out the specks in her eyes flashing like the gold in Storran's flag.

*

The next morning, the main street of the Unnertoun was choked with Separatists waiting to head up into the city. Cait hovered by Calan, who counted people under his breath over and over again as they passed by, and she wondered if he was aware that he was doing it. She watched the crowd of Separatists. Rifles passed from hand to hand. Friends laughed as they pinned navy sashes to each other's chests. They'd brought them from Gowdstane, but the Separatists' numbers were so few that there was no need to stitch any more. Instead, Cait had spent the night preparing a surgery in one of the rooms in the Unnertoun. She wound up bandages, and sterilised needles, and laid all her supplies out in a logical, careful order. *Just in case.* It gave her some sense of preparedness, even though her emotions were spinning wildly out of control.

Occasionally, a song broke free from the rabble.

> *Bring furth your best men*
> *Frae mountain and deep glen*
> *Bring furth your airms and your pipes and auld war sangs*
> *Gie nae surrender*
> *Ye stalwart defenders*
> *Join in oor chorus and fecht for the true king!*

Among the shifting crowd, a dart of red caught Cait's eye. She left Calan to his restless counting and waded through the bodies, neck craning, eyes searching for any sign of Aggie. She hadn't seen her since they returned to the Unnertoun the previous night, and she didn't want that to be goodbye. She had managed to weave her way almost to the exit with no sign of Aggie when a hand seized her wrist and pulled her into a dark doorway.

'Dinna let Calan see,' Aggie hissed, peering out into the street. 'You're covering for me, remember?'

She had parted with her coat, which left her looking smaller and frailer than before. The navy sash on her chest rose and fell with laboured breaths, her lungs still struggling under the weight of recovery. Aggie picked up a rifle that was propped on the wall at her side and slung it over her shoulder. 'Do me a favour and see if you can find any drink down here. We'll need it when we're done. I like a single malt. None of that blended pish.' Then she reached into her pocket and pulled out her knife. She let the blade pop and tossed it in a quick arc before she sheathed it and dropped it into Cait's hands. 'Hopefully you won't need it.'

Cait stared at the polished handle of the knife. It was spotless, any sign of its violence in the Dorcha Pass long since gone. 'What if you need it?' she asked.

Aggie laughed and nodded at the bayonet prying over her shoulder. 'I've got a bigger one. Deagh fortan agus na bhàsaich.'

Cait's heart fluttered at the sound of Leid on Aggie's lips. It sounded like magic — beautiful, but strong and unyielding, like the woman before her. 'What does that mean?'

Aggie smirked. 'Good luck and don't die.'

Cait rolled her eyes. 'That's not funny.' She struggled through a smile. 'Please be safe.'

'I will,' Aggie said. Her eyes sparked with vibrant life and purpose. 'See you on Oathlaw for a victory celebration?'

'Already planning?' Cait asked.

'It's going to be the party of the century,' Aggie grinned.

Unspoken words lingered in the air between them, and all that bridged the gap was the rise and fall of Aggie's breathing. *I'll see you again,* Cait told herself. A story like the Fox of Thorterknock couldn't die. Not before she'd had a chance to finish the book. She looked to the floor, breaking from the bright ale of Aggie's gaze. 'I ...' but she didn't know what to say. She looked back up to find Aggie staring at her, lips parted, and brows furrowed as if she, too, were right on the cusp of words she couldn't grasp. Cait's heart pounded with the anticipation of *something* that belonged in this moment, but wasn't. She suddenly felt too hot in her skin.

'I should go,' Aggie said, and made to move past her.

Cait stepped in her way. 'Aggie —'

They collided. Aggie's faint freckles starred across Cait's vision.

She'd never noticed them before. Briefly, their noses brushed, and then Aggie's lips were on Cait's. Cait's breath hitched. At first, she thought her heart would drop dead in her chest, but it soon settled into a spirited canter. Aggie's tentative hands brushed the small of Cait's back. Cait's fist unclenched and found Aggie's hip. She let herself sink into Aggie. Sinking into Aggie was like sinking into cool silk sheets in the middle of summer. She wanted to stay there all day.

Then Cait saw the Dorcha Pass in her mind, and Aggie's boots pacing over blood, and Kenzie's face, twisted with betrayal and rage, and inexplicable guilt churned in Cait's throat.

'No.' The word burst from Cait's mouth, and she stepped backwards, hands flying to her lips. Aggie's eyes widened as she recoiled. Cait immediately regretted pulling away. She made to reach out to her.

'I'm sorry,' Aggie whispered, and dived into the street.

Cait's thoughts caught up with her too late. She cried for Aggie to wait, but by the time she had rushed into the street after her, the current of Separatists had carried Aggie away, and she was nowhere to be seen.

Cait's first thought was that she'd regret leaving things that way for the rest of her days. Her second thought, for some reason, was about Oathlaw.

*

There was one person in the Unnertoun that was dissatisfied with their role and would jump at any chance for something else to do. Cait pushed her way through the crowd of departing Separatists and hunted empty rooms until she finally found Aidan in a room tucked away in a secluded corner. She faltered at the door. His ceremonial plaid from the coronation looked somehow more magnificent in the Unnertoun's gloom. His curls were smoothed back, the crown placed carefully on his head. He talked quietly with Elsie, who seemed to never leave his side, and they both looked up as Cait entered.

'Go, Elsie. Calan will be waiting,' Aidan said. The girl gave a dutiful nod then hurried past Cait and out the door. Aidan watched Cait from the other side of the room. 'Did he send you to chase me up?'

'No,' Cait said.

He didn't say anything, but lifted something from the table in front of him and fastened it to his hip. Cait realised it was a sword. 'You're not going with Calan, are you?' she asked.

He nodded at the door and the people beyond it. 'I need to be with them. And …' He chewed his lip. Doubt crept across the determined set of his face. 'I'd feel safer on the frontline.'

Cait's heart fell. The price on his life would be hanging over that boy's head like a guillotine. 'You're one of us, Aidan. No one will give you up,' she said. The look he gave her told her that he didn't believe a word she said. She forced her voice to brighten. 'I've got a better job for us.'

'What's that?'

'You remember the treaty I told you about?'

'Aye.'

'And what it would mean?'

Aidan's eyes narrowed. 'Storran would belong to the people. So … Afren would have to let us go.'

Cait nodded. 'I think I know where it is.'

Chapter 39

A Puppet Parliament

'You know, there's an old wives' tale about Daibh's Airch,' Elsie said. Across her nose, her pale skin was already tinted pink from the early sun.

'What's that, then?' Tavis asked.

'They say that couples who exit at opposite sides of the bridge are doomed.'

Tavis tutted. 'Well, that certainly explains a few of my failed romantic escapades.'

A small barricade constructed mostly from sandbags and old furniture from the Unnertoun was well underway on the New Town side of the little cast-iron bridge, and the Separatists worked away quietly, their low mutterings humming like a hive.

'Make sure it's as strong as possible,' Calan called to them, which earned him a few exasperated stares. He didn't care. Because Daibh's Airch stood over the narrowest part of the river, it would be the easiest point for the Lealists to cross, so the barricade needed to be sound. One of the Separatists dropped a barrel, and the thud it made against the ground made Calan wince.

'Let me help you wi that,' Elsie said, brushing past and helping the Separatist hoist and secure the barrel onto the barricade.

Calan cringed as her Lealist cloak snagged behind her. 'Watch your uniform!'

Their short rescue mission in Hart Hall had been a blessing in disguise because it left Calan with three Lealist uniforms at his disposal. While Calan sweated beneath the thick layers, and the one Tavis wore was clearly too small for him, Elsie looked every bit the polished Watchman.

'You ready, lad?'

'That's the signal,' Elsie said, shouldering a rifle.

It felt much quicker than it should have. Calan had ensured he was happy with the progress on the barricade before sending their scout out to the meeting point, and he could only hope the other bridges were suitably secured. 'Aidan's still not here,' he said.

'We're on borrowed time,' Elsie said. 'I can fetch him if you want but …'

'No,' Calan said. It was too late now. The signal had been made, which meant the sand in their timer was already pooling. Calan released a slow breath and allowed himself a moment to watch the last of the embers fall quietly to earth, then clapped his hands together. 'Let's go.'

*

The four of them — Calan, Tavis, Elsie, and Fraser — moved through the New Town as quickly as they dared, though no patrols seemed to have reached that side of the river, so their movements were easy. Despite its weight, Calan was glad to be wearing the Lealist uniform. It made him feel impenetrable. As they walked, Elsie gripped Fraser's shoulder.

'He's not our prisoner,' Calan said.

'Well, I'm certainly no your ally,' Fraser muttered.

Calan ignored him. 'Elsie, let him go.'

Elsie's hand held fast. 'Aidan told me to watch him,' she said.

'Then watch him,' Calan replied. 'But stop manhandling him.' After a moment of hesitation, she released her grip.

They paused just around the corner from Parliament Square with its flat grey frontage. The statue of Anndras cast a long shadow across the ground. As expected, two City Guards watched over the entrance to the Parliament. They looked bored, and Calan hoped that would err in their favour. 'Tavis and Elsie will go inside with the taller guard, and once he's secured, give me the signal and we'll deal with the other one,' Calan said in a low, slow voice. They knew the plan, but it didn't hurt to hear it again. They could do with Aidan for the extra numbers, but Calan could make it work.

'Just like in the museum, lad,' Tavis murmured, patting Calan gently on the shoulder as they strode out into the open. His words settled Calan's racing heart somewhat; they reminded him that they had done this before. They had been tour guides rather than guards, and despite the setbacks, they had succeeded.

The guards straightened as the three Separatists and Fraser crossed the frontage of the Parliament. 'Morning,' Calan said with a dip of the head, climbing the low stairs towards them. The burly, dour guard eyed them suspiciously, and his impressive garden of a moustache twitched. Calan continued. 'We've had some information about suspicious activity around the area this morning, and I'd be grateful if my colleagues could scope the building to check it's secure.'

The hairy guard's thick eyebrows lowered. 'Haven't seen anything. It's been quiet aw morning.'

Calan looked at him in mock-surprise. 'Did you not see that almighty blast?'

The second guard, a younger woman who had been looking up at her companion for the duration of the conversation, nodded. 'Aye, we did, actually. Any idea what it was?'

'Can't be sure. We have a couple of leads, but really ought to check this area to rule a few things out,' Calan said.

The man didn't so much as twitch as he regarded Calan. 'Like I said, been quiet aw morning.'

Calan spread his hands. 'Look, I'd rather not be up at this time either, but when the Brigadier tells you to look into something, you do it.'

'Let's just go back to Hart Hall, lad,' Tavis said. 'No point in wasting our time.'

Calan feigned resignation. 'Get their names, then. I'm sure the Brigadier has dealt with plenty uncooperative types in his time.'

The woman's face went ashen as she looked to her companion, and the large man sighed. 'Mon, then.' He indicated one of the sets of doors behind him and pulled out a set of keys. 'Make it quick.'

'Much appreciated, sir.' Calan nodded for Elsie and Tavis to follow the guard inside. 'I'll watch your post.'

Calan stood next to the other guard and scanned the area, schooling his face into what he hoped was neutrality. He strained for the sound of gunfire, or screaming, or any sign that things had already fallen apart, but the morning was quiet.

'So, the Watch, eh? Is it as good as they all say?' the guard asked.

Fraser opened his mouth to speak. Calan gave him a hard look. *Don't say a word.* 'It's money and a bed at the end of the day.' Then, seeing an opportunity, he added, 'Can't take anything for granted right now, though.'

'Oh? How's that?'

'With this pretender news, word in Hart Hall is they'll start looking at making cuts if it all calms down.'

'Ah, they're stubborn, those Separatists. Can't imagine them lying low for long.' She turned to face Calan, leaning lazily on one hip. 'You'll have your job for a while yet.'

'I hope you're right,' Calan said.

She took a conspiratorial step towards him and lowered her voice. 'So, between you and me, what's it your lot are looking for in there?'

'They're Separatists,' Fraser blurted.

Calan's blood ran cold. The guard stared at Fraser. Thankfully, she laughed. 'Well, of course it's them behind this. But what did they do, like?'

'Don't trust them. They want to take the Parliament,' Fraser said.

Calan kicked Fraser in the shin. The guard looked between Calan and Fraser, then lifted her rifle.

'Building's secure,' came Elsie's bright voice from behind, and Calan breathed a sigh of relief as they both rounded on the guard in one swift motion, catching her unaware. She yelped as Calan wrested her gun from her hands, and Elsie secured her arms behind her back and marched her inside.

Calan turned to find Fraser struggling to his feet, rubbing his leg. 'Get inside,' Calan snapped, shoving him ahead towards the door.

The Parliament was as magnificent inside as it was out. It was elegant, yet understated, with a vaulted ceiling held aloft by slender marble columns. Their boots squeaked on the polished white floor, and a skylight high above let the morning spill across the marble. Elsie and Tavis manoeuvred the second guard towards her counterpart, who was slumped on the floor beside a large, oak reception desk. She managed a cry of, 'What are you going to do?' before the gag was shoved in her mouth. Calan finally let his cloak drop to the ground and stretched out, feeling much lighter.

There wasn't time to relax. Calan could almost feel his watch pulsing away in his pocket. 'Here's what's going to happen,' he said. The two guards glared up at him. 'You're outnumbered. There's not a Lealist on this side of the Cath. We're going to keep you here, and if you don't make a fuss, you'll get home unharmed.' He was glad they were gagged and unable to challenge him on what would happen if they didn't cooperate, because Calan knew fine well they'd come to no harm regardless of what they did. He turned back to the others and found himself looking down the barrel of a gun. Fraser's hands shook as he held the discarded rifle of the younger guard and pointed it straight at Calan.

'Fraser,' Calan said. 'Think about what you're doing.' Slowly, he lifted his hands above his head.

Fraser shifted his grip on the gun. 'I won't let you get awa wi this,' he said.

Elsie lifted her rifle, too, pointed straight at Fraser. 'Aidan said he would be trouble,' she said.

'Elsie!' Calan snapped. 'Put the gun down.'

'That's twice he's tried tae flee. He'll just keep trying.'

Fraser was an asset. It didn't matter if they could trust him or not, Calan needed him. He took a step towards Fraser. 'We don't want to hurt you.'

Fraser thanked him for the sentiment by spitting at his feet.

'Stand back, Calan,' Elsie said. She stared down her gun, eyes trained on Fraser, but if her aim wavered, Calan would surely be caught in the crossfire.

'Elsie, stop. We need him.'

'He'll lie,' Elsie said. 'He'll get you to send all your messages to the Prongs. They won't reach anyone.'

Calan's pulse surged in his ears. If Fraser's blood was spilled across this immaculate floor, it may as well be over for them. 'Elsie,' Calan looked her firmly in the eye. 'Drop the gun.'

'Aidan warned me,' Elsie whispered. 'He trusts me.' Her finger rested on the trigger. She was Aggie, fist poised over the glass case in Eadwick.

'There are two outcomes here,' Calan said more calmly than he felt. Elsie's eyes flicked to him and back to Fraser. 'If you execute Fraser, we will have eliminated a threat, yes, but I will have to work out how to send messages to our potential allies myself. It'll slow us down, and we're already on borrowed time. Every second I spend making mistakes is a second gifted to the Lealists. If you let Fraser live, we get that time back. The world will learn of Storran's freedom far quicker than if I do it alone.'

Elsie looked desperate. 'What if he lies?'

Calan shrugged. 'If he lies, he lies, but if we dispose of him now, we're shooting ourselves in the foot.'

'I won't help,' Fraser said, squeezing his finger on the trigger.

BANG. Calan flinched. Smoke billowed in the air. He looked up, and Fraser's gun clattered to the ground. He staggered, but he was unharmed.

Elsie's shot had arced wide, splintering the wooden reception desk. Calan wiped his forehead. The first shots of the Separatist uprising had been fired, it seemed, their mark in the Parliament made permanent. This was real. This was happening. There was no time to catch lost breath. 'I'll need someone to escort me and Fraser to the comms room and stand guard.'

'I'll come,' Elsie said quickly, eyes still trained on Fraser, who seemed resigned now. They set off, leaving Tavis to keep watch over the foyer and the prisoners. He suspected they were in for a good few tales.

*

An empty parliament was an eerie thing. Calan flinched at the echo of his own footsteps down long expanses of corridor, and the offices he peered into were, for the most part, empty. The ones that did house desks and cabinets were sparse, with little sign of work. The building and its workers were a symbol for what was supposed to be an equal system, and nothing more. Petty bureaucracy was the most action the building ever saw. The Five Realms were supposed to have their fair share of power, but they were useless when Afren had ultimate control of finances and tax. This building was a puppet, but one day it would burst with people the best in their field. The corridors would ring with fresh ideas. They would hold a grand re-opening, a celebration after so much division. It would be something that all people in Storran could get behind. It would be the restarting of a bustling, beating heart.

When they reached the lonely communications room, Elsie wished them luck with a brisk salute and took up her position in the hallway. Calan let the door swing shut behind himself and Fraser, trapping them in the dark. He lit one lamp and refused to open the blind on the window. The thought of raw, natural light felt too exposed. He'd always conducted his schemes in secrecy and that wasn't about to change.

He had expected chaos. He had expected desks strewn with papers. He had expected typewriters of every model, and frantic scrawls of ink in margins. He had expected a well-connected centre of power, but the room was bare. The telegram sat at a lonely table, with nothing but a dusty typewriter for company. When he sat at the desk, the chair was too low and the desk too high. How anyone got work done here he wasn't sure.

'Sit,' Calan said to Fraser, who hovered by the door. When he did nothing, Calan shrugged. 'Or stand.' He looked at the telegraph in front of him. A wire sprung from the transmitter into a switchboard with dozens of numbered inputs. At the end of each input lay another telegraph and an operator just waiting to hear the news that Storran had been claimed by its people. 'Is there a direct line to Hart Hall?'

Fraser remained silent and it wore on Calan's patience. He gripped the knob and peered over his glasses at him. 'I didn't save your life for you to stand there and waste both our time.'

'I'm no Separatist,' Fraser said.

'You're not,' Calan said, 'but you're supposed to be dead. Twice over. What do you think the Lealists will do when they find you here? Will they welcome you back with open arms?' Fraser's throat wobbled. The next words Calan said were risky, but he could see that Fraser wouldn't take to force. 'You're free to go, but if you help us and we win, I promise you'll have a life. If we lose, we'll protect you as one of our own.'

Fraser took a step back towards the door and hesitated. A long moment passed where Calan thought he had lost him, but eventually he crossed the room and lowered himself into the chair beside him. 'Line three runs between Hart Hall and the Parliament.' He opened a drawer in the desk and started rifling through. 'There's usually a directory of where each line goes.'

Calan turned to the transmitter. He plugged the wire into line three, then quickly tapped out his message to Hart Hall. It was nothing more than a diversion, and a bid to make sure things didn't get more complicated than need be. He informed them of a Separatist incident in the north of the Old Town near the Skemmels and advised that citizens should remain indoors. He hoped they spread the word.

By the time he finished, Fraser had located the little book and laid it open on the desk. 'Where next?'

'Eadwick,' Calan said. 'Whatever line gets us the Council of Five and Queen Ana.'

Fraser didn't need to consult the book. He reached over and plugged the wire into line one. Calan clasped the grip and smoothed out the message in his mind. It wasn't new to him. Even before he had conceived of this plan, the words had played across his mind before sleep. He steadied his breathing, then pressed the grip up and down in a clear pulse. These were the words that could change the tide of history, and they couldn't be misunderstood. Slowly, carefully, he formed the message that the parliamentarians of the Council of Five would find written on a little card when they sat down at their desks for the day.

FAO Queen Ana. Chancellor Borden. Council of 5. All members.

Calan wiped the sweat from his hand onto his trousers, then started again.

Occupation of Storran's Parliament by King Aidan and supporters. Storran henceforth independent of Five Realms. Autonomy will be respected.

Chapter 40

A Gathering Storm

The thirty or so Separatists on Aist Bridge decided they wanted to beat the other barricades to completion. They laughed and joked as they stacked high the pieces of iron and timber scavenged from dust-yards and the backs of factories around the city. Aggie, smarting from the effort of the short walk from the Unnertoun to the bridge, wasn't much help in the barricade's construction, but she celebrated with the others when it sprung up in less than thirty minutes. It was at least double the height of her.

As she perched on the bridge's balustrade and shuddered against the fresh June morning, she started to regret abandoning her coat. Since her brush with the Shadielaunds, the cold seemed to cut straight into her bones and gnaw her stiff. But that wasn't all. It was as though a remnant of shadow had lodged itself inside her, like an unwelcome souvenir, and it dampened each of her senses. Food tasted like dust. The world seemed to exist behind a thick pane of glass. Sleep came in fitful bursts, and when she did manage to rest, her dreams were stalked by the Fox of Thorterknock with its brimstone glare. Worse still, the skittishness of her dreams followed her into the waking hours, and she lived with her eyes over her shoulder. She could see herself as Cait must see her now: a zealot and a terror.

After that morning, she feared that Cait's startled face would join her haunted dreams, hands forever shielding her lips. Aggie longed to hurl herself in the Cath. She'd wanted to kiss Cait since the lochside, but if stories had taught her anything, it was that a kiss was never just a kiss. For once in her life, she'd battled every brash instinct within her, and made herself handle it carefully. But when Cait had stood before her in the Unnertoun, eyes glossy with worry — worry for *Aggie,* no less — all she could bring herself to care about was how soft her life had become since the brave and kind-hearted doctor's daughter had swept aboard their Eadwick-bound train. For the first time in a long time, Aggie had felt a timid sense of peace. With Cait around, even a lifetime of fighting Afrenian rule didn't seem so damning. The fact any individual had the ability to soften her edges and calm her ire both terrified and delighted her. Standing in the Unnertoun that morning, Aggie had realised she adored Cait. She had also realised she could very well die today, and if that happened, they'd never know what could have been. And then Cait had stepped closer, and Aggie had foolishly given into the hope that she felt the same way.

Aggie groaned and dropped her head into her arms. *Let the Lealists take me.*

'There's a sight for sore eyes.'

Aggie turned at the sound of the familiar voice.

'Ey up,' Jamie said. She stood, as always, with her thumbs hooked into her braces.

Aggie turned her eyes back to the river. 'What are you doing here, Talasaire? I thought the front would be too hands-on for your sort.'

'I was promised a completely peaceful revolution,' Jamie said, leaning against the balustrade at Aggie's side. 'And if I don't get one, I'll wring Calan's neck.'

Aggie sighed. 'Ah, the peace-loving ways of the forest folk.'

'Aye,' was all Jamie said.

Aggie couldn't pretend to understand much about how Talasaire abilities worked, but something about Jamie had seemed off since Aggie recovered. 'Calan told me what happened with you and the crown,' she said.

Jamie shrugged. 'Did what I had to do.'

'For Storran?' Aggie asked.

Jamie nodded once, looking out over the Cath. 'Aye,' she sighed. 'For Storran.'

*

The frontline was a lot less exciting than Aggie thought it would be, but she took it as a sign that Calan's plan was working. By half past seven, the first pinstriped lawyers and clerks trickled onto the bridge, setting a course for an early start in their New Town offices. When they found their way blocked, some turned to seek an alternate route, while others lingered in the shadow of the barricade, inquisitive necks craning. By the time the clock struck nine, the crowd of anxious workers stretched back halfway down the bridge.

Jamie hopped down from the concealed vantage point where she had been watching them from. 'They're getting angry, and there's a handful of Lealists behind them now, too.'

'What are they daein?' Aggie asked.

'Just standing there, watching.'

The Separatists lingered aimlessly on their own side of the barricade. It was easy to hold off the Lealists when the soldiers were merely watchful spectres, but how long until they decided to attack? Half an hour later, the Lealists still hadn't moved, but the civilians caught between the soldiers and the barricade had worked themselves into a ruckus as more arrived and had the unhappy realisation they wouldn't be going to work today. It wouldn't be long before the crowd posed a bigger threat to the barricade than the Lealists.

Maybe the feartie bastards are going to let the public do their job for them, Aggie thought. The racket rattled the morning peace: demands to be let through, name-calling, pleas for the Lealists to shoot the Separatists down where they stood. With every passing moment, they grew in anger and confidence, and soon people started tearing chunks out of the barricade and throwing them over the side of the bridge into the river below.

'We need to do something,' Aggie said, the Fox within her snapping at its restraints.

Jamie frowned. 'We can't engage the civilians.'

'No,' Aggie said as a couple of sections from the top were pulled down to jubilant cries. 'But they'll tear us apart when they get to us.' Aggie looked up. When she was fitter, the barricade would have been no problem to climb, but now even looking at it she felt her limbs aching. Still, they didn't have a lot of choice. She put her hands to the wood and dragged herself up the side of the barricade.

'What are you doing?' Jamie called after her.

Aggie's muscles throbbed by the time she made it to the top. Her legs wavered under her weight as she rose, and she wished she had a rifle to lean on, but she couldn't give the Lealists an excuse to shoot. At the sight of her, some of the public turned and left, and those who didn't roared louder.

'Get hame!' Aggie called, though the effort tore her breath away. 'There'll be no work today.' This didn't earn her a warm reception. The unintelligible clamour turned venomous as faces reddened and contorted with rage.

Ungrateful. Can't they see we're doing this for their sake? The Fox snapped inside her head.

'Surely a day's wages is a fair price for yer freedom?' she cried.

The crowd roared straight back at her. 'We don't want yer freedom.' 'Give it a rest already.' 'They'll string you up, Fox!'

Bankers. Lawyers. Professors. Doctors. Their clean suits and shiny shoes showed exactly what freedom would mean to them. She wasn't fighting for their sake. 'Try thinking with your heads and not your pockets for once!' Her frustration ribboned at the end of her words. 'If you knew what was good for you, you'd throw your support behind our King.'

'Fuck yer pretender!' someone shouted.

Aggie laughed bitterly. 'Our pretender has mair richt tae govern here than the Chancellor of the Five Realms.' She paused to catch her breath. 'I've heard the stories frae Gowdstane. He sought their permission before he put any crown on his head, and the folk cheered when he did. The sovereignty of Storran rests wi the folk, no in a bloodline. Our *pretender* is proof of that.'

'Not in my name!' A voice shouted. 'Where's your prince hiding?'

Aggie grit her teeth. It was ignorant fools like these that stood in the way of progress. 'He's busy winning you a better future while yous aw stand here complaining —'

'I work for the Five Realms! How can you promise I'll still have a job if that boy drags us out?'

Aggie opened her mouth to explain that any government jobs left by leaving the Five Realms would need to be replaced by Storran's own roles, it was really that simple, but her words died when she caught the gaze of the woman who had asked the question. Beneath the fury in her eyes lay brittle fear. In the weeks and months following her brother's death, Aggie was a pendulum that swung between anger and listlessness. The cleverest boy she knew was swept away, and with him, the answer to all her questions. Time and again, she had sat in the room they once shared and asked aloud how the soldiers who were supposed to protect them could have hurt him. But no matter how many answers she had come up with, the future was still dark, and lonely, and so, so questionable.

You have power in your words. There was no argument or prediction that would remedy these people's fear if they couldn't see cold, hard proof of a better future, and Aggie was many things, but she was not a prophet. *You have power in your words,* Aggie told herself again, and as she looked over the crowd, she realised that the civilians outnumbered the Lealists five to one.

'I can't say what our future will look like,' Aggie said. 'I can't guarantee there won't be hardships. What I can promise is that we'd be in control of it all.' She waved an arm behind her towards the New Town. 'It's about filling that big, empty Parliament back there wi folk that care about *you* and *your* needs. How does a politician living in Eadwick know whit it's like up here? How do they know whit it's like tae be crammed intae workhouses, or working long hours, or sacrificing breid for coal? They never will. But we know.' Anyone travelling to work from the Old Town each day would know what that looked like, regardless of their station, regardless of how tidy their office was or how clean their shoes were. The crowd met her with contemplative silence. Rain pattered across the ground, cool and fresh. Aggie turned her face to the sky and caught her waning breath. She looked down at the civilians. For so long, her anger had been her weapon, biting, and scratching to be let loose, but it was *their* anger that could turn the tide. She only had to stoke it. 'How many of you have been to Eadwick?' she asked. 'Because I have. You think the New Town's posh? Eadwick's ten, twenty times that. They've got palaces, and river cruises, and I'd bet half yer weans don't even hae shoes.'

Knowing glances were exchanged between crowd members. Murmurs of resigned affirmation.

'Down there, they don't care about you. They care about what you can do to keep feeding the beast that is Afren. That gluttonous, golden boar only wants glory and riches. It'll eat up our resources until it's fat and fed and there's nothing left for us. It's doing it already. You know. You've lived it.' The rain hammered harder, but no one ran for shelter. 'There's a storm coming,' Aggie said. Just then, somewhere far away, thunder rattled the sky. Aggie watched the faces of the people as they heard it. Their eyes widened, their heads whipped to and fro. *How did she do that? A trick, surely?* But there was no witchcraft, no cunning trick or hidden drum, only a coincidence that shook the familiar ground these people stood on.

Emboldened, Aggie lifted her voice. 'When I look out at this crowd, I see inventive folk. I see good-herted folk. I see unyeildin folk.' Her mind strayed to a borders lass that might never look her way again. 'I see all of this, and yet we trail behind Afren like a loyal dog and take nothing but scraps frae our master's golden plate.' Another clap of thunder rolled overhead, louder now, closer. It rumbled in her chest and shook her fragile bones. 'There's a storm coming.' The rain kissed her head, her skin, the ground. 'It's here, and you can go and seek shelter, or you can staund in it with us. Either way, when the skies clear, this land will be changed. Things will never be the same again.'

Aggie hadn't planned to stop, but she had run out of breath to carry her words. She stood panting above the crowd as the rain built to a downpour. Heads shook, eyes rolled, backs turned, but a ripple broke from the centre of the crowd, and Aggie wondered if it had all been for nothing and she was about to be ripped apart. *A martyrs' death wouldn't be so bad,* Aggie thought. But slowly, a single woman pushed her way towards the barricade, her eyes trained on Aggie. Aggie recognised the woman as the one who had demanded answers about her job. She moved cautiously, and paused at the foot of the barricade. For a moment, she just stood there, watching Aggie with wide, watery eyes. Then she reached a hand up and began to climb. Trembling, Aggie reached out and hauled her up on top of the barricade, where they stood watching each other, both breathing hard. Aggie said nothing, but the woman gave one shivering yet determined nod, and Aggie understood. It meant *I'm with you. Show me what you've got.*

And Aggie grinned, because it didn't matter if no one else joined her up here, because this woman had, and this woman believed. And no one had bled for it.

A cry from below grabbed Aggie's attention, and she turned to find Lealists battering their way through the crowd. Some tried to back off the bridge, but the Lealists swiped them out of the way and marched over them. 'This is a peaceful protest!' Aggie shouted. 'We're not here to fight!' The line of Lealists stopped. Their figures straightened, legs bracing. They raised their guns. 'Stop!' Aggie screamed. The sound of Separatist guns anchoring themselves over the top of the barricade surrounded her. '*Hold*,' she commanded.

A voice from the Lealist line cried, 'Ready!'

The crowd of civilians charged forward, and Aggie looked on as the barricade changed from a symbol of division to a beacon of survival.

'These are innocent people!' Aggie growled at the Lealists. The guns behind her clicked. 'I said *hold.*'

But the Lealists didn't flinch. They wouldn't do this. They couldn't.
Let them, the Fox hissed in Aggie's mind. *Let them see what Afren can do.*

'Take aim!'

'They can't,' Aggie whispered.

Of course they can, the Fox snarled. *Don't you remember what they did to your brother?*

Aggie understood now. One convert was simply too much of a risk. The cry for fire was lost to Aggie's pained scream as she hoisted herself behind the barricade and snatched up a gun. She made it to cover just as the sound of gunfire struck the barricade and brought with it the sound of death.

Chapter 41

Oathlaw

The rain built up to a frenzy, and by the time Cait and Aidan had made it to the foot of Oathlaw, they were soaked through. Cait strode ahead, lungs and legs burning, rain spotting in her eyes. She could hear Aidan panting behind. He was probably struggling under the plaid he still had slung over his shoulder, but she didn't wait for him. She had to keep moving, because if she stopped, she'd be consumed with worry and thoughts of, *What if? What if I hadn't pulled away?* Maybe Aggie wouldn't have gone.

The hill was a common green space, so it was well paved on the ascent, but that didn't stop its slow curve around the hill being a tedious and exhausting climb. By the time she reached the top, Cait's legs were ready to give way. She paused only long enough to wipe the rain from her face and catch two shallow breaths. Then she started to dig. She tore at the ground. Grass ripped like hair. Wet clumps of earth piled under her nails like dry blood.

'Cait!' A distant voice called her name. She ignored it. She kept digging. 'Cait, haud on.' Hands grasped her shoulders and pulled her upright. Aidan, just as drenched as she, stared at her. 'Whit are ye daein?'

'It's here.' She tried to pull away, but Aidan grasped her shoulder harder.

'Is it, aye?'

Cait looked down at her muddy hands. She hadn't even thought about it. All she knew was that the treaty had to be here, somewhere on this hill, and that if she had it, she could shield her friends from harm's way.

'Go from the start,' Aidan said. 'Mind me of the line in the ballad.'

Cait tried to think through the haze, but her heart pounded too quickly. Her breaths came too shallow. 'Um ... a ... a stramash. I ...'

'Breathe,' Aidan said. 'Take your time.'

Cait tilted her face to the sky and let the rain spill over her cheeks. She let her breath come as quickly as it needed, and then slowed, until finally her thoughts cleared. She squeezed her eyes closed.

'A stramash three years in its length
A Keeng withoot a throne
A chairge enshrined within the law
Fur freedom jointly owned.'

'Nice one,' Aidan said. When she opened her eyes, he was grinning at her. 'So where does that leave us?'

Cait cast her eyes about the hill. *A chairge enshrined within the law.* There was no proof that the treaty would be up here, or even that Oathlaw was the right law, but she needed something to cling to. Cait scanned the area until her eyes fell on a large, conical structure a short distance away. 'What's that?'

Aidan shrugged. 'Some kind of cairn?'

They made their way over to it, and the closer they got, the bigger Cait realised it was. It was taller than Aidan by at least a couple of feet. As they looked up at it, Cait cast her mind back to facts about history and folk tradition her father had thrown her way over countless tea times and fireside chats.

'We need to take it apart,' she said.

Aidan glanced at her twice. 'Whit?'

In the present-day Storran, cairns were merely wayfinders. Some were new; monuments that had been built over time by each person who reached the summit and placed a stone to mark their journey. Others, and Cait hoped she was right about this one, were ancient.

Cairns are like crowns, her father had said. *They mark the most important places, or at least they did before we started building them everywhere. They're sites of pilgrimage. The structure is strong. It can hold anything from a tomb to a memory.*

'What if this cairn was built to mark where Anndras pledged himself to Cathal's cause? And where they signed the treaty?' Cait said. 'The promise that Storran belonged to the people wasn't just enshrined in *law*, it was enshrined *on the* law.' She pulled a stone from the structure.

'Do you really think it's in there?' Aidan asked.

Cait tossed another stone to the side. 'It has to be.'

Aidan watched as she discarded five stones, and then he joined her. 'This feels wrong,' he said. 'Feels like I'm digging up a grave.'

'Don't think about it,' Cait panted. 'We'll put it back together.'

Three hours passed. Cait's hands were blistered and sore. Her arms burned from the effort. They had brought the cairn to knee-height, and so far, they'd found nothing; no ancient box containing a yellowed piece of parchment, no cryptic clue of where to look next.

For a long moment, they stared at the pile of stones that remained, until Aidan said in a quiet voice, 'Is it definitely real?'

'Yes!' Cait groaned, dropping to her knees, and pushing aside more stones.

'Maybe it was just something added to the story, or just a promise, or —'

'My da can't have been wrong,' Cait said. She wanted to cry. She hurled a stone, and it bounced along the ground and down the side of the hill.

Aidan watched it go, then stilled. His gaze drifted to the south side of the hill that looked out over the river and bridges. 'What was that?' he whispered.

All Cait could hear was the rain. 'What?'

'Listen,' he whispered. Slowly, he drifted to the edge of the hill. Cait followed, and soon, she heard it, too. Screaming, punctuated by a faint popping. 'Shadielaunds,' Aidan whimpered from his vantage point. He lifted a hand to his curls and clutched them.

Cait couldn't see. The bridges and everything beneath the hill were a blur to her. 'What's happening?' Her heart skittered in her chest. She didn't want him to tell her.

Aidan's eyes were trained on the bridges below. 'They're fighting.'

'Who is?'

'The Lealists. The Separatists. Shadielaunds, the civilians, too.'

Cait's heart sank. 'Which bridge?'

'Aist,' Aidan said. *Aggie's bridge.* His eyes trailed along the winding Cath. 'All of them. They're *all* fighting. I —' Cait took his hand. She didn't know what else to do. It was trembling. So was hers. 'I can see bodies.'

'Stop,' Cait said. 'Let's keep digging.' No good would come from watching the slow massacre happening in the city below. She had to keep Aidan calm and preoccupied with the task of dismantling the cairn. She needed it for herself, too. She tugged at his hand to pull him back, but he remained rooted to the spot. He shook his head.

'No. It's too late.'

'It's not. The treaty's up here.' She tried to steady her voice, but it wobbled as she spoke. 'We can find it.' Her friends were down there. Aggie was down there. 'We'll find it.' Maybe she was only kidding herself.

Aidan shook his head again. 'We need to end this.'

Cait glanced back at what remained of the cairn. They had decimated it, and she had the sickly feeling that Aidan was right. The terrible cacophony of horror only seemed to grow louder by the second. Any one of those screams could be Aggie's; any one of those bullets could pierce her heart. If the treaty did exist, what good would it do? If they kept looking, it was likely they'd only succeed in wasting precious time. Fiction couldn't protect her friends from gunfire. Perhaps it was time to let fairy stories be fairy stories. Anndras and Cathal couldn't help them anymore, and it was time to let them rest in the verses of song. When Cait looked back at Aidan, she found him staring at her. 'What do you have in mind?' Cait asked.

'I think I have a plan.' He glanced nervously back at the bridges. 'I need to abdicate.'

*

As the fighting seemed to be isolated to Thorterknock's bridges, they made it back to the Unnertoun with relative ease. Only on a couple of occasions did they have to hide from groups of Lealists freshly released from Hart Hall and marching towards the bridges. Some of them were leading civilians, armed and angry, to their deaths. The city shook with gunfire and screams coming from the direction of the New Town, but the streets of the Old Town were eerily empty.

In the Unnertoun, Aidan strode ahead of Cait. He barged through groups of people that Cait hadn't expected to see down here, bloody, broken faces with wide, scared eyes. Cait briefly noted their injuries, but she pressed after Aidan. He hadn't spoken since the top of Oathlaw. He pushed his way into the room in the Unnertoun Calan had used to plan their strategy, and immediately started rifling around for a pen and paper. Cait closed the door behind her and watched from the opposite side of the room.

'What are you doing?' she asked. He ignored her, trembling hands frantically scribbling out a message. 'Aidan,' she pressed.

When he finished, he straightened, and crossed the room to her. He pressed the letter into her hands, then wrenched the ring from his finger and held it out to her. 'Get this to someone wi sway. Anyone that can make it public.'

The letter was barely legible, but the jagged script revealed Aidan's plan. He wrote to the Council of Five, Queen Ana, and the people of Storran, and the words sent chills down Cait's spine. Aidan had relinquished his crown to the people of Storran. He stated that Storran's sovereignty belonged to them, and no person or state had the right to rule them.

'Do you think this will work?' Cait asked.

'Dinnae ken,' Aidan said. He sighed and shook his head. 'I *don't know.*' He tightened the sword on his belt, then removed the crown and laid it on the table. 'I need to try.'

He made to walk by her towards the door, but she stepped in front of him. 'What if it doesn't?'

He didn't answer her. 'Do you know where to take it?'

Cait wasn't sure, but she cast her mind through the New Town for someone that might hold sway. Her first thought was Kenzie and his Brigadier, but anyone could guess that that would only end in shredded paper. She remembered the blonde journalist at Hart Hall and the article that had sparked this mess. 'I have an idea,' she said.

'Good,' Aidan nodded. He made to pass her again.

'And what about out there?' Cait asked. As if in answer, a volley of gunfire sounded overhead, and they flinched.

'I'm going to the Parliament,' Aidan said. His next words seem to take great effort. 'It's me they want.'

'Aidan ...'

'I can stop this,' he said. He looked more like a boy in trouble than a soldier. He gave a weak smile. 'It's my job.' And then he was gone. He barged past her and through the door, past the gaggle of frightened Separatists gathered outside. They watched him go but said nothing. Then they looked at Cait. She pocketed the letter and ring. She'd go to the journalist, but she had to set up some order here first.

Chapter 42

Fireworks

It only took Cait around half an hour to delegate jobs to those gathered in the Unnertoun. These were Separatists who had sought shelter when the fighting started, and the news they brought from the frontline was grim. Luckily, the injuries before her were unserious, but Cait guessed that the worst casualties hadn't made it off the bridges. There were around twenty of them.

Cait had searched their faces for Aggie, but she wasn't there. Instead, her coat lay like a ghost by her stack of books. With the bullets roaring up above, Cait pulled it tight around herself and searched the pockets for Aggie's courage. In the lull, she allowed her mind to wander. She knew she shouldn't dwell on frivolous things when battle raged above, but dwelling on something as frivolous as a kiss felt like a small luxury. *But it wasn't frivolous at all,* Cait thought. To her, it was earth-shaking and history-making, yet as fragile as a folktale. She was afraid to relive the moment too many times in case her mind reshaped it into something it wasn't. Ghostly fingers touched the small of her back. She shivered. *Snap out of it.*

Mirren, a young Separatist carried back to the Unnertoun after breaking her ankle on the Barter Bridge barricade, whimpered from her chair as a new round of gunfire shook the Old Town up above. 'This is it, isn't it?' she said as Cait knelt beside her. 'It's not like I can run from a Lealist.'

Cait pressed her cheek against the arm of the scratchy armchair. 'It's not going to come to that. Even if it did, we'd all help each other out.'

Mirren looked at her leg, propped up on a footstool in front of her, and let out a shuddering breath. 'I want it to stop.'

'I know,' Cait said. She had to pretend she didn't feel vulnerable and claustrophobic, too. 'But really, if you close your eyes, it sounds a bit like fireworks, don't you think?' She had never liked fireworks, but she hoped

Mirren did.

Mirren screwed her eyes shut. 'A little, aye.'

'When was the last time you watched fireworks?'

Mirren appeared to think hard, then her brow relaxed a little. 'There's a winter market up Oathlaw in January time. There's drinks and dancing and all that, and they set off fireworks at the end.'

'Do you go often?' Cait asked.

Mirren nodded. 'Every year.' She screwed her eyes tighter as another, louder, volley sounded above. Cait hoped the backs of her eyes sparkled.

Cait glanced around and saw that things seemed well in hand. She still had a job to do. 'Can you keep an eye on things here?' she asked Mrs McTavish, a tough but soft-faced woman who had somehow managed to fight on Grace Bridge and lead the injured back to the Unnertoun without gaining a single scratch.

'Aye, all in check, hen,' she said.

Cait nodded and turned to Mirren. 'You'll be okay.' Mirren didn't say anything, but kept her eyes closed and nodded adamantly.

As Cait made her way along the main street of the Unnertoun, she realised how dark and eerie it was compared to her visit there. The street was so alike the ones above ground that it was easy to forget she was underground at all. Something caught her eye in the open door to what once would have been a shop front. She hesitated and glanced inside. The floor was littered with the brown tubes and cylindrical packages of fireworks that Calan had been sorting through the previous night. Thinking they could be dangerous, Cait entered the room and carefully set about stacking them. Her fingers crinkled so delicately over the wrapping that she forgot one spark could unleash a dazzling torrent that would ravage the Unnertoun and shake the world above. That was all it took: just one, weak flame.

Aggie swept into her thoughts yet again.

I did find some fireworks, and I did plant them in the house of a member of Prosperity.

She'd looked so smug.

That's heinous, Cait had said.

And Aggie cackled. *She's heinous.*

Those were not the words of the girl she had stood with on the roof of The Crabbit Corbie, and, perhaps only so she could let herself have the memory of Aggie's lips, she had to believe Aggie had changed her course.

She only realised she had been clutching the same large firework when she heard shrill voices from the street outside. She quickly placed it on top of the pile and followed the voices into the street. Two Separatists met her there. Their clothes were bloody and their skin sooty, and Cait immediately started inspecting a nasty looking cut on one of their arms. 'What happened?' she asked.

The boy winced. 'Loads of Lealists. Civilians, too.'

'We tried getting into the Parliament, but they're all over the bit, so we came here.' He tried to touch his wound and Cait moved his hand away. 'Do you have stitches?'

That was when Cait felt it. It was a sigh of cold air that didn't belong. It swept like a wraith down the street, shifting their hair and clothes, and chilling Cait through. 'Were you followed?' she asked.

The two Separatists looked at each other. 'Naw, don't think so. Can we get those stitches now?'

Cait hushed him and listened carefully, but the Unnertoun was quiet, and the cold breeze had gone. She shook the uneasy feeling off and led the pair to the building where the others were. Once she'd got them settled and briefed Mrs McTavish, she set about finding stitches. The pair of newcomers mumbled between themselves, and Cait was all too aware that across the room, Mirren was listening.

'Wonder how many made it to the Parliament in the end,' said the boy with the cut.

'Couldn't have been that many,' said his companion.

Behind her, Cait heard Mirren stir. 'What happened on Aist?'

The boy with the cut shook his head as he spoke. 'Nothing at first. The civilians were all getting angry, but the Lealists just stood there and watched. And then Aggie got on top of the barricade and started saying all this stuff.' Cait's hands stilled in their search through the medical pack. 'And then this woman, this civilian, climbed on top of the barricade, and that was when it all went to shit.'

'What happened?' Mirren asked.

'Started shooting,' one of them said. 'Us. Civilians. The lot.'

'*Civilians?*' Mirren cried.

'Aye. Got them fighting, too. It was a bloody slaughter, so it was.'

'That's enough,' Cait said, turning from the counter towards the two boys. She knocked over a bucket of water in the process. She'd interfered for Mirren's sake, but she also didn't want to hear how their story ended.

'I'll be back in a moment.'

They fell into silence and Cait clunked her way downstairs and started rifling through cupboards to find something to mop up the water. She was tearing through a cupboard by a window that looked out into the Unnertoun's main street when movement outside caught her attention. One shadow, and then another, flitted by the window. Cait froze. Sure enough, two Watchmen were poking around the house opposite. Cait's pulse hammered in her ears, and she slowly closed the cupboard and backed away from the window. She steadied herself against the opposite wall and tried to think straight. They were preoccupied by one building for now, but eventually, they would sweep the whole Unnertoun. They weren't just here for a nosy. They were out for blood, and they had just struck gold. When the officers vanished into the opposite house, Cait gulped in a breath and hurried up the stairs. She had no idea what to say, but she heard her mother's level words: *People are grateful when you're honest with them.*

When she entered the room, Mirren and the uninjured newcomer were engaged in a conversation about the best bookshops in Thorterknock, and Mrs McTavish was humming quietly away to herself as she carried out some knitting. Cait hovered at the door.

'Mrs McTavish,' she said softly, and the old woman looked up. 'Can you get everyone on their feet?'

She had tried to keep her voice steady, but Mirren's wide eyes stared at her from across the room. 'Why?' she said.

'It's okay, Mirren,' Cait said.

'They've found us, haven't they? They've found us and they're going to kill us!'

Be honest.

'There's a couple of Lealists downstairs, yes.'

Mirren's face paled. 'Shite ...'

'They don't know we're here, and they also don't know their way around, so we need to move quickly.'

'Well, I can't do that!' Mirren cried, indicating her injured leg.

Cait fought to keep her voice steady. 'Mirren, I'm going to need you to keep your voice down.' The girl watched her the way a child with a scraped knee watches their parents: waiting to find out if they had the balm to ease the pain, or if it was time to scream. Cait helped Mirren to stand and slung her arm around her shoulder. When they reached the bottom of the stairs, she left the others in the shadows and slowly opened the door to peer into the street. She spotted the Watchmen a couple of doors down and whispered to the others as she kept her eyes on them, 'Where's the nearest exit?'

'Butcher's,' Mrs McTavish said from behind.

Cait shook her head, remembering how the butcher had to move a pile of boxes out of the way when she and Calan entered through his shop. Besides, he might very well be a traitor. 'Anything else?'

'There's a way that goes out near the Cath.'

'You know the way?'

'Aye.'

They had precious little time, and the group moved slowly, but she told them that the moment the Watchmen had entered the next building along, they should hurry towards that exit and not look back. She told them that if anything should happen, they should run to The Crabbit Corbie and find the open window. When the coast was clear, Cait gave the word. The going was steady, and Cait stood at the centre of the street as the others began their slow journey up through the Unnertoun. They had almost made it to a corner that would conceal them when Cait heard the Watchmen stepping out into the street. Mirren heard them, too, because she stopped dead and looked over her shoulder. Cait waved for them to keep going, and unsure of what to do, she hurried down the street towards the Watchmen and ducked into the open doorway of the building where the fireworks were. She was concealed just in time for the Watchmen to emerge and settle their gaze on the Separatists.

'Bastards!' one of them cried, rifle already in hand.

Cait's hand reached into the pocket of Aggie's jacket. The lighter was still there. Without thinking, Cait seized the largest firework from the top of the pile and burst into the middle of the street. The Watchmen startled, which bought her valuable moments.

'Go!' Cait shouted over her shoulder. 'Get to cover!'

She lit the fuse.

Heinous, Aggie's voice said coyly in her mind.

Cait hurled the sparking firework into the room with the others and bolted.

Time to give you that firework display, Mirren.

She only had time to throw herself out of the way and cover her face as the Unnertoun shook, the world pulsed, and everything fell into silence.

Chapter 43

The Bluidy Brig

When the last bullet had been fired on Aist Bridge and the last Lealists disappeared in pursuit of retreating survivors, Aggie dragged herself from her hiding place behind the barricade. The cut on her arm where a bullet had grazed her skin stung beneath the rain, and Aggie clenched her jaw to stop her teeth chattering and body shivering. The wound on her stomach ached, and though blood oozed through her clothes, her stitches hadn't yet burst. Slowly, she used the barricade to pull herself to her feet.

Aist Bridge was a sorry sight. The bridge was built on a slight incline, and the rain washed the blood towards the New Town and over the sides into the Cath. Bodies lay where they fell, some shrouded in Lealist cloaks, others with navy Separatist sashes twisted around their necks and chests. Among them were the dead who wore the smart attire of New Town workers. White smoke bled into the air, carrying the taste of copper with it. Aggie hauled a piece of the barricade from its place and hurled it into the Cath with a roar. The effort forced her to her knees, and she stayed there, watching blood curl through grey puddles, just like she had when she was fourteen.

She wasn't sure how much time had passed when she spotted a figure running from the direction of the Old Town. At first, she thought they might be a lost civilian or Separatist, but when she spotted the cloak flapping behind them like crows wings, and the light hair turned a dirty brown by the rain, her despair hardened into a cool blade of anger. She took cover behind a table that had tumbled from the barricade and seized a rifle from the stiff hand of a fallen Lealist. As Kenzie jogged past her hiding place, Aggie swiped the rifle into his ankles. He sprawled forward, smacking against the ground with a gasp. He rolled over onto his back and stared, wide eyed, as Aggie stood over him. 'Fox …'

Aggie hammered the back of her gun into his face. His nose cracked and he cried out. 'That's for Cait,' she said.

Scrambling to his feet, Kenzie pulled out the pistol that had almost sent Aggie to the Shadielaunds, and they walked in a slow arc around each other at the centre of the bridge. 'She said you were dead,' Kenzie spat.

Aggie managed a weak bow. 'I rose.'

'It's over, Fox.'

Aggie lifted her gun and rested her finger on the trigger. 'That's not my name.' Besides, she could still hear fighting from a distant bridge. It was far from over. 'Look at you. The proud Queen's Watch,' Aggie said. 'Look what you've done to this city. Look what you've done to its people. You sent them running to us for shelter.'

'You caused this,' Kenzie said.

'I don't recall firing the first shot.' Kenzie lifted his gun higher. 'Do it,' Aggie said. 'But before you do, you should know that Cait called for you when she was being led to her execution.' A maniacal laugh escaped her. He deserved to die alone with Cait's name on his lips and her knife in his back. Not that Cait would ever do it. But Aggie could. 'Where were you?'

Kenzie's gaze hardened. 'I don't know who you're talking about.'

Bang. The force of the bullet leaving Aggie's gun sent her staggering backwards. It missed Kenzie, and he was on her before she could right herself. The fingers of one hand cut into her cheeks, the other pressed the pistol to her head. Aggie's rifle slipped from her grasp and clattered to the ground. 'I'm glad it came to this,' he spat, his sweaty, bloody face inches from her own. 'I can make sure you stay dead this time.'

Aggie barked a laugh in his face. 'If only your parents could see you now.' *His parents were murdered by Separatists,* Cait had said as she glowed like a wisp by the loch. It felt good to use Cait's confession against him, as though Cait was guiding the hand that Aggie clutched the knife in. It was a small amount of retribution for all he'd done to her. Kenzie's grip slackened and his face fell. Aggie seized the opportunity and rammed her knee into his gut. She ripped the pistol from his hands as he stumbled back. She raised the gun.

'Go on, then,' Kenzie said, straightening.

Aggie's finger found the trigger, but she hesitated. The Fox wanted to tear his heart out and mount it as a trophy. But Aggie thought of Cait.

I think you're more than the Fox of Thorterknock.

'Surely this is second nature to you,' Kenzie sneered.

Aggie stared at him. The gun quivered under her poised finger. He was caked in battle, but now all Aggie could see was a borders lad whose parents never returned from the city. In his eyes was the same hopeless wondering that she still carried with her. 'End this,' she said. Kenzie chuckled. She took two steps closer. 'They'll listen to you. Call them down.'

'I don't command them,' he said. 'They'll keep fighting until the Brigadier calls them off.'

But Aggie had never heard of a Lealist who rose through the ranks so quickly. 'Call. Them. Down,' she repeated, taking another step closer. The gun was almost pressed against his skull now.

Kenzie's eyes flashed and his teeth bared. 'I'd rather die.'

Then die, the Fox snarled somewhere within her.

Aggie. Cait's eyes, purple hued under a northern moon. *Don't hurt him.*

Kenzie's foot cracked against her chest. Aggie's vision exploded into white as she hit the ground, and the air left her lungs. The pistol skittered along the ground at her side. As she coughed up blood and gasped for breath, she saw Kenzie gliding closer through her swimming vision. Her limbs were heavy. She pushed herself onto her elbows, then fell straight back down again. Her heart pounded. He was going to put her down like a dog, right there on Aist Bridge. He had almost reached her, his body already stooping to collect the gun, when the whole bridge trembled. The bloody puddles shivered. The Cath below them lapped. Through the ground, Aggie was sure she felt something explode.

The bridge had scarcely stilled when Kenzie looked up and his eyes widened. He backed away, and Aggie turned just in time to see the barricade teeter, and she curled herself into a ball as timber and metal came crashing down in a cloud of dust between them. Kenzie caught her eye through the rubble. They watched each other, then he grabbed a discarded rifle and took off in the direction of the Parliament. Surrounded by fallen debris, Aggie lay her cheek to the ground. Her wounds pounded against cold wet stone, but the icy rain started to numb her. She had no more strength to give. She let her eyes close and her breathing slow. *Run,* she thought, picturing Cait's face as it drank in the views of a midnight city. *Run, and never let him catch you.*

When she opened her eyes, familiar shadows curled into her vision, and Aggie was happy to see them. They took her pain away. They made her drowsy. She looked forward to finally sleeping. The world doubled, and she wondered if she would be able to watch what happened next from the other side of the smoky screen. A bloody hand reached down. Aggie lifted her eyes to see the Fox of Thorterknock bearing over her.

Is there a single hero in that book of yours who just lay down and died?

I'm so tired. She wasn't sure if she spoke the words or thought them.

You told me, "next time."

Her eyes closed. *I want to rest.*

Rest, then, and let Kenzie Bell be the man who slew the Fox of Thorterknock. Let him have his little dove. Let him bolt the door on Storran's cage and dig your friends a tomb.

Aggie looked up at it. *No.*

The Fox grinned. *Then trust me.*

Aggie's numb fingers curled around the handle of Kenzie's gun. She reached up to take the hand of the Fox of Thorterknock, and the shadows receded.

Chapter 44

The Land of Mosaics and Fine Wine

Calan's fingers ached, but he couldn't bring himself to stop. Hart Hall had ignored him, Eadwick, too. He had reached out to the cities of Carse and Witteneuk, and a number of countries on the Continent, but no one replied. At first, he sent messages systematically. He drew up a priority list in his mind and made his way down it, but when the sound of retreat reached him from below, he started to fire off messages indiscriminately. He paused only briefly when the door opened, and Aggie entered. He nodded at her, then returned to his current message.

'Hi,' she said, as if he was expecting her.

When his mind caught up and he realised she shouldn't be here, Calan spun his chair and glared over his glasses at her. She looked a mess. 'You're supposed to be in the Unnertoun.'

Aggie smirked. It meant she had proudly flouted the rules and was lapping up the resulting outrage like cold cider. He normally hated that smirk. Right now, he loved it. 'It was boring down there.'

He watched her standing there and he couldn't explain why, but something seemed different about her. It wasn't the blood soaked into her clothes or the gunpowder covering her skin and hair. Something was off. 'How bad is it?' Calan asked, though judging by her appearance, he wasn't sure he wanted to know.

Aggie slanted herself against the door frame. 'Grace Bridge retreated first. Then Aist, Barter, and Wast. Daibh's Airch held up the longest.'

Calan sucked in a breath. Somehow, he felt the worst news was yet to come. 'And the Lealists?'

'They've surrounded the Parliament, but they've not tried to attack.' She paused. 'They shot at civilians.' She delivered the news as though it meant very little to her at all, and he understood now what the change in her was. Her restlessness was gone. She was steely and calm. 'The ones they didn't shoot at, they recruited.'

'Shadielaunds,' Calan breathed, rubbing his face with his hands. He closed his eyes and saw Iffega's streets lined with body bags. He needed to get back to work, if not to find their salvation, at least to occupy his mind with a monotonous task until the end came to meet him. Aggie staggered, and Calan got to his feet. 'You need to sit.'

'I'm grand.'

He scowled and pushed Fraser's empty chair towards her. 'Sit.'

Aggie gave in and dropped into the chair. She blinked, seemingly just realising Fraser was gone. 'Where's that telegraph lad?'

Calan pulled the book of line numbers towards him. Fraser had hardly needed to consult it. 'I let him leave.' The man had wasted no time in bailing. They fell into a hopeless silence, and Calan watched Aggie carefully. She looked around the room casually, as if perusing a house she wanted to buy. It was like the restlessness that always seemed to follow her around had been smothered. 'Are you alright?' he asked. It was probably a stupid question.

'Fine,' she said. 'Any word from Afren?'

'No.'

'Hart Hall?'

'There's been no word from anyone.'

'I bet Fraser cut the lines. It's been tampered wi.' She tried to lean forward to investigate the telegraph, but winced and sat back down with a hiss.

It didn't matter now. If Fraser had tampered with it, Calan could just add that to his growing list of oversights. 'How many are left?' he asked.

'Of our own, forty-five. A few civilians decided to join which takes us to roughly sixty.'

Calan tapped his finger on the desk. The numbers were far bleaker than he had expected. 'Okay,' he breathed, tying to steady his thoughts. They ran wild. When he tried to reign them in, they strayed further. 'We just need to hold the Parliament. The Lealists are regrouping, but if we can hold them off —'

'Calan.'

He counted the minutes and hours. How long could sixty people withstand the might of the Queen's Watch? How long until someone responded to his increasingly desperate pleas for help? He started rifling through the book again. 'If I can just find the right embassy to contact —'

'*Calan.*'

His thoughts sputtered to a halt, and he looked at Aggie. Her expression softened, and in that moment alone, he felt she was truly herself. 'You should go,' she said.

There she was again, stealing the apple for him and taking the cane. Calan imagined himself creeping out the backdoor and going somewhere, *anywhere* that wasn't here. He glanced at the telegraph book, half the pages still unturned. There were people out there who hadn't heard from him. There were potential allies unreached for. He rested his hand on the telegraph's handle. 'I have too much to do.' Aggie said nothing. 'Take your chances,' Calan said. 'It wouldn't make you any less a patriot.'

The vulnerable look on her face disappeared and her expression steeled. The darkness that stalked her into the room deepened. 'I'd rather die.'

Calan knew that. It was silly for him to even suggest she go. He'd always known that maybe one day he would stand in a free Storran, but that the Fox of Thorterknock might not be there to see it with him. Calan managed a weak smile. 'Are you regretting dropping out of school now?'

Aggie grinned right back at him. 'Not on yer nelly.'

A fuzzy crackle from the telegraph's earpiece made them both start. They stared as the tape slid out of the machine with its face freshly printed with the dots and dashes of a message. When it finished, Calan just stared at it.

'Go on,' Aggie whispered.

Calan tore the paper gently from its rest. His hands shook so much that he had to lie it flat on the table. Briefly, he forgot what a dash represented. Aggie stared at him from the other side of the table. 'It's from the Government of Leja,' he said slowly, carefully, checking that he had deciphered the code correctly. He fought to keep his hopes in check. 'There's a chance they may support us. They've called an emergency meeting to discuss, and they'll vote on how they'll respond in the morning.' He looked up at her. 'They might speak in our favour.'

Aggie's face, frozen with disbelief at first, cracked into a grin. 'We've done it,' she whispered. Her eyes flashed. Then she laughed. No, she cackled. 'We've won!'

'Not yet,' Calan said. Her delight unnerved him, especially when they were surrounded by Lealists.

'It's the land of mosaics and fine wine, Calan! It's *Leja.*'

Leja was a firm ally of Afren, that much was true. They were one of the most robust trading countries on the Continent. If it really was Leja, if they really did declare their support, surely the rest of the Continent would follow. Calan folded the paper up and pulled the telegraph towards him, punching in a message that forwent all formality: *thank you.*

'What now?' Aggie asked.

Calan adjusted his glasses. 'We just need to hold out until morning when they have their vote. I'll have Leja contact Afren directly about their plans. Afren need Leja, possibly more than they need Storran. They won't be willing to risk the agreements and trade deals they have.'

Aggie's eyes sparkled. 'So, you're saying they'll stand down by morning?'

That wasn't what Calan had said at all, but he risked a smile up at her. 'They just might.'

Chapter 45

The Seymour Suite

Cait wasn't sure if her eyes opened at first. She went through the motions of lifting her eyelids, but the world was black. The air around her rung. When she eventually managed to push herself to her feet, dust and fragments of rubble rolled off her back and she felt for the wall as her boots struck stone. Her head weighed tonnes. It lolled on her shoulders as she felt her way through the dark. A dense wall of smoke slammed into her as she stepped out of the building she had taken shelter in. She spluttered and choked. It tasted like bonfires and cooked meat. She doubled over with the force of it. It stung her eyes. She hacked into her hands.

When she straightened, she wiped the acid tears from her eyes. She'd made it into the Unnertoun's main street. Rubble lay everywhere. She stepped forward, and her foot struck something, toppling her onto her hands and knees. When she looked at what it was, she realised it was a corpse. A Separatist. She didn't know their name, but she'd known their desperate expression when she'd told them the Lealists had found a way into the Unnertoun. The Lealists were dead, too. Their bodies were burned and blistered and buried. Cait swallowed the sob in her chest and stumbled to her feet, wiping her hands over and over again on her dress, but the soot was stained deep into her skin.

'Hello?' she croaked, straining for a voice.

She found two other Separatists beneath the rubble, but they gave no answer. The Unnertoun hung in stunned silence. There was no one alive down here to save. She didn't know where she was going, only that she needed to find a way out of the dark before the smoke filled her lungs. Her head spun. Her throat burned. She couldn't even be certain her feet walked her in a straight line, but they were moving, and that was all that mattered. As the ground beneath her sloped upwards, Cait reached her arms out in front of her until she collided with metal, then pulled herself up the ladder. She banged her head against the grate at the top, pushed it, and light swarmed in. It blinded her. She gasped in fresh air. The world buzzed quietly, and as her vision cleared, she made out the streets of the Old Town around her. She staggered in helpless, swaying circles around streets that all looked the same, with their slanted, brown buildings leering down at her. She turned one corner, then the next, and walked straight into a couple of people she hadn't heard coming. They were civilians. Their voices were muted by the ringing in her ears, but she could see they were terrified.

'Wait,' she said, but they hurried by her before she could finish.

She kept walking until she saw the shape of Aist Bridge appear before her. It was quiet. The barricade had fallen, and no one was around. She stepped onto the bridge. The first bodies she encountered were on the Old Town side and belonged to Lealists, but the further she walked, the more the dead began to look like civilians and Separatists. Each face bore a slick mask of familiarity: people she had passed in the street, people from the Unnertoun, people who had once crammed inside a tiny waiting room. She wanted nothing more than to look away, but she hunted each face for signs of life. At the other side of the bridge, she strode off into the New Town without looking back.

The Seymour, Kenzie had said on their first day in Thorterknock. *It's where all the Watch's visitors stay.*

*

The casualties seemed to be concentrated on the bridges, and Cait passed very few bodies on the way to the hotel. The New Town looked untouched, as though the workers were holed up in their offices and could spill out at any moment to go home for tea. The front door of The Seymour was locked, but she saw a flurry of movement inside as a receptionist ducked behind the desk. Cait hammered on the revolving door. She was ignored.

'Let me in! Please!' she cried. Through the glass, she saw the receptionist peek tentatively over the desk. 'Help!' Cait screamed, hammering harder. Cautiously, the receptionist slipped out from behind the desk and crept towards the door. He fumbled for a set of keys in his pocket and unlocked the revolve, which gave way against Cait's weight. She pushed through it, and on the other side she immediately grasped the lapels of the receptionist's jacket. 'I need to know what room Heather Bruce is in.'

The receptionist opened his mouth, face paling in shock at being accosted by the seemingly helpless girl he had just saved. 'I'm not allowed —'

'It's an emergency,' Cait said. 'Just tell me what room.'

'No can do,' he said, freeing himself and quickly locking the door behind her. 'It's a security thing.'

Cait gave a laugh that was somewhere between a sigh and a cough. 'Security?' she looked over her shoulder at the street outside, where a fresh group of Lealists were running by. She looked back at the receptionist. 'At a time like this?'

'Aye,' he said simply.

Cait's hand enclosed around the pocketknife Aggie had given her. She considered using it for just a moment, but she'd already taken one leaf out of the Fox of Thorterknock's book, and she wasn't going to do it again.

'Okay,' Cait said. 'Where do the Watch usually put their guests up?' The receptionist gave her an incredulous look. 'You don't need to tell me anything else,' Cait said quickly. 'Let's just say I'm with the Watch and wondering where I'd be staying.'

The receptionist sighed and covered his face with his hand. He seemed to decide that today was far beyond his pay grade. 'Our main suite,' he said, walking back towards the desk. Without turning around, he pointed a finger at the ceiling. 'Up top.'

Cait took the stairs two at a time until the third floor where she was forced to slow down and catch her breath. Her skin prickled with sweat by the time she reached the seventh floor. The Seymour Suite lay at the end of a lengthy corridor that seemed to stretch on forever, and Cait felt like she was trapped in a dream where she never reached her destination as the world slowly ended outside. When she finally reached the huge door to the suite, she tried to push it open. She didn't know why, because she knew fine well it would be locked. She knocked three times, politely. There was no answer. She tried again, more forceful this time, but the door mocked her with its rigid stillness.

'Heather? I'm from Hart Hall,' she offered it, but it still didn't move. Cait sighed and pressed her forehead against the door. She knew exactly what was likely to work, and she hated that it would. 'Kenzie Bell sent me,' she said.

Heather must have been waiting right behind the door because it instantly opened a crack. Heather's steel-blue eyes watched her behind the thin security chain. 'Why?' she asked.

'Follow-up story,' Cait said, suddenly aware of how dirty and clammy her face was compared with Heather's flawless porcelain skin.

Heather arced an eyebrow. 'About?'

'The pretender,' Cait said. 'Something new Dr Hardie discovered.' She pulled Aidan's letter out of her pocket. It was crumpled and stained now, hardly looking like something sent straight from Hart Hall. 'He said to give you this.'

Heather's eyes sized up the paper, as though calculating if the gap in the door was wide enough for her to slip her hand through and snatch it. Then the door closed, the chain rattled against the other side, and it swung wide open. Heather was a slight woman. She was around the same height as Cait, but everything else about her was petite and compact. Her suit fit neatly, with no baggy sleeves or stray threads. Her hair curled sharp at her jaw. Nothing about her took up any more space than it was intended, and yet, Heather Bruce's presence dominated the doorway, and Cait felt very small.

'Come in,' Heather said, stepping inside. She must have noted the state Cait was in, but she didn't say anything. Cait followed her to a pair of armchairs by the window. 'Water? Wine?' Heather asked, reaching for a decanter on a dainty silver tray and pouring herself a large glass of white. Hart Hall had certainly been taking care of her.

Cait was about to politely decline when she realised how rough her throat felt. 'Water, please.' As she watched Heather pour her a glass, she suddenly felt envious of false bravery and dulled senses. 'And wine,' she added quickly.

Heather's red lips curved upwards as she handed Cait a full wine glass. It was empty in four gulps. Heather's eyes trailed the glass from Cait's lips to the table, and she raised her eyebrows. 'Long day?'

Cait wiped a hand across her mouth. 'What do you think?' she hiccuped.

Again, Heather smiled. 'Out with it, then,' she said. 'Why did that blond bastard send you down here?' Cait flinched. She didn't know why. Kenzie wasn't here. Heather chuckled. 'You don't like him either.'

Cait temporarily forgot about Kenzie, so lulled by Heather's voice. It was plush rose petals on a bath's surface, or silk skirts against a soft thigh. When the feelings it elicited started to smell like leather and cigar smoke, Cait suddenly felt a flush of guilt for being drawn in. She shook her head, unable to form words. She held out the letter from Aidan. Heather took it and read it with puckered lips. Cait watched her eyes glide across the page, one hand clutching Aidan's letter, the other tapping a nail against her glass. She could suddenly understand the stories of the mermaids or fairy folk who infatuated their victims and stole them away. 'Interesting,' Heather said at last. 'Where did you happen across this?'

'The King,' Cait said.

Heather rolled her beautiful eyes. 'There is no king, sweetheart.'

Cait held out Aidan's ring. 'This is from him.'

Heather slipped the ring onto her middle finger and held her hand out to get a look at it. 'It's a fine piece of craftmanship.'

'It's an heirloom. It belonged to Anndras. It's proof that the letter's from Aidan.' Every word was a struggle to form as she watched Heather. She had to snap out of it. Cait forced her gaze to the claw-footed bathtub at the other side of the room. 'We need you to publish that letter in as many places as possible. The same way you did with the article about Cathal,' she said quickly.

'You're not from Hart Hall at all,' Heather said, though Cait was certain she had worked that out a long time ago. She lay the ring down on the wood side table and fixed Cait with a probing stare. Cait fought every urge to meet it. 'I saw you there with Bell, but you're a Separatist. And now you're here, grovelling for my help, just like he did.'

Cait's gaze snapped back to Heather. 'He ... grovelled?' It took her by surprise.

'Oh, not at first. When I answered his gentle summons, he swept me into one of their lovely Hart Hall offices and started firing off demands. Prick.' Cait flinched again. Heather took a sip of wine and savoured it for a moment. 'But when I didn't give him what he wanted, when he realised he couldn't order me about like one of those soldiers of his, now *that* was a sight to behold.'

Cait should have told Heather she was changing the subject, but she was completely drawn in. 'H — how?'

Heather laughed. 'I have plenty experience navigating troublesome editors. Men like Mr Bell aren't rare.'

A loud scream and volley of gunfire came from somewhere outside, and it was enough to flinch Cait out of whatever spell Heather had spun over her. 'Will you do it?'

'I don't control the papers,' Heather said.

'You must have other ways.'

'You're not the first Separatist to come begging. You lot have no grasp on reputation.'

'Please.'

Heather drained her glass and placed it back on the tray. 'I can't. I couldn't even if I wanted to, which I don't, because there is no benefit to me.'

She poured another glass for Cait, who took it and swallowed another large gulp. The alcohol was starting to take away some of the throbbing pain in her bones. Good. 'Don't make me beg,' Cait said.

'Oh, I won't make you beg, sweetie. That's reserved for my favourite clients. I'm just saying no.'

'What have you got to lose?' Cait said, though she realised she was almost shouting, words fraying with desperation, senses dulled and unsteady.

Heather's expression turned cold. 'Everything.'

Cait instantly wished she could take back her words. She knew what she was asking was huge. She knew too well the sacrifices that came with picking this side, she'd seen the pressures laid on Calan's shoulders thanks to his choice. But if the "everything" that Heather had to lose was the finest suite in The Seymour, she could surely stand to lose *something*.

'Then Kenzie wins,' Cait said quietly. Heather paused in pouring herself a new glass and looked inquisitively up at Cait. 'And everyone like him. They'll just keep pushing us down, and making excuses, and doing it all over again,' Cait said. She'd seen Kenzie beg, too, and she knew it meant nothing. 'And it'll never stop.' She tilted her head as she regarded Heather. She didn't know much about the woman, but anyone who treasured their position so dearly surely had a history of battered sails. 'Aren't you tired?'

Heather watched her, mouth slightly parted, bottle hanging above her glass. Then she placed it down. 'I think you should go.' She didn't point at the call wire on the wall beside her, but her gaze slid to it, and back to Cait.

So, Cait left. She left the letter. She left the ring. She left her hopes all stacked on Heather Bruce's hotel room desk and prayed that something she said had hit home. For now, she had done all she could, and as she saw Watchmen outside, swarming towards the Parliament, she knew she had to be where she could help her friends.

Chapter 46

We All Have Our Autumns

The battle had passed in a blur. Jamie wasn't sure if it had been mere moments or hours. Gunpowder had stung her eyes. She had tried to fire the gun that had been thrust into her hands, but despite being untethered from the Cy, she'd felt the air slice as though it were her own skin as the bullet passed through it. Civilian hands had reached over the top of the barricade. Jamie had clung to them. She'd pulled them up. Some had been shot before they reached safety. Then she'd started dismantling the barricade. She'd wrenched timber after timber until her hands prickled with splinters, urging civilians to clamber through. Someone had ordered a retreat. Aggie had screamed that they were cowards. She'd stayed behind with a few others, and Jamie was surprised to see she'd made it back at all.

Now, they were holed up in the foyer of the Parliament. The night was getting on, and Jamie could only be impressed that they had lasted this long. Aggie, broken and bleeding but somehow still standing, delivered Calan's news to them through shortening breaths. There was someone out there advocating for them, and if they could only last the night, it may all just pay off.

A sombre camaraderie fell about the Parliament as defences were reinforced and shifts were selected to keep an eye on the Lealist lines through the night. The Separatists and the handful of civilians who had chosen to fight with them sat in little circles, telling stories of their youth, and singing songs from their hometowns and childhoods. There was something so much more organic in the way they shared their stories compared to the Groves. In the Groves, you learned a story. Sometimes it would change with telling — you'd emphasise a character trait or draw out a fight scene — but, for the most part, the story was all the same. Listening to the Separatists compare stories that were the same, in essence, but different in so many subtle ways from Witteneuk to the borders, was refreshing.

'There was a dragon on the hill that watched the village,' someone would begin.

'Naw, it wasnae a dragon! It was a snake!' another would interject.

'Well down *my* way it was an eel,' a third protested.

'And it could sing.'

'Naw, it could predict the future.'

And so, it continued. Jamie remembered a similar conversation she had with Cait on the way to Gowdstane. Cait had told Jamie about the version of the Crone of the Cruin that she knew as a resident of Storran, as opposed to the one learned in the Talasaire Groves. It was much sadder, much lonelier. Jamie hated to think of the poor Crone still wailing up there today, straining against the elements. If she had the choice, she'd like to be a mountain. She'd like to be strong. It all reminded Jamie too much of her Grove, and it made her sick with envy. Storran was her second home, but the songs that the Separatists sang were nothing more than a fascinating insight into their lives and lore. Jamie missed the songs of her Grove that often didn't have many lyrics at all. She could recall what a harp being plucked in a clearing sounded like, or the hum of a flute on a bright starry night, but since her connection to the Cy faded, the memories of how those sounds *felt* were slipping away.

She spotted Tavis sharing swigs out of a hip flask with a group of older Separatists. He was laughing, his trusty whittling knife in hand. Jamie lowered her eyes and pulled her cap down as she passed. She longed to share her homesickness with someone who understood, but she wasn't sure she could look Tavis in the eye and tell him she had lost the crown he had sacrificed everything for.

At one end of the foyer was a long, oak desk that was bare save for a couple of potted plants. Jamie picked one from the top of the desk and slipped behind, tucking herself into the hollow corner. She dug her hands into the soil, but the vibrant personality, and life, and memory that normally pulsed through the roots felt so far away. Oak was proud. Hazel was wise. Birch was optimistic. The Storrian Silver Birch was particularly stubborn. The little sunflower in her hands? She had no way of knowing its personality.

'Well, if it isn't Jamie?' Jamie looked up to find Tavis standing over her like a pine. 'May I sit?' Jamie nodded, hugging the pot tight to her chest. He unfolded himself beside her, and they sat in silence.

'You fought?' Jamie asked at last. It surprised her.

Tavis shook his head. 'I joined them on Grace Bridge, right enough, but only to lend a hand where necessary.' Then, as if nothing had happened between the last time they spoke and now, Tavis unclipped the knife from his belt and began whittling a half-formed spoon.

Jamie watched him carefully. Even though her own senses were dampened, she still felt a hollowness when she looked at Tavis. 'Your connection is still severed,' she said.

Tavis paused as if he had forgotten, which Jamie knew was impossible, then nodded slowly. 'That it is.'

'For good?'

Tavis' weak smile tugged at his little white beard. 'For good, aye.'

'So, being back in the Grove didn't help?' she asked.

Tavis clicked his tongue. 'Truthfully, Jamie. I didn't get that far. When my Grove realised what happened, they wouldn't let me return.' He gave a forced chuckle. 'Luckily for me, that was when our dear Calan summoned me.'

Tavis was an exile. *That's what happens,* Llyr clucked. *He meddled where he shouldn't have, and he paid the price. He knew what he was doing.*

But it's not fair! Jamie wanted to scream. It was Tavis. There was no better Talasaire in the Five Realms — he was practically a walking stereotype. He'd only wanted to do what was right. *He only wanted to save me.* Jamie reached for her own connection, but she couldn't find it. 'I tried to save Aidan's crown from the fire.'

Tavis scraped too much off his spoon and frowned at it. 'That must have hurt your hands,' he said.

'I changed my mind at th'last minute.' Jamie paused, afraid of what Tavis would say next. 'You said your duty was to Storran.'

Tavis stared silently at his spoon, but his knife had fallen still. 'I was wrong,' he said at last. Of course he was. She had hoped that if Tavis could make peace with his sacrifice, maybe she could, too. Now she felt her last shred of hope fade. 'It will come back to you,' Tavis said. His eyes crinkled at the corners. She hadn't told him, but he knew.

'You thought yours would come back.' She regretted the words the moment she said them. Still, Tavis didn't flinch.

'Do you still feel it?'

'Vaguely.'

Tavis gave her a warm smile. 'Then there you have it.' His white caterpillar eyebrows cinched together as he watched her. 'Regain its trust, Jamie, and when you do, do not let it go. Not for anything.'

Jamie nodded and bit back her tears. 'I wish I stayed home,' she said.

She had heard of Storran's folktales and wanted to hear them for herself. She had wanted to know what heather sounded like, and to see if the sky really was a different shade of blue up here, but she'd fallen in love with this place and its people, and the way they talked, and the way they lived, and it had only taken one telling of *The Ballad of Anndras and Cathal* to make her a Separatist. Somewhere along the line, she had become a citizen of Storran, and now she didn't know where her old self ended, and her new self began. She had sacrificed so much for Storran.

'What did you leave behind?' asked Tavis.

'My lessons. My family.'

Tavis raised his eyebrows. 'A lover?'

Jamie smiled. 'No, just the Grove.' Dappled summer light in oak leaves was better than any lover's eyes.

'The trees are ancient, they can stand to wait a couple of years for you,' Tavis said.

Jamie smiled, but she shook her head. 'I don't think so.'

'Ah,' Tavis said with a long, slow nod. Then he added, his voice lifting. 'My own Grove was always very sombre. I loved it all the same, mind you, but it never quite sat right with me. I always felt it lacked a certain spirit.'

Jamie laughed. 'Oh, mine were spirited.'

'Troublesome youngsters,' Tavis tutted, but the twinkle in his eye told Jamie he had once been just like her. 'I suppose you don't enjoy ceremony, then?'

'Actually, I do. A lot of my friends never came to the Circle on the Day of Shadows. They always said it was too cold and boring.' It was no wonder. The day to honour the dead was in the depths of winter, and always from sundown to sunup. It was hardly ideal conditions to spend all night holding vigil around a stone circle.

'I would have to agree,' Tavis chuckled. 'I can't say it was ever my favourite ceremony either.'

'I always liked it,' Jamie said. 'I liked paying tribute to my ancestors. I always felt there was this unbroken line of us, and that their legacy is mine.'

Tavis nodded. 'That's a very wise thing to cherish.'

Jamie ferociously wiped a tear from her cheek. 'In summer, our tents always got so hot. We used to paddle in the stream.' A racket sounded from behind: shouting, doors being flung open. Panic seized Jamie's chest and she turned to look over her shoulder, despite the strong arms of the desk blocking her view. 'What was that?' her voice ragged with terror. *They're here. This is it.* 'Tavis ...'

'You should know by now that we all have our autumns.' Tavis lay a hand on her knee, his voice a steady bough beneath her trembling legs. 'Keep telling me about your Grove.'

'I've got this mate, Darcy. She always gets excited around the Midsummer festival when the flags go up above the tents. It's always the same flags every year, but she'd always choose her favourites, and they'd always be different to the year before.'

Jamie's voice shook with every word, but Tavis chuckled. 'My favourite in my own Grove was shaped like a fish. Of course, it was the one above my own tent, but all the more reason to like it.'

Jamie squeezed her eyes against the din from behind. 'I loved Midsummer the most. We'd all walk to the Singing Stones and there was always someone with food on the fire. And there was singing. And dancing.' It would only be weeks away now. The flags would all be up. Darcy would be choosing her new favourite. 'We used to dance on the stones. The elders were never happy about it.' She laughed. They only wanted to observe their ceremony in solemn silence, but Jamie saw Midsummer as a day to celebrate life. She didn't see why there couldn't be room for both. Gunshots cracked behind them. Jamie flinched. She squeezed her eyes tighter. 'It's loud.'

'Midsummer is a special time,' Tavis said. His voice was perfectly steady.

Jamie breathed hard. There were people shouting. Footsteps pounding. The pop of gunfire followed by screams. She blocked it out. She dove back into her world of songs and stones. 'It felt proper special. It's like we were connected to something people have been doing for thousands of years.' Then she felt it. It gave her a fright a first, jolting through her whole body. A sharp heat cracked across her senses, an unmistakable feeling. *Sunflower.* She could feel it pulsing beneath her fingers. It was bold. It was steady. 'It was a celebration. We stayed up all night for it,' she

348

continued. She felt the Cy watching her, tentatively stepping closer. In her mind, Jamie reached out a hand. She realised that she would not make it out of this building, and if the last thing she could feel was her connection to the Cy, she could make peace with that. *We all have our autumns.*

The shouting drew closer. The gunfire spilled into the foyer behind them. Jamie shook.

'Keep talking to me,' Tavis said gently. His voice was a breath of wind through a willow.

'It always got tricky in the early morning,' Jamie said, remembering countless bitter mornings where she almost went home before the sunrise. 'It were cold, the ground were hard, but then the sky would lighten and everyone would gather in the centre of the stones.' There was a scream of 'Lealtie Ayebidin!' and then a shot and a thud against the wood at Jamie's back. 'We knew the sun would rise, but we cheered like its rising depended on us. And sometimes we'd cheer, but we'd timed it wrong. And then, when it did rise …'

In her mind, Jamie's hand touched the Cy, and warmth flooded through her. The flower in her hands sang. It was a long, low drone, and it filled up the dark spaces within her. She could hear the chatter of the other potted plants in the room. She could feel the distant heartbeat of the oak desk, quietened by carpentry. She could feel the Cath thundering by outside. '… it took my breath away every time.' She smiled through her tears, now uncontrollable. 'Feeling that morning sun warm you up, it must be how the earth feels in spring.'

The sound of quick footsteps and panting stole Jamie away from that place, and when she opened her eyes, there was a Lealist boy standing over them with his bayonet raised.

Tavis rose to his feet, his hands spread wide. 'Come now, son. Let's not have any of this.'

'Tavis —' His name was barely out of her mouth when the boy stepped towards them. The blade was already wet with someone else's blood. She was back on the pier watching Tavis sing to the canal, and she was back in the little cottage watching the crown melt. The Cy roared in her veins, and she couldn't watch Tavis die. She stretched for it, the words *I'm sorry,* on her tongue. She called to the potted plants, the desk, the River Cath, anything that she could use to save him. She hungered for the command to rush through her veins. As quickly as it came, the Cy retreated. It raised its hackles and slunk from her, hissing over its shoulder. Jamie screamed as the Lealist boy ran Tavis through with his bayonet, once, twice, three times, before discarding him like he was litter. Jamie's body seized in terror as the boy turned his eyes to her, and she scampered deeper into the hollow of the desk.

'Please,' she begged, hardly able to see through her tears.

There was a *crack,* and the boy's head snapped sideways, blood oozing from his temple. Aidan was behind him, the back of his rifle raised. He reached down to her, and Jamie took his hand. She couldn't feel her legs. She couldn't feel anything.

'Tavis.' She scrambled for him. He lay face down in a pool of blood, his murderer crumpled over him.

Aidan pulled her back. 'We have to go.'

'Let me see him!' she screamed, but she wasn't strong enough against Aidan's grip. As he ushered her through the foyer, she registered the full extent of the carnage. Lealists, too many to count, flooded through the doors. Separatists lay lifeless on the floor. Any who remained, ran for their life, or made a stand in huddles with rifles poised.

Aidan pulled Jamie away from the foyer and down the Parliament's dark corridors. Their footsteps rang in the empty halls, and Jamie paid no attention to where they were going. She let Aidan drag her as her mind emptied. They finally stopped at a pair of large wooden doors, and Aidan heaved them open, revealing the debate chamber within. A huge skylight above them let the budding daybreak spill through. Wood-panelled benches curved around the room in two semi-circles, and at the head of the circle was a raised chair where a Speaker, or a Minister, or a Chancellor might sit. Aidan slammed the doors closed behind them and dampened the sounds of unfolding defeat. Jamie braced her hands against the oak wood of the benches, but she felt nothing. She felt numb.

Brennan, she thought, invoking the name of a legendary Talasaire who once walked the Shadowlands. *Let it be painless.*

Chapter 47

In Dreams

The debate chamber was a wide, round room. Curved benches in polished wood spiralled around the perimeter, and shafts of rose gold dawn struck the floor from the skylight above. Aidan had never been here before, not in the waking world at least. In his dreams he had. He knew these benches. He knew the shadows of the viewing gallery above. 'I dreamed about this place,' he said, perhaps to Jamie, perhaps to no one at all. He recounted the images of the joyful songs and Storrian flags, of Anndras at the front of a proud procession, the language he didn't speak, but understood every word of. He paced the room slowly, letting his fingers trail the polished wood of the benches. Jamie stood by the doors and watched him, but she seemed very far away. 'We all crammed into this room,' he said. He remembered that his mother had been there. She told him she was proud, her little hero, her duck. He paused in front of the chair elevated above the rest. The light struck it, staining the mahogany red and gold. 'I sat right there,' he whispered, lifting a trembling hand to point at the chair.

'Did you see another way out in this dream?' Jamie asked.

Aidan ignored her, walking slowly towards the chair. He imagined a leader sitting there holding Parliament. He imagined a king. He almost expected Anndras to be sitting there, but he hadn't seen the King since the ship. He stepped up towards the chair and placed his hand on the armrest. He had expected it to feel higher, for its size to dwarf him like it did in his dreams, but it was the perfect size. He looked up at it, wondering what it would feel like to sit in it. It was only then that he realised how much his hands and legs shook with exhaustion and adrenaline. The chamber was peaceful, but beyond the sanctity of these wood-panelled walls, the sounds of gunfire and fighting continued. In all his dreams, his arrival at the Parliament never sounded like this. Freedom never sounded like this. It didn't smell like blood or taste like tears. It didn't reek of despair. In his boyhood dreams, he'd never led his people into a bloodbath. He'd led them into a brave new world, and they'd followed.

And they'd followed now, too. Even with Calan's plan, they had known the stakes and still they took to the streets. And what did Aidan have to show for it?

The sudden sound of footsteps in the Chamber started him from his thoughts. He stepped down from the chair and backed himself towards the door, quickly putting himself between Jamie and the noise. He touched his hand to his sword as a door at the opposite end of the room opened. Cait stumbled out. The tension ebbed out of Aidan's bones. 'It's jist you,' he sighed.

'What happened to you?' Jamie said. Her voice was flat and eyes hollow. She was right to ask, though. Cait was covered in ash and black soot.

She hurried across to them. 'I'm fine,' she said.

'How did you get in here?' Jamie said.

'Back there,' Cait pointed at the door. 'I got in through a window into a basement.'

'That's our way out,' Jamie said. She started walking towards the door. 'Let's gan.'

Aidan watched her go, and he watched Cait hovering between them.

'Did you get the letter out there?' Aidan asked. At the door, Jamie stopped and looked back at them.

Cait nodded. 'It's with Heather Bruce.' She flinched as gunfire ricocheted outside. It sounded closer now. So much closer.

'Good,' Aidan said. It was out there. All wasn't lost. Once everyone knew that he'd abdicated and given Storran to the people, they'd have no choice but to stop.

'Aidan,' Jamie said. 'Let's go.'

'Come on,' Cait said, taking a step towards the door. She stretched out a hand. 'We need to leave.'

But Aidan knew how it ended. It ended with cheers and nostalgic songs. It ended with victory to the people. 'Go,' he said. He started towards the chair. 'Anndras showed me the future.'

'Aidan,' Cait said.

He stood face to face with the chair. 'They can take everything from us. *Everything*.' He looked around the room. 'But no this. Never this.' He climbed up the two steps to the chair and lowered himself into it. 'This can't die.' If they came, he'd meet them here. He'd meet them and tell them that Storran was theirs now, and they could choose to do what they would. The choice was theirs.

As Aidan sat in the chair and looked over the debate chamber, Jamie paled. 'Listen,' she said.

It took Aidan a moment to realise what was so wrong. The entire Parliament lay in silence. The fighting had stopped. A desperate laugh escaped him. 'We've won.' The cheers of jubilation and sounds of surrender never arrived. A soft murmur came from the other side of the door, followed by a click.

'No,' Jamie said. 'We're surrounded.'

Chapter 48

Rebel Heart

Calan's incessant tapping on the telegraph wasn't enough to block out the commotion boiling on the floors below. When the Lealists had undoubtedly breached the Parliament, Calan calmly rose, propped a chair under the door handle, then placed the telegraph's headphones over his ears, drowning the battle out with empty static.

A shot from directly outside the door cut through, but he continued furiously tapping out his messages. The door rattled. The chair quivered. Calan tried his best to ignore it.

Successful takeover of — over of — Successful —

The chair flew halfway across the room as the door burst open. Calan kept tapping. His messages couldn't be unsent, even if he was shot halfway through.

'Stand.'

He recognised that voice. When he spared a glance sideways, the first thing Calan saw was Elsie lying on the ground, her eyes wide and glassy. Kenzie stood over her with blood smeared across his face. Calan returned to his work.

'I said,' Kenzie lifted his rifle and pointed it at Calan. 'Stand.'

The message he sent with his dying breath could be the one that saved his friends. Though his fingers trembled, Calan continued to batter out a message home to Iffega.

Kenzie's gun clicked. 'What messages have you sent?'

'Will you unsend them?' Calan asked, feeling braver than he should. 'I've been in touch with Carse, Witteneuk, Eadwick, even as far as Ravo. Leja are voting on our cause as we speak. If it goes in our favour, Storran is as good as free, and everyone knows what the Watch did here today.'

A heartbeat passed before Kenzie said, 'What the Watch did?' he lowered the gun ever so slightly and paced slowly towards Calan. 'I was out on the street defending the public from your people.' Calan said nothing. 'I heard how they screamed when the Separatists fired at them.'

Calan gritted his teeth. 'That's a lie.'

'Were you there? Or were you holed up in the safety of this office while innocent people bled for your cause?'

'The Watch shot first.'

Kenzie laughed, long and low. 'Who told you that? The Fox?' The way Calan stilled was enough to betray himself, and Kenzie leaned across the desk and spoke softly to Calan. 'She would tell you that, wouldn't she? She knows that you, of all people, wouldn't stand to hear what truly happened out there. She knows you'd abandon this cause the moment things turned sour.'

'The Fox isn't the only one with a slick tongue,' Calan said, but he'd been there with Aggie in the Dorcha Pass when she'd almost killed someone. Who was he to say what Aggie would and wouldn't do for a taste of freedom? The flat calm way she had told him about the slaughter on the bridges returned to him. He couldn't even be certain Aggie was Aggie right now.

'My offer still stands, MacKenzie,' Kenzie said. 'We could use you. You could give back and make sure no one ever needs to become a Storrian refugee.'

Calan paused. 'And what happens when they come for me?'

'We could see to it that you were protected. Your family, too.' Kenzie watched him expectantly, but when Calan said nothing, he continued. 'Afren will hold to their deal. Just tell me where the little king is.'

'After everything?' Calan asked.

Kenzie nodded. 'That's what it means to be gracious. I wouldn't expect you to understand.'

If Afren gave them those powers, it might mean that the carnage wrought here today was worth something. 'I don't know where he is,' Calan said.

'Then come and help me find him,' Kenzie said. 'All anyone on the outside needs to know is that you led me to him.'

Calan almost said yes. He had almost breathed the word to life for the sake of the people he loved, when the telegraph stuttered and a message from Iffega rolled out into his hand.

Iffega stands with Storran.

The boy he once was had seen people chewed up and spat out by regime. He had also seen those same people punch the teeth from the regime's jaws. He had seen fields strewn with corpses. He had also seen the wildflowers that sprung from them. The boy he once was had gifted Calan a rebel heart, and it was beating yet.

'Go fuck yourself, flag shagger,' Calan spat. If he lived to see Aggie again, he would have to tell her that he said that.

Kenzie swept across the room and seized Calan's shirt collar. When Calan tried to push him off, Kenzie's grip went for his hair and pulled his head back, and he found himself with a blade at his throat. 'Walk,' Kenzie said. He steered Calan out of the room. They stepped over Elsie's body. Her blood left red footprints down the corridor behind them.

Kenzie marched Calan directly to the debate chamber, and Calan realised just how utterly surrounded they were. The fighting had stopped, and now Lealists crowded around the door to the chamber, their guns locked and loaded and waiting.

'I'll handle this,' Kenzie told them. 'Be ready.'

As Calan was thrust through the doors, he suddenly wished he could have sent just one more message while he had the chance: *Storran stands with Iffega.*

Chapter 49

Pretender

When the doors to the debate chamber flew open, everyone, apart from Aidan on his throne, hit the floor. Cait ducked behind a row of benches, hands pressed over her ears. She braced for the firing squad she had cheated, waiting for the bullets to finally catch up with her. When they never came, she peered out from her hiding place. Kenzie marched through the door, holding the glinting blade of his bayonet to Calan's throat. His face was set with white-hot fury, and Cait couldn't bring herself to rise.

'I want your pretender, and I want the Fox,' Kenzie said. 'I know she's here.' Cait thought she might be the only person in the world who could hear the tremble in his voice.

'We don't know where she is,' Jamie said, rising. 'Just let us go.'

He pushed the blade closer to Calan's throat, and Calan lifted his chin with a grimace. 'Where is she?' Kenzie said. His hunger foamed at his mouth.

Aggie's not here, Cait thought. *You'll never have her, never again.*

'We don't know!' Jamie cried.

'You're lying,' Kenzie hissed.

'It's the *truth*.'

Kenzie pressed the flat edge of the blade against Calan's throat, and Jamie begged him to stop as a voice echoed across the chamber from above.

'Get your haunds aff him.' All eyes in the room lifted to the viewing gallery that encircled the top of the room. Aggie was unseen, but her voice prowled the shadows above them.

'Come down or I'll kill him!' Kenzie shouted, turning on his heel, looking up in all directions.

'Is Queen Ana's thirst for blood still unsated?' Aggie said. 'Will she ever be satisfied?' Her words rung through the chamber. It chilled Cait.

357

Her voice lacked its usual warmth, sounding only like denuded moorland now. She pulled Aggie's coat tighter around her. In the years before moving to Thorterknock, Kenzie used to recount epic tales of the Fox's crimes that he'd read about in the paper. It was like some twisted version of her father's stories, complete with a savage and rasping impersonation of the Fox. Right now, Aggie's voice sounded uncannily similar to that impersonation.

Kenzie turned in a circle. 'Stop hiding, coward!' Kenzie's lips and skin shone with a frothing, furious sheen.

'You can have me when you release him.'

Kenzie pushed Calan away. He scattered across the floor to Jamie, who helped him to his feet. Above, Aggie's laugh reverberated vulture-like around them. 'Good soldier.'

A flicker of movement from above caught Cait's eye. A flash of red, the slam of boots on marble. Aggie landed on her feet before Kenzie with a pained grunt. She took a moment to gather herself, then rose slowly. 'You can hae your fox,' she said, then stalked towards Kenzie, spinning his own pistol into her hand. 'But you'll never have our King.' Her eyes were not her own. A dark oil had spilled across her gaze. Kenzie pointed his rifle at Aggie, who mirrored him with the pistol. Behind her, Aidan watched from his throne.

'He's no king,' Kenzie spat.

Click. Aggie cocked the pistol. 'Say that again.'

Kenzie cocked his own rifle and the sound snagged at Cait's heart. Either Aggie was too drunk on adrenaline to know that he would do it, or she didn't care. Kenzie placed his finger on the trigger. Time moved too slowly as Cait rose. She was certain she wouldn't make it in time. One step, another, a stumble, and she slid to a halt between Aggie and Kenzie, her arms spread in a fragile wall between them. Kenzie's face fell. She was supposed to be a dead woman. She was his rotted childhood sweetheart who had paid the price and met the firing squad. Now, she was before him, alive, and draped in the skin of the Fox of Thorterknock. His expression bore the horror of seeing a corpse, and Cait realised what that meant. *He never even tried to see me.*

'Cait …' His face drained of the flush it had carried before. The gun sagged in his grip.

'Stop this,' Cait pleaded.

'How?'

'Put the gun down,' she said slowly.

Kenzie's eyes darted across her face, perhaps trying to distinguish the traitor from his *little dove*. A breathy laugh escaped his lips, and he cupped a hand over his eyes. 'I thought —' He stepped forwards, tilting his head to the sky. He gasped. 'This can't be real.'

'They saved me,' Cait said as she backed away from him. 'They got me out.' She paused, fresh anger bubbling up in her gut. *He didn't even try to pay his respects.* 'You did nothing.'

His hand dropped from his face, and he regarded her with a sneer, teeth bared and bloody. 'You *deserved* nothing.'

'No. No, you're wrong.' She stepped back again, head shaking.

Kenzie took leisurely steps towards her. He walked like that when he was tipsy. He used to tuck her hair behind her ear and slur that she was the most beautiful creature on earth. 'You were always indignant, weren't you?' he swiped the gun through the air. Cait jumped back from the bayonet. 'Nothing was ever good enough for you.'

'That's not true.'

'You're pathetic.' He laughed and brandished the gun around again. 'Look what happened the minute I wasn't there. Shadielaunds, Cait, you couldn't even *die* properly without me there to hold your hand.'

'Stop it,' Cait said. She could barely recognise her own voice. The room swam. 'Just stop.'

'Turned my back for two minutes and you became a traitorous bitch. That's what they call you at home, you know. A traitorous little bitch.' He pronounced each word carefully, each punctuated by an ambling step towards her.

'Shut the *fuck* up,' Aggie growled from behind.

Kenzie jerked to attention. The delirium melted from his gaze as he focused on Aggie again. He aimed the gun over Cait's shoulder. 'Don't!' Cait shouted, raising her arms again.

It was then she realised that Kenzie was relying on a cumbersome rifle. She searched his belt for a pouch of ammunition, but there was none. She already had his attention. It was possible he only had one shot left. 'You've won, Kenzie. You saved Storran.' Cait took a shaky step towards him. The bayonet lay inches from her chest. 'Just let us go.' Kenzie's grip shifted on the rifle. His eyes flicked rapidly from Aggie and back to her. 'Please,' she said. 'Let's get it right this time. No guns. No death sentences.' He just watched Cait. *Yes,* she thought. *Keep your eyes on me.* She didn't want him to even think that there were any others in the room. It was just him and her, and the vast, knotted history that lay between them.

'You don't deserve grace,' Kenzie said, voice brimming with disgust. 'To think I used to call you family.'

'Family?' The word escaped on a laugh. Cait felt nothing as she stared into his blue eyes, the blue of Storran's sky, and Eadwick's sky, and the sky over Kerneth, and Prilwyn, and Tor. 'This isn't how a family should be,' she said.

'You need me,' Kenzie said, and it sounded like a threat.

Cait shook her head. 'You do nothing but hurt me.'

Behind her, Aggie took a step forward. Cait reached her hand out, closing it around Aggie's wrist to stop her. Kenzie's expression cooled. His grip on the gun steadied as he lifted it. 'I warned you.'

'Kenzie —'

The shot rang out across the debate chamber. It cracked in Cait's ear. The air sizzled. She stumbled, searching for the pain, her hand feeling her gut, her chest. When she turned, she realised the shot hadn't been for her at all. Aggie stared at her, wide-eyed, lips parted. The world seemed to slow as her chest rose with laboured breaths, and she, too, turned to look at where the bullet had made its mark. On the highest chair at the head of the room, Aidan stared at them. He slumped. His hands reached for the wound on his chest where blood oozed through his shirt. Cait staggered. The room's noise damped and the whole place spun. Aggie roared. Cait managed to catch her just before she threw herself on Kenzie. Cait wrenched the pistol from her hands and turned it on her. Aggie froze.

'Cait ...' she whispered. 'What —'

'Leave him,' Cait snapped, then she turned the gun on Kenzie. He stared at her. She knew what he would do next: he'd open the chamber door, then order his men to massacre everyone inside. 'Please,' she said. The pistol shook unsteadily in her hand. She realised she'd never held a gun before. It felt so cumbersome and heavy. She could hardly get one hand around it. It seemed remarkable that Kenzie had managed to make the shot at Aidan, and that made her sick. She tossed it to the floor.

'Kenzie?' A voice called from outside the room.

Kenzie's eyes darted to the side. Cait shook her head. 'You've got what you wanted.'

Kenzie's eyes lifted over her shoulder and fell back to her face. 'Not everything.'

'Let Aggie go.'

He faltered. 'Aggie?'

'Let us go,' Cait said. She imagined walking towards him, reaching up to his face and wiping the blood from his nose with her thumb, but it was nothing more than the ghost of a terrible habit. She stayed where she was. When he opened his mouth, she braced for him to give the order, but moments later, his gun clattered to the floor.

'You have five minutes,' he said, and marched for the door.

Cait held her breath. She waited for the sting of his treachery as troops swarmed in, but they never came. *He's leaving,* she thought. *He listened.* Then, *Aidan.*

He had been moved to the floor. Blood gurgled between Calan's fingers as he pushed down on the wound. Cait rolled her sleeves up and as Calan moved aside, she slipped her hands where his had been. Aidan's eyes bulged. Blood seeped out between his lips. Cait pressed down hard on the wound. 'Aidan, look at me. I need you to stay with me.' She fought to keep her voice steady, like her mother always did, but it betrayed her. She pushed, but the wound pulsed under her hands. Aidan's eyes rolled back for a moment. 'Aidan!' she cried. 'Look at me!' She had dragged Aggie back from the brink. She could save Aidan, too. Aidan tried to speak, but he coughed, and blood splattered over his face. Cait used all her strength to press down on the wound. 'Come on!' she groaned. Her hands slipped. Her arms quivered.

'Bess,' Aidan croaked. He lifted a bloody, trembling fist. 'Give.'

'Stay still for me,' Cait said.

'No —'

'*Aidan.*'

His fingers opened to reveal a sprig of white heather tinted red with his own blood. He pressed it into her hands. His head lolled back. 'How did ... how did I dae — do?' Aidan asked weakly.

'Brilliantly,' Cait said, smiling for him. She dragged her sleeve across her eyes and used a fistful of skirt to plug the wound. It was saturated in moments.

Aidan managed a weak laugh. 'Good.' He closed his eyes.

'Eyes open, Aidan,' Cait said.

He blinked blearily. 'Are you proud?'

Cait glanced up at him, but rather than looking at her, she found him staring up, glassy-eyed, at the empty chair behind her.

'Cait,' Calan's voice came through the chaos. His hands were on her shoulders.

'Just give me a minute,' Cait said through her teeth. She gave a frustrated scream.

Calan's face dipped into her view. 'Look at me.' Cait continued trying to stem the flow even when the wound stopped throwing out blood, even when Aidan's gaze fixed somewhere none of them could see. Calan took her face in his hands and turned her eyes to his. 'We need to go.'

But the only thing Cait could think was how disappointed her mother would be that she was sobbing in front of patient. 'I can heal him.'

'We're leaving. Now.' He pulled Cait to her feet. She reached for Aidan's arm, but it slipped from her grasp and fell limp at his side.

'We need to take him,' Cait screamed. If she could just get him out of this horrible room, she could heal him. Calan pushed her through the door she had come through, just as the main doors to the chamber burst open. Cait looked over her shoulder, and the last thing she saw before someone closed the passageway door was the young pretender's bloodstained highland garb, and the Lealists that swarmed around him.

Chapter 50

Witteneuk

Bess couldn't shake the dream she'd had last night. In it, she was running through Gowdstane. The weather was bliss and warm, the sky a thunderous blue. She was laughing. She laughed so hard she wheezed. She stopped running when she reached the ramparts that looked out over the Cronachs. The air was calm today and no wind rang through the Crone's halls. Bess forgot the reason she was running, or the game she was playing, and she leaned against the battlements to watch the kites swooping over the mountains.

Hands struck her shoulders from behind, and Bess screamed but fell into peals of laughter when she spun around into Aidan's arms. 'You did a rubbish job of hiding,' he laughed.

Bess gave him a light thump on the chest. 'You didn't give me enough time!' His laugh faded into a distant smile and his eyes softened. A curl on his forehead swayed against the breeze. His waxy gaze made her blush. Suddenly self-conscious, she covered her face with her hand. 'What? Why the look?'

He shook the look away and his eyes focused. 'Nothing.' Bess turned to look out over the mountains and pressed her head back onto his shoulder. 'Do you still have that heather I gave you?' he asked.

'No, I let it fly away in the wind when you ran off to Thorterknock to play hero.' She rolled her eyes. 'Of course, I still have it.'

Aidan's chin lowered onto Bess' shoulder, and he kissed her on the cheek. He hung about her waist like her favourite skirt. 'Do you think it's too late for me to come to Witteneuk?'

Aidan couldn't see the surprised look she gave the mountains. 'I mean, of course not. It's just that it would be hard to rule Storran from up there. It's quite remote.'

After a moment of silence, Aidan said, 'I abdicated.'

Bess started. 'You did what?'

'I gave it all away. It was the only way to win.' He brushed a hand through her hair. 'It was the only way to get back to you.'

She smiled. She shouldn't have, because she knew how much Aidan's purpose meant to him, but she didn't care. He'd thrown it all away so he could come with her. Her cheeks ached from her grin. Then she remembered she had agreed to meet her father that afternoon. 'Oh, Aidan. I'm late.' Aidan's arms held on as she pulled away. She kissed his lips. They were strangely cold. 'See you tonight? We can talk about it more, then.'

'Wait,' Aidan said, and that hazy look fell back over his features. 'Stay with me a bit longer.'

Bess grinned, walking backwards. 'I can't get in any more trouble. I'll see you later.' She blew him a kiss and hurried into the shady castle.

*

Now, surrounded by the comings and goings of Witteneuk's busy harbour life, Bess tried her hardest to focus on the scrap of paper and pencil in her hand. She sat on the edge of the pier, watching a group of women sorting fish as they sang in a lilting tongue Bess didn't recognise. It wasn't Old Storrian. When spoken quick enough, Old Storrian could baffle her, but she understood enough to make sense of it. This language was something entirely different. It was beautiful. It felt like it belonged to the sea, as much a part of the harbour city as the salt wind and seaweed. Bess sketched the fine lines and tough skin on the women's faces, trying to capture their hardy beauty. She wished Aidan were here to hear their song. Once again, her mind turned to her dream.

It had been two months since Aidan left for Thorterknock and she and her father had run to Witteneuk. Her father was unrecognisable now. Lister Burke was gone, and a rugged man named Angus took his place. He grew out his beard. He worked, and he worked hard. He took jobs on fishing boats, he tied nets, he shuttled passengers to nearby islands on ferries. He paid for a squat room for the two of them above a post office, and he kept his head down. He was quieter here. He was softer. Bess didn't know how to talk to him. There was no word from Thorterknock. Not that Bess had looked. Her first night had been spent sleeplessly tossing and turning and waking up screaming from nightmares about war on Thorterknock's streets, and she'd been so sick with worry the next day that she couldn't bring herself to eat. On her father's suggestion, they agreed she wouldn't read the paper. She knew Aidan would come for her when he was ready and had Thorterknock secured. She just had to wait and forget.

Bess had been so drawn into the women's song that she didn't see the group of seven Queen's Watchmen approach. By the time she saw them, they were mere paces away. She kept her face shielded by her hair. They wouldn't know her. No one knew Lister Burke's daughter.

'Oi, wummin,' one of the soldiers said, swaggering over to the group of fishwives. Their song died instantly. 'Funny wee tune you're singing there. What's that all about?' The women laid down their fish. They exchanged tense glances.

What are the Watch doing here? Bess thought. Her father had chosen Witteneuk as their refuge as it was the most remote of Storran's cities, and the Watch hardly bothered to police it. People weren't interested in separatism up here. *Of course,* she thought. *They've had to retreat from Thorterknock. Because of Aidan.* This was the last remaining place they could work, but soon Aidan would disband them all.

'Speak up,' another of the officers snapped. He kicked one of the women's buckets. The women said nothing. 'How much time would ye get for using that tongue?' the officer mused aloud.

'Oh, three years at least,' his companion said. 'Longer if you misbehave. Ten if you keep singing your filthy little songs.'

'Dùin do bheul, muc,' one of the fishwives spat.

Orders barked, old arms wrenched behind bent backs, it took them only a few moments for the Watch to detain the women and march them away. They sang in defiant whispers as they went, but the Watchmen stuffed their mouths with their gloves. Bess' heart hammered. The pier hung in tense silence. Even the waves felt like they'd stopped to watch. Bess couldn't stay here anymore. She shoved the paper into her pocket and hurried away. She kept her head low as she walked, but out of the corner of her eye she noticed more of their familiar uniforms. She certainly hadn't noticed them before, and she changed her route several times, not because she feared they would know who she was, but because part of her worried they could hear the song still wafting through her mind. She was almost back at the flat when she passed a squabble on the street. They looked to be fighting over a piece of fabric. *They're probably drunk,* Bess thought, hurrying by.

'Oi, I got it, it's mine!'

'Not anymore,' one of the men cackled, holding the fabric up in a victorious fist.

'Geez it back!'

'King's plaid could fetch a fortune!'

Bess halted. She turned back to the rabble and watched as a fresh person sprung into the fray, grappling with the first man over the fabric. There was a loud tearing sound, and they both fell backwards. The crowd jeered.

'King's plaid fer everyone!' cried the first man, holding his fragment in the air and tearing it in two. He tossed one half into the crowd. The crowd surged, each grabbing for a piece of their own. A piece of navy and gold plaid was thrown from the crowd and fell at Bess' feet. Her stomach swam. She ran.

King's plaid. The day Aidan was coronated, they danced and he playfully slung it about her shoulders. It weighed a tonne.

She grabbed a newspaper from the first stand she reached and rifled through the pages, heart racing faster with every page. There was nothing. No news at all from Thorterknock. It was like nothing had changed in the slightest.

Coincidence, Bess thought. *Or a good sign.* They'd said, "King's plaid," after all.

When she got back to the flat, her father was not home yet. The small room with its two beds felt dark and musty, so she threw open the curtains and opened the window. *Aidan will come,* she told herself again, gulping in lungfuls of fresh air. *You'd know if something had happened.* It was the mantra that she'd been repeating for two months now. She laid her head on her arms, and watched the fishing boats in the harbour bob and sway as the fishermen brought their catch in. The air was cold. Autumn was coming. Her eyes trailed the harbour to the spot where the fishwives had been. Their *funny wee tune* still lingered in her mind. If Aidan were king, he wouldn't let them be treated that way.

It's fine. He's fine. Breathe.

An hour passed, and then another, but her panic lapped in and out like the sea. She thought she might die without knowing. Her eyes flitted to the top drawer of her father's desk. Lister Burke hoarded newspapers like gold. It was a habit from his days in politics that he clearly hadn't shaken. If she wanted answers …

Her feet carried her to the desk, and she got as far as clutching the handle.

Have you lost faith? Aidan chuckled in her mind. *You know that papers lie. Whatever's in there will just upset you, regardless of what it says.*

But this is killing me, Bess thought straight back at him. She squeezed her eyes shut. *Missing you is killing me. Not knowing is killing me.*

In her mind's eye, Aidan smiled and tucked a strand of hair behind her ear. *Trust me. Not even Queen Ana herself could stop me getting back to you.*

'Okay,' Bess whispered. She reached out to touch his face, but her hand met air and she opened her eyes. The illusion vanished, and she was alone in the room once more. She left the drawer and moved back to the window. She'd wait a lifetime for him if she had to.

*

Lister Burke removed his boots at the door and hung his wool hat on the peg. The fire smouldered away in the corner, which told him the room was warm, but it would be a while yet before he felt it. The sea wind had a way of turning blood to ice, and he was yet to grow accustomed to it. He walked across the room and checked that Bess was sleeping soundly before moving to the desk in the corner and opening the drawer where he kept his newspapers. He reached inside his heavy coat and produced that day's paper, before carefully placing it in the drawer with the others. Each day that passed, and each paper stowed away were a relief, as they slowly piled over the headline he was all too eager to bury.

When the news had first broken from Thorterknock two months ago, he had been determined that Bess would not find out. He told her it was unsafe for them, that she should stay in the flat and not talk to locals in case she was recognised, and she was so beside herself with worry that she readily believed isolation was what was best for her health. When the papers stopped reporting what had happened, and the locals stopped gossiping, Lister finally deemed it safe for his daughter to wander freely.

Carefully, he closed the desk drawer and set about readying himself for a short sleep before his next shift. He glanced at Bess, whose breathing was strong and steady. Now and again, the temptation to tell her the truth arose, but in times like this, she looked so peaceful. He let her slumber. The headline, "Separatist revolt crushed. Young Pretender amongst hundreds dead," would remain his secret for as long as he could keep it.

Chapter 51

The Chained Stag

Cait tucked a strand of hair under her hat and kept her head low. Two months had done nothing but stoke the Watch's vigilance, and she wasn't taking any risks. In the days following Aidan's ill-fated insurrection, statesmen and public bodies had been careful to toe the official lin. The Separatists had done the unspeakable: they'd toyed with innocent people and used them as pawns in their messy revolt. But those who had been there and lived to tell the tale knew better. Each day Cait crept around the streets of Thorterknock, she heard fragments of the same hushed conversation from a dozen different tongues.

It was fine until one lass climbed the barricade. Must have given them a scare.

It wasn't just Aist. The Watch fired first on Grace Bridge an aw.

On Wast Bridge the Separatists didn't even fire back.

Sheltered us in the Parliament while they were slaughtered, so they did.

The day after the battle, Calan threw a newspaper on the table in front of Cait and Jamie. 'Maybe it wasn't all for nothing.'

Afren had chosen to be gracious. At first, the Council of Five had flirted with the idea of punishing Storran, but they'd chosen to do the opposite. In order to quell any discontent that led to the uprising, they'd promised instead to furnish Storran with some of her own powers. *A balanced settlement*, Chancellor Borden had called it. At face value at least, Afren had been sympathetic to Storran, and they hadn't thought it fair to punish innocent people for the misdemeanour of a few. Plus, it would please Leja, who had come so close to voting in favour of supporting the rebels.

'Kenzie told me if I took him to Aidan, he'd make sure Afren stuck to their end of the deal,' Calan had said.

Cait had stared at him. 'Did you?'

'I told him in no uncertain terms what I thought of him ... but maybe he had something to do with this after all.'

'Or maybe Afren are just that generous,' Cait had said.

'Bullshit,' Jamie had said. She stormed from the room, and when Cait checked on her later, she was gone.

There were other whispers on the street, too.

What ever happened to that Fox of Thorterknock?

I heard she summoned thunder with her words.

She did, I was there. Brought a whole storm with it.

Cait could believe it. She wondered what stories they told themselves about Aggie and what she was doing now. She wondered if they told their children that she was in hiding, ready to rise again. They would never think that the Fox of Thorterknock had shut herself in a dark room and barely used that storm-churning voice of hers anymore.

'Moarnin, Lorna,' the vendor said when Cait reached the usual newspaper stand. It was the very same one where she had first heard Aggie speak. 'How are we today?'

'Ah, getting by, Don,' Cait said, selecting *The Chronicle*, which Calan had recommended as a reliable paper, from the rack as she did every day. The front page declared that Storran's fishing industry had never been better.

Funny that, Aggie — the old Aggie — said in Cait's head. *Two months ago, that same paper said we were running out of fish and could only rely on Afren's waters to keep the industry afloat.*

There was nothing about 'The Stag's Revolt' as it had come to be known. Even the tabloids seemed to have forgotten. The only physical remnant seemed to be the damaged foundations around Aist Bridge that had revealed a system of long-forgotten buried streets.

'One o these days I'll make a sale off ye, lass,' Don said, chuckling to himself.

Cait glanced up from the paper and grinned. 'Don't count on it.'

There was still no mention of the powers Afren had promised, and Cait almost let down her guard and asked Don if he thought they would ever come, but she bit her tongue. Talk of separatism travelled fast these days, and it was growing far too common for the wrong words to the wrong person to lead a gang of Watchmen to your door. Cait sighed, replaced the newspaper on the stand and dropped a Bodle into Don's hand. It wasn't much, but it kept him sweet about her daily visits. 'See you tomorrow,

Lorna,' he said as she skulked away.

Every week, Cait made the journey through the Old Town up to Hart Hall. She changed the route each time. She had started to grow familiar with the Watchmen patrols and hadn't had a near-miss in a while now. She turned up the narrow, winding street that curved around the back of Hart Hall's indomitable walls and found Innes was waiting for her at the door that led to the execution yard. 'I don't have long,' he said, looking over his shoulder.

'Busy day?' Cait asked.

A grim look passed over his face. 'Two,' was all he said.

Cait didn't ask who. There were hardly any Separatists left to scrape off the streets, which could only mean it must have been a couple of innocent bystanders who had muttered the wrong thing to their neighbour or looked a little too suspicious to the Watchmen. Innes passed her a jute sack and Cait peered inside. It held the usual cheese, and bread, and cured meats that she returned for every week. It was scraps compared to what the Watchmen enjoyed, but it was much better than starvation.

'Do you need any more medical supplies?' Innes asked.

'We're okay for now. Everyone's healing up well.' As Cait fished through the bag, her fingers closed around a crumpled brown packet, and she opened it up to reveal a small amount of shortbread.

'It's not much,' Innes said quickly, 'but I managed to swipe it from right under the matron's nose.'

Cait smiled. 'You didn't need to do that. Thank you.' She hated that he put himself on the line like he did. 'You should get out of Hart Hall. You don't belong here.'

He gave a weak smile. 'And let you lot starve?'

'We'd find a way.'

They'd had the same conversation each day she crept up here, and it always ended the same way.

'I need to get going,' Innes said.

'See you soon. Thanks again.'

He vanished through the door, and Cait hurried back down the street. When she reached the bottom of the hill where the street forked to the left for Hart Hall's gatehouse, and right for the main streets of the Old Town, she risked a glance up, and froze when familiar blue eyes met her own. Among a group of Watchmen marching back into Hart Hall, Kenzie halted and stared at her. Cait knew she should run, but she couldn't bring

370

herself to. They watched each other, and Cait noted the two extra gold chains on his cloak. She wondered which one was for Aidan. Eventually, Kenzie's gaze was taken by the shade of his cap, and he disappeared into Hart Hall with his comrades.

*

Cait checked over her shoulder when she reached The Crabbit Corbie and let herself inside. The main floor of the inn was empty, and Cait made her way upstairs, ducking beneath the dock leaf she had pinned to the ceiling. She slipped into Mirren's room and found her in a chair by the window with her foot propped up on the end of the bed. She gazed at the street below, unaware of Cait's presence.

'Mirren, close the curtains,' Cait said. The girl jumped at the sound of Cait's voice and slid the thin, purple curtains over the window.

'Sorry,' she muttered.

Cait reached into the bag and tossed Mirren a slice of shortbread. Her eyes lit up. 'Don't tell the others,' Cait said.

Of the fifteen Separatists she had helped in the Unnertoun, twelve had made it out. She looked in on all of them, then stopped by Calan's room to tell him there had been no change in the papers and no signs of Afren keeping their promise. When she reached her old room, Cait paused and took a steadying breath. She shoved the door open over the carpet and found Aggie sitting on the edge of the bed with her elbows braced against her knees.

'Hi,' Cait said. Aggie didn't look up. Cait hovered by the door for a tedious moment, then sat down next to Aggie. The bed groaned. She left a hand's span between them. 'Can I?' she asked, lightly touching Aggie's damaged shoulder. Her touch felt altogether too clumsy. Aggie nodded, and Cait gently peeled back the bandages. They were dry, the wound beneath healing, and the same went for the wound at her gut. Her ribs, which at first Cait worried had broken, were only bruised, and Aggie seemed to be able to breathe easier now. Her emotional wounds, however, were something Cait didn't know how to fix. Aggie had gone somewhere after the revolt, and Cait kept chasing, but she was yet to reach her.

Cait set about changing the bandages, carefully and wordlessly manoeuvring Aggie's shoulder to where she needed it. She worked in silence until the silence was too loud. 'Calan's taken a shine to Bram's whisky,' Cait said. 'And Innes packed us some shortbread this time.' When

Aggie didn't respond she added, 'And I've been thinking of learning Leid, if you'd be up for teaching me.' Still, nothing. She sighed. 'When are we going to talk about what happened?' They both knew that "what happened" didn't refer to what they'd endured that day at the Parliament. Cait had mustered the courage to talk to Aggie about the kiss so many times now that it had stopped being scary, because she knew Aggie would refuse to talk about it. This time was no different. 'There's no rush,' Cait said, as per usual. 'Whenever you're ready.' She wished there *was* a rush because she hated this veil that seemed to hang between them.

'You're well on the mend,' Cait said, fixing Aggie's shirt and getting to her feet. 'You'll be good as new in no time.' When Aggie didn't respond, Cait filled the silence with, 'Are you coming for some food?' Aggie said nothing. 'You need to keep your strength up.' Still, she said nothing. Cait sighed as she watched her. She made a mental note to bring her a plate, but there was no food or medicine that would clear the haunted look in her eyes. 'There's a library in Hart Hall. I thought I could ask Innes to get you something.'

At that, Aggie's head lifted, and she watched Cait with dark, spiritless eyes. Cait's chest ached. 'That would be nice.'

'Okay,' Cait said, moving to the door. 'But only on the condition that you come and eat some food with us tonight.' Aggie dropped her head again. Cait lingered, but when she found she had nothing else to say, she opened the door.

'Cait.'

When Cait turned, Aggie was still looking at the floor. 'Did they find him?' she said softly.

Cait's heart snagged on Aggie's words. How long would she languish in this denial? 'Aggie ... he's gone.' She didn't have the heart to tell her that the Watchmen had strung Aidan's bloodstained plaid up over the city gate, or that they had taken the crown and melted it into ceremonial coins celebrating the primacy of the Five Realms.

Aggie's hands clenched around each other. 'I see.'

*

When she returned downstairs, Cait sorted through the bag Innes had given her, and at the bottom, she found a crumpled letter. Her hands shook as she recognised her father's handwriting scrawled across the page.

My dearest Cait, it read.

A friend of Kenzie's at Hart Hall wrote and told us that you are safe, and we are so pleased. Things are tricky here, but we only want you home.
That revelation about Cathal was certainly something, wasn't it? I've been cooking up a few theories. Let's talk when you're back. You did always say those characters were confused.
Hope to see you soon, pet. Don't be a stranger.
Love,
Your da.

Cait wiped her tears as she folded the letter and tucked it into her pocket. Seeing her father's jagged handwriting made her ache for home, but the words *things are tricky here* unsettled her. They sounded like a kinder way of saying *traitorous little bitch*.

*

Aggie never appeared for dinner, and she was asleep by the time Cait took a plate to her room. Cait and Calan stayed up talking and sharing some of Bram's homebrew. She suspected more of it had been consumed in the past few months than in Bram's own lifetime. They toasted to Bram. They toasted to absent friends. They circled the same conversations, dodging the one day in Thorterknock they both wanted to forget. They talked about nothing of consequence because nothing was of consequence anymore. Then they each staggered to bed to try to fight off the memories alone.

In the early hours of the morning, Cait jolted awake to the sound of movement downstairs. Her heart lurched, her instincts telling her it was Kenzie. She should have known that he wouldn't just walk away from her, and here he was now, knowing exactly where to find her. She should have run the moment he saw her. She should have packed up and left Thorterknock for good. Slowly, she crept across her room. She couldn't hide from him. When she reached the top of the stairs, she peered over the banister, but found the floor of the bar empty. She caught her breath, then jumped when Aggie emerged from the darkness below. She was pulling her coat over her shoulders.

'Where are you going?' Cait asked. She paused at the bottom of the stairs. Through the windows, dawn spilled purple shadows across the floor.

The sound of Cait's voice made Aggie halt, and without looking around she said, 'For a walk.'

Aggie continued trying to wriggle into the coat, and Cait stepped behind her and helped ease her arm through the hole. They were close enough that she could see the individual red strands of Aggie's hair; close enough that she could feel the warmth of her skin. Cait stepped back. As soon as she was in the coat, Aggie pulled away, too. The distance between them was unnatural and deliberate. 'You're not just going for a walk,' Cait said. Cait had toyed with plans of their next move since their retreat to the inn. Her father's letter had revealed that there was a place for her, even if others didn't want her there. Cait just wasn't sure where Aggie fit into this new world they found themselves in. What she did know, was that she wanted her there. She'd carve out a place with the old pocketknife if she had to.

Without meeting her eyes, Aggie said, 'Someone needs to set things right.' She walked to the door. 'Someone needs to pay.'

Cait hurried after her. 'It's *us* who need to pay. We brought this to the city.' She hadn't meant to snap, but she had felt the permanent scars out there every day she walked the streets of Thorterknock.

Aggie turned on her. 'I was there when the first shots were fired. I saw who started the killing.'

'I know. I'm sorry, I just —'

'The Lealists will pay. So will every coward who supports them.' Her voice broke on the word *coward*. Cait tried to see that she was grieving. She had lost her friends, her King, everything that she devoted her life to achieving. But the low fire in Aggie's eyes frightened her. This was more than grief. It was rage.

'What are you going to manage alone?' she asked.

Aggie's jaw clenched. 'There will be others.' Then she hesitated, and the fire in her eyes dwindled a little. 'You could join me.'

Cait glanced at the door. Was there truly a place for her in Briddock? Could she walk the fields of her youth hearing Kenzie hiss *traitorous little bitch* at every turn and in every breath of wind? Maybe her place *was* with Aggie on her burning crusade. She felt powerless. She had done for two months now. Maybe her power lay in becoming the traitor that Kenzie was so certain she was. For a moment, she let herself wonder what she and Aggie could be if they both crossed the threshold and left The Crabbit Corbie for good. Cait could see herself following. Aggie would get on with what she needed to do, and Cait would dampen her flames. Maybe then the veil between them would lift. That path had the potential to heal, but it also had the potential to burn, and she knew that if she followed Aggie she *would* get burned.

'I can't,' Cait said. Aggie's walls built themselves back up, and she opened the door. The early morning rushed in. 'Aggie, wait,' Cait said. Her voice shivered. 'Just stay here. Stay with me, and Calan, and maybe one day —'

'It's not enough.'

Cait's eyes burned. How could this feel worse than Aggie's heartbeat staggering beneath her fingers? 'You're wrong.' She took Aggie's hands. They were freezing. 'You can't do this.'

'Why?'

The truth? Because Cait had somehow managed to forget what the world was like without the Fox of Thorterknock. Because her heart had never beat to this bold, new rhythm before. Because she was falling, and she didn't want to hit the ground alone. She wanted Aggie's smirk back, and she wanted it to be hers. She wanted to know the girl beneath the musty cigar smoke. She wanted to know who she was without the weight of Storran pressing on her shoulders. She wanted to finish that kiss. Cait made to brush a loose strand of hair from Aggie's face, but when she caught the zealous look in her eyes, she stopped. It was the same look that was there when she had stormed towards the Watchman girl in the Dorcha Pass. 'Because you're better than this,' was all Cait said.

Aggie's eyes searched her face. They settled on Cait's lips for a moment, then flicked quickly away. For a moment, her ire dimmed, her mouth turned upwards, and Cait thought she had won. 'You think too much of me,' Aggie said with a smirk, then her eyes darkened. 'This is who I am. If I'd realised that sooner, things might be different.'

'No, things would be exactly the same because Afren —'

'Afren is going to pay,' Aggie said simply.

Cait shook her head. 'Is this about freedom or revenge?'

'Can't it be both?'

She dropped Cait's hands and stalked into the morning mist, her coat flapping at her shins as she went. Cait almost called after her, but she knew it would be futile. She sank to the floor and watched the mist dissipate with the rising sun. She tried to fend off grim visions of what Aggie might become, as well as the heart-crushing realisation that Cait hadn't been enough to keep her from that path. She knew that whatever happened next would have to be done without Aggie, or perhaps worse, despite her.

At some point, Calan appeared and sat down next to her. 'She's gone,' Cait whispered.

'I'm surprised it took her so long.'

Cait hugged her knees. 'She implied she could've single-handedly freed Storran.'

Calan chuckled, but Cait saw him swipe a tear from his cheek. 'Yeah. That sounds like her.'

In the quiet, Cait removed the letter from her pocket and read it over again. Her father's words were her absolution. If she went home, maybe she could try to leave behind the crushing guilt of what had happened here. Maybe she could start to rebuild her life. She could go back to being the doctor's daughter in the house near Puddock Bridge.

'What's that?' Calan asked.

Cait showed him the letter, and after he had scanned it, he passed it back to her and asked, 'Will you go back?'

Thunder rumbled somewhere in the distance. Cait spoke before she could think. She was tired of thinking. 'No.'

The Lealists had taken their King, their refuge, their people, but they had given them a gift: Storran's blood was all over Afren's hands, and the people were not blind to the stains. Afren would be lenient until the people forgot, but in time, Aidan's rebellion would bring their wrath down harder on Storran.

They sat in quiet for a long time until Calan said, 'What should we do now?'

Cait supposed he meant something more immediate, perhaps if they should prepare breakfast, or whether they should think about leaving Thorterknock. But somewhere out there, the thunder drew nearer.

Cait smiled. 'We try again.'

THE END

Acknowledgements

My deepest thanks to the team at Ringwood Publishing for picking up my fatigued, yet hopeful, query email in November 2022 and making this a reality. The interns at Ringwood are real-life heroes, and I cannot express my thanks enough for the incredible work they do on a day-to-day basis to bring stories to life. Specifically, I'd like to thank the team that worked on *Song of the Stag*: Rachel Harley, Annemarie Whitehurst, Natasha Chanse, Skye Galloway, and Annika Dahlman. I've loved every moment of working with you throughout this process. Thank you so much for guiding me with your talents and wisdom and working your magic to turn this shared vision into something real. Annika, you've been the most inspiring editor, for putting up with my silly questions, supporting my ideas, and most of the time, knowing the characters and story better than I do.

In all my wildest dreams, I never would have imagined that this could be a reality, and I owe all my thanks to my family for giving me the drive and courage to pursue it. Mum, Dad, Rachel, Granny Yule, and the Broons — thank you for always believing in me, whether I was writing primary school stories about dogs that didn't exist, or barely comprehensible stream-of-consciousness rambles at university. This book is as much yours as it is mine.

David, my co-conspirator, my questing companion, my husband. Thank you not only for your unyielding support, but for your patient ear while I'm figuring out plot holes, your sparkling wit always at hand when my confidence wobbles, and your seemingly otherworldly ability to craft all manner of things I need (websites, antlered crowns, and leatherbound copies of my proofs, to name a few). Thank you for being you.

My incredible friends, whom I don't know what I'd do without, and who have given so much advice you may as well be co-authors.

Rosie, a friend most steadfast. You weathered all those years of providing patient feedback on terrible manuscripts. I'd return the favour and do my time, but you're far too talented for it to be considered a trial.

Róisín, your wit and insight never miss, and you do it all while making me laugh so hard I need to hit my inhaler.

Hannah, you have been a light in my life since the start, and my original muse (Team Hannah the Horse Rider forever).

Taylor, who I can always count on for inspiring conversation with the greatest takes, or a good old vent about the state of politics. I'll always be glad we bonded over free cheesecake and local councillors all those years ago.

Joanne, our shared ordeal of creative writing classes may be in the past, but there's truly nothing like gushing about great books and Taylor Swift with you.

Rebecca, thank you for inspiring me with your endless font of talent, authenticity, and impeccable taste. You are who I want to be when I grow up.

Granny Broon and the Whites — my first ever readers. Thank you for taking the plunge and opening that early PDF draft. Your feedback gave me the confidence to seek out more readers.

It takes a village to make a dream come true, and by god, I have the best one.

About the Author

A proud Dundonian, Rebecca is an English and Creative Writing alumna and co-founder of the charity Folklore Scotland. Armed with an obscene number of folklore books, she and her husband strive to preserve the tales of the past for a new generation by digitising stories, recording podcasts, and of course, hunting for fairies.

She is fascinated by the transmutation of stories with each telling and loves to build this into her fantasy worlds. In her writing, folklore is a force to be reckoned with; it has the power to uproot lives and divert the course of history.

Her love of stories and Scotland go hand-in-hand, and her debut novel, *Song of the Stag*, was born after her family got bored of hearing impassioned rants about Scottish politics and history at the dinner table.

More to read:

If you enjoyed *Song of the Stag*, you will most certainly like these other Ringwood books:

Raise Dragon

L.A. Kristiansen

In the year of 1306, Scotland is in turmoil. Robert the Bruce and the fighting Bishop Wishart's plans for rebellion put the Scottish kingdom at risk, whilst the hostile kingdom of England seems more invincible than ever. But Bishop Wishart has got a final card left to play: four brave Scottish knights set off in search of a mysterious ancient treasure that will bring Scotland to the centre of an international plot, changing the course of history forever.

ISBN: 978-1-901514-76-6

£9.99

Revenge of the Tyrants

L.A. Kristiansen

The fight for the nation's soul has begun, and nothing will ever be the same. While the King of Scots wages a desperate, bloody war for Scotland's independence, four intrepid Scottish knights embark on a treasure barge. What follows is a journey directly to the heart of the conflict, and a vivid depiction of the scheming, treachery and violence it entailed. Meanwhile, Kings Edward the first of England, Philip the fourth of France, and Haakon the fifth of Norway have their own reasons to thwart the Scots, and each will stop at nothing to gain their victory.

ISBN: 978-1-901514-89-6

£12.99

What You Call Free

Flora Johnston

Scotland, 1687. Pregnant and betrayed, eighteen-year-old Jonet escapes her public humiliations, and takes refuge among an outlawed group of religious dissidents.

Here, Widow Helen offers friendship and understanding, but her beliefs have seen her imprisoned before. This extraordinary tale of love and loss, struggle and sacrifice, autonomy and entrapment, urges us to consider what it means to be free and who can be free – if freedom exists at all.

ISBN: 978-1-901514-96-4

£9.99

Bodysnatcher

Carol Margaret Davison

In the late 1820s, two Irish Immigrants, William Burke and William Hare, murdered 16 individuals and sold their corpses for use in anatomical dissections at the University of Edinburgh. Their killings ended when Hare turned King's Evidence, and Burke was hanged.

However, the question of whether their female accomplices, Nelly McDougal and Margaret Hare, were involved, has never been determined. Told by way of alternating confessions, *Bodysnatcher* is both a graphic depiction of one of Edinburgh's most notorious crimes, and a domestic story of a relationship unravelled by secrecy and violence.

ISBN: 978-1-901514-83-4

£12.99

The Hotel Hokusai

T. Y. Garner

It is 1893: When a young woman is found drowned in Yokohama Harbour under suspicious circumstances, downtrodden Korean eel salesboy Han compels the eccentric Glaswegian artist Archie Nith to help him investigate. Written from the perspectives of both Han and Nith, The Hotel Hokusai follows their journey as it snakes from Yokohama's harbour to its red-light district, stopping along the way to meet two of the famous Glasgow Boys and pay respects to the Dragon King.

ISBN: 978-1-901514-70-4

£9.99

The Bone on the Beach

Fiona Gillian Kerr

In 2002, in a tight-knit Highland village, a young woman named Deirdre mysteriously dies. Fifteen years later, Meghan, a lawyer, arrives in the village seeking a fresh start. But when a bone washes up on the beach, she is embroiled in the mystery. As the residents refuse to discuss the past, Meghan wonders what transpired in the village all those years ago. As she uncovers its storied history, she discovers that all is not as it seems in this village. Drawing on the ancient Celtic legend 'Deirdre of the Sorrows', and set in the otherworldly Highland landscape, this tale shows Deirdre as she has never been seen before.

ISBN: 978-1-901514-91-9

£9.99